Julie

Gabriella's Book of Fire

VENERO ARMANNO

Gabriella's Book of Fire

HYPERION

New York

Library of Congress Cataloging-in-Publication Data
Armanno, Venero.
[Firehead]
Gabriella's Book of fire / by Venero Armanno.—1st ed.
p.   cm.
Original title: Firehead.
ISBN 0-7868-6597-0
1. Italians—Australia—Fiction.
2. Sicily (Italy)—Emigration and immigration—Fiction.
3. Brisbane (Qld.)—Fiction.   I. Title.
PR9619.3.A69 F5 2001
823'.914—dc21   00-058058

Designed by Cassandra J. Pappas

FIRST EDITION

10 9 8 7 6 5 4 3 2 1

To my family

Contents

Contents

PASTA · 1995

Contents

LOVE ☀ 1975

Fresh Breasts

SHE USED TO SELL her kisses for caramels; her lips went for long licks of licorice and her touch for tangerines and tutti-frutti. You could get her in the dark of your cardboard cubby-house or down into the cobwebby underworld of the dirt under your home, if you could find something sweet to offer her. The other kids would run by unseeing, with scabby knees and split soles in their bare dirty feet, and she'd let you sit with her in the musk of a quiet corner where a hundred times you'd been told not to go and you'd gone a thousand times. You could give her a Valencia orange to peel and as the juice ran down her chin she'd let you hold her knee for whatever promise your fourteen-year-old mind could find there; and if she was in a good mood and her chaotic family life was on a high that afternoon or night she'd let herself be held, and you could take the spicy citrus taste from her mouth and her pink firm tongue, and when you did you knew it for sure, neither she nor you would be fourteen again, and life never so easy.

Not when you could buy such dreams for fruit and candies.

She came to our little corner of Heaven in the month of June in the year of 1975, on a Friday, the thirteenth, the black day. The first thing she

3

said to me over the back fence, in an accent as unruly as her hair, was, So what's gone wrong so far? and I looked up from my boy's collection of bones and murdering weapons and dead dogs' teeth and answered, Nothing yet, and she said, Wrong, and showed sharp teeth as white and tiny as my dead dogs' teeth were yellow and long. When summer hail-like rocks and stones fell out of the sky that night, and lightning thrilled the fat clouds alive, I knew she was right. She had that powerful accent of the Mediterranean, but she spoke perfect textbook English and she'd come into my corner of the world with her family all the way from that piece-of-dirt nothing place on the toe of Italy, called Sicily. Where my family originally came from, the difference being that my papà married my ma here in Australia in the fifties and I was born in their adopted country, whereas this girl and her folk were new arrivals, a perfectly foreign family unit fresh-moved to the Southern Hemisphere, the island continent. To Queensland and to Brisbane, to the suburb of New Farm and my big dreamy street, Merthyr Road, corner of the lushly green Abbott Street. To the house next door. We were to live side by side in an urban forest of deciduous trees, where crickets and cicadas sang their croaky songs and sparrows and starlings dive-bombed our heads whenever we played our backyard games; how would we ever forget such beginnings? From the very start I knew she was here to stay, in that way that means that even if she traveled to Babylon and married a sultan and turned his hair snowy white and his sad straining nerves into shuddering spasms of electricity, her small sharp teeth and red rampant hair and plastering of freckles would never leave my world.

In case I hadn't got the message she climbed my fence and trampled my ma's fennel bushes and gave a smile that was supposed to say sorry but was in reality full of devilment. She said, Put out your arm, and so I did, and with a big permanent marker she had in her back pocket, where she kept pens and folded sheets of paper containing strange notations and never-ending loopings of writings, she wrote on my arm in brilliant red letters: Gabriella. So put out *your* arm, I said, and she was delighted to comply, and I wrote on the soft white skin of her inner forearm the three letters of my name: Sam.

She shook her head and put out her other forearm for me to try again. In a very rough and exasperated Sicilian dialect exactly the same as my parents spoke or screamed in the home, she said, Sam? Who cares for a name like Sam? Where we come from it's Salvatore or even sometimes we change it to *Turiddu* and one of those is what you are. Understand?

I did, and that was why I tried it again.

In long strokes across that warm virgin flesh I wrote out the whole name, Salvatore, and she tried not to be tickled but of course it was tickling insanely, and I had to hold her by the wrist to keep her forearm steady, and because I saw she was bright in the face with something I'd never made happen to a girl before I carefully wrote out my long surname too, and there she was in my ma's ruined fennel bushes, blushing deep red and marked with my name, Salvatore Capistrano, and, I thought, she was very satisfied about it too.

Then that defiance I would know so well came up into her eyes.

Va bene, she said, are you ready to get the full treatment too? And without waiting for a reply she took that indelible marking pen and wielded it like a weapon, and I didn't blush but all the same something deep deep deep inside started to melt, slowly, languidly, inescapably.

Contradictions.

She looked as Irish as rain out of a sunny blue day and as English as green meadows where wildflowers grow, and her name was Gabriella Maria Santuzza Zazò. Her mother was Belpasso Agata, if you used that funny formal inverted way Italians have for saying their names, and for the rest there was her father Raffaele and her brother Michele—or as we say in English, Michael—and her only living grandparent was with them too, a thoroughly senile nonno from her mamma's side. His name: Belpasso Enrico, or to us here and evermore, Signor Enrico Belpasso. His surname literally translates as "beautiful path" or "beautiful steps" and maybe that's what he was taking, beautiful slow steps that led him toward Heaven, because I couldn't see him going to any other destination.

And so that was the clan who moved in next door. Gabriella told me the names of the places they had come from and to me, at first, though I could speak the old language and the old Sicilian dialect, these names were like stones that you had to put in your mouth to chew but you could just never manage to chew them right.

The day after they moved in Gabriella asked me for some caramels and we found our way into the dirt and cool dark under my house where the rope of an old abandoned swing was frayed enough to drop you on your backside if you gave it a try, and where rusty broken soldiers and one-eyed teddy bears with mangy fur gathered like deceased ancestors coming to bring their families gifts on the Italian Day of the Dead. We sat together and I discovered what you could barter for and what wasn't going at any price. A week later Shane Calder from three streets away said that for two dark plums the right side of ripe she let him put his hand into the leg of her wide sports shorts and play with the springy lawn she had up there, and I knocked him down for being such a liar.

Everyone knew then that I was in trouble.

Gabriella's papà couldn't speak the new language yet but her ma could, having been trained by her own daughter, who'd been teaching her English words and phrases for a whole year and a half before they finally migrated. I liked Gabriella's ma because she liked me, and because there was always something cooking on her four-ring gas stove. One day Mamma Zazò pinched her nose up when Gabriella gave her a kiss and said, Phew, darly, what you been eat? She went into the pockets of her apron and took out a packet of Kool Mints and popped one into her daughter's ready mouth. Then Mamma Zazò looked at me and held a few more Kool Mints out in her palm.

What about you, darly? she asked. You want the fresh breasts?

A little over a week they'd been in that house next door, me no more than twice in their home; I was already Mamma Zazò's darly.

Whenever Gabriella smiled all the freckles across her nose seemed to come alive. She was as light-skinned as her ma was the hue of nice ripe olives, and now Gabriella turned around and I could see every one of her freckles like they were begging to be counted. She was sucking the mint in her mouth and she had this look in her face that told me most of my days of bones and murdering weapons and dead dogs' teeth were over.

Ma asked you a question, Salvatore. She folded her arms, beautiful and small and red wild-haired. Salvatore. So do you think you want the fresh breasts?

The Case of the
Missing Newspapers

MY MA LIKED TO call me that too but only when I was in trouble and now she was yelling it through the house like the carpets were on fire.

"Salvatore! Where are you? Get to the front door! Quick!"

I mooched through the bedrooms because Ma wasn't the type to hold back with a slap across the face or a clip behind the ear when it was needed. It was my papà who never touched me, though when he was angry he could be scarier than any Wolfman or Count Yorga or It from outer space in the Saturday night TV monster movie. I was wondering what I was getting caught for out of the profusion of possibilities and probabilities of things I'd done wrong—or that my sister had done wrong and put the blame on me for. Luisa was like that. Three years older than me and she knew how to play me like a piano. In fact she was pretty good on a real piano even though plenty of times she didn't turn up to her lessons but instead went smooching with her secret boyfriend, Bob. Ma would have killed her if she'd known there was a boyfriend on the scene, especially some Bob who lived for weekend football-fixtures and had the brain of a weekend football-fixtures Bob. I called him Bobo and to his face too. One day when he got fed up he tried to smack me one but though he's broad in the shoulders he's slow in the legs and I'm fast, just fast, and he ended up screaming in one spot like the moron he was. Mrs. Dorrington, whom Luisa called Dogbone because of the way she was so goddamned skinny and dried up, was Luisa's piano teacher. Some days she was so far away with the fairies she didn't know who turned up to lessons and who didn't, though there were plenty of other days when she was as sharp as a carving knife and could pick out the flaws in Luisa's playing like wrong brushstrokes in an imitation Rembrandt. Luisa was too brave or too stupid or too horny to really care. She just took her chances and so far she'd been lucky and that probably meant Bob was getting lucky too. Dogbone mightn't have dobbed her in anyway. Luisa told me one day she was doing some arpeggios and when Mrs. Dogbone turned her back her light-blue skirt was stained dark with what smelled like cat's wee but was obviously her own, and when Luisa pointed this out the poor old incontinent begged her not to tell anyone for fear of what we Italians like to call the Casa di Riposo—the home of rest. So Luisa had a secret pact to rely on, if the need arose.

It never did. Bob got his back broken in a sub-mutant football scrum and they had to send him to the Gold Coast for recuperation and repair, and he just never returned. Luisa went quiet for months and months and her playing improved out of sight; she was probably the most nimble-fingered check-out chick our local Woolworth's ever employed to punch out the figures on an old mechanical cash register.

Anyway, this day the front door of our house was open to the summer sunshine and Ma was standing in a wedge of it, and there was Mr. Harry from the small corner shop looking all unhappy and hang-doggy. When he saw me mooching down the corridor he perked up a bit and rubbed his mustache like it itched.

"The boys must know something about this," he said to Ma. Mr. Harry's corner shop was one block up but he never made house calls. We purchased milk and bread and a few other odds and ends from him but we never knew his other name or if there was a Mrs. Harry, and so all in all it was a surprise to see him there. He said, "Come on, Sammy, what's it all about?"

"What's what all about?"

"Where the bloody hell are my newspapers?"

Ma said, "Mr. Harry, you no talk to my son like that."

I said, "Huh?"

"Every day between four and five in the morning the paper deliveries drop my bundles in front of the shop. There's a hundred newspapers there. Somebody's been walking off with my bundles. Nearly every morning." Mr. Harry looked like he wanted to jump from foot to foot with frustration and shake me by the back of my neck until I told him what he wanted to know. "They keep stealing my newspapers! Why? What's the point? You know anything about it?"

If it wasn't one of the weirdest crimes I ever heard about, it was at least the most nonsensical.

"I haven't seen anything."

"Listen, Sammy, this is bloody—"

"Mr. Harry," Ma cut him off, just like that. "If he say he no know, he no know. *Basta.*"

He had to go away even if he was grumbling about it, because he knew Ma wouldn't take any shit. After all, he was an Aussie and she was a Sicilian and her son had spoken. So to her that was all there was to it; I could be a bad enough boy sometimes but when I said I was innocent then I was innocent. *Basta* and *finito.*

I did end up feeling sorry for Mr. Harry. He had one of those horrible jobs where you get out of your bed at five in the morning and are still at your place of work at nine at night, and now he had to get up just that little bit earlier so that he could catch a thief—or at least rescue his bundles of daily newsprint. I heard that he started getting to his shop by four every A.M. and some days he saved his papers but plenty of other days the bundles went walkabout before he even had the chance to arrive. Me and my friends made a pact to stake the joint out some pre-dawn, but with every morning that came none of us could find a good enough reason to get out of bed so early.

In the weeks that followed Mr. Harry became more and more embittered, and the police he kept calling didn't really care, especially our local hero, young Officer Pietro Pierucci. Soon Mr. Harry was always looking sleepy and unfulfilled and sometimes we took to calling him Harry the Droop. Meanwhile, newspapers erratically disappeared. Someone in the neighborhood must have known what was going on but no one would let Harry the Droop in on it. He went into a spiral. He'd yell at us when we were in his shop too long and we didn't buy anything; he developed halitosis; his posture changed so that his shoulders were always slumping. I couldn't believe that such a little thing could drag a man down so.

Gabriella and I developed outlandish theories to explain what was going on. We discussed aliens, zombies from beyond the grave hungry not for flesh but current affairs, and a plot by some racist political group to keep New Farm Sicilians ignorant of world and Australian events and hence out of the greater running of the country.

It wasn't the world's most intriguing mystery, but at least it was ours.

It Looked Like a Salami

A FEW WEEKS AFTER Gabriella and her family became our neighbors my ma and papà asked them to come visiting. They thought we
could all be great friends, given that we were two Sicilian families living
next door to one another. My papà was a bricklayer and Raffaele Zazò
was a plasterer and at first my father thought he should try to find his
countryman some work, but what he didn't know was that the Zazòs
had relatives all over town who were already easing their way into
everything they knew about Australian life. These relatives were the
ones who helped them get here in the first place and buy such a nice old
Queenslander house, and so Raffaele didn't need any help at all.

When the night of the *visita* came, Ma made me put on a clean
white shirt and she opened a bottle of dark-colored Cinzano and put out
some ice cubes and sliced lemon and little bottles of tonic water. She'd
made some ricotta cannoli, which were a specialty of hers, and from the
Italian food place in Fortitude Valley, Sala's Delicatessen, she'd purchased pasta di mandorla biscuits, which are soft and bitter and sweet at
the same time. There were also some other biscuits that are as hard as
nails and threaten to break the fillings out of your teeth; these sweets

are called *ossi dei morti*—skeleton bones. Papà was in a good mood because it was the end of the working week for him and he'd come home early, which I knew because when I came in from school his car was already in the garage and the bathroom mirrors were still misty and the door to the main bedroom was shut. Behind that door there was a little talking and a little laughing and if you stood still and silent you could feel how the house was moving on its wooden stumps.

If it hadn't been for Gabriella's Nonno Belpasso it probably would have been a fine night and from then on all of us great friends, but he was about eighty years of age and unfortunately runny in the head like a soft-boiled egg, and anything he thought to say just came out very loudly, even if it was the most insulting or inappropriate thing on this earth. He didn't understand the concepts of yesterday and tomorrow and to my mind was weak about today too. Gabriella he called Fortunata, and his daughter Agata was Marina, and his son-in-law and provider Raffaele was *tu* and nothing else. He got very excited by Anna and Frida of ABBA, especially when they wore those satin outfits with the cute pussies on the front, and whenever he saw Humphrey Bogart on television he would shout, *"Cumpari, vieni 'ca!"* Comrade, come here! The son, the seventeen-year-old Michael, wasn't present on that night. He was out chasing skinny neighborhood girls with his new gang of friends, but I was the only one who knew about that.

Gabriella told me that fifty years after the Italian victory in World War I, Il Presidente della Repubblica conferred on Enrico Belpasso the title of Cavaliere dell'Ordine di Vittorio Veneto and gave him some medals for having been blown up in some forgotten battle somewhere. The old man was rarely with it enough to know that he was now officially a war hero. It had come too late. Sometimes, she said, he had great clarity and could tell stories and remember everything about his life, but I only thought she was being romantic and making it up. All I ever saw was a glaze in his eyes that was like looking into the horizon on an overcast day. The old man was as round as a great barrel of wine and there were three rotted teeth and no more residing in his mouth. He towered over everyone and was rock-melon bald and a dent in the side of his head accentuated the thick horrible squiggly line of a pronounced vein on one temple. Added to that, he laughed like a hyena when something struck him as funny. He was very unattractive. Nevertheless, Gabriella seemed to idolize her nonno; she cared for him and they looked like the oddest of odd couples, she pink-featured and freckled and petite, tonight with her red hair in braids like a sexy Pippi Longstocking, and he like some ancient bear staggering around because lightning just hit the side of its head and even left a dent there.

At first on that night of the *visita* Gabriella stayed by his side, giving him a drink and breaking up biscuits in her hands so that he could suck them and swallow them without too much chewing, but he kept pushing her away by the shoulder. He must have been in one of his worse phases and finally she rolled her eyes and gave up, keeping away from him, as did everyone else. He was in front of the television and agitated and muttering a great deal, maybe because he was disoriented in a house of strangers. Every now and then he would bellow Sicilian phrases like, "The vines need water!" and "Who out of those criminals in Rome can have clean hands?" and "Ugly bitch!" The final notable thing about him was the lump of wood in the front of his trousers that he kept moving around, possibly for pleasure but probably only for comfort's sake. The Zazòs must have lived with all of this for a long time because they rarely commented on his activities, and my ma and papà were at great pains not to notice any of his trouser maneuvers.

Luisa took one look at him and turned to water. She tried to make use of the driver's license she'd just got but Ma gave her that sharp sideways glance that meant she'd better stay right where she was, if she knew what was good for her.

So Luisa's presence was the other thing that helped matters get out of hand.

To start the evening off Ma served beer to the men and Schweppes lemonade to me and the women. It took the adults about seventeen seconds to work out that not only were they of course from the same country and the same little island, but that they hailed from the same small province too. Names were fired like bullets from an automatic rifle but our two families found no relatives or friends in common, which seemed remarkable. The real difference was that the Zazòs lived in the city of Catania and my ma and papà grew up in a little nothing of a town in its surrounding countryside. That still meant, however, that we were neighbors by probably no more than twenty kilometers, so with everyone relaxing and the beer and lemonade soon changing to that dark-colored Cinzano and tonic—and everyone oohing and gooing over Ma's cannoli—they dropped the formal High Italian strangers tend to speak so haughtily and changed to the good rough dialect we all knew so well, Sicilian. That included me. The thing about my parents was that they always made Luisa and me speak the old language at home and so we were nearly as fluent in it as in English. This pleased the Zazòs, and even more so Gabriella. She kept giving me this funny look that said we might have had secret kisses and fumblings to share, but better than that was our own secret language—and *vaffanculu* the rest of the English-speaking world.

After a while, with the adults animated and Luisa bored but drinking plenty of Cinzano, and Gabriella and I fidgeting, Gabriella said, *"Salvatore, posso vedere la tua stanza?"* The way she said it was the way actresses in the movies talk just before they slip out of their shirts to reveal a silk camisole and beautifully firm and large twin bulges.

Ma shot me a look. She wasn't going to miss that intonation, not even with all the happy and energetic half-yelling that was going on. But I did what Gabriella asked and took her to have a look at my room.

She studied the walls covered in posters of female rock stars in female rock-star poses and said, dubiously, this time in her heavily accented English, "So, have you been relieved of your virginity?"

Gabriella sat on the side of my bed and toyed with the cover of a Spiderman comic. She was in jeans and a western-style shirt with stud buttons, and she looked innocent and lascivious at the same time. She looked like she could eat you alive and you'd enjoy the whole thing. She was just plain sexy, and it took me the first few weeks I knew her and kissed her in the dark, and those moments alone in my bedroom with her, to understand that it wasn't something she put on with her wardrobe and braids, it was just the way she was. The thing of her was, she had this light inside and when she passed it on you were lost and grateful all at the same time because your spirit and your body just went up in a fire.

She said in Sicilian, her voice low and throaty the way it sometimes was when what she said came from a lot of thought, "Salvatore, you wouldn't want to make love if you weren't in love, would you?"

My feet were tingling and so were the backs of my arms. I guess it was from the realization that she was completely different from everyone and anyone I'd ever heard about. She wasn't a *Penthouse* letters section fantasy and she was no *Playboy* pinup and she wasn't a rock star grinding her hips and pouting into a camera. She was a fourteen-year-old kid whose skin could turn red when you touched it and she thought about life and she was kind to her grandfather. And the rest intrigued me too: a flame-haired, light-skinned, green-eyed girl in a Sicilian family; an Irish-looking kid who had a heavy, throaty Mediterranean accent and who didn't know what hell Australian schools would be for someone like her; a child whose kisses you could buy for no more than twenty-cent sweets, yet who carried a sensuality you'd never touch if she chose not to offer it to you.

"So, your virginity? I'm waiting."

Speak-swaggering is an art, the only sort of art there was to learn at the mean-spirited little Christian Brothers school I went to.

"You must be joking."

"You must be joking yes or you must be joking no?"

"The Big V is old news. That was two years ago at least."

Normally she could see through a boy's speak-swagger like looking through a shop window, yet it touched me that a trace of anxiety crossed her brow. It touched me that she had just a trace of a teenager's gullibility.

"Well," she said, "I want to keep something no one will ever get from me."

"Your ma will be glad she's got a good girl who won't give in until she's married."

"Who's getting married?"

"You. Sooner or later. Not like me."

"You're not getting married? You'll be the first." She was angry for some reason and reverted to rapid-fire Sicilian. "Fuck you, I'm the one who won't be getting married, I can assure you of that." Her voice went quiet. "I really, really won't."

"Why not?"

"I wouldn't be sure what sex I'd want to marry."

"You kiss the male of the species."

"I like to touch. I think it's nice. Lips and skin and the way you start breathing together. When people have fresh breasts, that is." She had a smile that didn't go with the sound of her voice now. "Oh, I don't know." Gabriella started to undo her braids and it was like she was stripping herself naked, just for my sake. I was scared. Even though I'd fumbled and groped with her and kissed chocolates and caramels and citrus fruits off her tongue in the many dark places we kids knew how to find, I really was scared. Because this was something different, something new. I barely understood the new word that was coming into my life via this Gabriella Zazò.

That word: intimacy.

And another one: complicity.

Add them together and what can they equal but love?

I sat on the side of the bed and put my hand on the leg of Gabriella's jeans and she said, "Don't do that now. I really want a true answer and you can stop trying to be so smart about it. I want to hear you say it. Are you a virgin or not?"

Lies were now things you used for everyone else and never for her.

That little playful smile on her lips became real. Her expression cleared of doubt. I was glad I'd made her happy. Again reverting to Sicilian, Gabriella said, "Sono contenta," and I couldn't tell if it was my information or my acquiescence to her will that pleased her. She said, "I think I like you a lot better now, Salvatore Capistrano," and she brought her pink hot face closer to mine and kissed me on the lips.

Even more than those lips, when she was so close I was transfixed by her sea-green eyes and the very smell of her. She was fresh, like the wind that comes in off an ocean, that rides to you over the breaking and crashing of great waves. Everything about her was just—different.

Gabriella let out a heavy breath. It seemed heavier than her.

"That's the first time I've kissed you without you giving me something."

Ma came in then, having measured about seven minutes' privacy for us. There was no such thing as knocking on closed doors in our household and Ma's instincts were too refined for that anyway. She was the way nature documentaries on television say a she-wolf is supposed to be, and her radar told her one of her cubs was gamboling too close to a precipice.

But no radar would have told her it was already too late.

"We're having some torta now," Ma said nicely. "Come on."

Gabriella kicked her feet out and said, *"Torta, signora. Bellissima!"* just like the fourteen-year-old Sicilian Pippi Longstocking she wasn't.

A shout went up from the other rooms.

There was some yelling—not the happy screaming of Sicilian camaraderie but the unhappy screaming of Sicilian murder.

With some sense of knowing, as if she'd seen it foreshadowed, Gabriella cried out, "Nonno!" and beat both me and my ma out of my little bedroom.

What my ma and I found in the bedlam was this: my papà wild as a boar and struggling old man Enrico out of the living room; Raffaele trying to tear my father by the shoulders away from his father-in-law and not getting anywhere, so then grabbing a good fistful of his hair; and Luisa looking dazed, befuddled, bemused—whatever—on the couch.

Out of all of this, to me the most terrible thing was Gabriella.

She looked like someone had slapped her face very hard. She looked like someone had jumped on her feet with boots. She was standing in one spot and screaming. At first no one was listening. Her fists were balled and her knuckles were white and her face was red and getting redder, her body taut like a high-tension wire. She screamed for everyone to leave her nonno alone, her voice getting louder and louder until all the glasses on the table and all the windows in the house must have been on the point of shattering. Then she launched herself like a human torpedo at the three struggling men. Her fists beat wildly and the sound her one little throat made was like that of a nation dying.

At first her ma Agata just seemed shell-shocked, then she came to her senses and she grabbed her child and tried to bury her head deep in her heavy bosom; it was supposed to be comfort but it was a lot like suffocation.

Gabriella fought and kicked against her.

Raffaele stopped dragging at my papà; my papà stopped dragging at Grandpa Enrico; Grandpa Enrico scratched in an abstract manner at the open front of his trousers.

Gabriella was still struggling not to be suffocated in her ma's ample front, and her father, in a rage, started to shout at her instead of anyone else. He was accusing her and, I think, meaning to shut her up.

"*Testa di fuoco!*" Raffaele Zazò yelled like a madman. "*Testa di fuoco!*"

Which means, literally, Firehead! Firehead! and I knew right then that this man was not her father, not by a long shot.

The rest is the rest.

Much later, in the aftermath, when my papà had finished swearing and my ma had shakily cleaned away the detritus of the failed little party, and we all helped wash, dry, and obliterate the night as if it had never existed, I sneaked into my sister's bedroom. It was two o'clock in the morning and Luisa was awake, lying there in her pink and white bed and staring into space. I finally got the chance to ask her what had happened.

"That stupid old man went to the toilet and when he came out his pants were still open and this thing like a salami was out and hard as a rock, and it was purple—purple!—and he came straight over to me on the couch and he put that thing in my face and he said, '*Mangia, signorina, mangia!* Eat, little miss, eat!' "

"Were you scared?"

Luisa lifted her head off the pillows to stare straight at my silhouette.

"Scared? Why should I be scared? It was a salami. The only thing I was scared about was that he'd hit me on the head with it."

Henceforth, in my house, the Zazòs were pretty bad news.

Sometimes Gabriella and I would send each other flashlight messages in the night, from dark bedroom to dark bedroom. Hey, are you all right? Do you miss me? Will you come and meet me later in the park, by the rose gardens?

We had our secret language all right, in voice and light, in rose gardens soft with late sunsets and parks that smelled of evening rain and new-mown lawns, and in kisses too, of course—sweet and silly kisses that went nowhere, forever and a day.

Crime and Punishment 101

TONY SOLERO SAID, "RIGHT, I know what it has to be."

"Yeah? What?"

"A silver cigarette lighter."

"Is that what they want?"

"That's all it'll take."

Treachery comes with simple words and even simpler desires, and though I loved Gabriella's kisses and her touch, so did too many other local boys. Sometimes after seeing her I ached with her unfulfilled pleasure in exactly the same way that I ached in the legs and the chest after a hard cross-country run. I wasn't her boyfriend and far from it too, but there were times I got carried away and imagined that someday before I was eighty like her nonno I'd marry Gabriella—and forget all the stupid things I said about never walking down the aisle. With Gabriella I wouldn't be walking anyway. I'd be waltzing like Fred Astaire toward that altar.

But the real thing about the here and now of our little corner of Heaven was that she was wed to the idea of virginity and I was trying to divorce its reality as quickly as possible. For all her hot and heavy breathing and the sweetness of her lips and the secrets we kept and laughed about together, she would not go that far. That was one step she didn't want to take and I was suspicious of what went on in her mind to hold her back.

So I thought very hard about what Tony told me.

We were wandering around the backs of the Fortitude Valley department stores, exactly the places put out of bounds by the school rules. Kids fought, smoked, and smooched around there; it was common knowledge. One early afternoon a flasher surprised a group of All Hallows girls in sports skirts who were standing around the loading docks of the Kmart smoking cigarettes. He showed them his cock and first they threw their burning stubs at him and then they dug in their bags and pelted him with things like cream buns and tampons. He must have felt like the goofiest flasher ever.

Tony and I were in our Christian Brothers school uniforms: appalling gray felt hats with a ribbon that carried the maroon and gold colors of the school badge; long socks with the same colors and crest; dark gray, daggy, show-your-knobbly-knock-knees shorts; and short-sleeved, light blue cotton shirts that had been washed too many times and weren't so blue anymore. And your collar had to be buttoned and the school tie sharp in its Windsor knot or it was four to six of the best from old Brother Reeves or young Brother Pierucci, the quiet and God-fearing brother of Pietro Pierucci, our local guardian angel. It was as if the school fathers wanted their boys to look as ugly and stupid as possible, as a character-building thing, but ours was the all-male neighboring school to the all-female All Hallows, and clandestine twosomes were already going on. If your love story was found out you got six cuts on the palms of your hands and detention for a calendar month. I never knew what punishment the girls got from the nuns. I felt sorry that Gabriella would end up there the next year, when her Australian schooling career started. For the time being she was occupying her days at home with her family, doing God knew what because she didn't have any girlfriends and the boys she knew were all in school. She was probably day in, day out scribbling on all her silly papers and walking the old man, dreaming of next year when she'd be like the rest of us.

Now it was a Wednesday, sports day, the easiest day to go missing and not be noticed, and Tony and I got away with it every four weeks or so. Without saying why we'd chosen to walk there, we were already at the back of the big Kmart, meeting place for wayward school students. We dumped our bags. Tony had some Marlboros and matches, so we smoked and considered the goods and bads of his plan.

"I don't think it'll work," I finally said.

"Sure it will. They're real."

"The girls? But it's only one lighter. It might split their vote, get it?"

Tony worked it out and nodded. "So all we have to do is get two lighters."

"Silver ones and maybe a carton of Peter Stuyvesant."

"Not Virginia. They say they like menthol."

"What's it matter? A carton of Alpine."

"Toilet smokes," Tony said. "That's it." He stubbed out his cigarette. "Got any money?"

"Nuh."

He pushed out his lips and made a sound like a wet post-pasta and fava beans fart. He had a soft, good-looking face and the type of floppy hair that in five or so years would drive girls crazy. For the present, though, the only female he drove crazy was his ma, who couldn't understand how her beloved boy Tony stayed bottom of every class he was in. It looked like a wonderful future in manual labor was awaiting young Tony Solero but whenever anyone threatened him with the fact he just smiled like he had better plans.

"If we get caught, Sam . . ." he said.

"Who cares?"

Tony sniffed and spat. "Incognito?"

So we stuffed our school hats and ties and badges into our bags and stuffed our bags behind an industrial bin. We rolled down our socks to hide the colors and school crest; Tony messed up my hair and I messed up his. Now we could have come from any school and—at a pinch, if no one studied us too hard—even a state school, which was the best thing to make people think because all the criminals of the world, it was believed, came from state schools and absolutely not the God-loving ones. We went into the Kmart through the back way and in a minute Tony was distracting a saleslady while I got my hands over and under the counter glass and helped myself to two nice silver butane lighters. Tony was telling her the true story of how smoking and cancer had destroyed his father's health, and how his mother wept at night, and how on earth could she justify it to herself that she took part in selling such wickedness, and the saleslady was listening, really listening, and then telling her side, so I went for the carton of Alpine and twin little bottles of lighter fluid too.

Greed was the wicked thing, not the gentle art of smoking, and I took too long and the saleslady turned and Tony and I were running like wolves through the store and out into the afternoon daylight, and then we kept going through the backstreets to where no one would find us, our school bags left behind to be collected late in the night when it was safe.

I F WE WERE the wolves then Andrea and Amelia Farmer were the lambs.

A little bit of treachery goes a long way and I was sorry that we'd arranged to meet up with them by the rose gardens in New Farm Park. That was where I normally met Gabriella, but with one look at their pleated Saint Rita's sports dresses and long white necks and long, long legs I forgot about her and anything real we'd ever shared. All the boys called Saint Rita's Saint Rooter's and the Farmer sisters were good to their word; Andrea lit an Alpine with her new lighter while Amelia took Tony down to the now dark riverbank. She relieved him and then Andrea took me down to the same place while Amelia and Tony sat under a bottle boab and smoked and couldn't find anything to talk about.

Andrea Farmer's breath smelled of menthol cigarettes and the garlic and pork sausages her mother had fried in oil the night before, and when she lay on the riverbank and flipped up her skirt and pulled down her yellow underpants nothing inside me worked the way it was supposed to work. There was cheap perfume and leftover tunnel-ball sweat on her skin and I kept thinking of how sometimes when I sat on a bench in the park with Gabriella and held her close the right angle could make her untied hair look like the blazing of the sun. Andrea Farmer used her hand to squish and squash around with me and then she said, "Oh, it happens, I won't tell," and pulled up her underpants and flipped down her skirt. She stood, brushing the grass off her back. For a little while I watched the new moon reflecting off the river's surface and the way a passing ferry's ripples and wavelets cracked that light into shimmery silver. Who was it who originally sang that old song, "Moon River," and wasn't it supposed to be Bobby Kennedy's favorite tune? Didn't they always play that as backing to documentaries about his assassination? Andrea walked ahead of me up the rise and when she got to the bottle boab and clump of other thick trees she said down into the darkness and without a trace of irony, "Mission accomplished." She used her new lighter on another Alpine and I saw Tony's unhappy face by the flame and that was Tony and my cue to disappear.

The funny thing was that neither of us had a lot to say and neither of us was swaggering along the streets the way we should have been. Was I fooling Tony as little as he was fooling me? No one was answering that question. Wouldn't it have been sick if he was still a virgin and me still a virgin and neither one of us game to admit it? And then, come about eight-thirty P.M., we were at the back of the Kmart again and our school bags weren't where they were supposed to be, or anywhere for that matter, and if our dicks had been tiny before, now they shriveled like garden snails that have the sense to turn in on themselves at the first threat from the outside world.

THE NEXT DAY, Brother Pierucci from school took us aside and gently whispered that we had to expect to see his brother the policeman soon because he'd found our bags. Lucky for Tony and me too, because Pietro Pierucci knew my ma from back when he was a boy in Sicily and everyone suspected he still had a younger man/older woman attraction for her. At weddings Officer Pierucci always asked Ma for at least one dance, in a very courtly and suave manner, but never without a friendly smile and a nod and a word to my papà, who of course couldn't mind.

The thing is, Pietro in Italian means Peter in English but more than that *pietro* is the word for rock and that was exactly what that young man was to the Sicilian families of those days, the rock upon which they understood the solid foundation of Australian law.

So, we were lucky because Peter didn't report us to his station the way he was supposed to, but that was where the luck stopped. The next night he did drop our bags off to our respective homes, explaining very carefully and very precisely to two sets of shell-shocked parents that he expected the castigation of two Sicilian families to prove more than enough punishment for two very stupid young boys. He said that restitution had to be made and not from a ma's purse or a papà's wallet but from sweat—good honest adolescent boys' sweat. Peter said that even if the Kmart never knew where the money came from or why, *he* wanted to see it before it was handed over, and it better be sooner rather than later. He finished by telling our two sets of parents that if their boys were stealing silver lighters then they were obviously smoking and he expected the families to put a stop to that filth as well. That went down very badly in my household because smoking was almost worse than stealing, but I knew that in the Solero *famiglia,* what with all those years of lung-cancer battles, it was going to be much, much worse.

As he was leaving Peter stopped and turned around and looked at me hard. It was half anger and half love and it struck me there and then the way it had never struck me before that that was exactly the way he looked at every one of us in those dreamy New Farm days.

P ETER   PIERUCCI   KNEW what he was doing; it took till nearly midnight before I could crawl into my room and close my door. Neither my ma or my papà hit me but I had as many oceans of tears drying on my face as my ma did. My palms were still damp with perspiration and my ears were ringing and I felt like I'd walked through a fire and a thunder wall of excruciating noise as well, and my whole body trembled in the wake of it. After the immediate admonishments, I was informed I'd have to work with my father on Saturdays and half-days on Sundays from now on, and all through the school holidays which were coming up, and I knew that was going to be the worst punishment of all. Everyone else would be in the crystal waters of surf beaches; everyone else would be having hot holiday flings cooled with milk shakes and midnight car cruises. Everyone else would be being teenagers and I'd be laboring in the killing Brisbane sun with my old man, who liked hard work as much if not more than he liked anything else on this hard earth.

The light went out and alone in my bed I hoped to give myself quickly to the black; I hoped I'd dream of Gabriella, because the way things were going I couldn't see how I'd ever get the chance to steal enough hours to hold her and to kiss her and to tunnel my way through her body into her white spirit, the way I was born to do.

The Dreamer in His Dream

BUT THE POUNDING IN my chest wouldn't let me get to sleep right
and I was kicking at the single cotton sheet over me as if it were a
funeral shroud. The night wasn't hot but it was warm and there were a
hundred people in my room just standing there looking at me, and then
there was a scraping near my window like a cat or a possum trying to
crawl from my ma's vegetable patch below up to the iron gutters above,
and I was staring straight into the dark, awake and scared, and I saw just
the one silhouette and it was in the window frame and I knew it was her.

Gabriella climbed over the sill, quiet as an expert thief. I was sitting
up and ready to get out of my bed but she came and lay down and
pulled me to her. It was the most dangerous thing to do with my parents
the way they were and two rooms away, and her own parents just next
door. Still, there was a long corridor to protect us and a bathroom in
between and my sister's room was up at the other end of the house. So
if we were quiet enough the three or four A.M. world was ours.

"What are you doing here?"

I had to speak right down into her ear. It was like breathing into
Gabriella, my whisper going into her little body and then further down

into her soul, calling it, invoking it, waking it, and when she wanted to answer me she turned my head with her small hands and breathed back into my ear. Her breath was warm, from deep inside her, soft, making warm words. It was like a game that wasn't a game because it made me feel strong and like an adult and more excited than I ever could have become in the uncomfortable and mildewy dark places we went to for kisses.

"What do you think I'm doing here? I couldn't let you be alone after what I heard. I thought they were going to kill you."

"Me too."

"What was all the screaming for? What did you do? What did you steal from Kmart?"

I told her and Gabriella shook my arm and whispered, "Why? Why did you do something so silly?" And so I told her about the Farmer sisters too.

She went quiet. We were in each other's arms in that small bed, something we'd never done before, not in any sort of bed. I thought it was smart and tough of her to climb up into my window like a Spidergirl, and it was something she must have worked out and thought about doing, and how to do, for ages and ages.

For a minute it was as if what I'd told her would make her push herself away from me but just like that she held me tighter. Her hands pressed on my shoulders. Gabriella moved herself a little bit under me and then I did what she wanted and I was on top of her, and that was something we'd never done before either.

"You tried to lose your virginity with Andrea Farmer? Amelia's sister? With that whore? The one with the ugly head and the horse legs? You tried to buy her with a cigarette lighter?"

Gabriella was crying in a way that didn't make a sound but her tears on my face seemed as hot as olive oil off a frying pan.

She said in Sicilian, "Salvatore, why? I don't understand. Why?" But I think she understood all right.

Gabriella kissed the side of my face and the tender part of my neck and for the first time I understood the power of pain. If I wanted to fuck my Gabriella and make her forget whatever reservations she had about sex, now was the time, and she was loosening what she could of her clothes and for the first time I tasted her nipples, and it was because of that pain in her and because of those hot fucking tears that I kissed her hard and ate up her lips and her tongue but didn't let her get herself out of the things she needed to get out of.

I went onto my side and she put her warm head against my shoulder and that was the way we stayed, and she came into my dreams and maybe I went into hers, but in the pre-dawn light Gabriella crawled out my window again and the last I saw was the sun through her red hair, and inside I cried out for her, really cried out for her in a way that scared me, and it was something like, Gabriella, stay close to me, whatever happens make sure you stay close, I promise that's all I'll ever want from you.

Enrico Belpasso's Very Long
Road to Heaven

UNTIL THE END OF the school year and a little beyond I walked the
straight line.

I didn't wag anymore, never smoked another cigarette, and I worked
with my papà under the cruelest summer sun and didn't complain while
the flies crawled like blood over my face. No curses came out of my
mouth when my muscles felt like they were going to break. My intention was only to save the money to repay the Kmart as fast as possible
and hand it over to Officer Pierucci.

This I did, and so did Tony.

We hung out when we could, though the families saw us as bad
news for one another, and I didn't see much of Gabriella either. It was
just the odd encounter for a kiss and a rub; somebody told me there was
some Polish kid older than us that she was seeing a lot of, but at the time
I never knew if that was true or not. When I asked her she wouldn't
answer and sometimes she'd go sit alone and take out her pens and her
papers and scribble away so that there was nothing for me to do but

leave her alone. The Zazòs and the Capistranos still despised one another anyway, and in a funny way that really did serve to keep us apart. She rarely came to my front door and though I often went to hers there was never much of a warm welcome from Mamma Zazò anymore. I missed being her stupid darly, I really did.

Our flashlight messages sometimes went unanswered, mine to Gabriella, Gabriella's to me. I sat my final exams for the year with a feeling of impending doom and then the summer holidays started. True to my old man's word I was up at five A.M. every weekday and sitting beside him in the truck every 5:45 A.M. as we trundled off to our next worksite in Hell. His idea of punishment was absolute and the straight line I was walking now he expected to continue until I was a hundred years old. He gave me Saturday afternoons and Sundays off to recuperate from being a boy-laborer, but it never seemed enough time to get the aching out of my back and neck and legs, or to see my friends and arrange a trip to the blue-breaking surf of the north or south coasts. I heard tales of drinking parties, of a wild week where a dozen young *cumpari* lost their virginity in the sands of the wind-churned beaches near Surfers Paradise, and of nights dancing to new rock-and-roll bands. I was excluded from everything and after a while too tired to care.

In the night, lying boneless and dejected in my bed, I sometimes hoped or dreamed that Gabriella would come creeping through my bedroom window again, but she didn't. We'd learned how to give the proper SOS by flashlight, which I did every now and then, and then gave up on because nothing came back. Instead, some deep nights when I was wide awake in that crazy way physical exhaustion can affect you, I'd hear a lonely bellowing from next door. It was as if some elephant were lost in our neighborhood streets but I knew what it meant: an old man was dreaming.

Gabriella's nonno, once upon a time anointed Cavaliere by the President of the Italian Republic for his contribution to the war effort, wasn't getting any better, and I wondered how that made his young granddaughter feel.

Love: 1975

• • •

I TURNED FIFTEEN and Tony Solero wanted to buy me one of the Farmer sisters again, this time as a present. He seemed to understand when I told him that I wasn't interested and he didn't take offense, but somehow the Saturday night of my birthday we all ended up in New Farm Park again, and in exactly the place of the last imbroglio too. What I learned was that Amelia Farmer had told Tony that she really loved the armed forces, especially the air force, and that one day she was going to marry a flyboy and get carried off to her honeymoon in an F-III. Before his interest in girls had started to raise its purple head, Tony used to spend hours and hours sticking toy airplanes together out of kits, and for his best model F-III Amelia Farmer was ready to put out one more time. To be fair to Tony, his original intention was that he was buying her for me, but seeing I didn't want the gift he treated himself and that was fine.

The Farmer sisters traveled as a pair and that was why I was there with them again; that was the simple reason and it turned out to be too simple for Gabriella.

Tony and Amelia were down by the riverbank and I was sitting without a word to say to Andrea. Around us the trees were dark and then one of them was an obscure shape that moved forward. Gabriella came out of the darkness of New Farm Park with her bear-for-a-grandfather in tow. Andrea, sitting cross-legged on the grass and smoking one of those cigarettes that smelled as eucalyptus-fresh as toilet cleaner, said, "Who's this?" in a way that meant she'd already seen all the shit and charlatans of the world and these two before her now were nothing to get excited about.

Gabriella shone her flashlight over us.

"Scared 'a the dark?" Andrea said. "Shine that on me again and I'll stick it up your arse."

Gabriella said to me, *"Buon compleanno,"* then continued in Sicilian, "I thought your parents would have a party for you."

"I spoiled my chances of a party. We had dinner and cake."

33

Andrea said, "What is this wog SHIT?" and bored and aggravated by a lousy night doing nothing she got up and stomped toward the slope and the riverbank shouting, "Ahmee-lia! Ahmee-lia!"

I rose to my feet and the brain-dead grandpa was looking through me like I wasn't there. Gabriella was holding his hand and I knew they'd been out for a late-night walk in the cool. New Farm Park was still like that in 1975, you could go down the tree-lined laneways and across all the different garden enclosures, and even walk by the glittering river just to watch the ferries and be pretty certain that no deadshit would come and stick a knife in your back or want to stomp you just for something interesting to fill his evening. The strange thing was that Enrico went on staring at me; his mouth was a little ajar and his three teeth were showing and his eyes were glazed but somehow sharp too, as if he were looking at something only he could see. I hoped I'd never be so old and ugly that a fourteen-year-old kid had to take me for a walk like a dog, and maybe even have to point my dick for me when I needed to piss.

I hadn't spoken to Gabriella for weeks and it felt good to see her, though it was easy to tell what she thought I'd been doing. And if I had, so what? What had the Polish boy been doing with her? And what about any of the others I kept hearing about?

We were stiff with one another and kept to Sicilian:

"Why is he staring at me?"

"I told him what you and Tony were doing down here with those sisters."

"I wasn't. Tony was."

Gabriella said, "We're going now."

As far as I was concerned my birthday was over and Tony could fend for himself. I said, "I'll come with you," and we walked together slowly because that was the only way the big Sicilian bear could go. He didn't walk so much as thump, but it was good to take in the quiet streets by the park and the sweet evening breeze that had blown the humidity out of the day. Gabriella's hair was loose and whenever we walked under some streetlamp or beside the passing headlights of some car I saw her cheeks were rosy. That meant she liked seeing me, even if she was angry.

"I had a nice birthday surprise worked out for you."

"I didn't think you'd know it was today."

"Of course I know. I went to your house and your ma told me you went out."

"You came to the house?"

"I had a feeling you'd be in the park. I took Nonno with me to find you. Now you'll never know what your present was."

"Come on. What?"

"Maybe another time."

We went along some more and three guys I knew were like some sort of shadowy football front row coming down the street, and I said g'day to them and they stared after us like we were orangutans or something because of the language we were speaking.

When they were far enough away one yelled out, "Fucken wogs," and another singsonged, "Go back to Eyetieland," and Gabriella shouted back, "Convicts," just like that, and I felt a weight on my shoulders that hadn't been there before. Gabriella and I exchanged a glance and with as little as a look it was she and I in the center of the world again.

It wasn't difficult to see how much the everyday insults from the boys hurt her. It was something people like us were supposed to be used to but it was a hard thing to shrug off, especially when it made you feel like everyone was in a nice warm place, and you were there too, but if something went just that little bit wrong you'd be the first to be shown the exit door. No wonder the sons-of-migrants boys I spent my time with made themselves into such perfect Australians. In those days of 1975 if you didn't transcend being seen as a wog you had bad breath and were thick in the head and were a mamma's boy, and therefore fair game for beatings and exclusion. Those fed up with that sort of tag used to kill to play cricket and fight to play football and would call any of their kind fucking wogs or dagos themselves just to prove how much they weren't a part of the horrible migrant circle. What made me proud was that Tony and I wouldn't play that game; the two of us knew without saying a word that we would stick together even if none of the others did.

So that's how it was for us boys; it never really crossed my mind to wonder how a girl might have felt.

Now Gabriella put the matter aside. She didn't refer to what had just happened and so it didn't happen. Instead, going back to things between us and us alone, she said, "Don't make yourself cheap with the Farmer sisters again, Salvatore." She looked me in the face. Her nonno seemed to nod, as if for emphasis, but I only thought I was seeing things. She said, "You know, it makes me think less of you."

"I've never touched either one of the stupid Farmer sisters. What about Robert Scholar-mouse-key?"

"Skolimowski. Do you think he matters? I want to hold your hand, Salvatore, I want to give you your birthday present, but I can barely even look at you. Those Farmer girls are so disgusting."

I looked at the old man, who was looking away into the street, when I said in a low voice, "What were you going to give me?" and Gabriella, like magic—did you see it, Salvatore, or didn't you—slowly and deftly ran the back of one of her hands down between her breasts and into the V of her shorts, and it was like some white bird had caressed her with its wings.

"Salvatore, there's so much I want to tell you. There's so much I want you to see. You have to know me. That's it. You should know everything about me or then it's not even worth it and that's how it is."

I moved toward her, and Nonno Enrico Belpasso, senses or no senses, loudly cleared his throat and spat into the bushes. If that wasn't a warning for me to just keep my distance from his granddaughter I didn't know what was.

"I told you nothing's going on with Andrea Farmer or her ugly sister." But I put my hands into my pockets anyway, because now there was no taking hers, not with that old man looming like a beast.

Gabriella said, "Birthdays are in the air."

"Yeah, yours." It was true, Christmas was coming and she'd once told me that close after Christmas came her day. Every New Year really was a new year for her.

"No, it's Nonno's before mine."

"*Va bene.*" As if I cared. "How old will he be?"

She turned her face up to him. Gabriella was so small she seemed only as tall as his distended belly. "On the first of December he'll be eighty-one."

"*Gesù.* Eighty-one."

Gabriella gave me a smile that could have lit up the street and made the moon look like a match ready for blowing out.

"Salvatore, how are your savings going?"

"Phew, they're fine. I'm doing so much work I'm practically a millionaire. I paid back the Kmart and that got Pietro Pierucci off my back. Now the rest is for me." For the future—my ma and papà's favorite English word. Future. Just hearing the word made me sick. Future, future, future. So of course don't bother living now, just work yourself to the bone.

"Can you use it?"

"The money? It's not in a trust account or anything."

"Can I have some of it?"

"Yes."

"Do you want to know what for?"

"No."

Gabriella didn't smile so much now. She said, in all seriousness, "There's something I've been thinking about. Tonight's helped. I want the money for Nonno's birthday present."

"Buy him whatever you like. How has tonight helped?"

"Well, the thing about your friend Tony and the Farmer sisters."

I stopped on the footpath and wasn't sure what Gabriella was building up to. I said, "Tony and the Farmer sisters?"

Gabriella let out a deep breath. She continued in Sicilian. It didn't seem to bother her that the ancient bear with her might have followed what she said.

"*Nonno è vecchio*. Nonno's old. He's lonely. He's really so lonely, Salvatore. Since his wife died he's never really been happy. He was different when I was little. Now he's going to be eighty-one years of age, can you even imagine it? I think he deserves something very special for that. He deserves something he really wants."

"And what is that?"

"*Una donna*—a woman."

"A woman." Then it arrived: "You want to buy him one of the *Farmer* sisters?"

"No, I'm thinking of a professional. Someone who'd know what she was doing, and who has some experience with older gentlemen. Someone who wouldn't be disgusted to touch him. But she'd have to be nice too. I've seen those advertisements for escorts. I want to get him a professional call girl."

"How can you say that's what he wants?"

Gabriella gave me an ironic look. "He's a man. And he's not dead."

"Are you sure? Look at him. He hasn't got a clue what you're talking about."

"We talk a lot. He's not a donkey, you know."

"He's completely senile! You'd be being cruel to him. Why don't you leave him alone?"

"Leave him alone? Can't you see that's exactly what the matter is? The world leaves him alone enough as it is. Nonno, isn't that true? Nonno!" Her nonno stared at the soft leaves on some low branches while his breathing rasped. Gabriella said, "We're taught to put men and women like him where we don't have to look at them. You'd like that? Salvatore, he's like a TV that's tuned to the wrong station. He gets nothing but snow and interference but if you spend a little time, sometimes you can get him right. Then he talks and talks and talks, and he feels things too, and he knows everything that's going on. If only you could understand. He really feels things."

Her lips trembled a little. She felt things too—maybe that was the real point. Such an intensity came out from Gabriella that I had to stand transfixed. I wanted to put my arms around her and save her and I had no idea from what. Her eyes were shining and then a small shiny tear fell onto her cheek and Gabriella almost smacked at it, as if her very emotions were an act of self-betrayal.

"All right. All right. What does he say?" I looked at Enrico Belpasso. What could a man with mush for a mind possibly express?

Gabriella slowly passed her hand over one eye and down the side of her face. She had herself in check again. That touch of her eye, that palm down her cheek, these were moves that made her seem twenty years older.

"What does anyone his age say? We talk about his younger years. He likes to tell me about his wife but he gets very emotional. Don't you, Nonno? He remembers every detail. The first war too. You remember I told you he's a hero? He got blown up in a very important battle. Then other times we just discuss silly things like how to grow good vegetables and how to make strawberries and figs bigger. Then other times he likes to discuss lovemaking."

"You're absolutely making this up."

"So that's what I've got in mind for him."

Nonno set off of his own accord and so we were walking again. Now Gabriella took my arm and the big bear didn't react at all. Did that mean he understood what we were talking about? Did that mean he was beside himself with some sort of half-remembered anticipation? Gabriella's body, close to me now, despite her smallness gave off a heat. She was wet in her armpits and as we walked past those trees outside the park and on through the fresh night air I thought I sensed the heat between her legs too. I felt confused; I was mad with wanting her and mad with wanting to know what distressed her so. Despite Gabriella's story and her outward calm I could see how forced these things were. It was as if she were trying to hold back a big bursting geyser of blood with only the force of her will. But why? Where did it come from? What stopped her from telling me about it?

Gabriella shivered, pressed close to me; for long moments I almost believed her life was some sort of a buried nightmare of chaos.

"Gabriella," I said, "is everything all right?"

"Yes." Her voice had absolutely no authority. "Will you really let me have the money?"

"I already said I would."

"But you will, really?"

"If you want money you can have money. You can have anything you want. Just tell me what you want and I'll give it to you. I mean it, I really mean it, do you believe me now?"

Gabriella turned her face away. She must have been thinking it all the way through, or maybe just adding details to her plan.

"I've got some of my own saved but I need more for a really good woman. And I'll need your help. That's the other thing, Salvatore. I don't want to do this alone."

"Then I'll give you my help."

"I know you've been in trouble. If we get caught it'll be worse for you."

"I'll give you my help."

Gabriella squeezed herself to me. She looked up at me and I gazed into her small sweet face. Green eyes shining. What a fool I was. There was no nightmare in her, there was no inexplicable sadness, there was only me and my need to believe that only I would ever make her happy. The drifting scent of roses from the garden beds in the vast park behind us filled these last bits of my fifteenth birthday. My spirits had lifted. Sometimes when I looked at Gabriella I thought I saw one of those young goddesses out of Greek mythology whose job it is to spread wildflowers and rose petals in the spring.

"So. One more time. You will help me?"

She made me take my hand out of my pocket and she held it in hers. Her mouth was a firm line of determination.

"Will you, Salvatore?"

"Jesus, Gabriella," I said in English. "Jesus. Yes."

Gabriella turned my palm over, her soft skin gently touching my calluses and the raggedy blood blisters that had burst and burst again. She stroked these things as if they hurt her and not me.

Then she took her nonno's arm, having to reach up to it, and with her in the center like a child, and we her protectors, the three of us drifted down the shadowy streets toward this whatever-it-was that our Firehead dreamed could be a little like her grandfather's past.

Dear Diary

Gabriella's Book of Fire

I<small>T'S</small> D<small>ECEMBER</small> 1<small>ST</small> in the year 1912, and on this day, a cold, typi-
cally winter's day in Sicily, with icy winds blowing off the Ionian
Sea and across the Riviera dei Ciclopi, and into the flat plains of fields
where Baron Giorgio's family presides over roughly one hundred and
fifty hectares of vineyards and citrus plantations, Enrico Belpasso cele-
brates the morning of his eighteenth birthday by sitting under an enormous flowering fig tree and helping himself to the miraculous pile he
has made of some of the best of this tree's ripe fruit. How strange the
seasons have been this year, he wonders. Neither being one thing nor
settling on the other. For instance: look at this fig tree in full bloom
when by now it should be as bare as the bones of a long-dead donkey.
Look how the seasonal cold has finally decided to come into the world
today when even as recently as yesterday the daylight hours were balmy
and the evening hours uncomfortable as July. When the world is ready to
end, he thinks—as many others are already willing to think—these
could be its portents. Summer in winter, autumn in spring, swordfish

and tuna spawning when they shouldn't, and didn't someone pass the word not a week ago that a goat gave birth to a dead monster with two heads?

Ah, what of it, when right here like this he has perfectly beautiful figs to enjoy on his birthday when usually he can have none. Instead of signs of doom, maybe people should see these things as signs of impending plenty. Maybe it's not the end of the world that's being heralded but the dawn of prosperity; Heaven knows, the island could use some. Maybe people take things far too seriously, that's what young Enrico decides, but whatever the case may be, Enrico Belpasso does truly love figs, and this crazy season of bounty is certainly not going to be put to waste.

Not by the likes of him.

Through the heavy branches he can see the southern ascent of the volcano, which with the abrupt change to late-autumn normalcy has had its peaks covered with snow—yet at the same time there is angry activity up there. Against the saintly white the fire fountains burst, sending tall towers of sparks into the heavens and raining down spectacular showers of red.

This is, of course, an everyday occurrence.

THE SICILIAN TOWN of Riposto, and its close neighbor Giarre, and all the areas surrounding these, are famous for their beaches and for their fishermen and boats, and for the spreading coastal markets that sell all the fruit of the sea. Swordfish, tuna, sardines, octopus, and squid, these are only a small portion of what the fishermen's nets reveal daily; this sea has no limits. The surrounding lands are rich too, rich enough to support produce of an almost infinite variety. The fools on the mainland would have nothing like this if not for their island, whose locals they call the black men of Italy. Sicily is, after all—at this time in history, at least, before the corrupting influence of intercountry trade agreements—the Italian nation's bread basket. Grapes, lemons, peaches, corn, maize: imagine something that is capable of sprouting from a seed and here is the place where it will grow to twice its normal size. This earth is wild, fruitful and lush, its grace owing in equal parts to the lovely temperate climate it resides in and to the towering Mount Etna, which strews the land with lava and ash—agents of terrible destruction first, yet when they cool they enrich the earth.

No wonder the ancient Arabic word for Enrico's island translates as Paradise.

Enrico, however, knows very little about natural landscapes or antiquity. If you asked him what provinces border his own *Provincia di Catania* he wouldn't be able to say. If you wanted him to tell you the towns descending from the northern face of the volcano, less than twenty or thirty kilometers away, he would mention several and then dry up, muttering something about the strangeness of people from "up there." If you asked this eighteen-year-old boy where and from whom the Sicilian population descended he would shrug and not be able to reveal the names of the Sikels and the Carthaginians, and barely the Greeks and the Turks. He wouldn't know the different Sicilian eras: the Byzantine period, the time of the Norman conquests, the Hohenstaufen accession and the end of Hohenstaufen rule, or the time of the Spanish Hapsburgs, to name just a few. He would be aware of course that roughly thirty years before he was born Italy had become a unified nation and that included his island, and he might even know a little about Garibaldi and his famous "thousand" of supporters, but that's about as far as the young man would be able to go into history. Because what is history to him? It's eighteen years, eighteen years working and living on Baron Giorgio's property, and for now Enrico would rather consider his next eighteen years and where they will take him—and he'd like to eat his miraculous figs and enjoy his privacy too.

For he is a very, very, very lazy young man.

WITH NO KNOWLEDGE of the past Enrico Belpasso has no sense of the future, of the world growing into a war which the unified nation of Italy will enter in a bid to finally rid itself of its remaining oppressors.

What all other nations will call World War I Italians will prefer to know as the Italo-Austrian war, the final phase of the movement for liberation from the Austrian nationals who still occupy parts of the mainland in the north and northeast. Enrico is enjoying his figs on his eighteenth birthday without suspecting that come the day of his twenty-first birthday he will be lying flat, face down in mud, struggling to cover his eyes and nose and mouth with his mask as mustard gas and billowing smoke from the exploded mortar that has just killed his two closest companions settles over him like a shroud. He will barely feel the burning of his skin or the way a whizzing piece of shrapnel severs his Achilles tendon and leaves him as helpless as a puppet whose leg string has been cut and whose puppeteer, anyway, has fallen asleep. No, all that is ahead and of course this young man doesn't presume a thing about it. What is the now of his life is his lonely birthday and the fresh taste of figs, a taste that he'll dream about, tossing and turning and crying out, eaten up with fever and screaming names like curses, when he's shipped to a base hospital in Bologna to recuperate after the failed Fourth Battle of the Isonzo that he had the bad luck to be an infantryman in. It will be a trench war on the Isonzo front and it will help to leave a total of 280,000 Italian soldiers dead at the hands of the numerically weaker but strategically superior Austrian army. The first day of December 1915 Enrico will turn twenty-one and be blown up and half gassed to death; by the second day of December the whole thing will be called off. General Luigi Cardona will be in command of the Italian army and all the southern recruits will rue this man's unfortunate surname; the Sicilian word that sounds too much like the general's family name is the word *carduni*, which in their southern dialect is of course the word for imbecile. No consolation, that.

All ahead.

So it's as Enrico is eating one of the nice juicy figs that no fruit bats have gotten to yet that Fortunata, then already twenty-three years of age, though she admits to twenty and no more, comes through the rows of trees and pushes through the low branches—starlings and sparrows and wood pigeons scattering into the gray skies above—to find him. She stands amid the deep green leaves. She is five years Enrico's senior in age but has at least twenty years on him in experience, maturity, and, to be blunt, focus. She's not a petite woman and neither is she lightly pretty, but she's handsome in the preferred style of the day and heavy in the right places too, in a way that Enrico has noticed long before now. Quite a few of the young men of the surrounding properties and towns have also noticed this, so much so that it's a mystery to everyone, and most particularly Fortunata, why such fine stock as she hasn't found a suitable husband yet.

Fortunata knows where to find Enrico because she has been watching him as closely as she can for at least a month now, and therefore she is thoroughly aware of his secret: in moments of quiet this work-hating boy disappears like a morning fog from the gang of laborers he belongs to. He disappears into this shady bower of fig trees where no one will disturb him, and the surprising thing is that the closer to the main houses he hides, the safer he actually is. Laborers are spread like locusts all over the Baron's one hundred and fifty hectares, yet here things are so much quieter and he is relatively safe. Safe from them, yes, but not from this one extraordinary thing.

Fortunata's focus.

Finely tuned toward marriage and plump and healthy bambini, her mind has truly been on Enrico Belpasso and little else. She knows that none of these "off" times are his own times. He should be in the fields laboring the same way everyone else does, for in the Giorgio empire the only rest periods are nights and Sunday afternoons. This particular morning of the inappropriate fresh new cold Fortunata should be working too, but she comes under the branches crouching, the sleeves and hems of her white and black housemaid's outfit catching on burrs and baby shoots. The deep pocket of her apron is bulging squarely but small with what she has for him, the boy who is already known as the most indolent in the province.

They've spoken before but not many times and never more than the most perfunctory words. She works in the main palazzo cleaning the rooms and cooking the less elaborate meals. She keeps the beds as soft as the clouds where angels sleep and the floors as clean as the heavenly plains saints roam upon. If she were to fall below this standard once, she would receive a firm rebuke; twice and Baron Giorgio, a hot-tempered man who lives by laws he has devised himself, would whip her shoulders and buttocks with a carpet beater; three times and, as in the American game of baseball that her United States emigré friends have written her about, she will be kicked out. Be assured, Fortunata has never once fallen below the Giorgio standard.

Enrico is one of the field laborers. As has done his father and his father's father so does he, except for the fact that none of these forebears ever felt as much loathing for physical labor as he feels daily. Enrico Belpasso wastes a great deal of time dreaming under trees and lying on his back in swaying meadows, and the things that go through his mind he can barely put a finger on. Within as free-roaming a property as Baron Giorgio's no one but his immediate group of workmates knows this, and they don't care, and now of course a lovesick housemaid named Fortunata has also discovered his secret.

Yet everyone else on this property has to pull their weight. Twenty-eight entire families manage to live on the Giorgio land, and this is neither large nor small by the semifeudal standards of this early twentieth century. A small society within a society hums with life here. Working men and women, adolescents, prepubescent children, babies and toddlers, still-working grandparents, and those who are infirm and need plenty of help just to get from bed to chair to bed again. Then too there are countless chickens and roosters, ducks and drakes, hedgehogs, rabbits and hares, dogs, pigs, cats, slithering creatures of the dark rich earth like green lizards, leopard snakes, Aesculapian snakes, and vipers. There are innumerable species of birds: buzzards, sparrow-hawks, barn owls, scops owls, tawny owls, long-eared owls, and quails. Foxes can be found, and weasels, and farther into the hills, have no doubt, there are wildcats. Peasants and nobles alike hunt them with rifle and *lupara,* and bring their skins and skulls home as trophies.

During the day Fortunata is busy enough in the big house to keep two like her fully occupied, and at night her mother and father barely let her take two steps out of the two-room cottage where she lives with the two of them and her two sisters; their cottage itself is barely two meters from the main palazzo's washing sheds. Every constraint on her life seems to come in this number and so she has promised herself that when she makes her babies they will eventually add up to more than a pair by some significant amount. Yet for now everything in Fortunata's life reeks of family, responsibility, work, and Giorgio. How else could she have arrived at this age, with nicely padded, flaring hips, and breasts as full as wicker baskets after a day's stone-fruit harvest, and still not be married? But here's the thing: those two steps of freedom her parents have so foolishly allowed her have finally proven to be enough, because a sweat-stained young laborer, tall, strong, skin unmottled by hunger or sickness, and hair as black as the lava covering the Sicilian terrain, has successfully caught her eye.

And once caught, Fortunata is not the type to be let go of.

AT FIRST ENRICO hears, then sees her coming. His spirits drop like a stone. This is his sanctuary and worse than the thought of being punished for being so lazy is the possibility that his hidey-hole will be given away and he'll have no chance to escape there again. Fortunata arrives so quickly through the moist undergrowth that he doesn't have the time or the presence of mind to take the half-eaten fig that is tantalizing his palate away from his mouth. It is jammed right there and that's the way Fortunata finds her just-turned-eighteen potential paramour, with that purple fruit filling his mouth, its juice dribbling down his chin, and him dressed in his already dirty, always torn, perennially shabby work clothes and boots, his back propped against the trunk of the tree, and one leg outstretched in his repose and the other bent at the knee, as if he hasn't a care in the world or a thing left to do. He drops his hand down but his mouth stays full of fig, and beside him the skins of the many he has already gorged himself upon lie discarded and pathetic, looking for all the world like the pelts of dirt-territory rats.

That heavy wind cooled by its journey across the Ionian Sea covers all the baron's prosperous hectares but here Enrico is protected from the cold. He is completely comfortable, if melancholy, and in his little world of stillness he would have stayed, if not for the intruder.

"Happy Birthday, Enrico Belpasso," Fortunata says immediately, standing there in her white and black maid's dress that is a little like a nurse's in a hospital yet not quite so. Her skin is dark and her face oval; her eyes are large and brown and take him in. Everything about this young woman is large. Her lips and mouth seem almost licentious in the way they dominate her features; her arms are thick, her hands are broad.

The sight of her here in this bower is dumbfounding, but more than that is the absolute impossibility of her four words. She knows his name and she knows the relevance of this day. Did she actually come here to seek him out rather than having stumbled upon him, as he assumes she has? Now Enrico really can't speak, and he chokes down his mess of chewed, pulped fig, waiting for her to say what he most fears, that her next move will be to report him to the *massaru,* or worse, to that most senior man on the property, the one who stands for the Baron himself, the *fattore.*

"Can I have a fig?" Fortunata says with a coquettish furrowing of her brow.

Enrico has to shuffle his backside over the dewy grass and the exposed roots because she is about to sit down with him. His mind is rocked by the enormity of her move, by her incredible audacity. Something like this has simply never happened to Enrico before: he has never sat next to a female who was not his sister or his mother or his grandmother, or at the very least some sort of relative. Fortunata smells of what he imagines is lilac-scented bathwater and something else like plums, and she fills her skirts the way skirts ought to be filled, and when she does sit down beside him (leaning her shoulder next to his as if there were no space and this a simple accident, her smile innocent as a baby blinking at its mother) she selects a fig from Enrico's ready little pyramid and surveys it with interest. Then she tears the skin with her teeth and puts the point of her tongue right inside the pink and the purple of the fruit, and Enrico, watching this as closely as he has watched many a traveling magician's act in the Riposto market square, feels his head swimming and without notice—faints.

When in a moment he is awake, with Fortunata still shaking him by his shoulder and her concerned face before his as large and white as the face of the moon, pins and prickles cover his skin and he knows this for what it is—sheer and absolute desire.

She Had Wings Too

By telephone, Gabriella had made an afternoon arrangement, in advance of the big Sicilian dinner her ma would be making that night for the old man's birthday.

The grand old timber house in Spring Hill that we took Nonno Enrico Belpasso to looked like it had once been a piece of palatial, colonial splendor, even if the neighborhood it was in was no more than halfway decent. It was one of those Queensland places that had obviously been built at the turn of the century by some family with a lot of money, and a few servants or maids or whatever to boot. It was immense, and you could tell from where you stood outside, just by the many layers and plateaus of tin roofing, that there were plenty of rooms and stories and winding staircases in there. The only thing was, the heyday of this great house was gone: every scrap of its outside paint peeled away in strips to reveal the bare brown splintering wood beneath, and gutters seemed rusted right through in neglect. Windows were cracked and crooked and some hung off their hinges. Surrounding the house, what must once have been spacious gardens were now no more than vast stretches of weed; only the hardiest or the luckiest flowers still grew among all that guff that strangled the good. At intervals, the house's wire fence was bent and twisted into crazy angles and declensions, as if wandering drunks or escaping clients had knocked portions of it down with their weight, and the little iron gate that was supposed to afford a visitor's main welcome was red-rough with rust. Added to that, the property was three-street-cornered and faced a busy, busy intersection where the local council hadn't as yet seen fit to install traffic lights. The blaring of horns, the near sideswipes, the pedestrians dancing through the lines of cars—well, it was generations since this Queensland palace had been genteel.

Gabriella hadn't needed to answer ads in the newspaper; I got the name and number from Tony Solero, who didn't say too much about how he'd come by the information, other than to mention something about his older brother Lino—whose full name was Pasqualino because he was born on a Good Friday—and his bad-crowd mates and their Saturday nights in Fortitude Valley and Spring Hill's illegal casinos and brothels. These were the places everyone knew about and could pinpoint without a street map, to which any taxi driver could take you. Of course the local joke was that the police were the only good folk claiming to be completely unenlightened about such establishments; no one had any doubts that this had to do with the old brown-paper-bag-stuffed-with-cash and a lousy-government-too-long-in-power syndrome. That was the tenor of the times. Brisbane's illegal activities flourished and were police-protected; old buildings that should have been revered and heritage-listed were razed to the ground in the dead of night, just to make way for ridiculous steel and glass high-rise office blocks that no one wanted; developers and criminals prospered and so did the state government politicians whose potential objections were salved with kickback money, free trips to exotic locations, and good-time gals. These were the urban myths that filtered through the city like an ongoing pestilence. It would take more than a decade before the whole shithouse fell down, and when it fell it buried some people and sent others on the strangest journeys—me included.

But back in 1975 it was a totally different story.

Gabriella hadn't let me be the one to make the telephone call. She wouldn't even let me stay in the same room when she spoke to whoever ran Nocturne, but she must have been very clear and very convincing because when we arrived in the midafternoon of that first day of December, a nice woman in a deafening floral dress was waiting for us. I could see her loud raiment and her pale, mottled, veiny shins behind the lattice railings of the manor's front verandah. I could see the cover of the *Women's Weekly* she was reading. On the front page there was a picture of the ice-goddess features that made up Grace Kelly's scaringly perfect face. We went through the rusted gate and walked along a cracked concrete path through the weeds, and Gabriella gave two confident knocks on the front door. Through the lattice I saw that magazine go down and those ugly shins move, then the front door opened.

Our welcomer looked straight at Nonno Belpasso, into Nonno Belpasso, and winced, a sea of wrinkles turning her face into parchment.

Her first words were, "Oh, I see."

She looked dry as an old bone (in fact, she could have been Miss Dogbone the piano teacher's heavily made-up twin sister), she had a slash of brilliant red across her wizened lips, which made them brutal against that powdered pancake face, and her eyes were painted blue all around. Her long, sagging earlobes dripped with emerald and tiger-eye earrings that I thought didn't have much real emerald or any other precious jewel in them. The thing that was so nice about her, despite her hideous colors and dress, was that all those thousands of wrinkles managed to give her a kindly air. Her smile didn't look like the learned thing a woman like her would save for regulars and blow-ins; instead it looked exactly like the unconsciously captivated expression anyone would have for two dumb-as-shit teenagers wanting to buy comfort for a deserving octogenarian. At first I assumed she was supposed to be the comfort lined up for Enrico Belpasso, and out of the two of them I didn't know who to feel sorrier for.

Two dogs across the way in the teeming intersection of Boundary Street and St. Paul's Terrace howled at the midafternoon heat.

"Well," she went on, having gathered herself after that first sight of Enrico Belpasso. "You're Gabriella."

"Yes, we had a conversation on the telephone. This with me is—"

"Mother of God, you're tiny! And I wanted to tell you when we spoke, I *adore* your accent! The Italians have it all *over* any other nation of this world." She was taking Gabriella in, giving her her full attention, betraying a gamut of facial twitchings and tickings and tweakings that showed how the very sight of Gabriella was like being blessed with a drink of cold water on this stinkingly hot day. "You *do* speak our language beautifully. *Quando parle mi fai saltare il cuore!* And you know what, my dear, you could give lessons in enunciation to my girls. Some of them, my oh my." This woman—sixty-five years of age?—put her pale-white, pale-veined hands to the sides of her head, crushing her earrings, meaning to show how the Strine of her girls could grate against sensitive ears. "How long have you been in the country?"

"It's about six months now."

"That's all? *Well.*" She glanced at the man-bear, then at me. "It's certainly warmish out. Come in, come in."

Despite her cordial ushering we took tentative steps out of the direct sun and into Nocturne. Properly named too, because inside it was like night. We waited in the cool and dark of a long corridor that you couldn't see the end of for the poor lighting and the sun-glare still in your eyes. A drifting scent of incense, strawberry and sandalwood, and a television murmuring in some other room—that was what you got in there, and yellow lamplight in the distance. Then soft laughter came like the muffled tinkling of bells. There wasn't a whore in sight yet but something was already stirring my blood. It was the welcoming coolness, the softening darkness, the quietly chiming female laughter at some stupid television game show. Everything here was a promise; somehow a sweeter promise than Gabriella's kisses and somehow a truer promise than Andrea Farmer's menthol-cigarette and fried-pork-and-garlic mouth. Contrary to what I'd expected, it didn't feel bad to be in this place.

The object of our visit, the old man, had to be pushed farther into the corridor with a strong hand at the thick base of his spine. I remembered Gabriella telling me that he wasn't a donkey; pushing him like that, I knew he was. Nonno Belpasso shuffled in and waited unhappily, a beast shuddering on a hill in the face of a coming storm.

"Is this the type of thing—in your country, *tesora?* I've spent many years on the Continent and many thrilling times in, oh, Positano, Perugia, *Firenze*, so remarkably beautiful, but I'm not sure I've come across a custom like this one. Here you'll find it much more common for a father to bring his son, or an older boy to bring a young and inexperienced brother. The cherry visit, we like to call it. Half of us say we should give a discount because of the inexperience and the other half say we should charge twice as much for exactly the same reason. But I can't say I've had something like *this* before."

"You must have older men coming here?"

"*Carissima,* certainly. They're our bread and butter, though generally they're able to get here under their own steam. Otherwise, frankly, you'd have to think it was a bit of a lost cause. Now, who is this young man? Your brother? He's a very good-looking one."

"This is my friend, Salvatore."

"Salvatore-Salvatore," she said, really pronunciating the eight syllables nicely. "How *old* are the two of you?"

"Eighteen," I said.

"Not you, darling. And you, *tesora,*" she said, moving to tower her skinny-rake frame over Gabriella, "you are *fifteen*." She arched a pencil-line eyebrow. "Tell me it isn't so, dear."

Gabriella said, "I'm fourteen."

We waited.

"Spunk," the woman said. "I mean in the old sense of the word. Not what we swim in here. Spunk is something I admire, and you're not here for yourselves. What does it matter, anyway, your ages? I hardly have a license to lose." She came a little closer. "But if you ever tell—"

"We won't," Gabriella said. "We never will."

"And your uncle—"

"He's my grandfather."

"Well, your *grand*father seems of age. I think that's all that really matters."

She took Enrico Belpasso's hand and he pulled it away, perhaps the first real act of self-determination I'd ever seen him commit. If you'd told me that one day I would see hundreds more such acts I would have laughed out loud and rubbed your belly for being an idiot.

The colorful old woman said, *"Dear me,* though, if the gentleman doesn't want to."

"He wants to. Signora . . . ?"

"My name is Mrs. Veronica and as you can see Nocturne is my house of pleasure. You're all very welcome here. Will . . ."

"Enrico Belpasso."

"Will Mr. Belpasso come with me, *tesora?"*

"In a minute he will," Gabriella said. "I want to see the woman first. The one you have in mind."

"Darling, take it from me. Your dear grandfather's going to need more than one charming lady to help him through. When the spirit is willing and the flesh is weak it's challenge enough, but when the spirit seems so *distratto,* as you say in your language—well. Added to that, look at the size of the good fellow. I'm leaning toward *three* escorts for the afternoon."

"We couldn't afford that."

"Piccola figlia, as I mentioned on the telephone, it will be one hundred and twenty dollars for a languid two-hour afternoon—"

"Si, lo so."

"—per lady. And he will need two. Two. I can't let him alone with one of my girls. He's far too heavy and I don't care for that look in his eye."

"What look in his eye?"

"The one that says he's vacant as an old rotting Brisbane River catfish."

Gabriella bit her lip but she was clear-eyed and calm, her gaze never averting from Mrs. Veronica's—that sweet-talking criminal who was selling us up the way a smart used-car dealer will.

Gabriella said, "They'll be careful with him, won't they?"

"It's them I'm worried about, dear. They won't hurt him unless he asks to be hurt, and even then my girls are trained to be *enthusiastic* but agreeably *cosmetic* with what they do."

I leaned close to Gabriella's ear and spoke in Sicilian. "I've got extra money. But we should call it off."

Gabriella said to the woman, "I want to see them."

Mrs. Veronica led us down the corridor to a sitting room that was overstuffed with comfortable furniture. There was a lounge and armchairs, big pillows hidden in silk and patterned velvet covers, heavy mauve curtains with lots of frills, and all the colors of the room were saturated in blood-reds and purples. It spoiled the homey look of the place, but I had to remember this wasn't a family house where someone served you tea and biscuits and gave you polite conversation. Here it was polite *atto sessuales*—sex acts—in exchange for cash. The notes in my pocket felt like they were burning. Mrs. Veronica asked us all to sit down. On a two-seater lounge old man Belpasso was stuffed between Gabriella and me, and we were uncomfortable, shoulders and knees pressed together. The madam of this house of pleasure moved to a small but fully laden bar and asked us what drinks we wanted. As far as I could tell there were no other clients, at least no one else was in the waiting room. But there were closed doors aplenty down that corridor and I had no idea what went on upstairs. Still, the only sounds were that softly volumed television show combined with dreamy laughter. Mrs. Veronica let me have a glass of Fourex beer and I felt immensely worldly; Gabriella and her grandfather had a glass of lemonade each. The old man didn't drink. His stare went toward the floor, or some space in between him and it—who could tell? He couldn't or wouldn't raise his glass and his breathing was his usual rasp, his mouth half ajar and his three rotten teeth out in the open. A badly angled lamp made the dent in the side of his head look deep as a fissure, and the fat squiggly damaged vein was some electrical transmission system that gave this Frankenstein's monster abnormal life.

"My ladies are like nurses here. Especially with our older clientele. Firm, in a way that's best for them. Does he speak any English?"

"He understands some things."

Mrs. Veronica came to the couch and took his hand again and this time he didn't pull away. He stared into the crinkling lines of her smile and it was a mystery what he saw. Then he grinned, something I would have thought him incapable of.

"Dear man," Mrs. Veronica said. "Yes, he will need help to concentrate his inner *uomo*."

Enrico Belpasso seemed to be coming out of a walking coma. I said very plainly, for all to hear, and not in Gabriella's and my secret Sicilian either, "We could go home now," and the old man turned his great head and stared at me. At me, not past me or in front of me. At me. That, I thought, was a miracle, and I started to believe everything Gabriella had told me about their conversations.

Gabriella smiled encouragement at her grandfather but I could tell that the mechanics of this whole procedure were like a war of attrition on her resolve. She was wearing down, and looked hopelessly young. My heart was breaking.

Mrs. Veronica said, "Things are quiet until about six on days like today, though we do enjoy the odd afternoon jogger or shift-worker popping in on the way home. Sometimes on impulse a guest will wander in off the street, as much a surprise to him as to us. But I don't want you to worry, dear. Discretion is *assolutamente* assured. I think it will be easier if I bring the ladies to come visit a moment, then, *piccolina,* you can make your grandfather's selection for him."

"When I do . . ."

"Yes?"

"Maybe you could ask one of them to call herself Fortunata."

"Any name you like, *cara*."

There was high color coming into Gabriella's cheeks. *"Grazie,"* she said. *"Molto grazie, signora."*

Mrs. Veronica: *"Prego, cara.* Such a language!"

G ABRIELLA HAD WANTED me to come for one reason and that was to hold her hand while she waited for her nonno. She was nervous and then a little teary and I did hold her hand; we were two young terrorists terrified by our debut scheme. We sat in the room with the television, which smelled of the cheap lilac perfume of the prostitutes who had been occupying it, and of another, sweeter sort of scent that I knew was the leftovers of several marijuana sticks. We were waiting through our universe's two longest hours and I wondered, What could they do with him in all this time we'd purchased? Read him erotic Arabian tales and bathe him in milk and honey? Burn frankincense to arouse his imagination and anoint his great whale frame with oil and myrrh? I kept checking my watch and Gabriella kept twisting my wrist to get her own look. It seemed like an awful waste, this overindulgence of time. I knew very well and the prostitutes knew very well and perhaps only Gabriella didn't know very well that three minutes and no more than three minutes should have been enough to get the job done.

Yet I kept thinking of old man Belpasso being pampered like an ancient king and then being helped to sink into a welcoming dream of female flesh. Maybe it wasn't such a stupid thing to have organized. Maybe Gabriella had been right to carry out such a questionable kindness, but I kept wondering if there wasn't some cruelty here that she hadn't considered. For to my reckoning her grandfather was so lost in the head that he was probably confused by what was happening in his private room and therefore physically incapable of taking part in the act of his own servicing. And what effect would that have on his shattered spirit?

After a long silence Gabriella turned to me.

"Have I done the right thing?" she asked in our secret language.

"Yes, he's happy. He must be happy. But I want to know something. Why did you want to do this?"

"I told you."

We stayed close. She hadn't told me. She hadn't told me the half of it.

"Why did you ask for one of the girls to be called by his dead wife's name?"

"You know . . ." Gabriella moved uncomfortably. "It's who—I don't know how to explain it. She's what he desires most. I mean real desire, everything."

"Lust."

"Yes, but more than that."

"Love."

"Yes, but more than that too."

The leftover whore of Mrs. Veronica's trio came into the room and sat in an armchair. She didn't turn the television volume louder but started rolling herself a fat joint. Her fingers were expert and when she'd lit it and taken a few deep drags she passed the joint to us. I wanted to give it a try and so did Gabriella and we sucked too hard and our eyes watered, but then we got into the rhythm of the whole thing and the woman put a large square ashtray on her white potato knees and rolled another. The windows were shut and the room was stuffy but I didn't mind. I watched her as she worked and she smiled at me and I noticed that those misshapen knees of hers had burns on them, the same sort of burns I got when I crawled too fast around the carpet at home playing with the babies and little kids of my relatives. Added to that, she had the same features as the madam of the house, you could just see the way her horsey smile would one day be a litany of lines.

Gabriella had picked out two of the three women whom Mrs. Veronica had presented to us. They'd come into the waiting room and stood before us, Muriel and Melinda and Dorothy, looking a little uninterested, not wearing sexy lingerie or baby-doll nightdresses as I might have expected, but wearing housedresses the type anyone's ma would wear to go do the grocery shopping in. In fact, the women didn't look too different than our mothers. I thought they might all have been over forty years of age, which in my eyes made them supernaturally old. I thought they were like ancient villas that you would find your path through simply by following the direction well worn into the floors. At first they were all similar to one another and vaguely featureless, but that was a trick of my overanxious mind. What I was certain of was the absence of the slightest trace of Bunny glamour, and I knew I was a dunce to have expected otherwise.

Finally embarrassed, Gabriella had sort of half nodded that the first two were fine and she didn't say which was supposed to take the Sicilian name. I'd looked at the third and felt the last of my desire evaporate. She was Dorothy and her hair was dyed jet-black and she looked like Mrs. Veronica. Meanwhile, Enrico Belpasso had continued a slow climb into the real world. For moments at a time, until they led him away, he showed interest in what was going on. At one stage his heavy hands had quickly reached out as if to take a firm and desperate hold of the first woman's large breasts; Gabriella had turned to look elsewhere.

And Enrico Belpasso had said something.

He croaked just one word, *"Fico,"* which means fig.

The sweet smoke was getting to us; I was heavy and I could see how dreamy Gabriella's face was becoming, how sad and young she was revealed to be. Her pupils were dilated. They looked large and flecked with gray. She herself looked like she was full of longing and love, and the truth is that I really wanted her to be like that. Dorothy sighed with her last puffs and went and leaned with her hands on a wall and then she left the room.

Gabriella said, sitting close to me on the sofa as crazy television images flickered soundlessly, *"Mi voi bene, Salvatore?* Do you love me?" and I said, heart hammering, *"Si, ti voglio bene.* Yes, I love you."

Gabriella touched the back of my neck and put her lips there. "After the Christmas holidays, after my birthday, maybe I'll be your girlfriend. I mean, really yours. Maybe I can belong to you and no one else. I'll go to All Hallows and we'll walk to school together every day."

"Why do we have to wait? Why can't we do something together now? Why can't we go away or go to a hotel or just anywhere nice?"

"Maybe later—after." She kissed me as if in a sleepwalking dream. "I want to be old enough and then I want to belong to you."

"Me too, Gabriella, me too."

"Do you want to know something?"

"What?"

"It's a secret."

"Tell me."

"My papà's not my papà."

"I think I knew that."

"Yes. Everyone can see. My ma had a romance with a man from somewhere else. Strange to think that parents can have such passions. He was a butcher from Dublin on holiday in Sicily. My ma met him and fell in love with him and she ran away to Dublin to be with him. And after nearly a year she came back because it didn't work and by then she had me inside her. Can you imagine what that was like in the back-streets of Catania, where we used to live? Can you imagine what it was like for my papà? And for her? They carried that shame for years and years. I grew up with shame on my head. No one let me be Sicilian. I was something else. A foreigner who wasn't foreign. Everyone knew about it and it was never a secret, not even from me. My family was never normal. None of us are normal. I started to learn English on my own, already when I was in my first years of school. I thought one day an Irish butcher would arrive for me and take me to his paradise."

"Didn't that scare you?"

Gabriella closed her eyes, shrugged dreamily. "I just wanted to be ready."

"Why?"

"Because I've wanted to find my home."

"It's here—"

Gabriella shook her head. "I thought it would be. I thought it was going to be. Home isn't where you think it'll be."

"No. It *is* here. Listen. Because I'm with you. Where I am, that's your home. There's nothing else that you have to worry about. There's nothing else you have to know."

"I was good at English. It was my passion. It still is. I even write in English. I try to write like the people who write the books I read."

"But still, that man, he never came."

"No, he never came. But I think even the man my mother is married to . . ."

"Your father."

"My papà, I think even he thought that the Irishman would come back one day. Imagine the scandal of that. I think it was his nightmare. My papà. We had one thing in common. He was always so desperate to leave Sicily, just like me."

"He waited a long time."

"It's not easy to start a new life in a new country. Even I cried and cried when the time came. Animals that have been in terrible cages all their lives don't like to leave them when the door is finally opened. I was like that. Have you ever thought of leaving your home?"

"No. Why would I? What for?"

"I don't know," Gabriella said. "I don't know." Then: "Do you love me less?"

"Never."

"I'm half Irish."

"It's no surprise."

"Do you love me really?"

"Yes." I held her close to me and put my hand on the small warm mound of her right breast. The nipple was soft, an unflowering bud. "So tell me now, what is it that you're always writing on your little scraps of paper?"

"They're nothing. Just a pastime. Silly little things, things like dreams." Gabriella moved against me. "His name was supposed to be Brian O'Toole or Brian O'Connor or Barry O'Neil, or something like that."

"You know his real name."

"You're right, of course I do."

"What was it?"

"No, I just don't want to say it. Whenever I say it he seems real and

63

when he seems real I want to see him. I have to trick myself into not wanting to see him."

"One day we'll save enough money and we'll go find him together. I'll come with you. We'll go to Ireland and then after that you'll show me Sicily."

Gabriella murmured something that wasn't an assent. She shook her head. Maybe she meant to say that some things you have to take on your own shoulders, without any help. She whispered close to my ear, "You never want to leave me."

"That's right."

We spoke in Sicilian and we kissed in tongues, and her little hand slowly-slowly reached down far into me and squeezed gently and squeezed hard, and she was my Firehead, and my heart hammered because it wanted to break through the walls of my chest and explode into the stars.

"You know something funny, Salvatore? Every time I think about the story of how my grandfather met my grandmother, I have strong dreams. They're . . . rich. The other day after I told you about them, I was hot, down here." Gabriella slid her hand down her long throat, over her chest, over my hand still on her breast and down to her belly. "I dreamed, you know, that night."

"Tell me. Tell me what you dreamed."

In her dream Gabriella was tingling all over. It was as if there were tiny bubbles being made inside her, by the millions, the billions, these bubbles sizzling up into her skin and bursting, making her feel that she was more than just alive, that she was singing through every pore of her body. And then an even funnier feeling came over her, into her back and across her shoulders, and she was screaming with the pain of what was going on, and what was going on was that enormous wings were sprouting out of her. Huge in diameter, creamy in color, feathers long and perfectly formed, flicking, twitching, wanting to take to the air and ride the warm currents over our sleepy city of Brisbane. And a great bubble burst in her belly and the bubble in her belly was a baby, and she swept across the fat face of the moon cradling her child, whose skin was smooth and creamy and not freckled and pink like hers, and the baby's skin was creamiest at the shoulders and shoulder blades, which were hardly blades at all but soft and tiny mounds of creamy flesh, and there were no wings there and no promise that there ever would be.

Gabriella cradled me in her arms and her eyes were wet and large. Her lips when she kissed me again and again were soft and full, and those kisses—soft now, softer than ever before. Holding her, I could feel her heart and her breath. Her sighs were warm like spring breezes, and scented sweet, like caramels and tangerines, like tutti-frutti, a nice bagful for ten cents.

She said, "I wonder how he is. I wonder—"

"Do you want me to check?"

"Do you think you can? Yes. Check for me. See that my nonno's all right."

She slumped back into the sofa as I stood up. Shaky-legged I went to the door and when I looked back Gabriella smiled with her half-waking, half-sleeping dream. I felt exactly the same way.

"One day," she sighed. "One day I'm going to let you know everything about every part of me. Do you know that sometimes I can travel right into the heart of the stars? Right into them."

"Gabriella?"

"Can you imagine how big it is out there? Do you know that sometimes I can even see God looking straight into my heart?"

"Gabriella,"—I half laughed, half sighed, "what are you talking about?"

"Oh, I love you so much, Salvatore Capistrano, I really do."

"Really? Really truly?"

Her eyes were now not on me but somehow fixed on a point between us, as if there were some sort of invisible opening into a tunnel that led to beautiful places, and she said, "And when I say I love you, I just love myself too, I just feel so beautiful."

• • •

THAT PROPELLED ME through Mrs. Veronica's Nocturne. She told me she'd been busy in the rooms upstairs making several afternoon arrivals welcome.

"Boys are here." She smiled. "Lovely big boys the way you'll be one day. And there's one very timid gentleman waiting in his car outside, building up his courage I'd say by watching our walls."

Despite the humor in her voice, the idea of that frightened me. Sent a shiver right through me. "Police? Maybe it's police, checking us out?"

"Assolutamente no, caro mio," she laughed, clapping her hands at my childishness. She looked into my face. "Oh, how you've been indulging." That made her laugh again and I realized that what really amused her was the lost compass of my stupefied mind. "Everything is perfectly well, do you understand me? Listen carefully. Can't you guess that the good men of our police force would be amongst some of my best clients? Yes, that's the way it is. Low ranks midweek, high ranks Friday and Saturday evenings. That's the way their world turns, *figlio mio,* and so this is a sanctuary to all those fine gentlemen. We're safe here, darling, safer than in a church."

I smiled then. I was reassured. That's what I wanted, a churchlike safety for me and Gabriella, forever. So I told the old woman why I'd come wandering through the house. Mrs. Veronica smiled.

"Yes, I understand. Good. I've been casting an eye in every now and then myself, just to make certain all is well. He may be old but with the proper stimulation he seems to become *quite* competent. Deeply fascinating, isn't it?"

She took me into a room that wasn't the one where old man Belpasso was taking his birthday gifts. All the walking, the movement, the talking, the very idea of such deep fascination with an old man's powers, they made my head swim. When I put my hand out to a wall the wall wouldn't come.

Mrs. Veronica touched her hand against my shoulder. There was a little sliding door at face height in the wall, by a bust of some nymph with massive white hard marble breasts. There was a peephole. "Go ahead, see what there is to see, young man, there's no extra charge." Mrs. Veronica spoke through a heavy fog, and she had to gently prod me forward.

I put my eye to the aperture and what I saw was the world a million years ago.

Dear Diary

Gabriella's Book of Fire

H E CAN NO more move than if his legs have been numbed by hammers. He's transfixed by the fig juice on her chin, which she wipes with the back of a hand. With a secret smile Fortunata reaches deep into her apron. She says, "Here," and gives him a little gift that is wrapped in a colorful silk scarf and carefully tied with a pink bow. Enrico is as unworldly as one of the many hedgehogs that burrow deep into the Giorgio earth, but even he can see how her hand betrays her; she passes him the wrapped little package and her hand is trembling.

Still, she's in control, and she has to say, "Go on, open it, it's for you," because Enrico holds the gift and looks at it and seems stupid and senseless enough that Fortunata wonders whether she hasn't made some kind of a miscalculation and chosen to love an idiot.

"What is it?"

"If you open it you'll see, won't you?"

So Enrico does open it, and what there is to find inside that silk is a velvet case, and what there is to find inside the velvet case is a gold chain with a gold-medal pendant, and what there is to see on the face of the medal is no less than the face of *Nostro Signore,* sweet Jesus Christ. This gift, this glittering chain, is not only the most beautiful thing Enrico has ever held in his hard, knobby hands, but it is also the only such thing that was ever meant for him.

"I hope," Fortunata says, now showing some maiden shyness, but not too much because she knows it goes badly with her strong brow and heavy chin, "I hope that you'll wear it always."

"But why should I wear it?"

"Because it's a gift—from my heart to yours."

He contemplates this sentence, its enormity, not knowing that Fortunata has constructed it and retooled it and worried at it over many sleepless nights, over many strippings and makings of beds, over many sweepings and moppings and polishings of wooden and marble floors: Because it's a gift—from my heart to yours. And make sure the break comes just right, in the middle, with the slightest hesitation of breath.

He says, "Should I wear it even when I work?"

"Yes."

Enrico's confusion, sadly, is immense. Where could she have found such a beautiful thing? He cannot know that it was an inheritance from a great-uncle who died but who had once gone to Rome and made the journey back with his suitcase full of similar jewelry. Who is this Fortunata, Enrico keeps wondering, whom he only knows as one of the girls from the palazzo, one of the housemaids, someone he's gazed at from a long distance and never even dreamed of speaking more than two or three words to. Who is she to find him in his secret place on this of all mornings and give him such a thing? How does she even know about his birthday? His mind is busy with questions and doubts while beside him, under this strong and solid tree that protects them from the coast's icy sea winds, Fortunata needs to fidget like a child because of the as yet unrequited lust that is burning her up. At night in the bed she shares with her sisters she knows how to tame these feelings, while the two younger girls breathe heavily and snore, but in the presence of this man Fortunata is helpless.

The eighteen-year-old seems to be making no personal progress, so to help him along she offers these words:

"I've been watching you for a long time, Enrico Belpasso."

"Huh?"

"I've been watching you for a long time," and she waits for the absolute bluntness of this declaration to kindle some kind of animation in him.

In reply Enrico Belpasso only thinks that if his blood wasn't singing he'd be able to—think; if he was able to think he'd wonder what he could do about the cold sweat on his forehead and the heat in his trousers; if he could forget the heat in his trousers maybe he could run away. To a place where he could—think. So it's all a confusing spiral. Or circle. His tongue is the heavy log of a tree and then he finally asks the one real question in his mind.

"But why?"

Fortunata decides talk is futile and action essential. Acting the maiden will guarantee to keep her a maiden. Daintily she spits out some fig skin she has inadvertently chewed and she gets onto her knees and faces the stretched out, previously reposeful body of this long, muscular boy. She's soiling that matronly house uniform but isn't bothered. Let Baron Giorgio chase her with the carpet beater. Some things are more important than avoiding physical pain. No blows from Baron Giorgio could be worse than the anguish of facing a lifetime of spinsterhood. Fortunata has her own inner queries. For instance, this one: Why in the name of the saints doesn't this boy reach out and take me right now? And that question's brother: Why doesn't he push me down into the dirt and get over me? And that question's sister: Why doesn't he clamp his mouth onto mine and plunge his hand inside my skirt to take hold of the ripe fruit I've got there, just for him?

So Fortunata takes the velvet case out of Enrico's palm and makes to put the gold chain around his neck. Enrico has to lean forward for this, and he feels his face close to the heavy, frightening, tantalizing terror of her heavy, frightening, tantalizing, terrifying breasts. She snaps shut the clasp and he leans back against the tree trunk, his fingers delicately stroking the medal against his chest. His breathing rasps like a kitten's that has played with a ball of twine too long and is now exhausted. Close by, a group of men can be heard approaching from the lemon fields and they are calling out to one another, whistling, cursing at nothing, talking loudly.

There's a nice pinkness in Fortunata's cheeks that wasn't there a minute ago. Her lips, which before today he's not had the chance to observe closely, seem blood-red, as if she's bitten down on them. Her hair is thick and black as a raven's coat. Enrico has not expected to be so close to a woman until his wedding night; he doesn't appreciate just how close to his wedding night he is.

"You ask me why I've given this to you, Enrico Belpasso. You keep wondering why, why, why? But why even wonder? Don't you have eyes? Do I have to show you what's right in front of you?"

Enrico, finally comprehending her art of seduction, having got the message through his thick skull, nods slowly. He wants her to indeed show him what is right in front of him. So Fortunata slowly reaches for the buttons of her blouse. Watching her hand moving, unbuttoning the first, the second, the third, showing him the smooth ripe olive skin no man has ever seen, Enrico explodes into incoherent action. He throws his hands at Fortunata's breasts and hangs on to them as if they're the only things that will save him from falling off the edge of the world.

More relieved than excited by his awakening, Fortunata boldly looks him straight in the eyes and doesn't avert her gaze as she reaches down and picks out a nice fat fig from his waiting pile. She breaks it into halves and then into quarters and moves her fingers, carrying a piece toward his mouth. She touches his lips with it, caressingly, and he opens slightly and lets her put the quarter in, skin and all. His tongue runs over the pulpy flesh and his back teeth mash down; his palate reacts to the strong, luscious, out-of-season fig taste. That taste, in fact, somehow inflames the heat in his trousers more than even Fortunata's breasts do. He understands perfectly now, this is the age of miracles. She feeds the rest of the fig to him and the fruit is richer in tang and texture than it has ever been before. It is wine and blood and a woman's warm fingers.

Before he can swallow, Fortunata holds his face and she descends into him, kissing him so deeply and so ravenously that it's long seconds before he realizes, with a sort of terror, My God, she's eating a fig right out of my mouth!

But anyway, only a small and insignificant part of Enrico's young mind is still capable of rational thought, and so it doesn't interfere.

THAT NIGHT FORTUNATA doesn't need to tame her feelings in her bed while her sisters dream. Instead Enrico Belpasso is waiting for her in the blinding, freezing dark under that same tree. They topple into one another's arms; they kiss and grasp and clutch, and through the deep branches they can see their volcano's peak pouring flame over snow. In the black of their nest they eat more figs, ravenously, and then each other, just as ravenously and without inhibitions—he her tongue and her belly and her breasts, and she his mouth and his nipples and his hardened penis, which, she finds, has a mouth too, and it weeps a strange honey onto her tongue, and she has never imagined or expected that happiness could either be so carnal or so richly tantalizing to the palate.

In a week they've set a date and in a month that date has arrived, and after that the boy who was the laziest of the province is starting to be called the happiest, for his loneliness is gone and with it his dreaminess, and he can't stop smiling because of this, and he feeds Fortunata as much as she feeds him. Together they balloon with the sugar and meat of love, and he puts his seed into her as often as he can, and she always raises her hips and keeps them raised for long, long minutes after, so that the seed will take hold and sprout, and when finally this long-delayed fruit does, Fortunata swells and somehow Enrico with her, and they're fat as Sicilian hogs and twice as happy, and life for these two is as it should be—beautiful and agonizing and joyous—until their world goes to war.

Gabriella's Turn into
Some Other Place

THEY STARTED TO SHOUT and I was only capable of staring, one
eye blind against the wall but the other eye wide and looking into a circle of Hell.

"Is it his heart? Did his heart stop?"

Mrs. Veronica heard this as clearly as I did, but where I was in terror
she was without wonder, or even—I explained later to everyone, over
and over—a sense of surprise. She indelicately shoved me from my
place at the peephole. She wasn't drug-stupefied like me and she took
another look at the two female bodies working over the beached-whale
frame that was Enrico Belpasso. She'd already told me that she'd stolen
occasional glances at the naked bodies of her whores working over their
client's ugly expanse of flesh, and now they were still occupied but in a
totally different way. Mrs. Veronica hurried by me and used the adjoining door to get into the ruby-red bedroom. Her cultivated veneer was
gone and she took control and she started to bawl in Strine:

"Is that what ya call heart massage? And yew, before yew give him

73

mouth to mouth check if he's swallowed his tongue! Are ya completely bloody stupid?"

I followed into that place of heavy velvet curtains and red sheets and plumped pillows over a very large bed. It was as cheap and as fake as a setting in a department store display. A humming air-conditioning unit was set into a closed window and there were small hotel-type hand towels and a hot and cold water basin too. Outside that room, in the rest of Nocturne, I knew there were the faint traces of lilac, of drifting sandalwood and strawberry incenses, but here the unnaturally chilly air was sharp with secretions and seemed to quiver with the electric humming.

"He's going blue."

"That's because ya don't know what ya doing."

As far as I remembered from the school first-aid course, the technique of heart massage didn't start with beating on a man's chest with both fists joined as if trying to break down some stone barrier, but that was what the naked Muriel—or was it Melinda?—was doing. I was in no condition to do better. My face had grown cold and my arms and legs too. Needles were prickling in my scalp and I thought I was going to faint. In this emergency I was a piece of wood. With every blow of Muriel/Melinda's I shuddered because of the resonant *thwack* that vibrated through Enrico Belpasso's engorged pole like a tuning fork and made the white and blue feet protruding from the red sheets that covered him from knees to ankles and no more jump like animate toys. The other woman was clamped to his mouth, pushing the breath of life into him and then searching for a sign that he was breathing alone.

It wasn't coming.

Mrs. Veronica's face showed determination and anger. In an efficient way she pushed me out of the room and said, "We're lucky in Spring Hill, the ambulance headquarters isn't three blocks away. God knows, they know the way." She clapped my shoulder for encouragement and she wheeled me toward another room that turned out to be an office. This was where she did her work while her women did theirs. I wanted to go to Gabriella but Mrs. Veronica expected me to stay where I was.

When she lifted the receiver on the black wall telephone and started to dial the numbers she said to me, her veneer slightly restored, "I want you to write on this paper. I want your full name and Gabriella's and the old man's and your addresses. You're going to have to remember you came here of your own free will. You're going to have to remember that Enrico What's-his-name came here and personally asked for his pleasure and that you children waited in the waiting room and that I gave you lemonade to drink."

I wrote what she wanted and my fingers were thick and my hand slow. While Mrs. Veronica spoke into the receiver I stood in that office swaying. There were so many thoughts in my head I couldn't control a single one of them. The old man was going to die and Gabriella and I were going to Hell but before that the whole world would come down on us and that was because I'd never heard of two adolescents getting into as much trouble as this.

Some new young woman I hadn't seen before rushed into the office. She was pale and pretty. Mrs. Veronica covered the receiver and said softly, "Empty the rooms upstairs. Don't push for the money, just make sure everyone leaves immediately."

The young woman said, "It's all right. It's already done. They've been making so much noise the boys have already gone."

Mrs. Veronica seemed to sigh without a sound, then she repeated the name Nocturne into the telephone receiver.

I had to go to Gabriella.

Expecting her to now be in the room with the whores and her nonno, I went there first. It was not possible that she hadn't heard the shouting and the running up and down the corridor's bare floorboards. Even the people upstairs had heard the hullabaloo and hit the road. But Gabriella wasn't there. Exhausted, one of the women said to me, "For God's sake, you breathe him, I can't do it anymore."

I backed away and slid out the door.

So Gabriella would have to be asleep on the sofa in front of the flickering, silent images of afternoon television. The marijuana must have

knocked her out. No. She wasn't where I'd left her. Dorothy was, smoking a normal cigarette and ashing her dress in her agitation. Her attitude
spoke of trouble on the way and I wondered why she hadn't left.

"Where's Gabriella?"

"The kid? I haven't seen her. Where's my mother?"

"Your mother?"

"Mrs. Veronica."

"She's . . ."

But I backed out of that room without finishing. What could it
mean: "I haven't seen her?" That confused me. Those words meant
nothing to me. If Gabriella wasn't with her nonno by now, and she
wasn't in that waiting room, then exactly where could she be? I wanted
to go ask Mrs. Veronica but she would have had less idea than me. So I
backed up and searched through all the rooms I could find while whatever went on with Nonno Enrico Belpasso continued to go on. Time
was passing; I wasn't even sure if he was dead or alive. I searched everywhere in that vast old falling-down colonial mansion: kitchen, quiet
rooms, storerooms, bedrooms, bathrooms, of which there were three,
two up, one down, and toilets, of which there were three, one up, two
down. I checked outside in the backyard and then all through the house
all over again and by then I was screaming, "Gabriella! Gabriella!" in the
sort of panic that I could never have imagined afflicting me. It was a
sheer terror for her and a sheer terror for myself. How would I handle
everything that came next? What would I say? How could I explain
things all on my own?

For now I understood that the little bitch queen had abandoned me.
There was no other explanation.

M RS. VERONICA PURSED her lips and they became a thousand
dry cracks in a desert of parched earth. The siren's incessant
wailing seemed to irritate her.

Enrico Belpasso, with his own lips the color of dark figs, reached out
from the bed and grabbed me by the wrist. It was like being grasped by

a dead man. He tightened that monstrous cold grip on my wrist so that I couldn't get away. I wanted to follow wherever Gabriella had gone, but to where? It was as if the air had eaten her up. I wanted her here with me and I wanted to hold her so that everything would be all right. Her grandfather had taken a turn, but the next surprise was that he was back. He was back. So why wasn't Gabriella? Our families would discover what we'd been doing in Nocturne and the trouble we'd get into would be the troubles of the world's worst sinners—but together, somehow, everything would have been all right.

Together, you bitch Gabriella, we were supposed to be in this together.

I was already crying the way fools will.

Enrico Belpasso was rough with me. He shook my arm as if trying to wake me up to something, and I stared down into his ugly, ravaged face and into his twisting mouth. He was trying to say something but I didn't try to listen or understand. Words poured like water out of him but all I felt was horror and disgust and fear, of him, of myself, of the absent Gabriella Zazò.

The whores had dressed themselves and had made their exits. Dorothy was now by the bed. Mrs. Veronica, with her multicolors and charade, was back to her soothing snake-oil best. She caressed the old man's cheek and said, "Dear man, *tutto è a posto. Tutto va bene, non preoccuparvi.* All is well, don't worry."

Dorothy said, "Mum, he still doesn't look very well."

"He's well enough. Aren't you, dear man?"

He gobbledygooked more oceans of words, rattling his heels hard, furiously.

That was when I was able to wrench myself out of Nonno Belpasso's grip.

I went through the Nocturne house, down that long and dark corridor, and when I pushed open the front door and was out into the blinding sunshine my eyes were immediately dazzled. The heat that hit me was like a great breaking wave on some glittering coastline, and I saw there was some sort of crazy haze over the streets. I blinked and rubbed my eyes and shaded them with my hand, and in front of Nocturne the curious were gathering to stand by the ambulance and see what was going on and who was in trouble.

Two ambulance officers in crisp white shorts and shirts and long kneesocks were efficiently rattling their equipment out of the back of their vehicle. A police car was pulling up behind it, its siren not blaring, and when the driver's door opened Officer Pietro Pierucci's long frame stretched itself out into the sunshine. He took off his sunglasses and squinted at me. It must be said, he was the type of man who rarely looked happy, and right now he looked like a rock had fallen on his head.

He shouted, "Sam!"

Nocturne's front-door steps, though few in number, were old and wooden and unstable. I went down them and across the weed-cracked little path to the rickety gate. Where I leaned, looking up and down, up and down, willing Gabriella to come into view. My gorge was rising. I needed to bring up the contents of my stomach. Despite the ambulance and the police car and Officer Pietro Pierucci striding toward me shouting, the world was in its normalcy. Yet Gabriella wasn't among the people standing by the ambulance; she didn't reappear out of thin air; she wasn't waiting on some distant footpath watching and too afraid to return.

It was just too much for me to make sense of and that was how it would always be.

Gabriella Zazò simply wasn't anywhere, not anymore.

BLOOD ☀ 1985

Allegria

TONY SOLERO THREW A party that lasted most of the night.

It was the usual festive Saturday evening scene, only better. There was him and his older brother Lino and the two silent business partners who ran La Notte with us, a place that once upon a time and way back when was an old wooden Queensland palace named Nocturne. The smooth-talking harpy with bad colors who used to run that famously infamous Brisbane landmark didn't live forever, and when she went out and her daughter wanted to be rid of the business Antonio and Pasqualino Solero went in, and they remembered to take a couple of their most trusted friends with them. Which of course meant me. Our fine establishment couldn't have looked anymore different than that old dump because without a twitch of sentimentality about the rapidly disappearing colonial architecture of Brisbane's past we'd plowed down the house and its surrounding trees and scratchy patches of flower and vegetable gardens, which were mostly dense with prickly pear and wild sweet-potato infestations, and weeds, and we built a black steel and smoky glass nightclub in their place. Our club was a good enterprise but for the moment still running in the red—another year would get us into the black and well and truly so. Part of our setup and running costs was our ongoing wages, and Tony Solero, who really was the lifeblood of La Notte, made sure everyone was paid very well. Otherwise, he liked to say, what was the point?

He was generous as a kid and as an adult he hadn't changed. It was me who wasn't the same anymore.

For this particular Saturday night Tony had told his brother he wanted to try something different, that something being a Latin band he'd seen on some television variety show. So we got them booked and The Cuban Eight came along and really played their hearts out for us and made this, one of Tony's special La Notte parties, even more special. The thing was that ours was the type of place that well-informed night-prowlers under thirty or thirty-five always wanted into anyway, so anything better was pure bonus. We liked to think we attracted the city's cool set. Brisbane in the mid-eighties: an overgrown country town, hot as a four-piece pub rock band and steamy as a good Tennessee Williams play, barely out of its thongs and singlets and beach shorts adolescence, reeking of beery bumpkins who ranked ball sports higher than eros and art, the capital city of a state governed by farmers and right-wing types whose idea of stopping student street marches was to use the good offices of police batons, and who additionally believed that only money and economic development were to be obeyed, though of course there was much wet-lipped lip-service to God and fundamentalist notions of religion; that embarrassment of a government run with steely resolve and fascism in its soul—well, in a place like that a cool set was a misnomer as great as you were ever likely to get, but we told ourselves we got them, this growing city's stylish elite. In the end all it meant was that people knew they'd better dress well and show some good manners when they came to La Notte or they wouldn't get in. So come they did and dressed well too, and whenever our nightclub was full Tony and I, both only in our mid-twenties, felt like we already owned the world.

All the rest was a facade. The lights, the lovelies, the free-flowing liquor. It was a facade that said the world was a beautiful and romantic place, and this was the easiest lie to live when you believed in nothing higher.

So the girls who came there could be wild and the guys were inner-city, sportscar-driving flash maybe worth wanting, and the music and explosive cocktails our barmen made could curl the skin off your flesh. This particular Saturday night we took one step up the nightclub eminence ladder and cemented our reputation: our Latin band taking the place of the usual disco favorites and hot records of the week cooked everyone alive.

It turned out to be a joyous occasion, full of sweat and laughter and life, and whereas I should have been watching the door, in those days I had balls and Wednesday and Thursday and Friday and Saturday and Sunday night fevers enough that when the spirit took me I'd abandon my place and just get into the thick of things. I liked to dance my feet off with the crowds on the dance floor. Some nights Tony Solero would like to catch my attention and give me a wry and rueful smile. Other times I'd catch him mouthing curses at me, but he rarely tried to stop my wayward ways. Tonight less than ever. Tony had no illusions that I'd ever be one of the Solero brothers' more diligent associates. In fact they only had me there for the sake of an old friendship; for nostalgia's sake; for the ties that bind and that don't get broken until you're prepared to smash them into pieces. That time hadn't come. Everyone knew that to me the idea of drinking and carousing was infinitely preferable to standing at our horseshoe-shaped entrance watching for those club-night evils, blue jeans and running shoes, dags, hicks and bevans from the suburbs. We repelled what we didn't like. Kmart shirts dressed up with thin nylon and polyester ties and Woolworth's frocks glamorized with glass-diamond and fake pearl adornments, all such affronts could go back to the pubs and the beer gardens.

My small financial contribution to the La Notte start-up capital had earned me this job of looking into all the queuing-up faces outside in order to make a decision about who was too drunk to be allowed through the door and who was just too plain rotten to look at. And there was something else, that judgment you have to make about what people are like on their inside, about whether they will be troublemakers and scufflers and brawlers. The perennial disco question of guilt and innocence, of after-midnight good and evil. We took all of it so seriously. The problem was that to me, some nights everyone seemed to have a black and bad soul and some other nights I'd gaze at those perfumed, aftershaved, eager, and hopefully anticipating faces and see nothing but angels wanting La Notte to give them wings. When I was like that everyone was my friend. When everyone was my friend I gave off enough pheromonal perfume to attract the most attractive party-night girls back to my home. I was nothing like the businessmen who ran La Notte. No wonder Tony Solero always said I'd die in the poorhouse.

NOW, THIS NIGHT of the Latin band there were nothing but angels. The whole club was filled with drunken celestial bodies. Everyone was chanting and singing, showing high spirits that by the dawn hour would become either deeply inebriated sleep or slurred words of promised love, or good raw rooting in cars and homes and dark corners.

In deference to the fact that I was supposed to be working I didn't drink more than long tumblers of lemonade or Perrier mineral water, but I could see how that music made you want to throw down plenty of sudsy bottles of beer, or glass after glass of salty margaritas or licoricey rum and Cokes or lemony caipirinhas. Male or female, you'd eat fistfuls of the free hot salted cashew nuts and deep-fried corn chips smothered in piquant salsa and sour cream that continually went around on platters, and try your luck and your lines with some lovely, or if you were a girl or gay, give your smile to the hunk who best caught your eye. Some won and some lost and for some just being there was good enough. Tony Solero, even when he was counting our receipts and expenditures and contemplating the red divide between the two, always knew our La Notte gave people a measure of joy. The Latino dance night turned out to make all of us more joyous than ever.

It was like this:

The fast conga and timbales rapping, the staccato one-two-three/ one-two rhythms, the chiming guitars and thumping stand-up bass, the two-man horn section who without you noticing it would switch to violins or flutes, swinging in when you least expected it and sometimes jumping a melancholy minor chord into a major that filled your head with life; they made you want to shake every bone in your body and throw your hips around. No one really knew these old songs but it was easy as breathing when your body understood the groove. The singers, the guy whose name was Ernesto or Ranaldo, and the girl who did backup (and only occasionally got to take the lead from that suntanned strutting cock in a worsted white suit and a sky-blue shirt with lapels out to here), well, that pair really made you want to sing—with your whole goddamned soul.

The backup singer's name was Irina and she was a real coffee-skinned beauty from Cuba—or so I guessed at the time. Tony, with his trademark floppy hair offset by his bad-boy/good-boy grin, introduced us early in the evening before their first set started. At the time she was drinking plenty of spring water and loosening her voice and paid me no attention. Now, hours later, with long lean hard legs and nice high breasts under a gathered, tied-off halter shirt, and a naked midriff that could make a man woozy, well, she was just making everyone in the place all hot and horny. Perspiration helped her satiny skin to shine in the lights. The muscles in her thighs clenched and rippled, and she had this thing she'd do in the hotter numbers. She'd start off tall as a tree then slowly-slowly grind down into a sort of half-crouch, driving her pelvis perfectly in time to the rhythm, which got faster and faster with her. This Irina's torso would be straight but her breasts would beat and quiver and her arms would twist like snakes above her head. Perspiration would fly off her face, and her mouth would be wide in the purest, the most eternal smile, but that smile didn't show in her eyes. Instead her eyes would grow wide and wild and half crazy like a mountain cat's when it's about to pounce upon innocent flesh. They would glow right out of her coffee-skinned face. As if that wasn't enough, there were times you could see her nipples hardening with the passion or exhilaration of the Spanish canción, those little buttons jutting out through the half-transparent cloth and not being like buttons at all, but like beckoning fingers. With her dancing like that, exuding such a raw and primal wildness right up there on that little stage, you could be as fanciful with your imaginings about her as you wanted to be. I wanted to imagine a great deal about her; the night was still young but I was already telling myself I wanted her the way I wanted red wine with my pasta dishes. And then the next thing for me to consider was that other than her stunning looks and her honeyed voice and her sexy dancing behind the microphone stand, Irina sang a few of her lyric lines at me. It wasn't my imagination. I could see the wolfish grins on other young guys' faces. There was naked envy in some and honest *allegria*—happiness—in others. But her face showed that her animal was in the music and the music was in her animal, and me, well, I was just completely inside that spell she made.

Until somewhere approaching the wee hours.

The New Pietro Pierucci

SOMEONE SAID TONY SOLERO wanted me and I went to find him and even at twenty paces across the noise and narcosis of a nightclub there was a nice shorthand between us.

Fast as I could I pushed through the sweating crowd and made for the front entrance. The two Tony was worried about were wanting to muscle their way in. These boys were very well known to us; they were footballers or amateur boxers or something and they were bad news waiting to hit the headlines. They'd made it onto my shit list because the few times we did let them in they were snorting bulls badgering unwilling cows. When every girl rebuffed them they got rough. Their act and attitude was that they were two reckless sons of Mother Nature just wanting a good time, but the good time they wanted was to hurt you. To cause pain. So they'd slam dance like they were in a 1977 punk band dance pit. They'd hit you with their shoulders and bounce you out of your space on the springy floor. They'd conk your head good and hard while they were jumping and thrashing to the music. They'd give you a grin and drop their beers like you caused it then demand you buy them another one. In a crowd they'd pinch the cool flesh of a girl's bare arm.

They'd put an elbow in your sternum or they'd somehow manage to grind your toes under their boots while you stood talking and laughing with your friends. If you challenged them they'd be looking somewhere else as if they were deaf to everything but the beautiful music all around and if they thought you were sucker enough they'd fix you with a beery glare and a fist could just as easily come up and knock you down and in the confusion of the music and the drinking and the sex plays going on no one would be able to say for sure exactly what had happened. You, the sucker, the mark for this minute, wouldn't even see such a blow coming. Every nightclub in every fluorescent-lit city of the world knows the faces and the names of boys like these. These two were called George and Eric. The only redeeming feature they possessed was that they were stupid, which could make them susceptible to silky talk, which was supposed to be my specialty.

Carlo, our main bouncer, was doing his best to keep them in check but he wasn't doing enough. He was the type of bouncer who'd apply an excruciating armlock or even a gagging choke hold if he had to but he'd no more hit someone than I would; what made him special was his brick-wall build. Most potential troublemakers simply fell into a self-conscious silence at the sight of him—but tonight Eric and George had already shoved him around and his shirt was out of the waistband of his black trousers.

They were roaring drunk. They must have done a full night's pub crawl. I winked at Carlo to make him feel better but he was upset that he'd failed to get rid of them himself. At this hour there was no queue to get in, no one else was waiting outside, but a lot of traffic still headed up Boundary Street and down Leichhardt Street and into St. Paul's Terrace. I didn't expect things to get out of hand but the busy streets meant there were people who might see whatever might happen next, and that made me uncomfortable.

Tony Solero used to box down at the Police Boys' Club and he'd always told me I had a yellow streak that was only good for getting me hospitalized. He used to say that when a fight was coming I had to get in and get it over with. He used to tell me to shape up and strike. Strike now, not in five minutes' time. He said that talkers were wankers who got their faces split. He said goaders were fools who'd see stars and get stomped. He said baiters were cowards waiting for the other guy to throw the first punch, and his learned opinion was that to do so was like sticking your chin out and begging to be knocked into tomorrow. Then he'd come to the businessman's realization that all these fighter's qualities were only worth a lot more fighting at a nightclub door, and so now he preferred someone like me who hadn't been violent since school and had instead learned to sweet-talk almost anyone out of anything.

"Hey guys, how's it going?"

"This big fucken wog says we can't—"

"—come in. Arsehole. Smash his face in."

"Of course you can come in, but what do you want to come in for? We've got a Latin night. It's stuff from South America. You probably haven't heard of salsa and mambo but old people think it's all right. Anyway, it's like some over-fifties social club booked us in there or something. We're full up with middle-aged women and their husbands."

"Fucken what are you talking—"

"Maybe you wouldn't like it but the thing is the band's costing us a fortune so we have to charge twenty bucks a head to get in. You want to pay twenty dollars each for that shit?"

"It's not twenty."

"You know I'd let you guys in for free if I could but tonight twenty's it. Stupid. You know there's a lingerie night at The Beat?"

"Bullshit." They dug in their wallets and produced the cash.

"Well, I have to tell you you can't come in when you've both had so much to drink."

"We haven't."

"Come back next week, things'll be better."

George and Eric turned to one another. They looked like bulls dressed in Saturday night's cheap shirts and trousers.

I kept smiling. "So where've you been tonight?"

So much for sweet talk. George pushed me with both hands and slammed me back three steps so that my shoulder blades and skull bounced off the front wall of La Notte. A sound like a great church bell peeling rang in my head. I smelled foul body odor and beer and Brut cologne and was already as useless as a kitten.

Carlo cried out, "Hey!" and tried to drag George into a headlock.

Then Tony Solero was behind them and George, not the biggest but the toughest, got one in the kidney that with bad luck would get him into an emergency ward. The kidney is a very delicate organ, but that's life when you're a Saturday night fool. George crumpled, howling indignantly and holding his side all at the same time. Carlo made another move and got Eric from behind and pinned his arms, and Tony let him have two good ones that seemed to slip off his sweaty head and not faze him. Tony hadn't been boxing for a long time. His punches had lost their old bite. He'd put on weight but not where it counted. Still, he knew how to give Eric one in the belly and that was enough to put him down. I watched all this without participating. I was holding the back of my head.

Tony Solero was ready to stomp, but that was when I grabbed his shoulder.

"He's had enough."

"See what happens!" Tony's blood was still up. "Nice guy! What's the good of you? Huh? And you—Carlo. What are you supposed to be here for?"

I watched Eric coughing on the ground and bringing up a stenching bit of the numerous drinks he'd mixed, and the unmarked police car that often visited La Notte in those days chose that moment to pull up. So right there was the witness to the scene. Tony Solero was immediately pulling himself together and trying to keep the quavering out of his voice when he called to the lanky emerging cop, Detective Pietro Pierucci.

"*Cumpari,* how are you tonight?"

"Who're they?"

"Two stupid drunks. They've given us a bit of trouble the last few months. Tonight they pushed Carlo and Sam around."

I was still touching the back of my head to see if I was bleeding.

Pierucci nodded. He said, "They hurt you?"

"Nah."

Well-meaning Carlo said, "Sam got hit on the head. One of them knocked him right into the wall."

"Which one?"

"That one."

Pierucci looked at them. He knew them. He spoke their names. He crouched halfway back into his vehicle and on his two-way he called for a paddy wagon. He was wearing a brown suit and I remembered how his old police officer's uniform used to make him look better. Even though he was only mid-forties his once jet-black hair was completely gray and his skin was the color of ash. I felt sorry for him because his whole career as our old local hero had somehow only ended up eating him alive.

Eric was back on his feet and staggering around, then trying to drag his downed mate away by the collar of his shirt. Detective Pierucci went over to him and kicked the back of his knee out so that Eric fell down again. He kicked the side of his head while he was floundering and the *thunk* was clear as a branch breaking.

Carlo said, "No, it was the other one."

Pierucci looked up and nodded at his mistake and so gave George such a heavy kick in the side that it rolled him onto his stomach.

"Hey, Peter—"

"Tony. Shut up."

We all knew that when Pietro Pierucci was in a mean mood he was very quiet and right now his voice was barely to be heard. He returned to Eric and put his shoe onto Eric's face and pinned him there. The detective didn't feel the need to make a threat or give a warning about future behavior. Instead he pressed down hard and there was a little cry and then came the snap of Eric's nose breaking. Soon blood was seeping from under Detective Pierucci's sole.

"Sit in that gutter and be quiet," he spoke down to Eric, taking his foot away and scraping it once, twice, on the ground. With blood over his face Eric crawled into the gutter. He held his head but he cursed God and everyone else. Pierucci whispered, "I said to be quiet."

Eric shuddered like he thought worse was coming and so he stopped cursing. Sitting there in the dirty gutter he rocked to and fro, and then good sense prevailed and he put his head back to staunch the flow.

Detective Pierucci came over and looked at me. "How can you let people like that get the better of you?"

Tony intervened. He handed him the envelope he'd stopped by for. "Come in and have a drink, Peter."

"Not tonight."

There was never a night that Detective Pierucci came in for a drink, not in the entire year and a half since La Notte had first opened its doors. Inside the police car was his partner, some new man, a young detective, and this fellow knew what was going on but had maiden shame enough to not want to show his face. In a month or two he'd have his hand out and we'd feed it. That way we knew the police would come see us when we needed help; that way we ensured that most of the time we didn't need any help at all. Tony accepted it as part of life and if that was the way things had to be then that was the way things had to be; I didn't think it was so bad either. For us it was just a better type of business insurance. We often wondered how many establishments Pierucci visited to collect similar sums from and how much he kept for himself and whom he distributed the rest to. What was strange and what could prey on my mind if I let it was the way these piddling amounts we slipped him, of bean and beer money—as Tony used to joke about it—didn't seem to bring a shred of *allegria* into Pietro Pierucci's own life. In our situation at least he was helping to protect a business that was supposed to be all *allegria* and nothing else, yet he was completely the opposite, a man without a shred of happiness inside him.

"Any illegal substances in the club?"

Tony spread his hands and his unbuttoned double-breasted jacket fell open to reveal his white silk shirt and darkly patterned silk tie. I always wanted to tell him that double-breasted jackets should never be unbuttoned, they look wrong like that, but Tony's lack of style hadn't held him back in life. He laughed. He smiled his smile. All of us did. We knew Pietro Pierucci's question wasn't serious.

The detective tucked his envelope into his pocket and gave Eric a look that said, Move and I'll—and then he gave me exactly the same type of glare. What I mean by that is that it held the same order of contempt.

I stopped being stupid. I stopped smiling. This wasn't a social situation and this wasn't a friend.

The thing was, Pietro Pierucci knew my history better than anyone else, and like a father with a disgraceful son he was ashamed of me. When I was eighteen and I dropped out of law at university he heard about it and came to see me and swore at me, his spit spraying my face like I was a donkey that needed beating. Even my own father hadn't got as upset as that. Over and over in thick growly Sicilian Pierucci had called me a *cafuni*—which is the worst kind of fool, the kind who doesn't even know what he's got and so throws it away with both hands. Years after, when I went into the La Notte business with Tony and Lino and the silent others, he didn't say anything about it but I noticed that old half-angry, half-loving glare of his had cemented into something that was almost totally bad. The dreamy New Farm days of our migrant families and one young Sicilian-Australian police officer keeping an eye on us all were gone; enough years had passed to veil any sweet nostalgia Pietro Pierucci might have felt. But the thing is, I was nostalgic. I liked to remember him as one of the good guys, as our young local hero who courted my ma at Italian dances and weddings and always ended up watching her leave with me and my papà. I liked to remember him as the tough young blade who cared for us all. These days he was a divorcé with a child who called another man Dad and he collected bean and beer money from the very kids he'd tried to keep on the straight and narrow. His contempt for what I'd become might have been as unwavering as his contempt for himself—who could look into that corrupted man's heart and say?—but I just couldn't hate him back, not with the way I remembered him.

Of course the fact is, though we never spoke about it, I knew where our problems originated. There was no mystery. There were plenty of people who felt exactly the same way toward me. Because I was the one who lost little Gabriella Zazò. That was the thing wrapped in barbed wire around my neck. Pietro Pierucci blamed me for what happened and he blamed me for all the years he wasted trying to find her. Maybe he was gray and mean because he never found her. Maybe I couldn't hate him because he tried so hard. And maybe I was good for nothing but a good time for exactly these same reasons.

H E CLIMBED BACK into the car and we watched it pull away. Tony Solero sighed and shook his head. There was an element of idolization between Tony and Pietro, yet there was a sharp edge too. The man was paid to be on our side; he was mean but worse than that he was also unpredictable. On the one hand he could step on a boy like Eric's head and snap his nose, and on the other hand at his Christian Brother brother's burial last winter we'd watched him throw himself on the coffin and break his nails on the polished mahogany lid. There was more. When his father passed away he had some kind of breakdown that no one talked about, though we heard stories about a clinic he had to be taken to and prescription drugs they had to fill him with, and when his wife finally left him and took up with some counterculture guy who ran an arts and crafts store on the coast he disappeared like smoke and wasn't seen again until three months later.

Tony must have been thinking about it all too because he sighed and shook his head again and when I went over to Eric and gave him my handkerchief Tony didn't complain. I told Eric and the now sitting-up George that they better hurry along their way and not bother ever coming back.

We watched them totter off.

The paddy wagon, or the Black Mariah, or the booze bus, whatever you want to call it, arrived a couple of minutes later; like Nocturne before it, La Notte was nothing if not centrally located. Tony knew the young officers inside the van and he chatted to them like family when they wandered the footpath and wondered what the hell they were supposed to be there for. Eric's blood was smeared on the bitumen. Everyone went to look at it. Even I was drawn to it, though I preferred to go back into the club, back into the world of *allegria* where I could watch that lovely Irina sing and dance sexy, but when I passed the horseshoe-shaped doorway I had to lean with my shoulder against a wall and try to get the indelible redness of blood out of my mind.

Arroz Negro

WE HAD SOME FRENCH champagne that we kept in the coolers out back, away from the barmen and the punters, saved for special occasions. Tony had me open a few bottles as the band packed up. We stood drinking out of paper cups while dawn was a few hours away. Inside the club we were in a sealed environment and I liked the feeling that in there it could have been any hour of the day. The air-conditioning was sucking up the stale stench of cigarettes and sweaty bodies and spilled drinks, and the musicians were laughing and joking and rolling joints as they packed up. Tony was behind the main bar with the boys calculating the evening's take. Lino Solero had long since gone home to his wife and that was the way he liked to be; he'd stay a few hours, assure himself that things were going well, and leave proceedings to his younger brother. Tony also had a wife, and two children both under the age of three, and he was as devoted to them as you could be and still run an all-nighters' business.

The singer, Ernesto or Ranaldo or whoever, was mopping his face and neck as he came over to me. His white suit was soaked through and his toweling off had smeared some of his eyeliner. At the open collar of his sky-blue shirt there was a matting of very dark hair, with curling sproutings of white. He was older than I'd first thought, but oozed a scent of cologne and meat that said he was more potent than any three men put together.

"Hey. What's your name?"

"Sam."

"Well, you got anything to eat here?"

"Anything you want."

He looked to his musicians and at Irina, who was using a facecloth to wipe her legs right up to the little strip of leather that was the bottom portion of her stage outfit. "A paella would be good," he said, and then laughed heartily, slapping me on the shoulder and slapping down some more champagne. He lit a cigarette with a silver lighter, peered at me through his blue-gray pluming smoke, and said agreeably, "No, seriously, thanks for the drinks but we're starved. What time is it?"

"After four."

"That's dinnertime for us. What's ready?"

"Well, we've got plenty here," I said, sizing him up, "but if you want paella you can have paella. Seafood and chicken and I'm pretty sure I've got enough arroz negro for all of us."

"Black rice? What are you, Spanish?"

"No. But all the same, I'd like to make the dish for you and your friends."

He looked back at his companions, laughing again. They'd looked up, interested by the possibilities of what they were going to get to eat. The singer said, "You joking with us?"

"We'll have to share some taxis to my place. I learned a good recipe from my brother-in-law's grandfather. The family's Spanish, from the Galician region, and it just so happens I'm set up for it at home. Got chicken stock in a jug, made it yesterday. I don't feel like going to sleep either. That was a great night you've just given us."

His face was all smiles but it was as if he still couldn't make up his mind whether I was pulling his leg or not.

Tony called out, "He's not joking. He's a good cook. I'll come too. And anyone else who wants to."

"We don't want to put you to any trouble, friend."

"What trouble? And why does the party have to end?"

He stuck out his hand. "Julián Luna," he said, and I wondered where I'd got Ernesto or Ranaldo from. I also wondered if he noticed my glance past his shoulder toward Irina. She was tying her skirt around her waist, covering those long and dark and muscular legs.

She said, "Julián, he made it with cubes."

"Made what?"

"The stock."

"Well," the older man looked at me, "that's what my wife says."

I laughed, but in a funny way I was offended. I wanted this woman to think a whole lot better of me than that.

"I can guarantee you my stock comes from a free-range, corn-fed chicken the size of a turkey. It's made the traditional long slow method." Tony Solero looked up from his ledger and smirked at me. He knew what I was up to and I thought I was so transparent that Julián Luna would have to have seen it as well. "My place is on the river," I said. "We'll have a few drinks and by the time we're eating we'll be watching the sun come up. Want to try it?"

"Hombre!" Julián Luna laughed. "Why not?"

Champagne for Breakfast

THAT WAS THE WAY it was in those days. No one was up before the afternoon and the nights went on into the morning. Sometimes a group of people you knew, or strangers you thought you wanted to know, would drag themselves home with you and in your kitchen you'd make them some sort of early-morn supper while they helped themselves to your bottles of gin and whiskey and variety of mixers. The stereo would start thumping the latest music and the neighbors wouldn't care because you didn't have any. There were people a floor above and people a floor below and your apartment took up the twelfth floor all on its own—all two double bedrooms (both with en suites), one single bedroom, living room, lounge room, sunken something room, and stainless steel and polished kitchen off it. The place was spacious and light and thoroughly wasteful. It cost a lot. La Notte, or should I say Tony Solero, was good enough to put its rent through the official account books. Good that such a place was somehow a business expense, even if you personally didn't understand how. When you were going to sleep in luxury everyone else was on buses and trains or stuck in their cars in the start-of-workday jam. When you finally roused yourself it was well into the afternoon and you'd sit on your twelve-story-high terrace, under the striped awning, surrounded by potted plants and expensive Swedish outdoor furniture, having a coffee and a toasted slice of heavy German bread dripping with honey or smeared with too much apricot jam, and you'd watch the wooden old-style ferries come chugging, crawling, up the muddy winding Brisbane River. Students in baggy shorts and colorful shirts would be getting transported to the St. Lucia University stop and you'd watch them drift along in those ferries, wondering if they were learning things important to life and to love that you'd never fully opened yourself to. Then you'd forget about that and get up and lean on the railing, looking twelve stories down into the glittering green pool below, and wonder instead if the curvy blond in the yellow bikini had a boyfriend, or if the brunette in the black one-piece with a keyhole opening between the breasts was looking up from her place in that lazy chair dreaming about who you were and how she could meet you. Maybe, with her tanned legs stretched out and slightly bent in relaxation, she was only napping in the heat and you mistook the stillness of her head as the fixed gaze of passing interest. Never mind. It was the eighties after all, a time when love and money could fall into a young man's open hands if he was only smart enough to stretch them out and wait. You weren't smart but you knew enough to wait. So you'd turn your eyes away as the riverside's weeping willows caught a little of the hot breeze and their long weeping branches dragged in the water like sad spirits drowning. The afternoon sun would give a painful glint to everything and make the world diamond-hard, and with the usual ache from the long night before twitching behind your right eye you'd go to find your sunglasses and curse when they didn't come to hand, and you'd give up and stay back inside, drawing the curtains behind you. The sun still mutely coming through the fabric of those yellow and apricot curtains would light the rooms of your apartment with a sort of churchlike glow, and you'd still be in boxer shorts and a breezy cotton robe that you could never find the belt for. You'd wish for the cool drink that in reality you were just too lazy to get up and make, something like a Perrier with ice and a little slice of lemon, or a mango and orange fruit cocktail.

Soon you'd be stretched out with another jaded yawn, reclining like an indolent young prince on your plush couch, a sense of quiet and tranquility growing inside you, but sometimes with a vague sense of loss too, one that you knew well enough but could never quite put your finger on. You were only in your mid-twenties and you had no road. With the remote in your soft unworked palm you'd spend an hour and then two flicking through the daytime television shows, and you'd try to remember if you'd laundered your best linen shirts, or maybe the silk ones, wanting to decide which was ready for the coming night—which of all of them, really, was the right color and texture to lift your slow spirits and carry you through to another dreamy, smoky, wasted night and morning in La Notte.

But there were better wakings, weren't there, the times when someone sweet and special was in your bed with you, and dreamily and hungrily holding you, two midafternoon bedroom-cool bodies all twisted up together in the sheets and her already as mischievous and playful as a kitten. What was the name of the one out of all of them who'd been really something, the one you really liked, if not let yourself love? Come on, you haven't forgotten her. You haven't forgotten that twenty-one-year-old sweetheart who was as Rubenesque as your Firehead used to be slim, who was as jet-black-haired as your Gabriella was carrot-topped, who was as deeply olive-skinned as that littlest Zazò was freckled and pale and pink. Yes, her name was Rebecca, and you never called her anything else when you looked into those black eyes. You never called her Bec or Becky or some other sweetheart shortening because you loved those syllables, the sharp staccato sound of them so contrasting with the soft warm curves of her body, the warm smell of her skin, the silky luster of her black, to-the-shoulders, dead-straight hair. You could never get enough of those afternoons you'd wake together, not since that first one that happened after she came to talk to you at the door of La Notte, slightly tipsy with one too many vodka and oranges, the traditional Screwdriver that the barmen there made just that little bit too strong but liked to sweeten with dollops of sugar, the way Tony Solero had instructed them to do. His rule: if the drinks are strong the nights will be stronger. Remember how you were all hot and uncomfortable with that sultriest of summer nights outside, how utterly bored with examining the queues to get inside, how your brow was beaded with salty perspiration as you stood there fakely smiling, your body wilting in your nice Italian suit. She spoke to you and in your usual way you were nice back to her, but there was something to the way that her teeth were white when she smiled. Such a simple thing. Then she was home with you and you both went straight into your king-sized bed, naked but not making love, holding one another but not kissing, your hands on her fleshy strong thighs, yes, and her hands gently gliding over the thick hair on your chest, but neither of you making that first languid move toward something stronger. Instead you slept together, snored softly together, and somehow the intimacy of that bonded you, blended you, one into the other. In the afternoon, two or three in the afternoon, who remembers, you came awake and she followed you to the surface of your dreams, and though each of you was sweat-stale and stale in the mouth too, stale there with leftover drinks and cigarettes and nightclub snacks, she wanted to kiss, and kiss deeply. It was funny that she was ready to be kissed now that you'd slept entwined. It was good and nice too, her tongue slow and softly flicking at the corners of your mouth—and sweet, really sweet as a caramel. Remember that? She sensed some hesitation in you, sensed a spirit that wasn't as whole and strong and happy as she'd assumed, and so she guided your hands all over her body, along her strong hips, over the smooth cleft of her round buttocks, and deeper still so that she sighed and breathed near your ear in a way that was so passionate and yet so lost that you thought you would have to cry out with the pleasure of her.

Rebecca.

And then later, after days and weeks when you knew one another better, this sweet girl with the strong biblical name was a constant visitor. Waking, she would roll herself under the sheets so that she could lean with her forearms on your chest and watch your eyes as you stopped sleeping. She wouldn't hesitate but come and sit astride you, and take her breasts in her hands like she was offering you warm fruit, and she'd ask you to put the left nipple in your mouth, "Please, Sam, just do that," and when she was excited and breathless it was "Honey, now take this one," and you'd be deep inside her and thanking God and the saints for your physical body, for your young enthusiasm, for this beautiful angel who came out of nowhere to give you light. So enraptured, later you'd move into the kitchen ready to make her anything she desired. Anything. Lamb cutlets, pasta carbonara, peanut-oil-fried noodles with Chinese vegetables. She had a good appetite and an eclectic taste that wasn't shy to ask you to get in there and work. As if you minded. It made you feel good to cook for Rebecca, to watch Rebecca eat, to see her enthusiastic at her plate, her shining silver fork making frequent forays into that now happy, now chaste mouth. Breakfasts were breakfasts even at three in the afternoon. Fried eggs, scrambled with a little parsley, poached with a little salt and pepper, orange juice just squeezed, coffee coming through the dripolator and taking the scent of sex away from your hands, bacon grilling and sizzling, and diced tomato, onion and Worcestershire sauce cooking in the frypan. Bread toasting, butter ready.

"Are you hungry, Rebecca?"

"Baby, am I!"

And when she would leave your apartment there'd be a last squeeze at the door, a last longing caressing of her breasts jutting in that white T-shirt you lent her, a last touch of the slightly protruding belly you'd filled warmly, and your lips would meet and tongues meet too, and when the door was shut and you faced your big nicely furnished rooms alone, and the leftover traces of everything you'd done, for an hour it felt like life would be so good again, could be so good again, these afternoons of smooth-skinned sweethearts like Rebecca could give you dreams again, but the hour would pass and that feeling would go, and out of the lovingly framed photographs on the wall Gabriella Zazò's young eyes and childlike face would still be watching you, and you felt it in your heart, you knew it even more deeply than ever, while she was watching you you were waiting for her.

Waiting for your Firehead to come back to you.

Chillies for Courage

"WHO'S THAT IN all the photos outside? I was going to say your sister—"

"But she's got red hair?"

"Yes."

Mrs. Irina Luna, who looked anything but a Mrs., returned to the kitchen where I had the onions and garlic chopped, the pieces of seafood ready—sliced calamari, beheaded baby octopuses, pre-cleaned green prawns, green mussels in white wine—and was heating a good dose of extra-virgin olive oil in a heavy pan over the stove's gas flame. The jug of chicken stock was by my elbow and so was a big bowl of black rice. The boiled tomatoes were deseeded and lightly mashed and the juice strained so that I could use that too, seasoned with black pepper and saffron. Irina was drinking a glass of my champagne, not French but good enough, and she was bored with the men who spilled out through one room of the apartment and onto the spacious balcony. She was looking at the platter of pre-cooked chicken pieces: legs, wings, heavy portions with plenty of bone that the meat could tenderly fall away from when you ate it with your hands.

"Go on, take a piece."

She was ravenous and who could blame her? Irina ate a cold chicken leg with her fingers and when I glanced at her her lips were oily and the chicken flesh was already gone.

"Have another, there's plenty."

Irina did. "What makes it so spicy?" she asked when she wiped her mouth with the back of her hand.

"Red paprika."

"So why are you all set up?"

"I've always got something ready to go. I like to cook. I was planning something but this is better."

I liked to cook but Irina liked to lean on things and she liked to talk. She was taller than me and even without the spell she made on a stage she was utterly magnificent. Her wrap-around skirt was multicolored and multipatterned, with great broad-winged, green and yellow–feathered parrots and parakeets and macaws flying wild in a jungle. Above that, she was in a black cotton halter top. Her lean strong waist was the color of mahogany and her brown-gold hair was braided back away from her face.

"I've never seen so many oranges and lemons and grapefruits in a kitchen."

They were in cut-glass bowls, little hills of citrus that I always kept ready.

"We're too lucky in Queensland, I get carried away. Take a look at this grapefruit." I picked one up, weighed it in my hands, passed it to her. It was the size of a rockmelon and nearly as heavy. Irina held it and rolled it between her palms. "I have things the other way around. I like champagne in the morning and fresh juice at night. Usually two oranges and one grapefruit before bed. Then when I get up I squeeze a couple of lemons into about a litre of water to remind me to get enough fluid during the day. Good for when you drink too much booze. Or just for stress."

She smiled as if a person like me wouldn't know the meaning of the word. "I'll have to remember that." Inquisitive as a child, she took a look in the pantry and opened the refrigerator door. "You do like to have good things."

"It's just an interest."

"Julián always gets me to cook Cajun. He's pretty good with a bouillabaisse." Her voice, so honeyed in song, was throaty in speech. It was as if it didn't stand up to a lot of use. Her accent was very, very mild, almost indistinct to the ear, and her English was the same as mine. It was only when she'd been singing those Afro-Carib and Spanish-flavored songs that she'd had a distinct inflection from somewhere else. "So now you have to tell me. You've diverted my attention long enough."

"Have I?"

"Yes, you have. Who is the child in the photographs? You're too young to have a daughter, not of that age anyway."

"I haven't got a daughter of any age. It's not my sister either. She's married to a Spaniard herself, and they live on this nice little stone-fruit farm near Stanthorpe. They grow things like peaches and apricots and plums and at the moment she's pregnant for the third time. The girl in the picture is a very old friend of mine. We were close when we were kids."

"So many pictures. What was her name?"

"Gabriella."

"Then she was your first love."

"Maybe," I answered, and cracked a fistful of garlic though we didn't need anymore. "First love." I shredded the delicate, sticky white husks away. The oil in the pan was just starting to smoke so I started cooking things. The sizzling filled the kitchen with flavors. "What are the others doing?"

"Them?"

Irina's husband and Tony Solero and even Carlo had made themselves at home with the musicians, pouring lots of drinks like whiskey and sodas and rum and Cokes and laughing while they got out a deck of cards and tried to get a game of poker going on my dining room table. There was only one woman to lighten our early-morning dinner party, which consisted of nearly a dozen men. Ronnie Hughes was one of our older barmen and he'd come along for the food and drink and because he and Carlo were inseparable once they were outside the limits of their own wives and children. Julián's band members had first names like Oscar and Alberto and Miguel, and family names like Montoya and La Fuente and Galvan. There were others. I didn't remember any of them well enough to put two names together, other than their leader and singer, Julián Luna.

"You found some music?"

It was a Billie Holiday record and Irina had picked it well to suit the mood. The jazzy swing of "What a Little Moonlight Can Do," recorded in 1954, floated over the sound of the loud masculine voices.

"Listen to how she sings," Irina said.

"Yes."

"You know when Billie was a teenager she worked in a whorehouse just to get the chance to listen to the madam's records?"

"And then she turned into a prostitute too."

"Well, when she was very young. Later she said, 'If you expect nothing but trouble, maybe a few happy days will turn up. If you expect happy days, look out.'"

"Do you believe that?"

"Oh, times are different now." Irina came and took a good whiff from the pan. As she did I enjoyed the nearness of her. Then she looked out the window for the dawn that wasn't so far away and she leaned her right hip on a cupboard. "This record was made about five years before she died. She was lonely and she didn't have any money left. Her voice wasn't that great anymore either. The years of abusing it caught up to her. She doesn't have any range left and can you hear there's too much vibrato? Even her diction is a little slurred. But you can hear *her* in that voice, can't you? That's what makes anything Billie sings so special. You can hear her whole life."

The garlic and onions were sizzling and I gave them a good turning, over and over and over, letting them blanch but not burn.

"My mother used to say that when you get an idea about a person's life and what it's like, you start to fall in love with them."

"Maybe that's why people love Billie."

I was going to add that my ma used to say the same thing about food, that the best cooking had the best of the chef's life and love in it, but I would have felt foolish saying something so Sicilian-romantic; instead I kept turning the onions and garlic.

Irina didn't want to leave the kitchen. She said, "You've got so many records."

"Three or four hundred, I think. I used to have more but I sold a lot of the old ones. The ones I had from when I was a teenager."

"Did you get sick of them?"

"Kind of. No, maybe I just thought it was time for a clean-out. You know, like when you decide to get rid of all your childish stuff? It was probably one of the stupidest things I ever did. Hundreds of records. All those memories that I got maybe fifty or seventy-five cents each for. I probably spent the money in one night out. The funny thing is that as soon as I sold the records I wanted to hear them again. Every single one of them. Now I go around secondhand record stores trying to buy them back again. Some I'll never find but it does makes me feel good to hear the old music."

"Why?"

"I don't know. It just connects."

Irina shook her head, smiling, and I had to look at a smile like that.

"What?" I said.

"God you're a romantic."

It was good that Irina Luna wanted to stay in the kitchen with me rather than join the men outside. While I cooked and filled the space with the type of aromas I knew could make children and adults sigh, the smell of cigarette smoke wafted around too. I liked the sounds of men's laughter in the other rooms, the clinking of glasses one against the other, the bottles slamming down from hands eager to pour that drink and drink it and get back to the card game. Billie Holiday with her ruined voice and her great ruining past that somehow hadn't ruined *her* drifted above it all and she was the weeping ghost in the river. Really, she was. But her voice said her tears came from strength as well as sadness, from bravery, from the beautiful memories that battled the terrible. In the end, from a life lived. So it was a good morning. With these things my place didn't feel like some spoilt kid's den paid for by illegal book-keeping, but a home where good lovemaking could take place and where people could gather to be with one another and drink and laugh. Where you could really live. My authentic Spanish paella was going to warm a dozen grateful bellies. The dawn was going to come up over the river. I was going to kiss a beautiful woman named Irina.

She was watching me cooking, her eyes as intent on my hands as I'd been when watching the Galician *abuelo* of my brother-in-law as he taught me his family's way of making the dish.

It didn't take long to get the vegetables right and to mix things through. There was color aplenty, lots of variety. After I crowded the chicken pieces in I gave it the stock, the liquidy base of the paella turning a rich, rich gold. When that bubbled I poured in the rice and with my fingers slipped in and folded in the pieces of seafood. There would be more than enough for all of us and even a little left over for the person I'd meant it for in the first place. I covered the pot and turned down the heat and wouldn't touch it again until the dish was ready. Timing was everything, and the trust enough to leave it alone.

"I see," Irina said. "What now?"

"Twenty minutes." I took a look at the wall clock and went to get a little pyrex pot with a glass top.

"What's that for?"

"I'll be saving some for a friend of mine."

"Someone else lives here?"

"No."

"So—twenty minutes?"

"But I'll smell it when it's ready. The paella will tell me when it's done. Believe me. And I think in about twenty minutes the sun'll be coming up. It's going to be another hot day. What—Sunday? Work Sunday night, but then I've got Monday and Tuesday nights off. Where's my drink?"

She poured me a glass of champagne, the bottle nicely chilled from the freezer compartment. Irina seemed so much taller than me, so lean and so dark-skinned, almost African. But she told me I was wrong about her coming from Cuba; she was Catalan-born, from a poor country town not far from Barcelona. Her parents moved to Australia when she was nine and she'd been brought up outside of Adelaide, in the wine-growing district where her father had found work. At the age of seventeen she'd married the nearly twenty-five-years-older singer, Julián Luna, and they'd commenced an itinerant life, always starting up little bands and orchestras and taking them on the road, putting on shows in clubs, doing variety spots here and there, sometimes employing dancers and then getting rid of them when the money was no good. They'd break their bands up and then start again. For Julián and Irina Luna there was no real home. She told me they kept a little flat in Adelaide but they'd been in Brisbane six months and were thinking to stay longer, maybe somewhere on the beach, up the Sunshine Coast. They might take another six months and make it a semi-retirement before moving on and getting new musicians together. Or maybe tomorrow Julián would clap his hands together and say, Come on! We should be in Sydney. They'll love salsa there! She told me he could sing and play all the styles: salsa, Afro-folk, mambo, son, the musician Los Van Van's patented songo beat—which Irina explained was a mixture of jazz and rock—and sometimes he even liked to get together a group to play pure brass-driven jazz. Irina was thirty-one and she thought her voice was going. She thought it wasn't strong. No—she knew these things and had had them confirmed by three throat specialists in a row. The late nights and the drinks and the cigarettes were making her vocal cords scratchier and the beginnings of polyps were showing. Soon would come the first operation to get rid of them. There looked like being at least one more after that. Such was what she told me about her life.

The rest I made up.

Like this:

She thought Julián Luna was a ham and that his ego needed more attention the older he got. She thought his bowerbird approach to music had taken away their chance of a good recording career. She thought he was becoming more embarrassing and more of a strutting peacock with every new white hair that he dyed jet-black. She wished he would let himself be a man in his fifties and not try to live up to the old macho image from an old macho world that nobody wanted anymore. She was bored with dancing sexy in front of drooling crowds of men and she didn't even want to sing. At thirty-one years of age she knew a backup voice just wasn't good enough for a solo career, and what she had was never going to let her get out on her own. Julián Luna made sure she knew that so that she stayed submissive to him; he shamed her every time he looked at some dancer's gracefully supple body and she was sick of the fact that he probably slept with one or two of them, when he could, and lied about it.

Of course, Irina didn't tell me these things; these were the things I decided were true.

I put four eggs on to boil. They were for slicing up when they were hard and cooled with running water. They would garnish the top of the paella, as would asparagus spears. I'd make a neat, kitschy little pattern of egg and asparagus spears over the surface of the happy and colorful dish, to please the eye as much as to amuse myself.

Irina didn't want me to put my hands on to her narrow waist and reach up and kiss her very dark and very full lips. That was the other thing I knew. She didn't want me to do it because if I did it she wouldn't let me stop.

Irina Luna, married too young and married for too long, ready to get out if she could find the way.

"You should have put in chillies," she said. "For strength."

"In Sicily they're for courage."

"It's the same thing, I think."

"Three chillies. The dish'll be medium-hot. We might sweat a little."

She made to clink champagne glasses with me.

"For courage."

"For strength."

Why me? I wanted to say to her when she let me kiss her. I tasted the champagne on her lips and she put one hand in my hair and then she backed away. There was nowhere for her to back away to. I kissed her against the refrigerator door. I kissed her with her hip pressed into the sink. I kissed her with her dark long body half in and half out the walk-in pantry. She was hungry for kissing. I hunted her but she'd called me. Yes, yes, yes. I did want her like red wine with pasta and now like champagne with paella. It was a funny thought and that's why I was smiling. So why am I so lucky? I wanted to ask her. How did you hear my wish and choose to answer it?

Irina leaned with her elbows against my shoulders. Her breasts crushed into me so that I could feel her heart pounding the way mine did. Her breathing was so low it could barely be heard. She was thirty-one and ready to get out of her life.

"When?" I held her by the waist, not caring if that painted old dog that was her husband came in. I kissed her face and smiled at her and she kissed my face and then she smiled back. Eyes wide the both of us, excited and already planning her getaway: "Tell me when, Irina?"

From the other room a man was shouting.

Julián Luna, winning his hand, "See! See what I've got!" Laughing loud to show what a little strength and courage—not Billie Holiday's moonlight—can do.

Enrico Belpasso's "la Notte"

ENRICO BELPASSO WAS WAITING for me because he knew I liked to come visit some Sunday afternoons and bring him something good to eat. He was waving from the bottom of the five-year-new Zazò brick house and would probably have come to meet me at the bus stop if he'd known which one I was arriving on. Mamma and Papà Zazò would never have come out of their house to greet me. They barely ever spoke to me. Bad blood is bad blood and the thing ten years between us was about one thing and one thing only. They never balanced the loss of a daughter with the revival of a father. As if I would have. But it was my place to visit Enrico Belpasso. I visited him because he was my connection to Gabriella and today more than ever that was true, because Mrs. Irina Luna had asked me about those photographs in my apartment and I'd found it impossible to answer.

The paella I'd had ready to go in my kitchen had been mostly meant for the old man. It had been my plan to cook up a mountain of the golden dish for Enrico Belpasso so that he could keep it in his little bar refrigerator and day by day get through it. I did things like this for him every now and then. It made me happy. One Sunday afternoon I'd bring him a lasagne, some other time fettuccine with a spicy meaty sauce, and often a dish he really drooled over: beef cotoletti, slow-oven-baked in extra-virgin olive oil and rosemary, with hearty, similarly done vegetables such as whole onion and wedges of potato, sweet potato, and carrot. In the preparation, the thin slices of fine-grade beef (like eye fillet or rib fillet, nothing tough) I dipped in egg yolk, dusted with flour, caked with a special mixture of breadcrumbs and grated pecorino pepato cheese that was strong and had hot black-pepper grains in it, and a little parsley and garlic. Slow-bake that in your oven for two hours, and for two hours try to resist the aroma that fills your kitchen and your home and the homes of your neighbors. When I made that dish people who lived in my building rang on my intercom and wanted to be my friend. Swimmers in the pool twelve stories below got out and toweled themselves off, looking upward with their mouths open. Hearts broke too, because you can't be tempted by such pleasure yet be held so far apart from it and not be disappointed deeply, deeply, deeply. Enrico Belpasso liked the cotoletti—made my ma's old way—and he would eat with a truly Sicilian pleasure. I never held him back. He said that if one day his heart couldn't take the strain then that was all right because the taste would take him home, and I knew where that was.

I shaded my eyes and watched him waving to me as I walked from the bus stop to the Zazò mausoleum, that brick and concrete monument to prosperity and to loss. In my arms, of course, I had the paella left over from that early morning's drink-soaked breakfast shared under a burning dawn. The Pyrex dish was wrapped tightly in a tea towel. The tea towel was twice knotted at the top. Enrico Belpasso would like that touch. He'd especially like it. He'd notice it without commenting on it because it was a Sicilian thing. That was how you always had to bring good food, wrapped and knotted as if you were carrying it to the sun-baked workers in the vineyards and fruit and grain fields.

That was the way, even if this wasn't old Sicilia or the piece of it the old cummari and cumpari had originally made for themselves in this city.

I thought too many of the families had moved out of "their" suburb of New Farm. They'd left to show that they'd done well in the new country. It was their way of demonstrating progress. Too many of them now lived in big brick houses. Too many of them were in distant Brisbane suburbs nicely planted with trees in rows on the footpaths, where the surroundings were as whistle-clean as the grounds of a retirement estate. Everyone laughed at the ornate rococo, Arrivederci Roma, La Dolce Vita counterfeit Italianness of these places but my sense of humor always deserted me. I didn't think they were funny. I liked the rougher days in New Farm, when mothers and fathers and children weren't afraid to bellow at one another across rooms across streets across three sets of backyards. The old relatives and friends and neighbors used to all be in one another's pockets, and because of that proximity we always ended up fighting and eating and playing games together. At night the kitchens of those creaky wooden homes were crowded with hungry visitors. The smell of cooking would be in the air and if you wanted to you could go outside and be apart from the fervent laughter and conversations (so much like angry yelling that it sometimes terrified and infuriated your Australian neighbors, but at least in those days no one called the police on you) and just look up at the millions and millions of stars crazy-patterning the night sky. You could sit in your Uncle Antonio's fabulous just-delivered EH Holden, with its column shift and white, bone-hard steering wheel, and wrap yourself in the smell and squeak of most excellent new vinyl. You could sneak a cigarette with your cousin Joe under the gigantic deciduous trees of Abbott Street. You could ask little Suzanne Steggles from down Merthyr Road, a ribbon falling loose in her yellow hair and sunspots across her cheek and Vegemite still as black as mud on her tongue, to pull down her pants and show you the very surprising difference between brute Sicilian boyhood and gorgeous Australian girlhood. There was nothing wrong with losing yourself in the family vegetable and herb gardens if you were feeling moody, but if you were feeling good you could get into the hot, loud adult fray of the kitchen and eat your fill. There used to be energy, there used to be life; to my mind it had all gone too quickly and I blamed that on Gabriella's disappearance—but who knows, it might just be the thing that happens to immigrants in any country. They stay together as long as they can but then life intrudes and the old connections get lost.

In new estates like the one the Zazòs lived in children didn't play in the streets anymore, though there seemed to be more nature strips and traffic-calmed avenues than roads with cars on them. If you were a kid here you kicked a football in your rumpus room. Instead of randy slobbering pets that you fed, chased, and buried if they died, you sat in front of a television and let the radiation radiate all over you. If you were ever lucky enough to find a dead dog's teeth you still kept them in a matchbox at the back of your closet, beside your never-polished school shoes, but such everyday voodoo was harder to come by. No one can build a heart into a prefab community; whenever I arrived there I couldn't help imagining how Gabriella Zazò would have screamed all those brick houses down.

E NRICO BELPASSO, ALL ninety-one years of him, was waiting. He was smiling and he showed his nice pearly false teeth. Walking in the mornings or the afternoons and being a little more active than he was in his dark days had trimmed him down, though of course he would always be a very big man. The confused look was long gone from his face. The jagged, purple vein in his temple was still there but he wasn't vacant anymore. On the contrary, he seemed more attuned than people a third his age.

Beside him, for just a second, there appeared his other granddaughter, shy and skittery as a colt. She was eight years of age and born after Gabriella had gone. Her name was Sandra Elizabeth Zazò and she preferred Sandy and there wasn't anything of the Firehead about her. There were no freckles and not a trace of red hair. She was dark and tall for her age and she didn't look like she would ever stop growing. We never really spoke; she was sweet-tempered some days and touchy some others and that was everything I knew.

But I liked to look at this young child. I liked to see her running or hiding behind the old man or picking jasmine and honeysuckle from the garden. She was a miracle meant to take the place of another miracle. Her father wasn't some Irish butcher on vacation in the Mediterranean but the man who should have been her father. The reason I didn't know much more about her was because Mamma and Papà Zazò kept the kid from me. I wasn't anyone's darly anymore. They couldn't stop me visiting the old man but they wouldn't let me come upstairs into their part of the house for Italian coffee and a plate of skeleton bones. Our families never communicated. Gabriella's disappearance smashed everything and everyone. My family had moved far north and the Zazòs far south and that told the ten-year story.

There was at least one good aspect to this mausoleum the Zazòs had built themselves and that was that they'd organized their house to cater to the nonno. They must have decided he would end up living forever. It was certainly looking that way. He had the downstairs to himself, a cool and separate place with a tiny kitchen and a smaller bathroom, a bedroom, and a little corner of sitting room where he liked to watch television until all hours. He liked the late-night evangelical preachers. He liked the early-morning sitcoms and police show repeats that no one watched. To him they were brand-spanking new. He had his privacy. He also had his life.

So to the real thing about Enrico Belpasso.

For ten years now he'd been living in light. That's how he described it. That he could even talk was yet another miracle in the Zazò household, but he talked all right, and he thought, and he imagined and he dreamed. He fed himself. He had returned from wherever he'd been. Once, telling me about it, the blackness, he'd called that place *la notte*, the night. At first I was bothered by his choice of expression and there were moments when I would walk through the horseshoe entrance of the nightclub and remember his strange terminology, and have to wonder about the lives Tony Solero and I had made for ourselves, then I would put such thoughts aside. Omens didn't exist. The true thing was that during our long-ago afternoon at Nocturne, through an alchemy of prostitutes and a little marijuana and the visits of ambulance officers and Pietro Pierucci, Enrico Belpasso had traded places with Gabriella. Maybe in the end it was an everyday sort of voodoo, that switch, but it was the irony that ate at all our lives. She went away. He came back. In our hearts every single one of us involved would have traded a hundred scrofulous old men like him for one beloved child named Gabriella Zazò.

There was another reason Enrico Belpasso described his new life as being lived in light. For more than that resurrection into awareness he was also graced with visions of stars and universes, of exploding constellations that invited him into their vortex. Flashing colors whizzed by him as he fried a steak. Neon signs reading nothing shone bright as a comet's tail while he stood at his bathroom sink scraping a cut-throat razor over his white-bristled chin. When he dreamed he saw rivers in the sky, flowing into the sun. The red planet Mars was behind his head. The colored rings of Saturn encircled his brick home and sometimes an afternoon breeze was the color of a flowing torrent of lava.

Fancifully, there were moments when people's speech hung in the air like black clef notes and sudden simple certainties about individual destinies would strike him in the pit of his stomach. He'd tell you about these: My friend, you will fail in business; *Cumpari,* your wife imagines the body of a certain soap opera star while you make love to her; Salvatore, your tax return is wrong and you know it and for your dishonesty a nasty fine is arriving in the post. When it did arrive I was stunned and then a little scared and then I promised myself never to visit him again. As if I could have—but other people stayed away and that was nothing new so he didn't worry about it. Instead, Enrico Belpasso lived happily with the totality of these terrors and delights because the alternative was *la notte.* And what interested me more than all these half-eerie things was that he remembered lightning-flash moments from the old days in New Farm. These always involved Gabriella. Out of the acute dark, a memory of the warmth of her hand when she held his. Out of the silence, her voice saying, Will you push me on the swing, Nonno? Out of the nothing that used to be his colorless ocean of thought, Where is the child this morning? Why hasn't she come to see me yet?

Enrico Belpasso was back.

W HAT IS IT? What's troubling you today?" he said to me in Sicilian. There was no other language in his head as he'd never tried to learn English. Maybe he knew some words and phrases, I remember Gabriella used to say he did, but if so he never chose to use them.

Little Sandy had run as soon as I'd arrived. She was scared of me because her parents told her she had to be. Then a hail of pebbles had rained down on my back and when I turned, Sandy's bare dirty soles were disappearing around a corner. Enrico Belpasso roared after her like a primitive man shouting at scavenger birds.

"Get inside before I crack your head open! If I get my hands on you you'll be sorry!" That was the true Sicilian dialect at work. Sandy's disembodied giggling reached our ears; that was fearless childhood at work. The old man turned to me, wheezing a little, wiping his nose, laughing. "*Minchia*, you've got a big hole inside you today."

"No—what are you talking about?"

Then we were walking down the neat streets of his suburb. In a few hours I would be dressing myself for my own La Notte but for now I had time for our usual stroll.

"Do you understand what I said, Salvatore?"

"No."

Enrico Belpasso jerked his chin scornfully. "Your hole is so big and so black, if I put my hand in and reached hard enough I could drag the devil out by his nose. Tell me what's gone wrong."

"Nothing. Except I think I've met a woman."

"You're like a dog who's got a bone as big as this and doesn't know where to bury it." He grinned at me but his eyes showed that he had more than just a joke in mind. "There's always a woman."

"That's all it is."

"So what's new about a woman?"

"I think she's different."

"Ha," he nodded. "Now I understand my dream."

"What dream?"

"Last night I saw you were in the moon with Gabriella." He stopped on the neat footpath and clapped my cheek twice, his hand heavy, actions as anciently Sicilian as his words. "You are both flying over the mountains of the moon."

"There aren't any mountains on the moon."

He started to walk again, a slow lumbering because of old knees and sore feet.

"Who says? You've been there? In my dream Gabriella's wings are getting old and broken and the white feathers are coming down out of the sky. You as always are strong but you let her struggle. Now she is falling with all her ragged feathers around her and you are ready to fly to a star that is burning in the eye that watches us all."

"I don't care about helping her because I've got an appointment with God?"

He shrugged. "Do you know what this dream says?"

"Nonno," I said. "Nonno, I haven't a clue."

"It means you're waiting just like everyone else, Salvatore. Waiting. Why must you lie?"

The old man smiled his perfect false-teeth smile. Inside myself I jumbled those words: a smile, perfect, false.

My humor disappeared, just like that.

I wanted to scream, How can I be waiting? I know she's dead. Why do you think I'm waiting for a dead person? She must be dead. If she's alive she's not even twenty-five years of age. If she walked up to me now little Gabriella would be a young woman, a young, young woman with a whole world inside her to give—but, you stupid old man, what's the point of imagining such a thing?

She was gone and I knew it; at nights I still pictured her dying with blood, plenty of blood, because some maniac had kidnapped her and raped her and killed her with a knife—it always seemed to be this way, always with a knife, because that was the weapon that would make the most blood. Her body was buried somewhere, dumped in some grounds that were never explored, dropped down a gorge or weighted and thrown into the sea. There was no other possibility.

There had never been the slightest sign or clue of her. That afternoon at Nocturne she must have panicked and run and some monster out of the Void had snatched her. That was that. Even Pietro Pierucci had given up the investigation. He'd followed it from when he was a police officer to when he was a detective and then a senior detective. He tracked down the "boys" who'd been upstairs but that gave nothing because two of them were young cops from a station in the western suburbs and the third was their friend. Then there was the mystery of the car that had been waiting in the street, with the timid potential client staring at Nocturne's outside walls, as Mrs. Veronica had put it. She said the car was Japanese and yellow and her daughter Dorothy said it was a Chrysler and silver. Neither variation turned up. So was that the monster who'd made a child invisible?

Entering dead end after dead end, the investigating team tried to make Mrs. Veronica and the prostitutes give them every detail they knew about every man who had ever walked, blundered, or staggered drunk into their establishment. Soon Pierucci's enthusiasm for the case helped him make the rank of detective and he officially joined the team, and then in no time it seemed he was heading the whole thing himself. He had his women and men make lists and lists of names and lists and lists of clusters of male characteristics and they headed them with labels like "Freaks," "Fuckwits," "Perverts," and "Animals." They made sure they had the best in forensic psychology to help them but a kid like me was never to learn the key to what would qualify a man for one label but not the next.

Even people not involved in the case discovered what a maddening exercise the whole thing was; the papers followed the story. Working whores went to jail when the answers the police wanted simply didn't come. It was a sort of retribution, this blind crackdown. To me it seemed the authorities were determined to squeeze the truth out of Brisbane's underbelly and this was what I wanted; at nights I would lie in my bed silently begging Pierucci and all the police of the city to beat the truth out of anyone or everyone. Prostitutes complained about harassment and Nocturne and places like it were shut down for over a year. No graft was good enough, not in that first twelve months.

At the very beginning of the saga, people like Pietro Pierucci might have entertained the suspicion that Gabriella had somehow whisked herself off the face of the earth, and with the facts that came to light about her family many began to speculate that maybe some misguided romantic ideal had made her set her mind on getting to Ireland. This was by far the best hope Joe and Joan Public held to explain her disappearance; if it was true then might she not still be safe? Yet no customs records or flight lists or ship's manifests ever supported this particular belief. On Mamma Zazò's information it took Interpol no more than a few days to make contact with Gabriella's biological father, and very shocked a recent retiree caretaking on a horse stud outside Dublin was he, having never had any communication with his daughter, having never even suspected he had one. Mamma Zazò, when she'd left him all those years ago and returned to Raffaele in Catania, hadn't told him about her condition. So this part of the story was only another dead end that served to add a little extra dirt to the dying lives of Agata and Raffaele Zazò.

Gabriella's description and details went out around the world. The Zazò family hired an investigating firm and half a dozen times they took out full-page advertisements in local and national newspapers. Only well-meaning people with no information and nuts with plenty of information ever made contact. The main files on Gabriella Zazò never went into Pietro Pierucci's cabinet, someone told me. They were always scattered on his desk and around his desk and in the drawers of his desk, close at hand no matter what other case or cases he was working on. At the end an assistant reported hearing him mutter *Vaffanculu miseria*—the most bitter Sicilian way to say, Good-bye misery—as he finally put them into deep cardboard boxes and marked them to be moved into records. Records was a place he called the Police Department's dead-letter office. Years earlier the state coroner's necessarily inconclusive findings had mentioned words like "misadventure" and "person or persons unknown," and the subsequent memorial service held as much significance as a ceremony for the passing of a puff of wind—but the moving of those fat tattered weathered files from the environs of Senior Detective Pietro Pierucci's desk and into some cavernous basement central-filing system was Gabriella's true burial. That was when we all wept again.

After that Pietro Pierucci transferred to the Licensing Branch and gave up Death, hopefully forever, but, as I've explained, Death chose not to leave his side.

A FRANGIPANI TREE the old man and I passed smelled sweet, like a good memory of walking by New Farm Park on a soft summer's night.

Enrico Belpasso yanked at my arm and said, "We all have to wait because Gabriella isn't dead." This was what he often said, or things like this, and just as with my own such thoughts they only infuriated me. They infuriated me because I couldn't divorce myself from him and therefore I wasn't totally divorced from what he believed. This made life excruciating but I preferred that to—what would it be called in a psychoanalytic sound bite?—letting go.

The old man said, "But my dream tells me that you will deny her. That's what it is all about."

"No," I said, "if it means anything it means something else."

He hawked into a patch of some neighbor's daisies. "Maybe. But your hole is black. Black. Understand?"

"Yeah, I understand."

"*Allora.* Let's start remembering her."

This was how it went. This was why we met. This was the memory trail that kept Gabriella alive.

"I don't want to go first," I said. The morning champagne and the excitement of holding and kissing Mrs. Irina Luna had left me with a daytime headache. The bright sunlight hurt my eyes even through sunglasses. "You."

There was one unspoken last hope. I knew it existed. I knew it existed because if I'd thought of it then her parents must have thought of it, and if we'd all thought of it everyone else who'd ever loved Gabriella must have thought of it too. A certain invisible energy therefore surrounded this hope. It was simply that there'd be a miraculous event when Nonno Enrico Belpasso died, a miraculous event to match the one ten years ago when he'd come back to life. The miracle would be that at the moment his spirit departed, Gabriella's would return. And not just her spirit, her. They would swap places again. We'd bury him and she'd walk out of the air that had swallowed her. I lay awake some nights dreaming about this. I tossed and turned imagining her face and wishing the old man dead. But the bastard didn't die. He became healthier and happier; he was here and she was gone.

So there was no waiting. How could there be?

E NRICO BELPASSO HAD nothing to say. Despite his vivid dream and his unshakeable belief that Gabriella wasn't dead, today he couldn't remember her. It was almost as if my own lack of energy afflicted him too; what I mean is, my low spirits seemed to dampen his own, like throwing a shroud over some radar or transmitter.

His mouth worked but he didn't come out with a memory. Many times in recent months he'd told me little things about Gabriella and him in New Farm Park: how he used to push her on the swings, her little skirts flying and her white legs heading straight up toward the blue sky, toes pointed, or something about some wonderful Sicilian dish she'd cooked for him just the way Fortunata used to do, or some birthday card she'd made for him with her own hands, or how she used to spend hours and hours in a sort of concentrated pleasure, with her pens and her papers, writing, writing, writing God could only knew what silly things.

But today we were both blank. My black hole sucked Enrico Belpasso into it.

He said, "It is this woman." He nodded. "She's in your way. You'd better go to her. Today is a waste. Come another time, Salvatore."

It seemed like the worst betrayal.

"You know," I started, forcing myself to see an image of Gabriella running with me across the old suburban backyards of our neighborhood. In her excitement she'd make me climb the high paling fence that separated our two houses, even though I hated to climb them because they gave off big splinters. "You know, we used to have this little mystery back in New Farm. Gabriella always said we'd have to work it out but we never got around to it. Did I ever tell you about our mystery?"

The old man must have liked my determination. He said with animation, "No. I don't think so. What was it?"

"It had to do with the little corner store, the one run by Mr. Harry. It's a coffee shop now. Anyway, I don't know if you remember him."

"Mr. Harry?" Enrico Belpasso shook his head. Mr. Harry was someone he'd lost in la notte and who hadn't emerged, if he ever would.

"He had a mustache. He was an unhappy fellow. Well, it doesn't matter. But this thing was something we used to laugh about. Gabriella and I called it The Case of the Missing Newspapers."

"Newspapers? Huh."

"Yeah. We couldn't explain it. Will I tell you what it was about?"

"Newspapers." Enrico Belpasso repeated the word but this time it was something passed to him by a red hand from Hell. He twitched his head. "Huh. I see lights."

Enrico Belpasso might have been back, but sometimes he was still runny as an egg in the head.

"Lights."

"Different lights. Like a lamp. Not electricity. Something burning. A flame—in an oil lamp."

It was the tone of his voice. I felt like a fool to believe in him.

"What is it?"

He said, "Bundles of newspapers. Bundles. Tied up."

"Bundles, yes, that was it. But you can't remember that. Do you remember it?"

The old man shook his head and a look of nausea crossed his features as if he were pained and sick in the stomach. "No. It's nothing."

"Nothing?" I watched the way his big hands were so frail when they started to tremble. "What's nothing? Tell me."

Enrico Belpasso's weathered and worn face looked at me and I had to hold him steady by the arm. There was no bench we could sit down on. The footpaths around this street corner were dry and sun-scorched. Whoever was responsible hadn't been doing their council-allowed, handheld watering of the grass strips. It was too far to get him back into his home straightaway so I took him into some shade under a collection of short and very droopy palm trees. He took out his handkerchief and ran it around his face.

I said, "Why does it hurt?"

Enrico Belpasso looked through the shade, turning his face to the sky.

He said, "Look at the light, Salvatore. Look at it. To live in such light and still be blind. I am blind. Shit of a world, I still am."

I remembered very clearly the way he used to be, a vacant bear of a man led everywhere by his granddaughter, him slow-eyed and oblivious to everything and her as alive as electricity. But hadn't Gabriella always said that they'd been able to talk and recount stories for hours and hours? Hadn't she felt his pain and his desires and even his dreams?

Enrico Belpasso held onto my arms because he was afraid he was going to fall.

"There's one thing to remember," he said to the palm branches spreading over us, to the glinting sun above them. "It's Gabriella's room."

"What room?"

He touched that ugly electric jag down one temple. I looked at his eyes and the dark brown pupils were impossibly large in their dilation.

"Gabriella's room. The newspapers are in Gabriella's room."

There was an expression in his face that made me understand he didn't hear his own words. Or that if he heard them, he believed they came from some place other than himself.

"What are you talking about?"

"And so is Gabriella. Do you know it, Salvatore? Salvatore, can you imagine it? Our Gabriella is in Gabriella's room. And from there she's everywhere. No walls can stop her flying."

"What are you talking about?"

Enrico Belpasso was back from la notte but he was as mad as can be. Maybe he wasn't back at all. His mind swirled with crazy colors and he thought he could see the fine detail of people's destinies. In the hurting daylight of a Brisbane summer's afternoon prickles of hope and fear alike traveled across my skin. Gabriella is in Gabriella's room. It was like a scary twist in a twisted fairy tale.

Enrico Belpasso held onto me and he wept and it was easy to see he didn't understand why.

Orange Juice at Night

THE CUT-GLASS BOWLS OF oranges and lemons and grapefruit in my kitchen must have made an impression on Irina Luna. I came into my apartment soaking with perspiration and heartache and didn't expect to see her in there, in my white cotton bathrobe, her brown legs sticking out below, her breasts making the front bulge, her braided gold-brown hair damp from the shower, and her long hands firmly squeezing and straining citrus fruits. The sight of her made my heart soar. She could have been standing there in the world's ugliest tent dress and not in my bathrobe and my heart would have soared just as high. Irina was a shaded pool out of the sun; she was a gust of sea breeze on a forty-degree day; she was the fucking cavalry. No more than twelve hours had passed since the crew of musicians had left my apartment joking and laughing, their bellies distended with early morning paella and green salad and their heads singing with mixed drinks and champagne. Now the Sunday afternoon with Enrico Belpasso had drifted away and early evening darkness had descended; in a few hours more I'd be standing at the entrance to Tony Solero's La Notte, doing what I was supposed to be doing.

She hadn't heard me come in. I was dead in my tracks, overwhelmed by the surprise of her. I didn't say anything. I wanted all the time in the world to watch her, but in a moment she sensed me and she raised her face from the lemons and grapefruit. Then she smiled, a really sweet smile that said she'd been caught in the act and was glad to be. Her eyes were smudged with faint tiredness yet there was a low sort of playfulness in her voice when she said, "You need a cool drink, don't you?"

Irina resumed her slow and methodical squeezing, that liveliness never leaving her smile.

"Julián's gone to watch Juventus play Azzurri. Then he and his *compañeros* will find some bar somewhere and drink too much. Then they'll go for a pizza and eat too much. That's Sunday, when we're not working." She looked for oranges to add to the sour fruit juice. "So I thought I wouldn't put it off. I thought I'd come and see you."

"I didn't expect you."

"Why not? You gave me the key." Irina quickly squeezed the oranges and poured the combination of juices into a pitcher. She went to the freezer and collected ice cubes, perfectly at home. "It would be a crime to put sugar in this."

"Kills vitamin C. Maybe just a little water to protect our gums."

"That only applies to growing children." She filled two plastic tumblers, the type you use for iced coffees on the balcony or Bloody Marys taken on a pool's deck.

"And you look like you could use all the vitamin C you can handle. And maybe a few others." She handed me a full-to-the-brim tumbler and kissed hers against mine. Juice splashed onto the tiled floor I paid a housekeeper to keep clean for me. "Here's to that wonderful shower of yours. I helped myself. Do you mind?"

"No."

"The one at our flat has no water pressure and the hot water goes off as soon as you've started to relax. So thank you. Now tell me something. Why do you look so terrible?"

"Maybe I always look like this."

She stood back from me, then leaned against the sink. In my robe she looked like she belonged. There wasn't a trace of awkwardness to her presence, and somehow it was as if it were four in the morning again, only our roles had changed. Irina gave me a nice long up-and-down.

"No, you don't always look like this. You're one of those bastards who looks good no matter what they've been up to. How old are you?"

"Twenty-five. Going on twenty-six."

"I thought you were older."

"There's only five years between us."

"Six years. And six years depends on what you did with those six years."

Then Irina averted her eyes. It was as if she couldn't keep up her game. On a stage there always comes the time when you bow and leave, but here she was just with me and the way out had to be of her own making. She looked into her glass—and I realized she was just that little bit shy. Just that little bit unsure. Her vulnerability made me like her more.

"So, are you happy to see me?"

"Yes."

She drank and I watched her. She wiped her mouth with the back of her hand. Beneath her eyes there were those little charcoal smudges but her eyes themselves, they were awake and alight, dark and alive, just like her.

Irina said, "Do you want me here, Sam?"

"Yes."

"Then why on earth don't you show it?"

That was Irina Luna.

HER HANDS TASTED of the oranges, her lips tasted of the lemons and grapefruit. She ran her fingers through my hair. When I kissed her she sighed and all the aches of long, long troubles made this little bit of loving somehow soft and sweet. She let me lift her onto the kitchen counter, where I'd chopped a hundred pieces of garlic and a thousand brown onions, and the thought made me want to laugh, her sitting there, right on that place, in my white fluffy bathrobe. I was standing between her legs and her thighs squeezed my waist. We kissed long hard light fast—happy like children at the pleasure of it. I ran my mouth over her neck and the hollow of her throat and the fast pulse at the side. Irina opened the robe so I could kiss her brown breasts and darker nipples, but I stopped then. All I did was wrap her in my arms and press my head against her shoulder, holding her so tightly she could barely breathe.

She was only half laughing now. "What's the matter?"

"I'm happy," I said. "I'm really happy."

Irina got herself free from my hug and held my face in her hands. She said, "Sam Capistrano, why the hell shouldn't you be?"

T HAT MADE HER wonder. Irina picked up my glass of juice and helped herself to almost all of the last of it. Then she looked me straight in the eye again.

"If I didn't think you were ready for me I wouldn't have come here. Tell me what happened today."

"It's about the girl in those photographs."

Irina had this way of making little creases in her high brow, but it was her eyes, her mouth that kept drawing me in. Her lips were so full and dark with our kissing they were almost as ripe and purple as—figs.

"She broke your heart?"

"Yes, in a way."

"And is she here now?"

"No."

"Do you see her anywhere in this apartment? Here in the kitchen, or waiting over there, or hiding behind the couch?"

"No."

"Will she be coming here?"

"No."

"Will she ever be coming here?"

"No, she never will."

Irina thought about that.

"All right. So I'm here now. And then, Sam, I'll be gone. If you want me to go right now just say it and that will be all right. What happens with that girl or any girl isn't my business. This is a nice moment that can be for us, just you and me, and then it's over. But if you need some time to forget that girl or think about that girl or whatever it is that's going on, then just tell me."

Irina looked at the photographs. Then she looked back to me.

"But," she said. "But Sam, she's just a child."

"Yes, she is."

Irina didn't understand and I wasn't going to explain.

Because she was only offering the same old usual. It was exactly as she said. Irina was here now and then later she'd be gone. Somewhere inside I still had dreams of romantic love but no one wanted me that way. Maybe women saw the walls they'd have to knock down. Maybe they sensed the chaos behind those walls. So Irina Luna wanted to be just another nightclub gal, this one a Saturday night one, and married too, ah well.

Irina leaned forward and pressed her forehead to mine. Her skin was hot and her hands, now clasped behind my neck, had become damp. She shut her eyes and seemed slowly to drift into a sort of dream. It was nice; I closed my eyes too.

She said, "You know what you need?"

"What?"

"On a day like today, a nice long cool shower. It'll make you feel better." She opened her eyes and tousled my thick hair. "And clean as I am, I think I'm going to join you."

So I GOT into a nice cool shower, and it did turn out to be long. Because Irina followed me in. She turned me and turned me under the nozzle's nicely pummeling massage spray, and she took the waiting bar of soap and with it caressed my shoulders and chest and belly. It didn't seem to matter to her that she'd been in here not twenty minutes earlier. Irina doused herself, gasping at the coldness of the water, and I watched her buds grow out beautifully. The thick curling fronds of her wet pubic hair were like a collection of some sort of strange and exotic seashells. She made me lift my arms and she scrubbed me under there, and she got me down below, and she smiled in my face until we forgot about cleanliness and were kissing long and hard. When she put the soap aside and wiped her eyes, she turned her supple, muscular back to me and leaned with her breasts pressed against the dimpled safety glass of the shower door. She put out her tan but not tanned, heart-shaped rump and her narrow waist twisted easily when she looked back at me and said, "Please, Sam," and then Irina closed her eyes, flying away.

Letting go.

A Memory Like a Dream

GABRIELLA'S LAUGHING WHILE SHE takes me by the hand and
we run across the backyards, from mine to hers, climbing over the splintery wooden fence in between, watched by droopy neighborhood dogs
and her two pussycats, Gina and Sophia. One of our mothers will be in
one of the kitchen windows, slicing eye-fillet steaks or scaling some fish
like whiting or bream for the evening meal, and watching down on us.
When Gabriella laughs the way she's doing now I haven't got a care in
the world. I'm not a boy with scruffy black hair that ought to be cut and
scratched knees that ought to be smeared with ointment, but somehow
I'm everyone. I'm anyone who ever laughed and anyone who ever cried,
I'm anyone who ever dreamed of making a home in the stars and anyone who ever turned their hopes-dashed face to the wall beside their
bed and asked God for the easy release of sleep. She makes my secret
thoughts come alive; that's Gabriella. Somewhere inside I already
understand that there are people who will go through their lives and
never know a person like her, who will never find that someone who
will add a strange and wonderful zest to their existence the way
Gabriella does to mine. She's like a skyrocket that thrills alive a dull old

carpet of night-sky stars. The constellations have to be in awe of her. I will never die among sorrows and I will never be adrift; I am meant for this world, just the way she is.

I might as well ask her to marry me.

Well, some silly day.

We dash beneath her timber house and stand together in the dirt. We're panting, holding hands in the dim light. My hunger for her is so strong I'm in agony, my body screaming for release. This is the way it goes: the more the weeks pass, the more she means to me and the more my body needs her. Gabriella likes to kiss but that's as far as she likes to let herself go. Fair enough, because I like to kiss, and talk, for hours and hours in our nice dark places, but I'm still human too. I stare at her hard so that she might read my desire. But there's something different. What do I read in her face today? It's funny, for all her chocolate freckles and red hair and usual pinkness of skin, today she looks like she's lost all of her color. I can count the freckles standing out on the bridge of her nose one by one. She's white like a sheet but I still want her so badly I'm prepared to get down on my knobbly knees and kiss *her* knobbly knees. She seems oblivious to my plight and is instead lost in her own edgy happiness. Gabriella radiates sunshine but today it seems dampened with steel-gray clouds, and she seems—I don't know—brittle.

Gabriella says, "*Cosa c'ai per me, Salvatore?* What have you got for me?" and I feel around in my pockets for sweets but believe it or not I've forgotten to buy them. Wait. Here's something. In my back pocket is a tatty novel I found under a seat in Lino Solero's utility truck when he was driving me and Tony to the pictures to see that new movie someone told us is a sex movie about beautiful lost schoolgirls—and it isn't—*Picnic at Hanging Rock*. The book I found is called *Sexus* by Henry Miller. That at least is about sex, but in a way it isn't either.

"Supposed to be good," Lino Solero told me. "Piece a shit." Lino was after dirty stories and the creased and pulpy pages I first had a look at did read like the randy slobberings of a dirty old man, but there was something else, something about being wild and crazy and alive. That's also in those moldy pages and I think Gabriella will understand.

"Madonna," she says, because we're in our secret language. "I've heard about this man. I've heard about this book. My mother would kill me if she knew I had it—even if she can't read a word of it." We laugh together and Gabriella flicks pages. She says, "I've been reading stories by a Spanish writer. They mean a lot to me."

"Spanish?"

"Jorge Luis Borges. There's one story—" Gabriella's white cheeks slowly streak a crimson blush. Suddenly I'm confused. Is the color coming into her face because of what I've given her or because of this other writer? After a pause, still looking at pages, she says, "Ma will know this word. And this one. Shoo, and this one! Thank you. I'm going to put this in a safe place. I'm going to put this in my secret place."

"What's that?"

Gabriella gives me a look. Next will come a little white lie or something I absolutely didn't know before. She says, "Why do you think it's called a secret?"

"So tell me."

She crunches her bloodless face up like a pixie's and then she passes the backs of her fingers up and down my cheek, nice and slow. I think Gabriella is actually making up her mind about me.

She steps closer and says, "Oh, Salvatore," and gives me a kiss and the taste of just the warm tip of her tongue. "Do you really want to know?"

"Sure."

"Are you scared?"

"Why should I be scared?"

"Well," Gabriella says, "it's all the way down there," and she points to the gathered gloom of the far depths under her house.

"So what?"

Of course there's nothing to see but black. There are no lightbulbs, no light switches, not even the most rudimentary electrical cabling runs to that part of the Zazò household. That's because it used to be just open air around the rotted wooden stumps that held the house up, until

Gabriella's father bricked everything in, restumped the house with concrete pillars, and made a little separate room for himself in those far recesses. Now where Gabriella points to is the cool and gloomy place where he keeps the many wooden cases of wine he transports up from his relatives' vineyards in Stanthorpe. I've seen him heading there with a candle or a flashlight, a minute later emerging with a dusty bottle or two of vino.

Actually, it's not gloomy. Gloom implies some sort of obscure radiance, doesn't it? No. Down there it is perfectly black.

Gabriella smiles. She draws a big sigh. She takes my hand and tightly wraps her fingers in my fingers.

Gabriella says, "You and no one else. All right?"

"All right."

The thing is I'm not afraid and I don't see why she should be. I've never been the type to be scared of the dark. I watch ghost stories on television in the dead of the night and yawn all the way through them. Yet Gabriella's fingers are cold and a little trembly. That amuses me. If she's got a secret down there what's she nervous about? She holds my hand and then she holds my whole arm, her body pressed right against me. And this is perfectly fine. I like this mystery. I'm going to go into that little wine room with Gabriella and in the perfect dark ask her to lie down so that I can lie on top of her. What do I care about girlish secrets? Her ear will instead hear the soft things I have to say to her. Her face will feel the touch of a hundred feather-light kisses. Her little breasts will swell to the tenderness of my fingertips, and for once I'm going to gently slide the zip down on her white shorts. I'm going to touch her there, slowly, and I know that this time she won't let me stop.

"Wait a second, we'll need this."

On her tiptoes Gabriella reaches up into the rafters above a concrete pillar. Her hand catches on her father's waiting flashlight, which she flicks on, and I'm disappointed by this. I would have preferred the absoluteness of black, the cloaking of darkness that makes bad things good to do. Or good things badder to do. Now this spooky beam is flicking around and creating shadows, and the fantastic thing is it seems to only illuminate shadows too. We could make a great ghost story down here.

It's cooler. There's concrete underfoot. In building his wine room Raffaele Zazò fashioned walls and a doorway; the door is the old rattan type found at the front of falling-down workers' cottages built in the twenties and thirties. He rescued this one from where somebody had thrown it out on some tip somewhere. He sanded it down and repainted it; it's funny that he should go to such trouble for something that will live in a world of perpetual night. Gabriella reaches for the doorknob, turns it, and lets us in. I have absolutely no idea why she moves in such a slow and deliberate and pensive manner. It crosses my mind that this is actually a trick of hers. Maybe her "secret" is actually her secret desire to have me down here in this wonderful place, where she will turn the flashlight off and let herself fly into me.

Oh, but I'm beyond agony now.

The white beam passes over crate after crate and they're all stacked neatly on the floor and against the walls. They're mostly covered with ratty blankets to keep in the cool and damp. The walls are shrouded with thick cobwebs and if mice and rats wander through the Zazò house at night, this is where they sleep by day. Gabriella picks out the rat- and mousetraps ready and set in the corners, each with a fat piece of strong-smelling Sicilian pecorino pepato cheese set luringly in the iron jaws. Raffaele Zazò must think the rats and mice are Sicilian too, and when one trap reveals a squished mouse in it Gabriella twitches the light away and I know her father isn't stupid. The light beam passes over the wine crates again and it strikes me just how much these covered, neatly arranged things look in fact like stacked coffins. All right. I don't like it here that much anymore. Goosebumps break out over my arms and, my bravery a real thing or not, I'm glad my Firehead is with me. I put my arm around her waist and pull her to me, pressing my lower parts into her so that she'll feel the suffering I'm in.

Gabriella submits for just a few seconds, kissing my mouth and running her free hand over my shoulder, but I can tell her heart isn't in it. I feel her buttocks with both palms of my hands and then I creep one around to her chest and hold the small shape of her breast. Gabriella pulls away. I grab her again and hold that breast another half-second. Gabriella gets out of my grip.

"Is that all you ever want?" She thrusts the flashlight at me. "Here," she just about spits like a wildcat.

My chest is constricted. I say in a voice hushed with sexual torture, "Gabriella, what are you up to?"

"You'll see."

My bad temper tells her there's nothing very secret about her father's stupid wine cellar.

She smiles like the cat that has just stomped a rat. "Oh, this isn't good enough for my secret."

Then Gabriella goes funny again. A shadow passes over her face, and then it becomes a wince. Her hand goes down to her stomach. I pass the light over her and her palm is flat against her belly. Low down against her belly.

"Oh no," Gabriella says. "Don't tell me."

She tries to take the flashlight back but I don't let her.

"How can I be so stupid?" Her face screws up. "Get that light off me," she hisses, and then she runs out.

The old rattan door goes *bang*.

I open that door in time to see Gabriella's silhouette darting around the concrete posts as she heads out toward the distant, glowing sunlight. Which swallows her. It's been less than three seconds and she's already vanished, and then I very clearly hear her running up the front steps, and after that the sounds of her as she runs through the house. The floorboards *phunk-phunk* softly above my head. A door slams loudly. The bathroom or her bedroom? I guess the bathroom. Goddamn it. Poor Gabriella. It's shit to be a man when your thing is pushing like a fist against your zipper but it just might be shittier to be a woman; I want to kick myself for not having understood her pallor and mood. When she'd run out the flashlight beam caught the unbelievably red stain on the back of her white shorts. It was as if she'd been stabbed with a knife in that private place. How long was she bleeding before she felt it?

I shine the light around the walls, into the cheese-laden traps, into the one with the squished mouse, and over the coffinlike wine crates. It's musty and cool in here. But what kind of a secret is this to Gabriella? It just doesn't make sense.

Before I leave I pass the torchlight down onto the concrete floor between my feet. In that darkness there is one bright, yet dark, perfect droplet of blood. A red glistening circle no more than the size of a two-cent piece. My eyes are fixed with wonder, then I get down onto one knee and tentatively reach my hand toward it. This thing came from her; this is the essence of my Firehead. This here, this is what a secret really is.

Therefore Gabriella won't like it to stay there.

I don't touch it though I would like to taste it. I dig in my pocket for a tissue or a handkerchief. There's nothing. I untuck the tail of my shirt from the waistband of my shorts, twist it around and get down really close, and wipe that beautiful droplet away.

Dog Instincts

THE TELEPHONE WAS RINGING and Irina stretched and yawned, her whole long body arching. She rolled onto her stomach and crawled onto me, unhurried in her movements, her dark face rubbing against my skin, her forearms folding against my chest. We went together like sour bread and red wine; it was a lovely thing.

"What if it's Julián?" she sighed.

"What would he do if he knew you were here?"

Irina shook her head. It was not something to envision, but I imagined Julián Luna feeding me to the crows that lived in the river's weeping willows.

The bedside alarm clock showed that it was well after eleven P.M. La Notte would be humming and Tony Solero would be cursing my name. Carlo would be alone at the door and our disco lights would be flashing an eternal mating call into the infernal nightclubbing world. The person on the telephone line was more likely Tony than Julián and he'd have plenty to say to me. Friendship and a lot of years aside, things weren't really so rosy for me down there; the business seemed fine but he was getting fed up with my weak ways on the door, and added to that he knew all about Senior Detective Pietro Pierucci's feelings toward me. Pierucci was someone he needed kept on his side, whether he was mean and unpredictable or whether he wasn't, because the man had the Licensing Branch in his palm. The money the nightclubs gave Pierucci might have seemed like bean and beer money individually but he used to say, Little fish are the sweetest, and that meant they were nice on their own yet when you added them together you got a great feast for yourself and your friends.

La Notte could have been closed down for a hundred health and safety reasons and it was the same with a hundred other clubs. What I was really suspicious of was the fact that Tony and Pietro talked a great deal, by telephone and behind closed doors. They were cooking up secret future plans and so it didn't help my cause that the detective hated me. In the old days, to explain inexplicable attractions and inexplicable enmities, Tony and I used to have this phrase—"dog instincts." Of course there was nothing inexplicable about why Pierucci's animal didn't go with my animal, but the phrase always stayed in my mind. The thing was, such dogs you just kept apart, and Tony knew that. So I should have been doing everything I could do to keep on Tony's good side but even while I was thinking that I snuggled Irina's head into the crook of my arm.

The ringing stopped.

"Hombre," Irina said in the same way Julián Luna liked to say the word. That's what you got after so many years with the one person. She rubbed her eyes. "I've been sleeping. Have you?"

That dream like a memory or that memory like a dream had been powerful in its clarity. Enrico Belpasso brought it into my room and so did making love with Irina. It had just been this little moment between Gabriella and me, and it hadn't gone anywhere. Ten years ago I'd forgotten about it almost as soon as it happened; there were better things to do at the age of fifteen than wonder about some dark cool place where I'd failed to seduce my beautiful little friend. The idea of a secret place hadn't meant much to me. It was no big deal. At that time I had plenty myself, scattered all over the suburb. There'd been the shadowy corners under my own house; the little wooden cubby in the big mango trees at Johnny Aitkin's place; the little patch of protected green under the bottle boab trees in New Farm Park; the always available back seats of various friends' older brothers' cars; even the half-dangerous concrete crumbling cloisters of an abandoned old powerhouse on the Brisbane River, just by the park. A boy had a million places to hide. Yet now I really thought about what Gabriella had meant to show me. I had to picture it in relation to what Enrico Belpasso had said.

Gabriella is in Gabriella's room.

Among my crisp white sheets Irina was naked as the day she'd come into this world wailing some salsa-drenched song line. She pushed herself along with her elbows and brought her face up to mine. Happy. She slipped her tongue into my mouth and pushed her breasts into my chest. She writhed languidly against both me and the bed, satisfied yet wanting just a little more. She pulled back, smiling down into my eyes.

"Young man. What are we going to do?"

"You mean will we see each other again?"

"Maybe that's what I mean."

I said, "Well, why don't you stay here?"

"When?"

"Now. Tonight. For as long as you like."

Irina took a very deep breath and gave me the look that said I was loco.

"No, I mean it. Make this your home. Look at all the room. How else will you ever get away from him?"

"You think I want to leave Julián?"

"Don't you?"

Irina nodded. The obvious was obvious. She said, "That man would come here."

"And?"

Irina's smile widened and then she laughed, mocking me. "You think you're so tough?"

"I'm just saying feel free to take the easy way out. So Julián comes here. So you sit down with him in my lounge room and give him a cup of tea and tell him it's all over. Or you both yell and scream and smash all my furniture. Or he tries to throw me off my balcony. He won't do it. And you'll be out of what you don't want to be in anymore."

"Why do you think it would be that easy?"

"Why does it have to be hard? Show me where it's written that it has to be blood and guts. Show me where it's written that you have to tear your heart out. Just tell him and that's it. Do what everyone does. Just walk out."

Irina kept contemplating me, working out how much cruelty was in my words. A less generous woman would have had a very clear idea.

My idea was that I didn't care that I didn't have a clue what I was talking about. It didn't matter that I knew nothing about the institution of marriage. To me everything was transient anyway. The city changed on a yearly basis, everything nice got knocked down to make way for plate glass and black steel, and in just the same way if you loved a special partner you loved them until you didn't care to anymore; or if you were attached to someone wonderful sooner or later the day would come that the air would eat them whole, whether by their own design or by circumstances we like to call by that nice unbloodied word, misadventure. So my commitments were committedly short term. At least I faced that. It was the rest of the world that pretended.

Irina said, "Do you know what thirteen years of being married is like?"

I laughed. "No, but the old prince in that Italian film *Il Gatopardo* said something like it's one year of fire and twelve living in its ashes. Sound familiar?"

Irina gave me the most quizzical look. Not for the obscure allusion to a European film of the sixties but for what I was showing her of my heart.

"All right, if you're so tough. Here's the truth." She sat up, naked, cross-legged, looking at me. "I never loved Julián Luna. I was excited by him. I was infatuated by him. I liked the moving life we had and I liked the safety of being married. When I was eighteen he was a worldly musician of forty-three and he seemed so fabulous. I'd never been with a man before. When I had my first orgasm with his *pinga* inside of me I thought he was God. I was mad for sex and I raped him three times a day. That was the first year. In the second year I learned to hate his vanity and that big swaggering *boy*ness of his and his eyes eating up every woman he saw. I learned to hate how he was happy when I was low because then he could be a man and lift me up. In the third year I realized I just had to live with the way we were or get divorced, and I never wanted to be divorced. But things change. He's getting older now and all the hair paint in the bathroom is making me unhappy. There are these big black bushes growing out of his ears and his nose and they make me unhappy too. Even his smell has changed. He smells like an old man. When he comes into our bed he's all soaked-up whiskey and stale cigarettes and cigars and age. That makes me unhappy. I'm not saying my feelings are fair. They're not. But he's slowing down and I'm sick of having little affairs to make myself feel better. I'm thirty-one and I think I deserve to be able to live."

"Then live. Stay with me. How about that? I want you to stay with me."

Irina rubbed her golden-brown hair against my shoulder. Then she held herself as if she were afraid parts of her were going to fly off.

"Just like that. Just stay." After a moment, a hesitation, a chewing up and a spitting out, she shouted, "Fu-uck!" so loud and so theatrically that I had to laugh. She pounded the bed with her knees and beat the pillows with her fists. She screamed like a mad dog was after her and I had to laugh and adore her all at the same time, and soon she was laughing too. She settled down into my arms, breathing nice and hard. "One week." She spoke in a more reasonable voice. "Maybe two. No more." Then as Julián Luna liked to say, and even with his intonation, Irina added, "Why not?"

W E M A D E L O V E again, not gently or sweetly but in a fun way, nipping at one another and rolling around the bed, singing bits of songs and nursery rhymes too, and that was the way Irina wanted it, but this time blood was seeping out of her as if I were her murderer. In a second Irina was a brown Aphrodite stumbling toward the bathroom, her hand cupped between her legs.

The renewed ringing of the telephone followed her out and the shape of a bright quarter-moon was hanging in the broad glass of my bedroom's vast picture window. Who was so persistently ringing? Look at it this way: Julián Luna had read the stars; Julián Luna saw newspaper headlines in that same quarter-moon outside; Julián Luna was ready for blood. Or it was going to be Tony Solero with his own blood boiling.

My hand wavered over the receiver and when I picked it up, instead of either of them, the wheezing voice of old man Enrico Belpasso came down the line. He wasn't one for using the telephone and definitely not so late at night.

"Nonno. What is it? Are you all right?"

His Sicilian was thick and slow, measured out like the emotions you spoon into a simmering saucepan of *sugo di carne*.

"I dreamed it the way it used to be, Salvatore."

"Dreamed what?"

"About Gabriella and her room."

"Yes?"

"Salvatore. I'm in colors. They're all around me. They're drowning me."

"What? What are you talking about?"

Enrico Belpasso was quiet, except for his breath, and I could hear the wonder and the fear that made the rasping so hard.

"I'm coming over. I'll get a taxi. I'll be there in twenty minutes."

Enrico Belpasso let out a little cry and then he spoke an Italian word I hadn't heard before: *"Il caleidoscopio, Salvatore."*

"The what?"

"That's where I'm drowning. *Il caleidoscopio* is trying to drown me."

"Where is it? What is it?"

"Everywhere. Salvatore, it's everywhere . . ."

Il caleidoscopio. It sounded like kaleidoscope. Is that what the word meant?

"Stay where you are." I was already out of the bed and dragging my clothes to me. "I'm coming, all right? All right?"

"But how can this be?" Enrico Belpasso asked of me and the stars and the quarter-moon. "How can this be?" and I knew he didn't expect an answer. He didn't expect an answer because he knew I didn't understand the question.

Into Gabriella's Room

THE NEXT DAY THERE was only this:

The universe's silvery trail taking Irina's rattly, rust-ridden old Datsun into the suburb of New Farm. I couldn't remember the last time I'd been there. Years and years adding up to not much less than ten. Adding up to cowardice. The car blew oil smoke and when it turned a corner you thought parts of it weren't going to turn with you. That took care of any romantic notions of discovering the ghost of Gabriella waiting for me at the end of a carpet of stars. I stared at new bits of Brisbane landscape. Here an apartment building where the old service-station driveway Tony Solero and I had learned to roller skate in used to be. There a snazzy cafe-bar-restaurant where yesterday there was a Laundro-mat. Some Yugoslavian girl older than me used to work there, smelling always of Pears shampoo and 4711 cologne. With unlikely charm and priapic perseverance one closing time the seventeen-year-old me got seventeen seconds to feel the entire firm mystery of her Maidenform D-cups before, laughing, their owner threw me out the back door into the semi-industrial wasteland that used to be that part of the suburb. Now there were apricot-colored apartment complexes and black-and-white eateries and polyethnic delicatessens sprouting up on every street corner. New Farm was getting so polished you wouldn't find a dog's mess on the footpath or a single catfish in that river that twisted so muddy through the lower reaches of the suburb.

Irina, not Brisbane born and bred, didn't see the changes, the gentrification. She wouldn't have seen them anyway. Sometimes she would reach over and hold my hand for a few seconds, until the next gear change. Then she would turn her head to look into my face.

The night before, Irina Luna didn't go back to Julián. I didn't go to my job at La Notte. She waited in my bed while I went to the Zazò mausoleum and tried to calm the old man down. Mamma and Papà Zazò treated me like it was my fault, and when the doctor came and helped him to sleep with Temazepam I went home and thought about the remarkable things he'd told me that now brought me here.

We'd curled up and slept in each other's arms, Irina and I. We kept the world away. I wanted her in my bed to stop me thinking. She wanted to stay so that she could take first steps into a new life, but the first steps she took in the morning were into a past she didn't know, into Gabriella.

She'd said, "Well, my car's outside. We'll go and see, all right? Will that cool you down?"

Then, while standing in the shower, I tried to listen to her voice speaking into the telephone. I was certain I heard her go from strength to weakness. It was like the sensual spiraling in some canción she'd learned at Julián's hairy breast. I thought I heard her saying, Sorry, my Julián, I'm so sorry. I thought I heard her crying. I thought that by evening she'd be back in his arms and Julián Luna would really be planning how to feed bits of my meat to the crows living in the Brisbane River's weeping willows.

I didn't care, because of that trail into Gabriella's room.

WHEN WE TURNED off Brunswick and drove up Merthyr and came to the place where the adjoining timber houses should have been, bad neighbors Zazò beside bad neighbors Capistrano, there was instead a sweeping, completely boarded-all-around building site. The houses had been demolished and the twin properties joined into one lunar landscape. No—it wasn't truly lunar. In a week it would be but for now bits and pieces of timber and roofing and bricks and mortar still littered the area in rough and dusty piles. With a sensation like drowning I wondered why I'd deluded myself into thinking that ten years on there'd be something worthwhile for me here.

"Keep going, Irina. I made a big mistake."

She parked her smoking Datsun beside the curb. She wanted to get a closer look at the deciduous trees on Abbott Street. Visitors to the area always did. They still were something, those trees, huge as elephants— no, far bigger—as all-encompassing as the sky, making a perfect shade, a perfect jungle, from the top of the street to the bottom. Ten years from now the Brisbane City Council would vote that street the most livable street in the most livable suburb of the most livable city in the world's most livable country. I draw no conclusions.

While she wandered among the lovely carpet of brown leaves, taking off her sandals and kicking her feet into the feel of them, I took a look at that new construction site.

A sign showed what this would all soon be. A townhouse estate of eight narrow three-story homes. There would be a small in-ground pool. The terrain would be landscaped. Merthyr Mews would make people happy. For now it was a hole in the ground. I found a break in the rudimentary wooden safety fences and saw that not a soul was at work. Shading my eyes from the morning sunlight I guessed that things had already stopped for the coming Christmas break.

I kicked some thick palings down and slipped into the site. Rusty nails stuck out of the ground and there were a hundred ways to hurt yourself. My old house was completely razed and so was Gabriella's; I stood where my bedroom used to be, the living room, the kitchen. The room where my parents lay together so many years and made their children. The room where my father washed his sweat and aches away. I didn't recognize the pieces of rubbish lying around for it was impossible anything there could still have been mine. In the time since my family had sold up there'd been at least one set of new residents, and who was to say there hadn't been two, three, four, whatever number?

I crossed over to the old Zazò property, where ripped-up galvanized-iron roofing lay in sheets reflecting the sun. Splintery painted timbers, once solid walls and floorboards and high ceilings were stacked in layers. The demolition had been recent. It crossed my mind that maybe all wasn't lost, but it was without very much enthusiasm that I walked the length and breadth of the old house and then measured what I thought would have been the distance to where the wine cellar had been. It was easy enough to find. The concrete floor gave it away. It had been smashed into heavy chunks and even that old rattan door was still around, now flung aside in two bits on a pile of broken bricks. How weird to see that little piece of memory discarded there. The whole area looked like some monster had wandered through and unleashed an inexplicable fury, crushing everything it met with fists like sledgehammers. I started sliding sheets of iron out of the way and cleared as many wedges of concrete as I could lift. The ground underneath this was solid. No foundations had started to be dug yet. In a way it was virgin territory. My head started to swim with the delirium of potential discovery. By the time Irina came to find me I had my shirt off and was sweating the way I used to when my papà took me bricklaying with him.

"What can I do?"

"Put on your sandals. There are nails everywhere. Help me here, what are you waiting for?" Without a second thought, just the way my father used to say. So I added, "Be careful with your hands."

Irina would always tell me later that she liked the strange work that morning. She said I was like an archaeologist in Egypt digging down into some ancient treasury. She would tell our dinner guests that she watched me and felt something hard throbbing in her breast and a sort of fluttery feeling in her belly. Butterflies. She would say she saw me naked for the first time, pretenses gone, defenses gone, mask fallen, and it made her want me, really want me. She would say there was no point in denying that Julián Luna was a good man. He was a good man, with an ability to shine brilliantly, with an ability to be solid as a wall, but he was masked even to himself and never once had she seen the mask come away—and then Irina would leave our love story at that.

Our future was so, but this was the past. Which was too much my present.

Even in his fear Enrico Belpasso had been clear in what he'd told me. I knew about the wine cellar, that dark, dark place of crates and mouse- and rat-traps, but he knew the rest.

Some shovels would have helped but once the larger pieces of brick and concrete were out of the way things were easier. Enrico said that when his son-in-law Raffaele had concreted that floor he'd had to con- struct it around a trapdoor. That trapdoor led into a World War II bomb shelter that went twenty feet underground. Surprised to find such a thing, Raffaele Zazò explored it once, considered it dangerous, bolted it shut, padlocked it, covered it with straw matting and his collection of Stanthorpe wine, and forgot all about it.

In the war years, their house, like ours, had been used as serviced rooms to board the overflow of American soldiers who had nowhere else to be billeted. Among other activities, which included helping to build the immense Cloudland Ballroom that until 1982 had graced the nearby peak of Bowen Hills, those soldiers had used their months and months of waiting to excavate a shelter. This was for when Japanese Minister of War Hideki Tōjō's airplanes wiped out Darwin and came to bomb Brisbane. Those Japanese forces had victories in Southeast Asia and the Pacific but they never made it to Darwin, much less to my city; maybe the building scheme was just something the army hierarchy cooked up in order to keep a lot of fidgety Yanks occupied and away from Australian brothels. No, in those days the threat was real. I remem- bered that in my growing up there used to be places where bomb shel- ters still existed, twenty and even thirty years after the war. There'd even been one right in the main playground of my old secondary school, secured with the biggest blackest heaviest padlocks in Christendom. What I was completely certain about was that my old house had no such excavation: the inquisitive boy I used to be would have found a juicy thing like that before his fifth birthday. If Enrico Belpasso was to be believed, Gabriella had found the shelter under her house and made it her special secret, her hidey-hole from the world.

Then I saw that none of us were imagining anything. After stripping and sliding away the timbers, the rotten mattings, the old bunched up rolls of carpeting that hid it—there lay the trapdoor. Intact and mysterious and locked solid. The sight of it made me breathless but the question now was, Had it stayed that way through one whole decade?

"Well." Irina leaned back, hands on her hips, perspiration beading her skin like she'd just given everything in a stage show. "That's what we're looking for?"

What if she was in there? What if all these years—?

"Help me. Get the other side. No—there. *There.*"

Into the Treasury of Hell

TRY TO SMASH HINGES and locks with broken bits of brick. Stamp with both feet on damp-decayed wooden boards. Swear and curse. Use a plank to pry that sticking trapdoor up. Won't budge. Throw great hexagonal wedges of concrete onto it like the Cyclops hurling boulders and sides of mountains at the ancient Greek settlement in the Sicilian coastal town of Aci Trezza. Watch the weapons of your assault bounce back, wanting to crunch your toes. All right. Breathe hard. Look at Irina. Have a flash of inspiration. Irina, get your car's tool kit. We'll use the tire wrench as a lever. Jump impotently up and down on the boards while you wait. Then she comes back, your long brown Aphrodite, with just what you need. Now your muscles strain but hinges pop. Rusted screws leap into the air. The padlock cracks clean in two. Nails groan. Wood breaks away from wood. Then a belch of dank air; a secret place sighs at its uncovering.

You go down a short, surprisingly sturdy staircase and wish you had a flashlight, but the slanting sunlight is in fact more than enough. A great house no longer squats above to hide this musty chamber. But how did Gabriella see down here? Not by torchlight, surely, not if she came into this room for long periods of time. With a lantern? Some kind of oil lamp? Isn't that the light Enrico Belpasso said he saw? Why didn't the soldiers make provision for electric bulbs—were they stupid and lazy or did they simply run out of time, the war in the Pacific finishing before they did?

Gabriella—?

It's not twenty feet down. It's cramped and claustrophobic. Watch your step and cover your mouth and nostrils. Stinks. Slanting light from on high but darkening down here. The smell is of putrefying wood, tree roots, a lot of old wet vegetable flesh rotting off a metaphorical bone. No, don't get carried away. It's more like the muddy, sulfury stench on the Brisbane River's banks at low tide. Still, this must be what a grave smells like when for some brilliant purpose a corpse is exhumed. And it's no place for a girl like Gabriella. Enrico Belpasso is crazy. She wouldn't have played down here. She wouldn't have stayed down here ten seconds. And if she had, her father should have known about it and stopped her. Raffaele Zazò, what kind of a parent were you? And you, Enrico Belpasso, loving grandpa, in those days a great bear lost in his hibernation, couldn't you somehow—during at least one of your brief excursions upward into the light—couldn't you have managed to put a stop to it? And Sam, Salvatore Capistrano, you yourself young man, what would you have done as a fifteen-year-old discovering your beautiful friend's silent place? Would you have made sure she stayed away or would you have followed her down smiling and wondering how to create the opportunity to lift her little skirt?

Gabriella—?

Look.

My God. My God. My God.

There are signs of Gabriella Zazò everywhere. Signs of her but not her.

So it's true. This was her place. Is she really still in some shadowed corner, white bones crumpled inside a moldering skirt and a fright wig of red rampant hair topping the nightmare off? Just move around slowly, for this place has been untouched since the last time she left it.

Since the last time her white legs walked up that staircase. Or down them. Since the last time her hands closed that trapdoor. Then she was gone forever and the house got sold and no one was the wiser about Gabriella's Room. This secret place stayed nice and secret. You actually want to cry, don't you? You'd like to call out her name and get her back from the Void. But is she down here? Is she here or here or here or there or there or there? No. Stop rushing. Look around. Is she anywhere inside this pocket of Hell? No. You believe not. So breathe again. So add this dead end to the accumulation of all other dead ends. It may be a far more interesting dead end than any of the others but, really, what good does it do to visit this place? What good can come of it? So you wrap yourself in old loving memories—then what?

But don't have so many questions now. Don't wonder about this and worry about that. Don't fret that a townhouse complex will bury Gabriella's Room forever. Yes, it should be a shrine but it's already too much like an underground tomb as it is, isn't it? Fill the place in. Bury it. You can see that the process began long before you entered because one whole side has caved in. A wall of red brick has crumbled backward from the pressure and there is a mound of wet dirt tall as a man. Foul earth the color of ocher has found a way to invade this forgotten womb. This isn't a bomb shelter, it's a death trap. Gabriella, what did you mean by spending your time down here? No. No questions now. Just look. Take it in. Take in the signs of her life.

"Can I come down?" the voice from above.

"No!" the voice from below.

For here, and here, and here—look! Almost too many artifacts to swallow all at once.

There are magazines like *Time* and *Rolling Stone* long-forgotten pop newspapers like *RAM* (Rock Australia Magazine) books like *The Wild Ass's Skin* by Honoré de Balzac *The Dane Curse* by Dashiell Hammett space operas like the Skylark of Space series science fiction by Ray Bradbury fantasy by Tolkien crime by Agatha Christie some Italian writers called Pavese Pirandello Sciascia. You knew she was a great reader but never like this. Sherbet Skyhooks Al Bano record albums. No record player of course it was upstairs for the family to listen to. Hanging off a warped and mottled mirror a brassière designed to hold tiny breasts more a vanity thing than any sort of necessity you know that better than just about anyone. A gray satin shirt with patterned giraffes do you remember when she wore it was it one day on a ferry ride up the river didn't you share a chocolate milkshake or was it a Mr. Whippy ice-cream cone laughing as the silly thing melted all over your hands down your chin her chin probably stained that very shirt lying there like the skin of a dead cat. A little pocket makeup kit a handheld mirror a brush a packing case to sit on some kind of old doona rotting on the floor over a bare flat mattress she must have dug up from you can't even imagine where. Dear Gabriella what if we could have got married you in my apartment with me right now we'd have a kid or two the world would have turned out the way the world was supposed to turn out there'd be no La Notte or *la notte* you wouldn't be in the ground eating wet rotten dirt just like this I would have made love with you every morning every night bent you back in our beautiful bed taken you to never-ending beaches with galaxies of sand screwed you under the stars made you fried eggs bacon in the morning cool drinks on some rocky outcrop watching the sea wondering why us why us why are we so fucking lucky?

Some old sheet music music anthologies music books poster of David Bowie in 375 shades of Revlon. The pencil case you kept your colors in a block of drawing paper nothing on it virgin white except for age and water stains it's still waiting for your indelible mark. Che Guevara in a poster looking like a romantic hero. No photos no school pads you weren't even there yet no love letters no secret thoughts jotted down put in a time capsule for the future Salvatore to hold to his heart. All in all it's just old stuff in an old place that's rotting won't exist past the next few weeks maybe you should just go upstairs into the burning sunlight think about being alive think to yourself well that was kind of interesting take Irina home forget about it put it to bed once and for all she's still dead no matter what you saw in her secret room, fair enough.

What about all this?

Lightheaded, you walk around stacked, tied bundles of newspapers.

Newspapers! You have to touch them. Feel the damp. Mounds of the things—hills of them—built up into chest-high walls of discolored newsprint. How can it be? The Case of the Missing Newspapers solved but the motive is missing. Look at those dates, look at those headlines. Fraser might be slightly ahead but close Liberal race. Joh says: my phone tapped. Iranian newspapers asked by authorities not to mention name of Miss Juni Morosi. Poll shows major slump over last two weekends. Labor at lowest since 1966, LIB-NCP 53%, ALP 40%. Soviet Foreign Minister Andrei Gromyko to shortly set off on a tour of Arab states. Two hundred women storm offices of the *Canberra Times*. Sudanese Army troops loyal to President Jaafar Numeiri crush attempted coup. World politics sport crime entertainment business travel tips horoscopes births deaths engagements marriages wanted to buys wanted to sells personal columns opinions a thousand other things all as they were unfolding ten years ago. Here sit discarded all Mr. Harry's woes. Why? Who? You, Gabriella, *you* were the one who stole his newspapers in the mornings? What for? Why didn't you tell me? What was your scheme?

Voices up in the sunlit world.

"What you think you're doing here? Where's that door lead to? You can't be here, this is a building site."

Irina sweet-talking some tough guy, putting him off, calming him down.

"Lived here when? This is private property. Are you waiting for someone? Is someone down there?"

What's that over there, tucked away in the dark between two piles of moldy newsprint—a big shoe box?

"Hey—who's down there?"

Not a shoe box, something else. Reach in. Pull it out of the shadows.

"You! Get up here!"

God, look at it.

A mottled-with-age-and-damp little cobwebby doll's house. You can lift the roof open and look down inside and find Patsy and Flatsy or whatever their names are lounging around in tiny armchairs, surrounded by tea sets and a miniature, fully stocked kitchen and entertainment things like a television the size of a pencil sharpener and a hi-fi the size of a fingernail. But that's not what you're looking at really, is it? What you're looking at is an exercise book, wedged in between the plastic walls. When you pull it out by your fingertips you see that it's very well thumbed and nearly used up, and when you flick through the pages there are screeds and screeds written in a variety of ballpoint pens. Blue black green. Do you recognize that writing? Come on, do you recognize that writing? Well, honestly, the answer is no, but you remember Gabriella and her pens and her papers and the way she used to scrawl those things you never read. With her head bent down close to the paper and her red hair falling along her pale cheeks and she said she was always writing in English and trying she said to write as well as all those writers she loved.

But what really makes your heart leap, leap right into the top of your head, where colors thud like sounds and sounds swirly-whirl like colors, is the handprinted legend on the once white, now mildewed-with-age-and-damp, very first page:

Dear Diary

Gabriella's Book of Fire

I T BREAKS MY heart to see Salvatore when he's looking at me like that. If only it would help him if I made an extra special sugo di carne, because that's one of the best things I like to cook when I'm so happy. He'd probably like me to baste his body in that garlic-and-oregano-fragrant pasta sauce and eat it right off his skin. Lick it off the insides of his arms, the soft meat behind his ribs, the silky parts of him that don't get burned by the Australian sun. Salvatore, what an idea!

I do like to rub those sorts of herbs all over my own hands. I like to taste them from my fingers and get lost in the kitchen with my mamma and do all those things with her that bring food to the table. Salt is the sea that separates us from home and garlic is the family all together once again and oregano is a brisk walk in the Australian countryside and rosemary is a leg of lamb getting ready in the oven—everybody sit down, Sunday lunch is coming.

But I like the evenings the best.

Every night my papà will come in when dinner's called, and he'll sit, his body washed clean with his after-work shower and his hair wet and slicked back so that he looks very suave and very handsome even in his shorts and white Bonds singlet. On his face there'll be a tired but contented smile. Is that smile because of the good food coming—after all, he'll have been smelling those aromas as soon as he drove his car into the garage, his belly and brain driving him crazy—or is it because of the women in his family? Or even maybe just the progress of his new life in this country?

Everything is better for him than where we came from. No one says a thing about what I came from. That's the point. He works like a dog but this dog is so happy with what he does I think he never even contemplates stopping. Retirement is his bad word. For a man like him it would be like dying. Let his red-brown skin keep baking under the sun and he'll stay happy. He knows some English now and he likes to say he has the letter H three times. He's healthy he's happy and he's here. He always laughs when he says that.

My papà's teeth are so white and his arms so big and burned, but when he sits at the dinner table and smiles he's a boy! My brother Michael will rush in two minutes late and devour two heaped plates of dinner that he'll swamp with snowy parmesan cheese, and then he'll be out again. Recharged for whatever things he does with his nights. Nonno Enrico Belpasso will gum his way through half a plateful of food, his faraway eyes staring at the place where Michael was sitting, and he'll probably wonder whether or not a lightning bolt of a boy was there a minute ago. Then the old man will rise, his great belly looking like a sack of potatoes falling off a truck, but him happy enough to now be quiet in an armchair until sleep comes to call him, a siren singing a lost sailor into the deep arms of the sea.

It doesn't stop there. Some time in the evening my papà will be in an armchair too and the television will be on and my mamma and I won't be able to hear it because he will have joined Nonno Belpasso in a strong duet of dueling snores. That's when I'll look at my papà and think, But he isn't my papà at all and the girl I am is my mamma and an Irish stranger and the surname I carry is one big fat lie.

That's when I don't like the evenings so much anymore and my thoughts go back to Salvatore Capistrano.

I have a stupid little wish. If only the rich meatypotatoeytomatoeybasily flavors of my pasta sauce could soothe Salvatore's spirits the same way they soothe my family's—but that horsey face he goes around with! He's carrying a hundred sorts of agonies and a thousand sorts of miseries and all of them start from down below. He's got the fire down below while I've got it up top, in my firehead.

Salvatore makes me want to laugh, and to cry sometimes too, that's the whole truth. I could give him what he wants but a boy can't take a single minute to wonder what the price of this will be for a girl. So today, after he brought me a pink rose he pinched out of New Farm Park—his personal, neighborhood florist!—and some white chocolate bears with caramel cream inside, I led him up into our neighbor Signora Sanguinetti's mango trees. Signora Sanguinetti's got nine children, at least six of whom have perpetually runny noses, and that makes twelve disgusting nostrils out of which slimy trails run straight into their waiting mouths, where they suck the stuff up like a sweet syrup. We managed to avoid every single one of those dirty brats, who always want to play chasey or brandy, throwing the tennis ball so hard at your back or your thigh you have to lie on the ground and howl like a wounded animal whenever you're hit.

Instead we climbed very high, as high as we could go, leaves sort of soft like fur to the touch, and with that ripe fruity scent hanging around us we sat on the thickest, the highest branch. Legs dangling in space. That was fun. It was cooler up there. There was a nice breeze. It was a bit like the salty wind that used to sting my face in the mornings when I stood at the water's edge at Riposto and watched my uncle and cousins' night fishing boats coming in. From there, from on high, there wasn't the Mediterranean to look at but instead the big sea of our greenturning-brown suburb. It seemed to drift. It shimmered as if you were looking at it through rain. The heat's the curtain, gauzy as a butterfly's wings, slowly beating the same way. There should be more rain. Things are too dry. Too hot. Too standing still. The heat makes me think I'm a girl pegged to a suburban washing-line, flapping with the breeze, forgotten there but always waiting for something.

And who out of all of us here can't say she or he isn't waiting and waiting?

Over there playing in the sun I can see some of the girls I want to make friends with, but I have to wait until the start of the coming 1976 school year. That's more waiting. At the moment they tease me and call me bad names because of my accent and my Sicilian family and my wrong red hair and the fact that I kiss boys. They added everything about me together and came up with the wrong sum. They're skipping rope. Five of them. I wish I could make six. I wish I could be their friend and help them brush their hair and take walks with them in the park on those hot lazy afternoons that slide into muggy hard-to-sleep-in nights. I wish they'd ask me to the Centenary Pool, where they swim like frantic mermaids in one-piece swimming costumes and tease all the boys with the flicking of their long wet hair and the swinging of their teenagers' hips. Sarah, Sally, Susie, Samantha, and Sonja, that's how I always think of them even if some of the names are wrong. I wish I could go to the movie matinées they go to for the air-conditioning. I wish they'd invite me into one of their kitchens to show me what they'll make for an Australian Christmas. They'll like me once school starts, I'm very confident about that. They won't call me wopwogdago anymore. They won't call me bikeslutslag anymore. I'll be joining them at All Hallows, the ancient Catholic all girls school just down the road from Salvatore's Catholic all boys school. I'm waiting all right, but with a full heart, no matter that girls and boys of the neighborhood want to put me down. No matter what names they want to hurl at me.

SarahSallySusieSamanthaSonja are laughing. They sound just like overexcited monkeys at the zoo.

I liked the view so much it was almost a pity to spend time kissing, but I have to give Salvatore at least that. I give it to Shane Calder Johnny Aitkin John Deadman Rico Falla Graeme MacKenzie Antonio Scuderi Mark (Marco) Santo Domenico once or twice Tony Solero whom I really don't like and who should wash himself more and once and never again to his stupid brother Lino, who's older beefier stupider and who smells of raw onions and smoked salami and who has obviously forgotten the meaning of the word *Basta!* Enough!

We kissed up there for twenty minutes. For the first few moments I was thinking about what I'd feed my cats Gina and Sophia for dinner, but what with the ripe smell of the fruit and the little bit of breeze and the leaves scratching my face, soon it started to remind me of the stories Nonno Enrico told about how he met his wife amongst the flowering fig trees of the old Sicilian property he used to work on. It was like a fairy tale, that story, with the seasons gone so wrong and the world such a different place so many years ago, and maybe that's why I liked it so much.

We gave the kissing a rest when our bottoms were too uncomfortable on the branch. The real truth is I got hot and a little carried away. My hand wanted to drift into Salvatore's lap. I felt dreamy and a blush was traveling up from my feet to my face in a nice swelling wave. It made me want to love him sweetly that he could make me feel that way. I wanted to lie back and feel his weight pressing on me, like the sky covering the earth. I wanted to lift my legs and raise my hips for him. Lucky that we were in a place where I was safe. I climbed and then jumped down to the perfectly mown, perfectly watered, perfectly rich green lawn of Signora Sanguinetti's backyard, and then I ran to the corner shop as if a burning tiger were after me—what else could I do? Give in? Mr. Harry was behind the counter reading the *Telegraph* and he was as unhappy as always. You'd think it was him frying up inside. I gave him twenty-five cents for a lemon ice and returned to find Salvatore sitting on the low brick fence at the side of my house. Now he was very unhappy. With some kind words I passed that cold confection into his hand. I tried to get him to smile. Unfortunately, if you let your imagination run away with you, that lemon ice was in the shape of a man's thing. A big hard man's thing. Salvatore loves lemon ices. When he put it in his mouth and started sucking with such determination I couldn't imagine a boy looking any more sorrowful.

"What?" he said because I was laughing at him. "What?"

Blood: 1985

• • •

THE WAY I look says just about everything about my past and who I am so I won't worry about saying my name is Gabriella Zazò and I'm fourteen going on fifteen years of age and I'm this or I'm that. Well, just these things.

I'm a Capricorn and we're very fiery, but then so are the Irish from whom I get my red hair and freckles. Add that to the Sicilian part and you've got a firecracker whose wick you'd better not put a spark next to. My temper is something that gets me locked in my room. That gets the relatives arguing. That gets my mother crying and my father very, very quiet. So I'll leave all that alone. What I'll talk about at the start is what I am going to be, because that's more interesting to me. I am waiting for what I am going to be. So I like to think about the future. In fact I have seized my way. It won't be easy where I'm going but I think the absolute force of my certainty will silence anyone who wants to get in my path. Who are the people that always want to get in your way and tell you all your gorgeous avenues are dead ends? The people who love you, of course. But once they see me where I'm going they'll be laughing and clapping their hands and cheering.

Gabriella! Gabriella Zazò! Za-zò Za-zò Za-zò!

I'm going to be a famous writer. In fact, even if I'm not famous now, at least I know I am a writer.

I'm a writer because my hands smell good when I work with rosemary and basil. I'm a writer because my father's lawnmower makes our green yard smell like baby's wishes. I'm a writer because when I used to look out to sea at those fishing boats the crests of the waves were white. I'm a writer because when I lie in bed at night the sound of strangers talking low and loving underneath my window makes a warm spot in my stomach. I'm a writer because the profile of Salvatore's face fills my stomach with butterflies. I'm a writer because drums make me want to dance. I'm a writer because of the sha-na-nas in any good pop song. I'm a writer because my mother touches my cheek and says, Good morning, darly. I'm a writer because dawn air is so sweet to breathe it makes me think of clouds floating through Heaven. I'm a writer because when I stand in front of my full-length mirror and take off all my clothes, piece by piece, I just feel so beautiful. I'm a writer because good words in a good book can make me sigh. I'm a writer because when I close my eyes I see a road leading me safely toward the future. And finally I'm a writer because I will never forget that in Heaven there are good angels and in Hell there are the ones who have fallen, and God made them all, so don't you dare hate any of them.

LAST SUNDAY MY father was very serious. He was very preoccupied. He kept coming into the living room where my brother Michael was watching sports on television and where I was keeping him company by lying on the couch reading *Gone With the Wind* by Margaret Mitchell. Papà's English is improving because he works hard to learn and remember words and sentences and little sayings. He speaks it around the house now as often as he can.

He came in once and said, "Michael, what you do?"

"Watching TV, Pa."

He came in a second time and said, "How it is?"

"We're winning, Pa."

He came in a third time and he said, "When the university she start for you?"

"Febbraio, Papà."

Then he was out for a long time and I could hear him in the bedroom talking to our mamma. They must have been sitting on their bed having a deep discussion. Something was on my father's mind. The next time Papà came into the living room, Ma was with him. They both looked very serious but they were trying to smile. Papà went to the television and switched it off.

"Is nice day, is terrible to waste, huh? We go for nice drive to the beach."

Michael, shocked and aggrieved to have his precious television turned off under his nose, said in rapid-fire Sicilian, "What? What are you talking about? What are we going to the beach for? It's already the afternoon. It's Sunday. It's too late. I don't want to drive all that way. There'll be too much traffic. You go, I'm staying here."

Papà said back to him, in Sicilian as well, and a little pompously, "I have spoken, my son," and Ma gave Michael that look that said, For all the smiles on your father's face, you better get up and come with us right now.

When I had a second alone with her I said, "But what is it? What's wrong?"

Ma said in a whisper, "Your father has to speak to Michael. It's too important to do it here. We have to go with them and give him our support."

SO WE DROVE an hour all the way to the pathetic little beach at Sandgate, where children and old people were swimming in shallow waters and parents were firing up or cleaning down their portable barbecues. There was a smell of steak and salt air, and maybe because he was hungry from the aromas Papà sent Michael and me across the road to the fish-'n-chip shop to buy four deep-fried Chiko rolls and two dollars' worth of chips wrapped in butcher's paper.

"What does he want?" Michael asked me.

"I don't know, but whatever it is you better listen."

"It's a bit late for the birds and the bees."

"Maybe it's something else."

"What else is there?"

Then the four of us were sitting in a row on a bench looking out at the gray water, eating. There was me then Mamma then Papà then Michael.

Finally it started, and for some reason, maybe to show how "with it" he was, Papà chose to speak to Michael in English again.

"Soon you go the university to do you dentistry. You will have you own car. I will buy you secondhand little Datsun, Toyota, I no know yet. What we can get best price."

"I know that, Papà. You've already told me."

"With this car you must be careful."

"You told me that already too."

"When you go to this university you must be very careful."

"Why?"

Papà chewed his Chiko roll like it was made of rubber. Ma's eyes were watchful. Every now and then she would murmur just two words, *È veru*—It's true—but quietly, so as not to interrupt. It was like the prayer responses you were supposed to give in mass.

Papà's eyes seemed to narrow. He said, "There is corruption."

È veru.

"Corruption" was one of the first words Papà had learned for himself out of the newspapers and it always seemed to be lodged in his mind. He applied it to everything—politics, politicians, private businesses and government agencies, even bad marriages. And now universities too.

Even so, Michael said, "Huh?"

"Yes. University money she goes into the pockets of the professors. Instead of new buildings the high-up men they get new houses. And then the people with money have children who do better than other children. They pay the professors, you know. This is the way in Italy she works too."

È veru.

"Then there are the drugs. People will offer these to you or put them in you drink without you know it. These are some of the things I mean by the corruption of the university."

È veru.

Sicilian: "Papà, you don't know what you're talking about."

English: "I know what people tell me and I know what I read in the newspaper. And if no one tells me and it isn't in the newspaper then I know it anyway."

È veru.

Sicilian: "Papà, you're thinking about Italy. Of course we know it's corrupt there, but this is different."

English: "Men aren't they the same in every country?"

È veru.

Michael sighed.

I looked at Ma and by the intense expression in her eyes it was easy to tell what was wrong. Their eldest son was going to this mysterious place called a university. He would have a car and freedom. These were all first steps toward a professional career and an independent life in a country they didn't completely understand yet, and so they were scared. Scared and sad for themselves just as at the same time they were thrilled for Michael and terribly proud of him. It was the first letting go in the inevitable process of losing their boy. I felt an ache come into my heart and a hard spot come into my throat. I held Ma's hand. We were all starting to lose Michael, but for my parents it was hardest of all. Never having had much schooling, they would never really understand what went on at a university, with all those weird students and sit-ins and bespectacled mustached know-it-all professors, and courses with names you needed a university degree just to be able to work out. Ma was nodding hard, her black eyes saying to Michael, Listen to your father, just listen to him.

Michael took a great bite out of his Chiko roll to cover up the fact that he wanted to make eye contact with me so that we could laugh.

Papà said, "I have something to say to you."

"There's more?"

"You must never forget this thing when you go to this university."

"All right. So what is it, Pa?"

Our father finished his Chiko roll and wiped his mouth. He looked at my mother, who still encouraged him with her eyes. He looked back to his son and he was as serious and trembling as I've ever seen him. Something in my soul wanted to cry out for my papà for this was being delivered from his deep Sicilian heart.

"You no forget this," he said.

"What already?"

"The woman is trouble and watch out for the poof-e-ters."

È veru.

My brother was a little stunned. He said, "What was that?"

"The woman is trouble and watch out for the poof-e-ters."

I got up and went to the nearest tap so as not to humiliate my parents.

When I came back Michael had settled down. He told me later that bits of Chiko roll came out of his nose when our father's message had really hit him.

Mamma was now holding Papà's hand and he was breathing easier. The load was off his back.

"All right?"

"Yeah, all right, Pa. I understand."

"Good. We go home."

"But we just got here!"

Papà stood briskly. His job was done. He probably disliked Sandgate as much as his children did, but he'd successfully delivered the longest and most heartfelt speech of his parental career. It might have come down to only one salient sentence, really, but in his mind it told his boy Michael everything he would ever need to know. That night Papà drank two or three extra glasses of red wine to celebrate, and he became light-hearted as a sparrow, dancing my ma and then me around the kitchen table to the scratchy melodies of old Italian 78s.

The woman is trouble and watch out for the poof-e-ters.

"Dance with me! *Piroetta, i miei belli tesori!* Twirl, my beautiful treasures!"

I THINK I know when I started to become a writer. The year, the month, the day, the long moments of the minute. The smells that were in the air and the way time held its breath.

NONNA FORTUNATA, DEAD a year. A thousand-wrinkles smiling face. Hands adept at cooking and sewing. Hands always ready to brush a girl's flowing red hair and embellish the tales a grandmother is always

ready to tell. Like the way she was in love with her future husband
Enrico Belpasso before she even met him. Like the time he was away
and she was alone in the house with her two daughters, asleep at midnight, and she had to fire a shotgun at three intruders. Old hands
stopped moving. Old woman a thousand-wrinkles face, down on the
floor. Old home-crocheted shawl still over her white cobweb hair. Body
eaten up by a disease no one but a doctor dares to name aloud. Body put
in the ground and spirit gone, just gone. One year. Confused eight-year-
old girl skimming stones into the Riviera dei Ciclopi wondering what
happened where she's gone why does Nonno stare into space so?

Then a small fold-out bed in a hallway.

The house lived in by one good-natured old man losing his senses.

Grandfather lonely war pension age pension still speaking to his wife
when he thinks no one's watching. An hour in a dream staring at a wall.
Ancient picture of a housemaid named Fortunata looking back at him.
Black and white uniform, luscious mouth, thick womanly neck, heavy
feminine chin. Happy birthday, Enrico Belpasso. Can I have a fig? For
him, more and more days alone in a wicker chair, with his old-style Sicilian *conca,* coal and ash smouldering between his feet, keeping old flesh
and bones warm. He drops black olives at the edges of the red glowing
coal lets them bake brushes off the white ash eats them hot watches
people and cars in the street outside going about their business and lives.
His worried family invites him and keeps him at their house as long as
they can. Eat more sit and watch television with us no I'm tired now I
want to go home. Why don't you move in with us leave that lonely
house the room downstairs will be perfect no I'm tired now I want to go
home. Day after day old man fading away only truly lively with a nine-
year-old little granddaughter.

So there she is with red hair tied in braids staying over weeknights,
weekend nights, whenever-she-wants-to nights. She wants to a lot. She
loves this great big bear with a surprise always in his pockets some sort
of sweet or sugar-dusted pasta di mandorla. Even maybe a chirping
cricket hidden in his fist or here take this poor little lost lizard put him
outside watch him scurry home to his mamma. Little girl squealing with

delight. Loves the way he holds her hand in the street and then lets her fly through the main town square on beautiful wings only he and she can see, fat seagulls and well-fed pigeons scattering before her. Loves to do his cleaning beat his washing hang it up cook for him shop for groceries with him.

Here Nonno smell this honeymelon do you think it's ripe enough?

Loves hearing him talking in his bed to the stolen away Fortunata while she rests her head on her soft clean pillow and drifts into the sleep world.

Nine years of age this little cricket and this particular morning playing a silly morning game. Old man stumbles out of his bed comes to her she doesn't open her eyes: Gabriella wake up I'll make you breakfast.

I pretend that I can't wake up. Nonno Belpasso stands by my bed and I hold myself perfectly still. Barely even breathing. He leans closer. I can hear the smile in his voice. Gabriella my little darling wake up I'll make you breakfast. He plays it sing-songy; he knows all the games. A little girl . . . who won't wake uu-pp . . . might get her feet tickled . . . with a fea-th-er.

Who knows where this idea came from, to lie there so immobile? My sense of playfulness married to my sense of drama, maybe. Something childish and unspeakable going through my mind: But I'm dead Nonno, I can't move. I'm like Nonna Fortunata now. Sometimes I rode his back and sometimes I chased him down the hallways, to end, laughing, rolling on the floor. See a grandfather bald and big kicking his legs in the air to make a child laugh. Good man, funny man, never a word of anger. This time this game see what he does.

Gabriella wake up I'll make you breakfast. You'll end up without anything if you don't come now.

He clears his morning froggy throat. He seems to sigh with acceptance at my funny ways. Nonno Belpasso shuffles down the corridor into the kitchen and I hear him moving around. Cutlery striking cutlery being placed on the table the pop of gas lighting. His footsteps soon return. Gabriella. Gabriella. That's enough now. A heavy hand touches my shoulder.

Blood: 1985

Gabriella wake up your grandfather's telling you that's enough now.

He softly carefully lifts the sheet from around my feet. Stubby fin-gers light as fea-th-ers gently play on the tender pink skin of my soles. I hold myself still and silent but he knows very well exactly where a child is weak.

About to burst into wild gales of happiness. Unable to contain the thrilling bubbles of a silly game. About to pop like a balloon. Even wet myself. Wanting to drag it out one moment two moments three moments more. One thing I'll never remember properly. Did I say it or only think it?

But I'm dead Nonno! I can't move! I'm like Nonna Fortunata now!

What did the poor man look at? His granddaughter's white face. What did he touch? Her wild red hair. What did he see?

Now that I'm older, I know. I might even have known then.

Nonno Belpasso took me gently in his arms. Gently lifted me into a half-sitting position. I let my head loll tragic and sad, a lost princess poi-soned by murderers and schemers and traitors. He cradled me. He caressed my hair and then he put his face into the crook of my shoulder. And he started to weep. Crying and crying and crying. Hot old man's tears dripping onto soft little girl's skin. Fortunata my darling Fortunata my wife come back to me please come back let me see your face again.

Frozen with fear. Tongue gone with terror. Then even a small girl has to understand a little. Nonno. Nonno. Nonno. There there. There there. My nonno please don't cry.

And in these long moments that made a minute, a grandfather offered his tormented soul to a nine-year-old's understanding. Face burning eyes brimming mouth working. The abyss in the expression, the hope in the sighs. Yes, even a small girl has to understand a little, and understand something else too—how a bargain can be made without words. See how naked I am you must care for me child as I must care for you, there are no boundaries now.

MY NAME. MY name is Gabriella Zazò. I'm fourteen years old and I'm a Capricorn and I'm half-Sicilian, half-Irish and I'm a writer. I'm a writer because I have another name. My other name is Enrico Belpasso. Enrico Belpasso is the other half of my soul and I've entered him as he's entered me. Together we tell Enrico's life, Gabriella's life, Fortunata's life, Salvatore's life, the lives of Enrico's children and the lives of the people Gabriella reaches out to in this new country and who do not reach back to her.

So many lives and so many stories, who can ever have enough time to write them all down?

YEARS LATER. One day. One sunshiny morning of green and yellow parakeets and budgerigars singing in Signora Sanguinetti's mango trees.

Nonno Enrico has gone downhill and his eyes have become empty and his mouth slack, and the last but three of his teeth have dropped out. People in Sicily said his soul dried up like mud caking in a midday sun. Or, better, that the heat of his flowing magma had cooled and cooled and cooled and all that he had left inside was black lava. That's the Sicilian way of looking at the world. He was dead, they said, but only halfway. That's why he can eat and drink and occasionally talk, even if what he talks is wayward and strange. These old friends and family who'd known Enrico Belpasso five or six out of his seven decades said that if you could design some contraption that will attach to a man's head and look into his dreams, young Gabriella, and you did this to your Nonno Belpasso, inside his dreams you would see only an infinite landscape of rocks.

My papà planned nearly three years for us to move to the new country. Michael and I prepared for the new language, studying it with an excitement and an enthusiasm that rubbed off onto all our other subjects and gave us good grades for everything. Of course, in my case, I had many years' headstart in English, having commenced my study of the language almost as soon as I knew where my true father came from.

Michael and I started to play games with our mamma and papà, telling them words and sentences and trying to trick them into learning English without them even knowing they were learning. It was during

these preparations that Nonno had finally to give up his home and move
in with us. Nonno needed help. Michael specialized in giving him his
morning shaves, frothing up thick white lather in a cup with a brush and
using no less than an old-fashioned cut-throat razor that he stropped
sharp on leather. Nonno Belpasso would stand perfectly still in front of
the mirror, allowing his face to be scraped clean by a boy, inclining his
head when he had to, puffing his cheek when it was needed, lifting his
chin to the pressure of Michael's fingertips, enduring his nicks and cuts
without complaint. I kept his room clean and cooked for him and
soothed his head when he went to bed and couldn't sleep for nightmares. I knew he saw more in his dreams than a panorama of rocks; to
most people the currency of old age has no value. Yet this man had a life
and loves and he still had longings and desires. He must have had, or
else he wouldn't have wept so.

Even a child can see this.

Mamma washed her father. When that was required, Ma wiped his
culo. She would sit him with her all day when I was at school. Papà
brought the money home to feed and clothe his father-in-law, added it to
the war and age pensions, denied himself the chance of spending any
extra money anywhere else. When I was bored with being the do-
gooder Papà would take him for a walk out to the salty waterside, out to
the main square in front of our cathedral, into the men's club where I'm
sure the male aged of our town still sit around in clouds of cigar and
hand-rolled cigarette smoke, drinking wine or coffee and playing cards.
I'd like to see them all again one day, if I ever go back. Papà would buy
Nonno Enrico Belpasso a cool drink, place him with his old friends and
neighbors, leave him there and let them tell their old stories around him.
These men would make sure his shirt was tucked in right and his tie was
straight before they walked him home. They'd deliver him to our house
somewhere before midnight, and leave fruit for Mamma and some
sweets for Michael and me, and bid their lost friend Enrico Belpasso
buona notte and see you tomorrow, don't forget. Then their chuckles at
their own little joke would echo down the cobblestoned street just like
the sound of their hard heels, but there wasn't any malice in their

humor, only a little sadness, and the next day they'd save his place and wait for Enrico Belpasso to turn up again. That's the way little communities used to be.

Nonno Enrico Belpasso didn't seem to learn one new foreign word in the three years of our preparation, and when we came to the new country he didn't show by gesture or temperament or expression or act of necromancy that he understood he was anywhere different.

But he clutched to me; to me, Gabriella. Twelve years of age, thirteen years of age, fourteen. He'd stay close even when he thought my name was Fortunata or Maria or Sweet Angel of Our Volcano; he never stopped telling his tales. But only to me, you understand, and in so doing we developed our special way of communicating—call it shorthand. A gesture, a cough, a lifting of the finger or a smoothing of the lines in that great brow of his, these were significant in the storytelling.

So, years later. One day. One sunshiny morning of green and yellow parakeets and budgerigars singing in Signora Sanguinetti's mango trees.

I found my nonno coming out from the far darkness under our new Australian home. That was where the little scary room was, my father's personal wine cellar, but my nonno wasn't coming out of there with any bottle. His hands were empty. I was at the laundry basins putting one of my cotton shirts, today stained from my cooking, into some cold water mixed with bleach for soaking.

"*Nonno, cosa fai?* Grandfather, what are you doing?"

He had his faraway expression but he grasped my hand and he made me walk with him back into the dark. He reached up to where my father kept his flashlight and he snapped it on. Numb fingers working fine. This didn't surprise me. I'd seen days when he was clumsy as an oaf and others when he was dexterous as a surgeon. We followed the white beam past the old rattan door and into the little room. I wasn't afraid, not even of the wine cases covered in blankets and the way in the half-light they were a vampire lord's many coffins.

"Nonno, what's in here?"

His back gave him trouble but he pulled aside some old pieces of carpet covering the ground and there—right there!—was a trapdoor. Leading below the surface of the earth and into that vampire lord's lair. I remember I was already enthralled with the thrill of this discovery. My nonno pulled the bolts and without a backward glance he followed his white light down a wooden staircase.

To here.

The first time I came down into this world.

I couldn't imagine what this place was, but then it came to me. There were shelters in our old beachside town and now I knew that the threats that came with a war could travel to every single corner of the globe. Enrico Belpasso reached into the pockets of his trousers for a box of safety matches. He struck one decisively. An oil lamp was on the floor. He lifted the glass and lit the wick and the corners of this room came alive.

There were witches' hats taken from Main Roads Department work-sites; there were letters taken from people's mailboxes; there were shirts taken from a neighbor's clothesline; there were bundles and bundles of Mr. Harry's missing newspapers. Here an old cane chair—stolen from where?—there a succession of wooden carpenter's horses. What poor carpenter or bricklayer or builder missed these? Bric-à-brac lay scattered on the floor, crazy things that didn't go together. A carpet beater, a rusted electric fan that would never turn and whisk air into your hot face again, a frying pan. Lost photos of me and misplaced photos of Michael and long-missed, long-lamented photos of all the family, every one of them here and pasted to the walls. A treasure trove of brotherless socks and sisterless gloves and the dollmagazineplasticracingcarsoapholder-skippingropebutterknifepencilcupplaterecordalbumscissorsbook-shoeshirtwhatever you put down one day and tore your hair out trying to find the next. There were even flowers, or should I say roses, pink and yellow and red, now black of course, snipped and stolen and sneaked from the New Farm Park flower gardens in just the way Salvatore did, all of them standing as dusty mummies in a crypt, in discolored broken vases, dry-dead, withered, heads fallen.

"Nonno—" I started, wanting an explanation.

The answer came in the way he closed his eyes. In the way the lines of age and suffering in his cheeks seemed to smooth out. In the slow breath that was a great sigh.

"When a wife hears her husband call—"

"Nonno, please. Please, that's not right. She can't come."

"When a wife hears her husband call. When a mother loves her children. When a grandmother needs her children's children—"

"But I don't understand. How can I understand what you're trying to say?"

The corners of his mouth moved.

"By listening to this, little cricket."

IT'S LATE EVENING in winter, wartime, World War II wartime.

Fortunata is living in our small town at the feet of the volcano. She no longer works in a rich man's house as a maid but is the mistress of her own home and her own family. She barely remembers those old days in the old mansion, keeping the floors clean, keeping the beds clean, keeping the padrone's family's faces and feet clean. Now she has me and we have two daughters and her past life is already a dream. Our first child is nineteen years of age and our second barely five. For weeks I have been a long way away, on the mainland, in the horrible and exciting criminal city of Napoli, where tales of thieving in the streets and bold-faced robberies out of the home and whoring at every level of life are all you ever hear about. As well—to get to the point—as tales of the American soldiers stationed there. Everyone talks about them. Their strange accents and attitudes, their love affairs with local girls, their money. I've gone to Napoli on a money-making venture with two cousins from Fortunata's side, Alfio and Agostino Lorenzano. We're selling Sicilian-made jewelry to those foreign soldiers, nice gifts that they can give to sweethearts back home, once they've rid themselves of the two diseases raging through Naples like wildfire, syphilis and gonorrhea. We sell the boys a little romance. We tell them they are buying Greek artifacts hundreds of years old and worth hundreds of American dollars. It's surprising how much these young soldiers want to believe us. We embellish our stories with true stories of how Sicily is home to the best Greek ruins in the world. We tell them about the gods who fuck inside our volcano and cause all the eruptions and troubles. The American boys are in a foreign country doing a terrifying job and they want to believe their efforts will liberate a worthy, noble, refined, and even mystical race. Little trinkets like these that they can one day use to part the thighs of their blond-haired, blue-eyed, long-legged, faithfully waiting cheerleader girlfriends are their proof of the worthiness of such efforts. This is how I tell myself that I too am serving a good purpose.

Fortunata's friends make these baubles and bijoux out of beaten metals like bronze and tin, glass and cheap stones, anything, really, that will eventually look authentic enough to turn a few hundred lire. The war has left Italy poor and Sicily even poorer—surprise, surprise!—and out of necessity young men like Alfio and Agostino and me have had to develop tongues of gold. The Lorenzano brothers have in fact found their true calling in life and we often joke that none of us will ever be sheep- and goat-herders again. While our enterprise lasts and these lovely GIs are still so easily duped, we send our women wads and wads of lire.

Now this story is about Fortunata, not me.

The fact is this. Fortunata has always feared that our scheme will go wrong. She is a decent and an honest woman who finds subterfuge like this disheartening. She is also, however, a woman who has to pick lice out of the heads of her daughters and who has to make them happy to eat things like fennel soup and boiled endives and potato pie, such is our poverty. Such is everyone's poverty. So despite her misgivings she goes along with our plan and even pitches in with the manufacture, and she dutifully saves as much of the money I send her as she can. Does she really have any other choice? No. Yet in her belly there's always a lump of rock, and this lump of rock tells her things will go badly. Our Lord Gesù will not be happy to allow a crooked activity like this to prosper. This is what Fortunata thinks constantly—and right now, at this very moment, these fears of hers are being made entirely real. The scheme has turned in on itself like the roots of a tree twisting insanely with disease.

Why, Gabriella?

Remember what I said at the start: we find Fortunata in a late evening in winter.

It's night.

Fortunata is in her bed, which is located on the second floor of the little house we rent for close to nothing from one of her uncles. It's that time of darkness and quiet when the chickens in their coops will not stir and the rabbits bury themselves in on themselves and sleep like brown-furred angels. Yet Fortunata has heard a sound. Then another sound. And she knows the money-making scheme has gone all wrong. Why does she know? Because this day that I'm telling about I've sent her the most money yet, and our youngest daughter Agata has opened her mouth about it in the streets.

One possibility leaps into Fortunata's mind. Could it be that stupid cat Nino thumping around the rooms downstairs chasing after some inquisitive mouse?

Yes, no, maybe.

So Fortunata forces herself to lie quietly, barely breathing, listening not to her heart but reaching into that cold space of air around her that might bring some new sound. At first nothing, then a sound does come. And another, and so on. Soft like a specter's lament but as real as real is. Fortunata looks toward her children sharing the bed with her. Lying on the far side is Anitta, as I've said already nineteen, and in the middle, warm as a heating stone, your own mother is sleeping, Agata, named for the patron saint of the city of Catania, and here she is, five years of age.

Fortunata doesn't like mysteries. Every night Fortunata lies restless and attuned for sounds out of the darkness. She does like Nino the tabby cat with his wonderful ability to hunt down neighborhood mice, but what Fortunata likes least of all about this whole situation is that all the money I've sent her over weeks and weeks, and that large amount of today too, is wrapped in a red silk scarf under her mattress. You cannot trust the banks anymore. What is open for business today is closed tomorrow and your money vanished with its officials. Such is wartime. Such is Sicily. The space under your mattress is the only certainty your money will ever have, but the problem is everyone knows that, and, worst of all, today little Agata went strutting through the streets telling all and sundry about her new porcelain doll—with flowing flaxen hair you must believe is real!—purchased as a treat with the special money her father has sent from the special place he has disappeared to.

Now Fortunata imagines my face and wishes that I was by her side. In such circumstances, I mean when I am there, Anitta has to move into the bed in her own room but Agata always stays between us. Fortunata hears her eldest sighing and her youngest turning, and she realizes that it doesn't matter that her husband isn't with her. It doesn't even matter that the Lord Gesù has raised His finger and pointed at her, saying, Now there is a price you must pay for your dishonesty. This is Fortunata's home and these are her children and whatever happens next is going to be up to one person, and this person is herself.

In her white nightgown, which reaches from the frilled lace collar under her chin all the way to the floor, even to covering her feet, she slides out of bed and lights her lantern. The flame always burns low to save fuel but here she turns it lower. Fortunata sees these things: little Agata's babyish cheek, nineteen-year-old Anitta's full lips, and Nino the tabby cat asleep and useless as a shadow in the corner. *Basta*, Fortunata thinks, *basta*. Enough, enough. To make matters worse, for weeks there has been gossip about terrible happenings. Violent robberies close to home. Break-ins. Who needs to worry about what's going on in cities like Napoli when even here houses are found torn apart for whatever might be secreted away inside? And is that all? No, it's the least of it. There have been beatings. Yes, since three weeks ago there have even been deaths. Murders. Doesn't every living man, woman, and child know the fate of that poor Belocchio family who were murdered in their own beds for who can imagine what wads of lire they had under their mattresses? And what are the police doing; who is to say it wasn't the police themselves?

Young Agata sighs and turns under the blanket and rests her face in the crook of her elder sister's arm. Fortunata, by the side of the bed, watching down, understands everything. She is a woman and she is past her prime and her husband is away. There is no mystery about the sounds she is hearing so it seems Gesù has turned His face away from her—but if this is so then there is even less confusion about what she has to do.

The soft spirit's lament downstairs has turned into the sounds of scufflings and slight wrenchings. There are no ghosts of course, only men. These men who are coming think the world is theirs to rape the way they would do with some gypsy madwoman who chooses to live alone in a forest. Their confidence soars over their heads. They are untouchable, Fortunata knows, because if police are easily bribed in any human era then they are even more so in wartime. Whoever they are, these predators, they are part of an organized network; Fortunata dwells less on this fact than on the more immediate fact that they have decided to get into the house by taking off the front door.

Hanging on the wall facing the bed is a crucifix featuring the tormented Gesù Cristo in His agony. Despite His anger at her Fortunata says a quick prayer. Beside the crucifix is a framed image of the Lamb of God, His chest open to reveal His fiery heart. Fortunata mumbles some words toward Him. Beside the Lamb of God, in its wooden crook, is my twelve-gauge shotgun. Here she says yet another prayer, a little longer this time, clasping her hands hard between her breasts in order to help her gather all her strength.

There are low voices. The front door rattles as if to a wild wind. The grinding sound is of locks being tampered with. Even Nino has heard these things, his useless furry head raised and alert. Fortunata goes to her window and peers down. The dark ensures there is nothing to see, but in the distance is our volcano Etna with its glowing red mouth showing high and clear in the black veil of the sky. Like the Lamb of God's, the volcano's heart is on fire—and if you forgive my saying it presumptuously, little Gabriella, at this moment so is my Fortunata's.

The one thing that has helped her so far is that the front door is a masterpiece of latches and bolts and heavy screws in heavier hinges. We Sicilians are a very anxious race. Our island has been invaded too many times by too many peoples. What is not helping Fortunata is that there is no back door. There is not even a window secluded enough for her to feel confident about getting her children and herself out of unseen. There is one way into the house and one way out.

So Fortunata lifts down the shotgun and hunts in a cupboard for the cartridges. She finds them immediately because she has visualized this scene for longer than she knows. Two cartridges she puts into her night-gown. She cracks the shotgun in half and feeds in the next two. She closes the gun and weighs it in her hands and wonders how long it has been since she has fired one. Her brother taught her and her two sisters to shoot when they were Agata's age; he taught them how to shoot and how to swim underwater and how to stun a rabbit with a blow to the back of its neck and have it skinned and in the pot before it even thought of waking.

Fortunata looks around. Our daughters are sitting up in the bed, their eyes wide.

"Men are downstairs and I have to send them away. I want you to stay in this room until I come back. Lock the door after me. Don't either one of you move out of this room, no matter what you hear."

Our two girls, disobedient to the end, crowd behind their mother as she goes downstairs. Fortunata doesn't argue. In a way it makes her stronger to feel their warm and trembling bodies pressed to her. She thinks, These are my daughters and this is my home and if I have to kill these men to protect what is mine then tonight these men will die.

Downstairs, she tells her daughters to hurry and to light the lamps. The rooms soon move with shadows. Three pairs of female eyes stare at the wrenching of the front door, at the jambs moving sideways to crow-bars and whatnot, to the way the locks are splitting.

Fortunata screams, "Go away! Leave us alone!"

A man's voice replies, in a very conversational tone, "Signora Bel-passo, we're sorry to be here like this. Open the door and let us in and we'll only keep you five minutes. You and your girls won't get hurt. You know what we have to have." There is a pause, in which there is no wrenching and creaking. "By the way, you should tell Enrico to teach his daughter to keep her mouth shut from now on, huh? So will you open up?"

The men don't wait for an answer. The door shifts on its hinges. There is a wood-cracking sound like a fishing trawler breaking in two.

Fortunata tries one last appeal: "We'll scream so loud everyone will come running!"

Anitta and Agata start to scream as if they are already being murdered. Agata runs with her bare feet in a circle, howling like a wind. Anitta's cries turn her face red and would wake the dead.

When they've finished, now hugging one another in a frozen dance of hysteria, the man's voice shows how he is laughing.

"Well. Well, well. What a song!" He pauses, then, "Wouldn't they be here by now, if they were coming? Your beautiful neighbors have already covered their ears, Signora."

Fortunata bites her bottom lip and then speaks in a voice full of agony. "You have to promise you won't hurt us."

"Fine, fine. We won't hurt you. Who wants to hurt anyone? It's the world hurting us. We're all Sicilians, aren't we? We're not to turn against each other. We men out here have got wives and children ourselves. Do you think we're animals? It's the Americans and the Germans and the Russians forcing us into this kind of behavior. We all just need to eat. Have the money ready and there'll be no hard feelings. You can even keep a fair portion for yourselves. Just let me see how much there is that we're sharing. You know, we're not bad men."

"I trust you."

"Of course you trust me. I'm not from this region but somewhere along the line, my family probably knows your family."

"I'm opening the door."

"Good."

And that's what Fortunata does. She slides the breaking bolts, turns the locks, and that poor abused door all but collapses inward.

The cold comes instantly inside. Three men are waiting outside. Three men who all look like Fortunata's father, who all could be any of her male relatives, or any of the men of any starving village. Three men with gaunt faces and sunken eyes and shabby clothes.

They don't come inside like the cold because they are staring into the black holes of the twelve-gauge shotgun's black barrels. One man stands close and Fortunata assumes this was the one who did the talking. Her arms don't tremble. Neither do this man's. His lips purse and for a moment he holds his crowbar up for Fortunata to see, but then he lets it go so that it clatters to the ground. He very slowly and very deliberately unbuttons his jacket. He opens it. His face shows how furious with her he is. His family needs to eat and he doesn't need to be delayed one extra minute. He reaches into his jacket and takes out his hunting knife. Fortunata knows these sorts of knives well. They're perfect for skinning rabbits. She uses one herself, and the soft coats always come off as easily as clothing.

This man says, "Woman . . ."

The other two don't move at all, or even draw breath.

Fortunata will wonder for the rest of her days if it was the man's anger, or fear, or hunger that really killed him. In her memory and her nightmares his expression will change. Sometimes he will have the impassive face of an executioner, sometimes the wet-lipped and trembling expression of a man weeping for his life to be spared, and sometimes he will have the blazing eyes of a god raging to strike insignificant mortals down in their tracks.

It's the sight of that knife that terrifies Fortunata. What more can talk achieve? So she pulls one trigger. The man takes the contents of one barrel in his chest and he flies back as if Heaven has already given him his wings. Blood splatters Fortunata's face, Anitta's face, even little Agata's face. Screaming, Fortunata jerks the gun high and fires the other barrel so that the shot booms over the heads of the other two men, who are already running like jackasses. She cracks the shotgun and loads it and fires twice into the black sky.

Little Agata, blood-flecked and delirious, jumps up and down on the spot, fists clenched, face screwed up, as she cries out gaily, "Shoot again! Shoot again! Shoot again!"

• • •

FOR DAYS AND weeks afterward everyone wanted to hear the story over and over but Fortunata told it three times in the police station and once at the magistrate's inquiry and that was enough for her. A never-ending stream of visitors came to her home and some she let in but most others she sent away. When a newspaper man came calling she didn't even open that new front door she'd had installed. Those neighbors and relatives and friends Fortunata did let in drank her wine or coffee and ate her pastries and gazed long and lingeringly on Anitta and Agata, the two of their little community they'd come too close to losing forever. These visitors, when the time came for them to go, always made sure to leave a gift. These gifts weren't exactly what you might expect, little Gabriella. They weren't cakes or biscuits or even chickens or rabbits. The gifts these visitors left were cartridges for the twelve-gauge.

So Fortunata had to collect them, and put them in a drawer, and when the drawer overflowed she put them in a cupboard, and when the cupboard was full she asked people to stop, but they didn't stop, not for a long time, because everyone was certain these hard times would continue, and if that was true then bad men would always come to a woman's door, in new guises and in new forms, in new bodies and with new words, and when they did arrive like devils wanting to carry you into their bedroom in Hell, and Fortunata was forced to raise the shotgun again, every single one of her neighbors and relatives and friends wanted it to be their cartridges that my fireheart used to drop the bad men down.

Understand?

YOU SAY, GABRIELLA, Fortunata can't come again.

How can you say this? For the heart is full of fire and the cupboards are full of cartridges, generation down to generation. Isn't she here already, Gabriella? Isn't she standing in front of me?

Who else do you think you are?

Blood

IRINA LUNA WAS TIRED now of the future's most leafy and livable street in the cosmos. She didn't care that there were many more pages of blue-black-green looping script to go and she didn't see that I was trembling like a dog that's been beaten with a fence paling.

Looking into the sunlight falling in glassy shards down through the thick branches, Irina sat on the footpath and took a sigh that turned into a yawn, and said, "Do we have to stay here forever, baby?"

WHEN I WAS a boy I would sit in that same place and dream of superheroes and treasure; when those superheroes turned into my haughty neighborhood girls the only treasure I imagined was what they carried under their breezy summer clothing. I wanted every female in the city and at the same time only one, little Gabriella Zazò.

She was the slightly built, red-haired, secretive, loving, angry girl whom I day-dreamed naked and night-dreamed forever with me. When I lost her I lost that part of me we like to call a soul. I felt this odd presence suffocating, squirming, fighting for breath but dying over days, weeks, months, and then years of nothing. My later teenage years were like an era that didn't happen. At university I wandered aimless and alone around towering sandstone buildings and lakes where ducks skittered and gathered, and through green playing fields where my so-called peers play-acted their little battles of blood and brutality. It was as if I saw and touched no one. So who noticed me leave and never return? Only my family. I then let myself slide into the daily sensual pleasures of food and sex and wine, but none of these could hide the dreamlessness of a wooden puppet.

But what is dreamlessness when so many nights I still saw Gabriella's face coming close to mine, her green eyes wide and her lips wet and bruised with kissing? What I think I mean is hope, its disappearance. The irony is that when I was young my parents' preeminent concept was The Future, so that everything they did was structured to give me a good one—but the future became the thing the most irrelevant to me, the most inconsequential, the most useless. Somewhere in those lost years I decided that if my heart couldn't be filled then at least my body would be sated. I rediscovered my old friend Tony Solero. My family lost their hold on me and anything left of that little stifled soul slipped out of my fingers. I did absolutely nothing inside a flurry of activity; I thought nothing through long nights of yabbering to sexy strangers over bottles of wine and whiskey; I was being, just being.

To come now to this point, holding Gabriella's time-damaged thoughts written in looping colors, these memories arrested in water-mottled pages.

I RINA TURNED ON the car radio because I was so quiet and 1985's rinky-dink synth and dance tunes, the ones we shook the fat to in booming nightclubs, made me long for the full-blooded opera-aria records in my home. Being so forced to face my own abyss made me want to drown instead in the richness of life.

In the mood I was in I'd dig out those record albums and play them the rest of the day through and long into the night. I'd turn them to top volume and cook a proper meaty, garlicky, cheese-filled pasta or lasagne dish, drinking a bottle of ripe and fleshy, wildberry-rich Merlot while I did it. Irina and I would have our dinner looking over distant lights and the dark winding of the river. Ferry reds and blues would blink and flash against the sounds of water lapping and the city's incandescence would seem like some strange Milky Way laid to rest down against the earth.

Most of all I wanted to feel the heaviness and drowsy satisfaction of food and wine weighing in my belly. My heart pounding to the strain. Then I'd climb into bed with my senses ringing because of those few final shot glasses of anisette. Two A.M., three A.M.; the deeper in the night, the better. The witching-warlocking hours. The lovemaking hours. The hours of tender secrets never to be spoken when the sun is shining.

I'm with you and my blood is like wine.

Come inside me, come inside me.

Hold me here, hard, push, bite me, break me.

Darling, my darling, darling, my darling.

Irina's breasts would come warmly against my face and I'd hold her supple waist and strong hips to me. Against my palms I'd feel the pulsing of her blood the way you feel the force of an animal when it crawls into your arms for protection. Her brown skin would be burning as if she were sunning herself on some infinite beach, and when she started to sigh a raw blush would spread from under her neck and all the way down and around her chest and sternum. I wouldn't let her finish until her muscles melted like chocolate. She'd know she was alive then, and, holding my wine- and blood-engorged cock deep against her womb, she'd have no doubt that I was either.

N O MATTER HOW I tried to lose myself in such longings, whenever I raised my eyes to the windscreen it was as if an awful cast had come down over the day.

It hurt to look five seconds full in the face of the suburbs and the streets we drove through. If you leaned on a wall it would have to tumble backward to reveal the desert behind it. If you met your best friend on some corner you'd find there wasn't a worthwhile opinion between you. If you reeled drunk and muttering into a gutter you'd peer into your own guts and see how much promise you started out with and how easily you traded it for comforts and obliviousness. Why does the past have angel's wings and the present a millstone around its neck? I wanted to ask Irina this question but she turned to me so curiously I couldn't say a word. I rubbed my forehead. I tried to equate her with the person dancing and singing onstage. The stage, where she acts. Where she puts up the moves and maneuvers that seduce an audience into wanting her. Where she takes off one mask only to reveal a more convincing one underneath. I didn't know anything about this woman's insides and in my hands I was holding the precious remains of Gabriella's being.

Irina's expression said, Don't you compare me. Don't you dare compare me, you bastard.

THE RINKY-DINK SYNTH and dance of today was over and the FM station was now playing a lovely kitschy song already two or three years old. "All of My Heart" was by an equally lovely and kitschy English band called ABC.

"Let go, Sam. Just leave it behind," Irina said. "Listen to this. Listen to what angels sing to you in Heaven."

There was an ache in my heart and an ache in my head, the twin aches of love gone nowhere too long.

So I did what this stranger said and closed my eyes and leaned back. Sometimes music is a holy water that can find its way even inside a stone. That melody was a first glass of champagne drunk on the hottest night of summer. It was stars seen through the porthole of a silent movie's cardboard spaceship. Irina had what I didn't have. She could find beauty behind many disguises.

You said it was what the angels sing?

But you were their song, Irina.

Blood: 1985

.　　.　　.

JULIÁN LUNA WAS waiting for us on the open landing outside my front door. In shiny black leather shoes and black trousers and a black silk shirt hanging loose over his belly, he was a latter-day Zorro. The chain around his neck was a living thing glinting gold in the sun, and the hair on his chest was black peppered with white and gray, the same as what was coming through on his unshaved face. The hair on his head, however, was the perfect luster and color of a bad-luck cat. He was a Zorro—or better, a Casanova got a little too old and heavy for the energetic pursuit of love. Still, there would always be something of the lover and fighter about him, even if it had to be a lover and a fighter thickened with age. His face was handsome and his nose aquiline and under that silk shirt there was no denying the good shape and muscular density of his bulk. If he was in the mood, a man like him could break the spine of a man like me while drinking a glass of chilled white wine.

Irina let go of my arm and approached Julián.

His eyes were mad and completely for her. At first he was leaning with his shoulder against my door in a way that said he didn't have any strength, but as Irina came closer he straightened, swallowed, and even tried to smile. A burning started inside him. He was smoking a cigarette and from the perspiration sticking his shirt to his skin it was clear the sun had been beating relentlessly down. I wondered how long he'd been waiting there; he hadn't even had the presence of mind to find some shade. When Irina reached for his hand the cigarette dropped out of his fingers and he burst into a wrenching sort of weeping. We took him into the cool of the apartment and I turned on all the ceiling fans and opened all the sliding doors and windows and Irina got him a long tumbler of water with ice. She let him drink and then she dipped her scarf into the glass and wiped his sweat-beaded brow and face.

I was already saying my good-byes to her.

Irina and Julián Luna whispered to one another, and cuddled a little, and within a half hour he was leaving, his burning over and the look in his eyes all empty and lost.

He put out his meaty palm and was very thoughtful.

He said, "If you can be a better husband than me . . ." and trailed off, letting go his hold of my hand and for a moment leaning his forehead against my door as if by some voodoo he expected to melt through it. His body sagged like a spent balloon. It was difficult to imagine a time in this man's life when he could have been more comical and more tragic. Finally he squared his shoulders and puffed out his chest and said as if only to himself, *"Vaya cabrón!"*

Julián opened the door and exited, his big black bull body disappearing down the landing and into the sun. I wanted to run after him calling, Get her back, you idiot! Fight for her! You're not too old! Who says you're too old? Why aren't you murdering me? Why aren't you making me pay?

When the door was shut Irina stood unmoving in the middle of the living room and she was looking down at the carpet.

I said, "What are you going to do?"

"Nothing. I want you to do it," Irina said. "I want you to take me to bed," and nice fat tears ran down her dark face. "One week I'll stay here, if you want me to. One week or possibly at the most two and then I have to go. I'm going. I really have to get away from this city and everything and I'm never coming back. Never ever ever. That's what I promise."

At least she had the heart to tell me, unlike Gabriella Zazò.

I went to Irina and kissed the trails of those tears. What I felt wasn't blood but its absence. The sheer frightening absence of blood.

Dear Diary

Gabriella's Book of Fire

THINGS TURNED AROUND after that first visit into the shelter. I mean, that was the start of how I decided to make this secret place of my nonno's into my own place. I stole it from him. We still came down here together and he still told me stories but there were more times when I was here on my own. Mamma and Papà didn't suspect a thing and of course my brother Michael's always out in his own world. If Nonna Fortunata ever visited here, attracted to Earth by all the talismans her husband placed in plain sight, I didn't feel her. I made a vow that no one would ever come here with me. No one would ever know about it, with the obvious exception of my nonno and the possible exception of Salvatore. But that boy will have to earn it. I'm talking about trust. You don't give a thing like that away for the price of nice kisses.

Salvatore must come to deserve it. I just don't know how to let him go about doing it yet.

•   •   •

TODAY I WAS with him, not down here but in New Farm Park. We were sitting on a bench on the slopes that look over the river, and because it was a Sunday little families were having picnics all around us. I was wearing my gray satin shirt with giraffes embroidered on it, and when we were taking a ferry ride up the river and then down the river just for something to do, I caught my foot in the open back of the chugging craft and spilled the chocolate milkshake we were sharing with straws. It stained my shirt all the way through. People looked at me and I got embarrassed and I think I might even have started to cry. Salvatore found some paper napkins from somewhere and he dabbed at my shirt, wanting to clean me up. By then people weren't looking anymore. Diesel smoke was in our faces and hair and everywhere, but so was the wind and the smell of water. Salvatore rubbed my breast through my damp shirt; of course he did it on purpose. We both watched my nipple show through. Then the other one, and I wanted him to touch them with his fingers, to softly squeeze them, to just hold me hard and tell me something good. No other boy I ever kissed made me think things like that.

So then we got off the ferry and he bought me an ice-cream and one for himself and we went and sat on that bench. When no one was looking we gave each other cold ice-cream kisses and he kept on touching my nipples and I didn't argue. It made me ache and bite my bottom lip with the way they waxed and waned. We were talking in our secret language too, talking low in the language I'm not writing in this diary, and it was on the tip of my tongue to tell him about my secret place. I wanted to say, Salvatore, kiss this corner of my mouth, here. Then this corner, here. Kiss me nicely and then I'll take you to this special hideaway I've got. Salvatore, you can come down there with me. Salvatore, down there I want you to do whatever you want to do to me. Salvatore, when we're alone with just that oil lamp flickering spooky ghosts onto the wall I'm going to eat you up like English jelly.

But the thing got spoiled. The thing got wasted.

Blood: 1985

It happened again. We got picked on again.

This stupid gang was going by.

One of them overheard our secret-language conversation and started to laugh and to call his friends over. They grouped around our bench like they'd discovered two members of the animal kingdom trying to speak like humans. Only some of those faces were familiar to me but Salvatore knew every single one of them, and very well too. A few were at his school and a few were older brothers of boys he was friends with. The tough-guy leader was this sort of good-looking nineteen-year-old cretin named something Hutchinson. He had hair down his shoulders and in golden rings. Girls liked him a lot and even I knew a list of the ones he'd more than "pashed," as they say in this country. He even came looking for me once because of the things he'd heard on the grapevine. Mamma used the kitchen broom to chase him away from where he was hanging around under my window. He never came back but when on a Saturday morning I saw him outside the local bread and cake shop, he spat at me right in the street—and his mates and his girlfriends hanging around him like flies just giggled and taunted me like they'd been born with a nice cavity where their brains ought to have been. It was common knowledge that he broke into cars and could do the movie hot-wire thing on them. He'd joyride himself and his cronies around, one time even dumping a one-week-old Holden car half in, half out of the Brisbane River.

Something Hutchinson was sly enough to never be caught. He had the gift of being able to do whatever he wanted in his kingdom of New Farm.

With those sort of people there was never a lot of preamble. A "fucken wogs" this, a "stupid dagos" that, the usual "fuck off, you Italian cunts." In the time I've been in this country those words have attached to me better than my own name. Then a few disgusting things came up about "the Eyetie-slut, slam her up the box with a bottle of tomato sauce," and Salvatore was out of the bench and shouting like a madman, fighting and punching while I screamed murder. They knocked poor Salvatore down and kicked him, and I tried to tear out some idiot's eyes with my fingernails, and some of the mothers who were having their picnics had to drop their chicken salads and creamed-corn side dishes and come running to stop it all. Two or three of the fathers yelled and shook their white-bread steak sandwiches at the running, laughing, yahooingly triumphant gang.

Salvatore's nose was bleeding and his bottom lip was open and the skin around both his eyes was the color of raw meat. I took him home. Signora Capistrano asked me what happened and I said it was this nineteen-year-old no-good, this something Hutchinson and his friends. She asked me what names they'd called us and I repeated every single one, even the thing about the tomato-sauce bottle. She took it all in and touched my face. Her fingers and her palm were hard. She's the type of old-style Sicilian mamma who still likes to scrub some of the more hard-wearing clothes her family wears on an old-style washboard, using lye soap. Signora Carmelina Capistrano thinks labor-saving devices like washing machines, vacuum cleaners, dishwashers, and electric blenders are not quite up to the standards a good wife and mother wants. I think she doesn't even trust mops. Many times I've seen her on her knees, diligently washing the kitchen's linoleum floor by hand and hard-bristle brush.

Right now there was something about her expression. Something in the kind creases in the corners of her eyes. Something that said all this information I was telling her was going into the back of her mind for future reference.

Then she got herself busy with her busted-up son.

Somehow, even though Salvatore was the one who was bleeding and bruised, I felt like I'd got a punching and a kicking too. When you accidentally step on a kitten it finds a hidey-hole where no one can reach it and stays there until its trembling is over. That's what I had to do. That gang gave me a shaking up. Though I'd kept myself composed while I spoke to Signora Capistrano, when the conversation was over I ran under my house and into the peace, quiet, and beautiful secrecy of my sanctuary. Then I cried for longer than I could ever remember crying.

I felt dirty and ashamed and I knew that all those horrible names I

was always called stuck to me because there was one thing about them
no one would ever deny: they were true.

ISN'T IT A fact that you can never really see the sicknesses that start
such a long way under the skin?

I've settled myself down, finally. I know how to keep myself from
crying like a baby again. It's not good to keep this inside like some sort
of a germ I've swallowed. So now I'm here to keep writing about what
I know.

I know I'm a writer. I'm a writer because I want to understand hope
and need and loss and pain. I'm a writer because I want to know how far
down love and hate can go. I'm a writer because I'm scared of these two
things more than I'm scared of vampires and ghosts and the bogeyman.
God created angels that fly and angels that fall and we carry the both of
them inside us. They fight with one another and their battlefield is
inside every human frame. I want to soar but I want to bury myself in
mud and filth too. There is knowledge that is beautiful and knowledge
that is terror, and the knowledge that's been coming to me first from my
nonno and second from my life in this country is beautiful and terrible,
one within the other.

I'm on the outside of things. I see this now. So far in my life I have no
home. And the one and only thing that I must demand from this life is
that I do have a home.

It's as if I've entered a big and exciting party but I'm apart from it
too because something stops me from joining. The cliché says I'm standing on the outside looking in. I think I'm a writer because I'm half this
and half that but really I'm just an in-between. Nonno's stories aren't
my stories. His country isn't my country, it never was. In Sicilia I wasn't
positively Sicilian, not with my genetic mixtures and the way people
pointed and stared and gossiped, and here in Australia the situation is
worse. In the old place I was *testa di fuoco* and in this new place I'm
bloody fucking wog. So where is my home? Where is my place? Where
will I make a real life? On the one day these strangers here can be nice

and give me their friendship and on the next day they can take it away with a "piss off, you dago." Or even the slightest curling of a lip. There's no solid ground under me. Everything shifts. It makes me tremble right down in my belly.

So I kiss boys so they'll let me be close to them. I climb mango trees and look into people's backyards so that I can see girls my age playing. Windows only, no doors. Is that the real reason I think I'm a writer?

And to Salvatore.

He doesn't have my trust, even though he feels this rejection the same way I do. He was born here and so he shouldn't feel like an alien, but I can see that he does. Every time he's called a dagowop-wogeyetiegreaseball the wonderful light in him dims. It's in his eyes even when he tries not to show it in his expression. There are times he turns himself inside out just to be accepted and there are other times he sticks two fingers up to everyone he sees. Even some of the Italian boys will call him those names: they're the ones who consider themselves to be really Australian. They're bigger they're cooler they're more arrogant. They kill themselves for football and cricket and have nothing but contempt for where they come from. They're ashamed of their parents. They turn red with embarrassment at the comical accents, at the waving hands and olive-colored skins, at the garlic and fennel and fava beans that fill their homes. They're ashamed even of their own cut lunches; they would rather throw their salami and home-grown tomato sandwiches into a ditch than be laughed at. To their friends in the playground they call their own mothers and fathers stupid dagos. Who would believe such a thing? This is how the schoolyard has trained them to think. They speak about their own flesh and blood with such disgust! Disgust that is so close to hate that you would never know the difference. Is this what living in a new country is supposed to do to the spirit?

Why in the face of such things can't I trust Salvatore Capistrano, my one real companion and friend? He is good to me. But my wariness comes because his good feelings are corrupted. His feelings are corrupted by lust. How can I think of pure love and pure trust when he's like a vagabond dog ready to mount my shinbone? I know this is exactly true because in a way I feel the same Fire.

Yes, of course. Because I'm the same. The differences between women and men don't mean a thing when you talk about love and you talk about lust. I've learned this already. I want to love Salvatore and I want to make love to Salvatore.

My hand is trembling and I feel a lump in my chest, but I feel excited to write this way. I'll continue. This is the truth and I want it to go on.

Make love? Poetically, like in a satiny movie full of flowers and meadows and young heroines and heroes? No. I want Salvatore Capistrano the way I've read that a strong woman can have a physically stronger man. On top of him, swallowing him into her, breaking her bones on his body. Salvatore Capistrano. I want to hold his thing and stare at it. I want to taste it. I want it to move so deeply inside me there'll be a whole world in there, of strength and spirit and life. I want him to kiss me, just kiss me forever. Until I do all this I won't know if I love him. Not at all. The one thing gets in the way of the other thing. Desire before love. It's the same for him, I know this. Love. Trust. At the moment they might as well be with the man in the moon. They're somewhere else. Somewhere behind this very first trap in the journey—lovely, weeping lust.

I FEEL so sick with what happened today. Afterward I had to ring Salvatore on the telephone. He sounded very depressed. I sent him a flashlight message as soon as night fell, from my window to his, saying, You're my hero. But there wasn't any answer.

After dinner and doing the washing-up I came back to my deep dark little room. It gives me such pleasure. Mamma and Papà think I've taken Nonno for a walk but he's right here with me. I'm writing in this exercise book and he's doing nothing. The light from the oil lamp shines off his pate and the electric-strike vein in the side of his head is thick and purple. He looks lost.

So I put down my pen and tell my nonno all about what happened today in the park.

To get through to a man with a mind so mislaid takes time and patience. I've got these things. Once he truly listens and the light comes in his eyes he becomes something else. The Red Indians of North America have a proper name: my nonno becomes a shaman. With me he's a witch doctor. In Sicily we say he's a *stregone*. He conjures the past with his muttering, a muttering which is so beautiful when you see past the words.

And if I have a story about blood to tell, then my nonno won't be outdone. From somewhere in the far reaches of his mind he will find a story to far outdo mine. Just give him a little time, and all your patience.

Blood Brothers

Tony Solero told me about it straightaway. He didn't beat about the bush or try to make me feel better about things. That's what you can expect when you've known someone so long. We were in his office on a Friday night. Disco music seeped through the walls and he gave me a drink. Then he just went straight in.

"Peter doesn't want you involved with what we're going to do. He doesn't like you and he doesn't want you around. He says you're taking the best of what we've got without putting anything back in. Yes, you're on the door but you don't do much there except try to pick up girls. We can hire two bouncers for less than what you cost us. If it wasn't for Carlo we'd have all kinds of shit coming in anyway. I know you're good for morale and we can rely on you for a little party all right. You're good for the barmen and the entertainment too but I've got to say what I see and what I see is that you're not interested."

The whiskey helped me to relate to being pushed back into the nothing world, but I only took a first sip and stopped there.

"Are you going to tell me I'm wrong? Huh? Sam. Open your mouth and say something. Come on, I'm giving you a chance."

"A chance for what?"

"A chance for what? Listen to you. To tell me I'm wrong, you fucking *cafuni*. Tell me Peter can't see past what happened all those years ago and that you really want to be here. Tell me that you want to be a part of my business. Tell me that you care about it. Do you think I want you out? Do you think I want to be tied up with Peter Pierucci and no one else?"

"What do you mean, no one else? What about your brother?"

"He's finished with La Notte."

"And the other two?"

"Them as well. Investors are silent until they lose money and when they're losing money they can't see the long term. But Peter does."

"So you're with him now." I shook my head. "And of course he says I have to go."

"What else am I telling you?"

We looked at various things in the office that were safely not ourselves. When it was clear I didn't have anything to add Tony went on with a little less assurance.

"But you don't want to argue with me, do you? You can't, can you? You're not interested, that's the point. You invested two dollars and for that you expect to live like a king. How can that bastard be so right?"

We stopped looking at inanimate objects and ended up staring at one another. I couldn't help it: I saw a fifteen-year-old Tony Solero buying me a birthday gift named Andrea Farmer and he saw a twenty-something Sam Capistrano wasting La Notte's time and money.

"How long's that Irina What's-her-name been at your place?"

"A few weeks."

"A few months. And you've been worse than ever. I thought she was only staying a week."

"Things dragged out."

"She's fantastic, Sam, half your luck, but that's not my business. La Notte is my business and the rats have already deserted the ship they think is sinking. Have you got a clue what's going on? Have you spoken to anyone or bothered to ask me? No. Well, here it is. The books won't go into the black. How about that? The way things are set up, they never will. I was wrong. I was fucking wrong. My accountant's a fucking moron. The bank writes to me every two days now. Every new expense we get is like another knife in a vital organ. We're paying money hand over fist and we can't even put up our drink prices or no one'll come anymore. So that's it. I have to throw up my hands. I have to give in. You know what that means?"

It was a good question and so I gave it due consideration. I swirled the whiskey but again didn't taste it because I didn't like the way my hands were unsteady. Losing La Notte was like losing my one place of anchor. Maybe the possibility of that felt the same for Tony. I had to wonder, So with this sort of business, in mid-eighties Brisbane, what does it mean to "give in?" And then I had the answer and Tony must have seen the recognition in my eyes.

"Don't get moralistic on me. There's nothing else I can do. We've been too halfhearted. I'm giving in by going all the way. La Notte used to be a little whorehouse and that's what it's going to be again, but this time I'm making sure the emphasis is on class. We're going to make these great rooms upstairs with en suites and everything and we're start-ing up a casino too. That side of it won't be much in the beginning, but Peter's got some friends showing me how to start small and then just let things grow. They're donating the blackjack table and wheel from Strip-perama, that place they closed down last month. Those Lebanese idiots wouldn't pay an increase so the Licensing Branch raided them to teach all of us a lesson."

"So why wouldn't they do that to you too, once you're set up?"

"Because I'm not that type of tight-fisted Lebanese fucking idiot. You insure your house and contents, every year don't you pay the CPI increase? Do you argue with your insurance company about it? It's a fact of life. Except here it's the Cop Price Index you have to worry about. Fair enough, I can live with that. And the other reason things'll be sweet as a nut is because Peter was able to get good-mate's rates for The Joke to look after La Notte."

"What are you talking about, The Joke?"

Tony stopped and sort of coughed a laugh, and then some of his more usual light spirits crept to the surface.

"*Cumpareddu,* you've really got to hear this. Who said the police don't have a sense of humor? This inside world they run is totally warped. I'll tell you once but don't ever try to get me to say it again. The Joke is the cops. It's their money-making operation. The Joke lets all those places in the Valley break the law and never have to worry about it. Soft drugs, roulette wheels, poker, strippers, prostitution—you know what I mean. To tell the truth, I can't even imagine how many things they're involved in. The newspapers are always going on about all those secret places in Anne Street and Brunswick Street and everywhere else but the system turns a blind eye because being a hundred years in power's taught the government how to win friends and influence people. There are bagmen cops just like you see in the movies, and not just some detective like Peter Pierucci picking up his weekly cash from the likes of us. Bags and bags of money get collected and distributed, and I'm not kidding about this, a lot of it goes up the ladder too." Tony indicated it with his thumb. "Up. They told me. The powers that be aren't going to stop a police force making a bit extra for its men. They figure that at the same time they're still controlling illegal activities. Nothing gets out of hand if you're right on top of it, follow? It's a *type* of law enforcement. Maybe they call it containment. Anyway, who really cares how it works? It works. So that's my current-affairs lesson."

"But think about it. Paying Peter a bit of money to leave a nightclub alone is one thing, but prostitutes and gambling, Tony, that's jail."

"As if I'll be going anywhere near a jail."

"What about your family? What do they do if—"

"Look. Listen to me. Didn't I tell you not to be so moralistic? Or are you just a coward? You can't stand there and tell me one bit of bad is all right but another bit of bad is too much. So what's so wrong with what I'm going to do? And why should it be risky? If prostitution is the world's oldest profession then protecting it must be the second. Why's that going to change, and who's going to change it all of a sudden? Someone'll pass a law that says men won't want to win money anymore? Someone'll pass a law that says men won't want to fuck any-more?" He shook his head. "I know there'll be trouble here and there but Peter'll make sure it's nothing."

Tony shrugged then tried to stretch his neck, a move that showed where his tension and doubt had made a nice home.

He said, "Anyway. That's all there is. You're not a part of it."

Tony paused, maybe thinking about the more than twenty years we'd known each other. Those twenty years made it easy for me to see that he wanted me to leave without making a fuss. He didn't really want me to tell him I wanted to stay. He already had enough to worry about—and the truth is, there was little conviction in my heart.

Tony said, "Okay?"

I put the glass down. I moved to the door.

"I'll be out of the apartment in a week."

"Take as long as you need."

Good-bye is good-bye and should never be dragged out, but I couldn't help thinking about Tony's new move. Maybe I'd even seen something like this coming, but what worried me was what I still saw coming.

"One thing you should think about is that if the government ever does change, the first thing they'll want to do is fix what's been wrong before."

"No." He shook his head and then one hand went behind his neck and he stretched again. "Peter says that's not right."

Conviction or no conviction, I wanted to hit Tony for that. For being so gullible. For talking himself into blindness. In the end, for having sided with Pietro Pierucci and rejecting me. I wanted to shout killing words about friendship and loyalty, about stupidity and greed. I wanted to push him against the wall and make him remember all the years that made up our history. Instead I opened his office door to the midnight fury of La Notte.

"If you could see your way clear, Sam," he said over the heavy sound of the beat, "I'm hoping that you can leave your investment where it is. One day you'll be making bags of money."

I didn't answer.

Yet the good-bye still wouldn't come. Even in this situation neither of us was prepared to smash over one knee those inextricable ties that bind. Maybe that's why Tony coughed. Maybe that's why he cleared his throat.

He said, "There's one other thing."

"What?"

That's right, Tony Solero could no more rid himself of those more than twenty years than I could. He walked behind his desk and touched a few papers and letters. He drew a long breath.

"You might want to take the back way out. Go down the alley and come out on Brookes. Hail the first taxi you see and get yourself home."

I felt the nightclub's rhythm through my shoes, in my flesh, deep behind my ribcage and even in the roots of my hair.

"I mean it, don't go out the front. Go home. Go home by Brookes."

So this was it. Finally. I understood where things had arrived. Now that I was out of La Notte my old friend Pietro Pierucci was free to hate me as much as he wanted—and so my long overdue account for the loss of Gabriella Zazò was waiting.

The thudding, thumping music, the screeching-laughing people, it made up a world always waiting to swallow wandering souls.

I said, to pinpoint him exactly, "Why don't you drive me home, Tony?"

He eased himself into his businessman's leather chair. He slipped on a pair of glasses that enlarged his eyes so much that when he wore them he looked perpetually surprised. When we were in nappies our mothers used to put us into the same washing basket to play while they shared a pot of coffee and gossiped. We were exactly the same age but he had a gut growing like a pregnancy and his eyesight wasn't what it used to be. He sighed. He looked more tired than tired.

Tony said, "That's not something I'm free to do."

The world outside that office door was loud and large, but the little world of Tony's office shimmered. It shimmered because this was one of those concentrated moments that's always been waiting to kick the guts right out of you.

Dear Diary

Gabriella's Book of Fire

Something Hutchinson's name turned out to be Barry. His friends called him Bazza. I learned that and would never forget it again, not after a jogger found him at about six-fifteen A.M. in New Farm Park one Thursday, beside the rose gardens that people said were supposed to be the largest in the Southern Hemisphere.

It was ten days after our altercation.

The boy was unconscious and in a terrible state. The dew all over him said he'd been there half the night. He had broken bones and the story went around that his head was the size of a football, so swollen up with beating that his eyes couldn't open until a week later when the swelling was going down. BarryBazza Hutchinson wasn't able to say who'd done this to him. He said that he remembered working under the hood of his father's truck, getting some bits of the engine ready for cleaning, then nothing. They found a convex dent in the truck's hood that must have been made by BarryBazza's hard head, then whoever it was took him away and had the rest of their fun with him.

What was left went into the park.

BarryBazza was probably lucky to be alive but that was where his luck stopped. The investigating police officer, our local hero Pietro Pierucci from up at the New Farm station, did some poking around the garage that housed the truck and he came across some suspicious things. He got himself a warrant and ended up finding stolen goods all over the Hutchinson home. The whole family confessed after that. The boy went to jail and so did the father, and the mother got a suspended sentence that later on turned into jail for her too, after Pietro Pierucci arrested her in a parked Peugeot in Brunswick Street, where he said he found her with one man's penis in her mouth and another man's fist in her anus and a lot of five- and ten-dollar notes floating around.

Salvatore never said the boy Hutchinson got what he deserved. He never gloated that some sort of divine justice had been done. We were all just sick and scared that something like this could happen so close to home.

Not many people had a lot to say about the whole thing either, because no one really knew the family well. At least, nobody cared for them. What I did notice was that boys wandering in gangs was just something you never saw in New Farm again. It was as if some new law had been decreed but at the same time went unspoken. Then the whole matter was something I forgot about. But one weekday midday something reminded me of BarryBazza Hutchinson.

Mamma sent me outside to pick some basil and rosemary and I got lost in the silly pleasure of watching an isosceles triangle of white and blue butterflies floating over the herb garden, and while I was there the back door of the Capistrano house opened. Salvatore's mother was crying and Pietro Pierucci was in his blue uniform and doing his best to comfort her.

They were speaking in Sicilian.

"It was right, Carmelina. It was more than right."

"How could it be? They say he lost all his teeth in jail. They say he's raped in his mouth and worse every night. How could it be right?"

And she kept crying and then the tall policeman left her there, walking into the sun and putting on his blue hat.

Poor Signora Capistrano. She had the best heart of anyone.

Bloodletting

I HATED MYSELF FOR being scared but this was a nightmare thing that had loomed over me for years. On watery legs I left the humping, bumping, sexy half-dark of La Notte and went down the alley behind it, where Brisbane City Mission workers sometimes came checking for drunks who slept in their own urine and feces, surrounded by bright-eyed cats.

It didn't help.

Two figures stood under a streetlamp between the alley—Silk Lane—and Brookes Street. Behind me was a dead end. The club's fire-safety door had automatically fallen shut and locked after my exit and there was no way back in. By the yellow light I saw that Peter Pierucci didn't do his own dirty work anymore. In the old days he might have stomped kids like Barry Hutchinson half to death but here he'd enlisted these two. I had a nice sharp moment to wonder if Tony Solero had sent me out the back way on purpose, but no, it couldn't be so. He would never become so complete a stranger to me; it was very simply that a man like Pierucci knew the world well enough to work out what warnings would be passed between friends, even breaking-apart friends.

The two were none other than George and Eric, the pair of foot-ballers or amateur boxers or whatever, the bad news waiting to hit the headlines who'd shared star billing on my front-door shit list. What could he have promised them? My legs weren't so bad that I couldn't break into a mad dash, circling an industrial waste bin, doubling back, sprinting toward light, three pairs of running soles clacking and echoing in the alley, but they were on to me, and they measured the beating the way they'd been told to.

It was nothing like what you expect from having seen all the action movies in Christendom. At first there was terror and pain, then after a few more blows my soul felt that drifting sort of serenity that only comes in deep sleep or heavy orgasm. I moved into a good place and it was only the mortal coil being treated like a mute side of beef. Instead of them and the night and the blood already spurting out of my nose, the thoughts in my head were for Gabriella and all the things that were written in her diary, the things that I'd memorized almost by heart in the many times I'd already read it through to a final empty promise on the last page. There were all the secrets of our past in those bruised pages, all the history of being young and full of fire and blood and not knowing what to do about it. There was even a revelation about my ma and a lovesick young police officer, if you knew how to read the words right. What else was he doing leaving our home on a weekday when I was at school and my papà was at work? She'd been his favorite at the dances at the Cloudland Ballroom and the Sorrento Lounge in Deagon. He'd always been so respectful to my father. He'd gone so easy with Tony and me when we'd stolen those silly things from the Kmart. He'd taken such care to make sure we two wayward boys had every chance to turn out right. All for my ma. Did Gabriella guess the significance of what she'd written down; had she seen the love story about a young police officer not yet robbed of the joy and the juice of life and an older woman who felt only God could say what for him?

Well, what did it matter, anyway?

Drifting without pain, I saw my ma and my papà as they were now, living in a quiet house in a quiet street surrounded by quiet neighbors. The days of partying friends and relatives and immigrant torments and inexplicable love affairs were over; whatever went on back so many years they still had each other, so for a bad son there was no need to forgive them their youth, merely to go on loving them.

So to you, Gabriella. You're lost in time and as close as my own hand. Writing to me out of the past and giving me stories faithfully deciphered from your nonno's muttering mouth. What was one of the last things you wrote about him?

"And if I have a story about blood to tell, then my nonno won't be outdone. From somewhere in the far reaches of his mind he will find a story to far outdo mine. Just give him a little time, and all your patience."

Time. Patience.

Yes, but God how these two men make the blood run out of me.

"GABRIELLA DARLING, WE went too far. Our days in stinking Napoli selling those rotten trinkets came to a very quick end. The young Americans never knew where to find us when they discovered they'd paid good lire and dollars for worthless baubles, but when we tried to swindle our own countrymen we should have known that greed had the better of us."

FUCK IT, I'M on my knees now, panting. Whatever part of me was drifting is being sucked back to earth. I'm beginning to feel things again, things that taste like drops of bloodied sweat, and fear and death. Agony too. It doesn't seem possible to beg. They won't stop. If I beg them they'll think I've got too much left and so they'll keep on going. Something inside me is cracking in half. One kick too hard will make me lose control of my arms. My bowels. My urine. If I lie down on the road they'll jump on my back and I'll be paralyzed forever.

There, a third shadow, coming down the alley.

Blood: 1985

. . .

"A T FIRST WE were laughing among ourselves because of the stupid thing that happened.

"Remember, there was me and there was Fortunata's two cousins, the Lorenzano brothers, Alfio and Agostino. We heard a crazy story that a certain Signor Raiti, to whom we sold jewelry for all the ladies in his family, was after us. We stopped laughing because we heard he'd been to the police. Well, that's not what stopped us laughing, not exactly. The police rebuffed Signor Raiti with puffed-up words about having more important matters to attend to, didn't he know there was a war on, and how could he be such a dupe anyway? So after that Signor Raiti went to see one of the local cathedral tradesmen, who was a friend of his. Now, this man also worked for the mafia lieutenant of the quarter, who derived all his power from private construction companies and a healthy business in the maintenance and restoration of sacred institutions. All those are, it goes without saying, political contracts. So the mire we found ourselves in was deepening. Signor Raiti explained to his friend that he wanted justice because the fabulously expensive jewelry he'd purchased and given to his prettiest daughter had rusted in her ears, creating a terrible infection, and though on the left ear only the lobe had to go, on the right the whole ear had to be amputated straight away in the doctor's surgery, so serious was the sickness. He described how she'd been screaming even with the anaesthetic; how he himself had to hold her down while the doctor performed his operation. What we further heard was that this friend of Signor Raiti's, the tradesman, terribly moved by the story, now took the tale straight to the mafia lieutenant, who also happened to be his uncle. Favored nephew speaking to powerful mafia uncle about three Sicilian *cafuni* who'd been selling trash in the streets and had caused the amputation of a lovely daughter of the great city of Napoli's ears. Alfio, Agostino and I started to run as soon as we heard that story. We packed our bags and ran out of our hotel. We ran for the train station like wild dogs with devils chasing them, and it wouldn't matter what train was leaving and where it was going, for we'd be on the very first departure from those cavernous tunnels."

T HEY ROLL ME over so that I can look up. My trousers are wet in the front and in the back. If they hadn't stopped hitting and kicking me convulsions would have set in. I'm senseless, lost again in a beautiful dream. It's like the hallucinogenic effects of the most wonderful drug in the world. Sex and sleep and champagne combined into one amazing pill. So they sit me up. George and Eric hold my bleeding head straight so that I can look Pietro Pierucci in the face.

"B UT THAT'S WHERE they were waiting for us. At Stazione Centrale. Did they have advance information? Did someone in the hotel denounce us? No. These people simply knew what three Sicilian *cafuni* would do once they heard the story. The story they themselves had put around. They'd flushed us out of our hiding place, just like that. And five men were waiting, armed with bats and axe handles, and one of them, the smallest and the wiriest, even carried a hammer.

"I hope you never discover what it's like to be struck in the face, my beautiful Gabriella. What your television doesn't show you is the utter contempt that is contained inside that blow. When a person strikes another person they are saying, You are not human, you are not even an animal, you are nothing. You are worth less than the price of an olive, and the steaming shit I leave under a tree is more valuable than your soul. If one day your husband raises his hand to you forget loyalty and forget forgiveness and gather up your children and walk out the door and never return. Gabriella, understand me, that's what you must do.

"And these men did hit us. They struck us down with their bats and their axe handles, and while I lay trembling in the tangle of arms and legs and flesh that was the Lorenzano brothers and me, that little one, that wiry one, that weasel one, came and stood over us with his hammer and then he delivered the final blows. I felt the numbing reverberation go through Alfio first, and Agostino second, and then that little man with the pinched face and the brush mustache and the burning little eyes raised the hammer over me and struck down, and good night.

"You see here, Gabriella. You see this on the side of my head? My bolt of electricity. My bolt of lightning. Alfio was dead without so much as a shudder or a cry. Agostino was disfigured. And I was turned into a fool. From then, that's when the troubles with my mind started.

"Troubles? There were plenty more. The local mafia lieutenant, with his government contracts and his political friends and the military police in his pocket, wasn't satisfied. He wanted all of his particular Neapolitan quarter to be aware that common con men and thieves would not be tolerated, not if they operated without his approval. Before we knew it, Alfio Lorenzano was in the morgue and Agostino Lorenzano and I were with the *carabinieri,* and there was a trial, and we were condemned to eighteen months' hard labor each, and what with one thing and another it became two then three then four years, and we had to spend the rest of the war era in jail, looking at one another and not at our wives and children, working chained together like animals, breaking rocks, yes, as you see in the silliest and the stupidest gangster movies from America, breaking rocks for no purpose at all."

"WHAT WAS THE reason?" Pietro Pierucci said. "Why didn't you watch her?"

Something went off and something went on.

I heard, "Wake him up."

George and Eric shook their rag doll. Pierucci's face hovered in front of my eyes like he was the devil. And a devil seeing good in the world couldn't have been more hate-filled than he. More coldly angry. This was the right time for it to finally come out. I wiped my chin and held my nose and when I looked at my hand it was completely red.

"I lost . . . my Gabriella . . ." Funny that Peter Pierucci should be the only person in the world I said that to. Still, the words could only dribble out. They were part utterance and part red-stained saliva. "My . . . Gabriella . . ."

That got an instant response. I cowered from a coming blow but what I perceived instead were the tears welling up in Pierucci's eyes. They focused my mind a moment, those tears. God but he must have loved us all in the old days. Loved the immigrant families and all the children. He must have walked around the streets of New Farm, through the park and under the trees, past the shops and all the wooden houses, and he must have felt brave and protecting, all of us safe with him our rock, ready for anything.

"Who's ever going to forgive you for that? Who'll forget?"

Simple words that sent me senseless and sobbing.

Then I talked and babbled in a dream that was hazy in the front and blurred at the edges. It was as if, at those edges, everyone I'd ever known and let down stood and watched, with a slight, red-haired girl at their center. Even if it was Gabriella right there, I couldn't appeal to her directly. That hurt too much. So Pietro Pierucci was my intermediary. No longer a devil but a fire-and-brimstone priest.

"What are you saying? I can't understand a word you're saying." He shook me, shook me as hard as he could.

"Where did she—why did she go—lost—why didn't she come back?"

Maybe Senior Detective Pierucci thought I'd be stronger. Maybe he didn't understand what Gabriella's disappearance had left me with. A certain confusion or doubt seemed to cross his hard face. Maybe it was only my scattered imagining. Yet it was as if over all the years he'd convinced himself I never cared and here he had to see that I did. The tight muscles in his jaw clenched.

He looked at George and Eric and said, "Go up into the street. Wait for me there," and their hands stopped propping me up and I had a sense of them walking away.

Then Pietro Pierucci took me by the chin.

"Are you shitting me?"

"What?"

"Look at me. *Look* at me."

I had to focus again on the devil-priest's face.

"Don't play games with me, you little bastard. You still think about her?"

"Course—"

"You were fifteen. Ten years—and you still think about her."

"Always always always—"

He was holding my face, keeping my chin up, but the image of him swayed and blurred as if I were watching an image in a river and it was disturbed by currents and ripples.

Pietro Pierucci, the toughest man I've known, the most silently angry, took out his handkerchief and pressed it under my nose. Bone, cartilage, things, creaked, cracked.

"Fuck you, Sam. Fuck you, *Salvatore Capistrano*. I've seen what's left of a teenage boy hacked to pieces by his father, and I understand why it had to happen. I've seen three out of four members of the one family decapitated in a car crash, and I understand why that had to happen too. I've seen a three-month-old baby boy fried in extra-virgin olive oil in a fucking frypan and even that makes sense when you think about the lives of everyone concerned. Countless brutal crimes. Torturing, cruelties you can't even report in a newspaper, all of them happening here in this sleepy little city. Here. Everywhere I used to walk when I was a cop I trained myself to look for the tell-tale signs of blood coming, not blood itself—you're never that lucky, or if you are you're too late—but the forewarning of it, the smell that says soon blood is going to be spilled, the feel of it in the air. And sometimes I could stop something bad happening but most times I couldn't, and I always told myself, I understand, I understand why things have to happen, and that way nothing got inside me."

He wiped his mouth, first with the palm of one hand and then the palm of the other.

"But Gabriella disappearing—Gabriella—that was different. I didn't understand how it could happen out of the blue. Where was the warning? I never understood. If she'd been hit by a car or struck by a disease—but this thing didn't have an answer. If someone took her why did he stop at one? Why didn't he try to take more? Where's the pattern, where are the clues? At first, at first when I prayed and lit a candle in the Holy Spirit Church my faith got stronger. I would find her, and I'm not talking about a body dug out of a ditch that was going to have to be identified on a slab by her mother and father or by her teeth. No. Gabriella Zazò was going to come home and she'd be clean and whole and I'd be the one taking her through the front door of her home. You understand?"

I nodded. That was all I could do, nod and dream with Pierucci.

"But after everything I did there wasn't anything I could use. Nowhere left to doorknock, no creep left to bash a story out of, no prostitute that wasn't already shaken down. Wasn't a single outback one-man police station left in this country that wasn't flooded with her photos. Airports, trains, buses, taxi companies, so sick of me they didn't even want to hear her name again. Interpol cut me off. All the networks let me down. Not a word, not a whisper. One morning I woke up to it. Bang. I'm in my bed and I know the truth, and God and the Virgin and the Holy Spirit Church are dead. They don't exist anymore. Bang. Someone snatched her, that's all there is to it. Someone did it to one kid then never did it again. That day at Nocturne, someone got a hold of Gabriella. My money says she ran outside in a panic when her nonno got convulsions and whoever the freak in that car was—" Pierucci snapped his fingers. "And gone. He took her away and he killed her. She's not somewhere else. She's not like in the films, brainwashed or suffering from amnesia or living with a nice new family without knowing where she comes from. The girl is dead. Stabbed, strangled, bashed, dead, buried, weighted down in a river or an ocean. I woke up to it. So what do you do then? Finally you say, *Vaffanculu miseria*."

Pierucci had to stop again, as if the decision to give up had hollowed him out like a dead tree.

"Who let it happen to her?" He shook me by both shoulders. "Don't faint. Don't faint, you bastard." Pierucci waited until he saw that I wasn't going to. "You. You let it happen to her. If it was up to me I'd write a new murder charge to put in the criminal code, just for you. Negligence. Stupidity. Dangerous as a loaded gun. How could you have taken her to a Spring Hill brothel? If you were going to get her grandfather fucked you could have done it on your own. Was it a game? See a senile old man trying to get it up with a prostitute? Gabriella was supposed to be your friend. Friends look after one another. You were supposed to look after her. Weren't you? You have the hide to ask why it had to happen? It had to happen because you didn't take care with her. Care. And then you say you loved her."

Pierucci shook me.

"I—still—love—"

"If only it had been you, Sam. If only whoever it was chose you. That would have been better. Don't you think? If you'd been the one to disappear forever?"

"Would have gone—would have been all right—"

"You broke her family's heart." Pietro Pierucci kept lifting my face whenever my chin dropped to my chest. Even through the cottonwool world I could see and feel how his hands trembled. These feelings were bigger than he was. His words came out of his chest in bits and pieces, they came out of whatever of him was still our old New Farm hero. "Then you went and broke your own family's heart. You had every chance in the world and look what you turned into."

That was the end. The end where the accounts are done and the value of a life is measured.

"You're nothing, Sam." Pietro Pierucci's lips were white. "Nothing."

"Nothing—without Gabriella—"

That stopped him shaking me.

And what happened then?

The universe was black where it didn't shimmer with stars, and this black was encroaching, swallowing those stars and putting out their light, but that wasn't the strangest thing of all, no, the strangest thing of all in fact came in two parts.

First, through a lovely wall of cotton wadding and rubber padding, and even of softly thrumming music, I had the sensation of strong masculine arms all at once being thrown around me. They held me hard, tight, crushing with emotion, and there was a sobbing and wracking that wasn't mine.

Next, a soft hand reached out of the black and took hold of mine and carried me away from Pietro Pierucci, a nice white hand that said, All of this is just a dream, Salvatore, there's no need to worry, and it was you of course, Gabriella, come to lift me away from this bad place and take me into your good, deep night.

Ti amo, mia cara Gabriella.

And I love you too, Salvatore Capistrano. You know that, don't you?

PASTA ☀ 1995

Allegria Once Again

IN THE KITCHEN, PLENTY of pots and pans bubbled with sauce. Shiny stainless-steel lids trembled. Steam scented the space with the lightly drifting aromas of garlic and herbs. In an hour or two that feather-light aromatic drift would be cloying, overly sweet and overly heavy, as express cooking took over and dish after dish was pushed out to the dining tables. This was the best time of the night, the one I liked most, when things were getting ready.

Great bunches of parsley and basil lay on cutting boards, beside them fresh meats trimmed of fat: beef, lamb, and chicken. There were veal shanks for osso bucco. Homemade Sicilian sausages rolled into coils like rope were stuffed with minced shoulder pork and fennel seeds and cracked pepper. Stacks of mushrooms were washed and waiting to be chopped, as well as onions, potatoes, red and green capsicums, green heads of lettuce, and bunches of fat red chillies the size of your fingers. Eggplants, zucchini, whole artichokes, and tomatoes proliferated in corners. There was seafood. Fish and crustaceans, side by side. Heavy pieces of tuna and delicate fillets of perch, even whole sole. Barramundi for the moment I stayed away from, because there'd been some questions about what exactly you were buying. That didn't stop the purchase of these rock oysters and green mussels, the squid and octopus, even the single brimming bucket of sea snails, as hard to come by as anything you can imagine. From the best of the local produce, here were broiled Moreton Bay bugs waiting to be cleaved in two and served either in a marinara sauce or with a garnish, like a piquant mango salsa. Sometimes we barbecued them basted in olive oil and oregano. What about all these dry pastas, waiting to be chosen? Straight, curly, white, brown, vegetable-colored, you name it. Vermicelli, tagliatelle, lasagne in sheets with frilly edges, and just made, flour-dusted ravioli overcoats waiting to be made pregnant with tender fillings of meat or salmon, or a more traditional mixture of something like potato, parsley, mint, and garlic. Penne pasta, pastina, pasta in the shape of bow-ties and butterflies and shells, and of course the grains—rice, couscous, and the lovely yellow mounds of fine polenta. Name the one you most want for the delight of your senses, I'd be mortified if it wasn't in a jar, right here somewhere.

It was good to see all these things, all these things that were mine. I was laughing with the chefs over a loud joke about one of our crazy young kitchenhands who was a cousin and who said he was sleeping with not one, not two, but three of the young women working here, and I was asking my papà to go out the back and see if the bread-delivery truck was coming or not; in the middle of all this I was remembering a stolen moment with Irina. Before I left the house for work she'd been having a coffee in our backyard's garden, beside the plot of tomatoes and lettuce and endives my father had established for us and that she liked to tend. We'd leaned like kids in the shade, her lips full and tasting of bitter Brazil beans, and we'd kissed for a long, long time, just the way we still liked to do.

M Y MA BRISTLED around the kitchen like a squat little general, giving an instruction here and a severe order there, supervising the cooks to make sure they stopped their jokes and did what they were supposed to do and did it right. She kept saying, "Don't listen to my son and get to work. You, what are you doing? Mario, Vince, hurry up with the peas, the shallots, the onions, have we got all night?" Then she'd look at me and shake her head and smile her old Sicilian mamma smile while my papà did what our bread-delivery truck collusion was supposed to do: give him a few minutes to go outside and take a breather from my ma the general.

It was a dream to have things going so well, a visitation of pure *allegria*.

Falsomagro

SO HE MIGHT HAVE turned one hundred and one years of age, but that evening when the news that he'd died came, most of that *allegria* went into the cupboard.

He'd said to me about a month earlier, in Sicilian of course, "Salvatore, it seems that I must live forever," and I'd just about believed it. He would simply go on and on like a watch that never winds down. He'd survived two wars, getting blown up in the first and hammer-smashed in the second, had made it through nearly five years of incarceration with hard labor, had lost his senses and been dumb as a boot on the surface and as cosmos-connected as a shaman underneath, then somehow had walked back into the light and for twenty years been something of the man he'd left behind. To age like anyone else. He'd outlived innumerable relatives and friends and could never have counted those who simply fell out of contact in the way people will. He'd had to watch his wife Fortunata turn out not to be so fortunate after all and die too young, and then he'd had to live through the disappearance and never-return of his first female grandchild, his Firehead, his soul mate, little

226

Gabriella Zazò. And these were only the obvious markers. What about all the other trials he'd survived, the ones inside, the doubts, the midnight questionings anyone must make, the can't sleep for wondering if his life had been worthwhile and how he'd be thought of when he was gone, good man or bad?

I always thought I'd be there at the end, that Enrico Belpasso would very considerately save his ultimate departure until he could give a final shake of the hand to me. *Ciao, Salvatore, ci vediamo, va bene?* Bye, Salvatore, I'll be seeing you, okay?

Like our Sunday afternoon partings.

I was looking around the restaurant and the kitchen, leaning there against the wall, the telephone receiver jammed in my ear and Gabriella's little sister Sandra, who liked to be called Sandy, now eighteen—or was it nineteen?—and whom I barely knew, still talking low. How much of the ringing around of relatives and friends did she have to do, or was I the only one on her shoulders, given that her parents didn't speak to me? At least they'd been kind enough not to leave me to find out from a newspaper obituary column or some death-notice mail-out. That was good of them.

"Thanks, Sandy. Thanks. Tell your parents . . ." but I didn't finish. What was I going to say, Well, now after all these years you're free of me?

"They're here," Ma said. "Hurry up. Come on, hurry." She fussed with my jacket and straightened my tie for me. "Go on, Salvatore, what are you waiting for?"

I had to welcome the ex-premier and his wife into Ristorante Notte e Giorno so there was no room for tears. There was only the sort of numbness that comes with any sad news. I would have liked to lie down but my ma, as yet ignorant of the fate of Enrico Belpasso, pushed me out of that noisy kitchen. Smiling nicely now, shaking hands, I got our two locally famous visitors seated at the secluded table we liked to reserve for them or visiting supermodels, should one or two fall out of the blue.

"Your mother's here tonight?"

"When she heard you were coming—tell you what, order something special, make her happy."

"I was thinking of that dish, the really Sicilian one. *Falsomagro?*"

"Oh, yes. That's only on when she's here. She won't trust anyone else with her recipe. Go ahead and order it, that'd make her happiest of all. You know, the name actually means falsely lean, because the very lean beef that surrounds it hides the rich filling inside. I hope you're hungry, it'll be enough for two. We'll give you a dish so you can take the rest to your children. Falsomagro is the proper Italian way of saying it, but in Sicily, where the dish originates—from Palermo, my mother says—the dialect makes it fassumauru. Hear the difference? It's like different countries. The only thing is, fassumauru takes a while."

"Are we in a hurry?" The ex-premier looked at his wife. "Not tonight. Let's have a look what chiantis you've got."

"*Subito, commendatore,*" I said, because he liked it when I played up.

He laughed but there was that new stone of unexpected sadness that kept me from laughing too. Maybe I'd learn from him how to laugh when things were tough. He'd lost his position, and his party had lost government only months ago, after only two terms in office, but he seemed all right. Better than that, really, for there was a joy in him. Maybe it was the joy that comes with freedom. It pleased me to think that he liked to come to my restaurant, despite the fact that it was his government and its late-eighties inquiries and trials that had shut down La Notte and other Brisbane places like it. The rest of the story was that Tony Solero and a few other people running similar businesses went behind bars, where most still remained. Even the police commissioner wasn't spared, not after so many police officials—including Pietro Pierucci—saved themselves and told how bean and beer money aplenty made its way into his office and then into his many family subsidiaries. No more than a handful of private citizens and police officers eventually went to jail but it was enough to unravel the fabric of The Joke. Pierucci for one escaped a prison sentence because of his blabbing, and then he went into permanent hiding, and the era was over.

"Maybe I'll have a beer to start. What about you, darling?" he asked, looking at his wife, fingering the wine card.

This man's government had tried to take corruption out of the police force and had closed down all the so-called secret casinos and brothels of Brisbane. They had less success in revealing the true nature of shady business deals with the old government and of how contracts were supposed to be awarded to companies with the biggest brown paper bags of money, but the mold was now broken and that was a fact. So maybe Brisbane was a little less ashamed of itself. Some people mourned the changes but the larger proportion were relieved that the old world was finally gone. This ex-premier who was so crazy about my ma's recipes had overseen the dismantling of a highly refined system of corruption, yet a few years later he was out of business himself. It was as if angels had led him to one great duty and then released him.

"You're putting on weight, Sam."

I shrugged, always a little embarrassed by the spare tire the restaurant trade and my thirties had put around my middle. "Maybe I should open a gym upstairs."

"I'd be a customer up there—nowadays, I mean."

The ex-premier laughed again when he said that and so did his wife. They knew the history of this place as well as I did. Tony Solero's La Notte upstairs area had been a well-worn den of hard beds and cheap white towels and lemon-fresh refresher towelettes. It all came out in hearings and the newspapers reported every salacious detail, which kept the city and even the country amused for ages.

On the whole it was still a good night, in that way that most of our nights were good. Ma stayed with the cooks in the kitchen but she came out later to see how her special dish went down and have a glass of marsala with our well-known guests. When they left she saw them to the door and right to their taxi, and there was a lot of banter on the evening breeze, creeping up the front stairs like a welcome little visitor who wants to surprise you. My papà was keeping himself busy with minor tasks like stacking dishes and cutlery for washing, though we had plenty of university-student kitchenhands. When he grew tired of making those kids jump for their ten-fifty an hour he went and cleaned the rubbish bins in the alley out back, having been too shy to go inside the dining room, with all its white and red, its candles in glass bowls and soft music, and shake a famous man's hand with his hard-as-old-leather, garbage-soiled own.

After I told her the news Ma said, "Go home and don't worry about Enrico Belpasso. He's all right now. We should all be blessed with such a long life."

"I don't know, I should stay."

"Go on—who needs you here?"

I'D BE HOME a good two hours earlier than usual. That was the round of running a restaurant, late to bed and waking up at five or five-thirty to get the best produce from the fruit and vegetable market and the fish market. After that there were the mid-morning preparations for lunch and then its heady rush, a little business work in the afternoons, then home and maybe a nap for an hour before the children came in from school. I liked to play with them for a while, or cuddle up and take a look at their homework tasks and hear about their latest adventures. Then it was a shower and fresh clothes and a big fresh smile to get the long evening started. It was good work and paid all the bills, and my ma enjoyed doing something better than hanging around her home looking for something new to clean. My papà too, he liked to be out of his retirement, which had only left him bored and morose for years. The dining room was big and so needed plenty of staff, and with my recent hiring of an experienced food-industry business manager, Larry Rowe, things got bigger and at the same time more streamlined. He'd counted up everything I'd been doing wrong and put them all right. We could seat a hundred and fifty now. Two hundred when we were specially set up for functions like twenty-firsts, engagements, and weddings. He made me take out ads in style magazines and invite food critics along. He got me to write little Sicilian food hints and simple recipes for all the local newspapers. With so many people coming in I was used to those occasions when strangers would arrive with awe in their faces and say something like, But I met my wife/husband/ex-wife/ex-husband for the first time here ten years ago—more! When it was the best bloody nightclub in Brisbane!

Nobody recognized me, not in that way of being a face out of the past. Sometimes, though, people wanted to talk about how the Fitzgerald Inquiry had closed the previous establishment on this site. La Notte's name remained as a piece of local folklore. Tony Solero, during the lead-up to the trial and then in the court case, had achieved some notoriety too. Maybe if he hadn't kicked me out early I would have been a part of this history, but luck had been on my side. Tony's picture was in the papers and his house staked out by current-affairs programs, and most journalists had tried to make him out to be a mafia kingpin with his fingers in every illegal pie. Tony Solero wasn't alone in the whole city-of-sleaze thing of course, but he'd been the youngest to go down, the most good-looking, the one who was the fastest with some ready-made-for-quoting quip. That made him a star. On television and in his nice suits he looked like an up-and-coming executive or political candidate. Once, for a joke, he'd even used the line made famous by Giulio Andreotti, the Italian Christian Democrats politician who was twenty times a minister and seven times Italy's prime minister, a man whose very blood was corruption: *"Ma io sono più innocente di Gesù Cristo!* But I'm more innocent than Jesus Christ!"

No wonder Tony got so much attention, but in the end everyone understood he was just a young, shortsighted businessman who'd paid a police bagman to keep all the other police from raiding his popular nightspot-brothel-casino. He lost his money and his properties, and through something funny he'd been maneuvering with his investment lawyer, this site came to me. Like the police commissioner, chains of ownership and absolutely legal trusts went every which way, and my original investment in La Notte, which I'd never withdrawn, left me with a gold mine. Our deal was that when he'd done his time we'd work something out. It was never any firmer than that and didn't have to be. Tony Solero was still a brother. When I visited him one time three years into his sentence he said, "Maybe when I get out of here I'll retire to a secluded beach somewhere, just like that cunt Pierucci," and though he wouldn't talk about it anymore than that I knew that somehow, even with all the backstabbing and informing, they were in contact again.

It was hard not to keep reflecting on these things while I waited out front for my taxi. On this street corner had stood Nocturne and then La Notte and now Ristorante Notte e Giorno. Here, daily, there passed all the cars and the buses and the bicycles, the schoolchildren and the office workers, the Spring Hill bums who had to scrounge for their breakfasts. They were Gabriella Zazò and now Enrico Belpasso too. They were me and my family and they were themselves. Everyone cast shadows within and without, and I liked it that all these years later I was still so tied to this place where my life took such strange turns. For all the bad, right here is where I understand hopes and dreams. Right here is where I know that death isn't a zero and a life is never forgotten. This corner makes me believe that every daybreak burning up the horizon is worth having.

And in believing such a thing, it's easy to keep the heart for love, what do you say, Gabriella?

"This Girl Caressed by Fire"

IRINA WAS ASLEEP ON the sofa.

A script was open and half covering her face, her glasses had half fallen off. She didn't wake when I used my key to come inside our many-roomed old timber house, and instead of going straight to her I went to the kitchen and poured myself a glass of water from the tap, drinking it and another, until Enrico Belpasso's pinched-up, 101-year-old face wasn't in my eyes anymore. When I was standing beside Irina she was still asleep and even when I squinted I couldn't read the title of her photocopied playscript. I eased her glasses away and put them on and read the words *Blood Wedding* by Federico García Lorca.

"They typecast me," Irina said, looking up, yawning a little, sleep still in her eyes.

I sat with her and gave back her glasses. "He-llo. What do you mean they typecast you?"

"The bastards. I'm a Spanish mother."

"It's what you do."

"The director's going to play with the text so that I can be Death as well, which appears as a beggar woman. That's the part I'm really look-ing forward to."

"But they did cast you?"

"I waited up to tell you."

I took her face in my hands and covered her in kisses.

Irina thought all of my emotion was for her news. "It's a full season. A real run. Two and a half weeks with Saturday matinees and every-thing. I'm finally going to get a chance." She looked at the wall clock. "You're early, Sam." She looked again, taking off her glasses.

"Enrico Belpasso died, it happened today. I just wanted to come home."

"Oh," Irina said, "did you want to go over?"

"As if they'd want me there. He doesn't need me anyway, not now." Irina loosened my tie and unbuttoned my collar for me. "One hundred and one. You can't ask for a lot more than that."

"Still, it's hard."

"Yes."

Irina said, "I wonder if the person who rang, I wonder if it was about that."

"Who rang?"

"Someone. She didn't leave a message."

"That was Sandy, their daughter. The old man's granddaughter. I don't really know her. She got me at the restaurant."

"Well," Irina sighed, "come on. You'll feel better after a good night's sleep."

I was frowning, glum as a lost dog. "How are the girls?"

"Today, fine. No sniffles, headaches, tummy aches, or fights at school. Homework done. All their dinner eaten and in bed at the right time."

"They wanted you to enjoy your news."

Irina smiled because we both knew selflessness was never going to be a defining trait in three children under the age of ten. She said a little sadly, "Well, you know our rule, tonight it can't apply. It'll have to wait."

That woke me up. That made me aware of where I was and who I was and what my world was all about. Enrico Belpasso was of something else, not of this place, not of this home.

Our rule was that when good things happened they had to be celebrated immediately. Irina always liked to say that to let something good that happens pass half unnoticed was to tell yourself that you didn't care. Soon you wouldn't care—and getting work in a real production was something Irina had waited a long time for. Her name was with an agency these days, who'd found her two no-budget student films to act in and one television commercial where only her hands were shown, slicing a steak with a very special, sharp-for-a-lifetime knife. With others she'd staged *A Midsummer Night's Dream* in New Farm Park and then a very haphazard, loud, and pedestrian-interrupted *The Crucible* on the steps of the City Hall. Since giving up singing and having her throat problems attended to by surgery—two operations to remove tiny polyps that were all benign—her life had been bordered by the twins and then our last, the four-year-old. And me and the restaurant, which I kept her out of except for nice occasions when it wouldn't really be work for her.

In spare time, which Irina made by using a combination of family, friends, and teenage girls who liked to baby-sit while they studied or watched our television, she'd immersed herself in acting lessons. She read everything on the subject. She went to night classes. Then she tried more advanced techniques with a friend she'd made who was an early-eighties NIDA graduate and mid-eighties soapie actress, until her looks went away and she discovered that that was her heyday and it was gone.

In the refrigerator there was a bottle of something non-vintage but French, and Irina must have splurged on it straight after hearing the news of her casting. I thought Enrico Belpasso, looking down from Heaven, wouldn't mind. Maybe he'd see us making a celebration of his life.

Irina was thinking the same thing. "To Enrico Belpasso."

"To Lorca's dream actress."

"What I really wish is that I was young enough to play the part of the bride. She gets some great speeches. Listen to this." Irina put her glass down and shuffled some pages. " 'Leave her! I want her to know that I'm clean, that even though I'm mad they can bury me and not a single man will have looked at himself in the whiteness of my breasts!' Don't you love it?"

"Let me see the whiteness of your breasts."

Irina liked that. We sat close, drinking. Dead old man or not it was good to be home early. I felt better. Irina could do that to me, make me feel better when a weight was dragging me down.

She said, "Do you mind about the rehearsing? There'll be a lot."

"Oh, we'll get organized. We can get all the help we need, and when things go wrong I'll just stay home and Ma and Larry can run the restaurant. Or Ma can stay here for when the girls come home. And you know how good my father is with the picking up and setting down. He won't mind going backward and forward from the school."

Irina fumbled with the playscript. "The mother and Death, what more would I want? They'll get some unbelievable honey to play the bride and I'll look like an old bag."

"No."

"I'm supposed to be an old bag. Listen to the poor bride again. 'And I was going with your son, who was like a child of cold water, and the other one sent hundreds of birds that blocked my path and left frost on the wounds of this poor withered woman, this girl caressed by fire.'"

With a sinking sensation I looked at Irina. She might have been happy about this turn in her career and she might have been drinking champagne but she was thinking about something else. I knew why she'd read that section. Speaking of Enrico Belpasso brought Gabriella Zazò back into this home.

"For God's sake," I said. "I *have* forgotten her."

Irina said, "You haven't, Sam, and I don't want you to lie about it. That's all there is, I don't want you to tell me lies."

So there was nothing to feel low about.

Irina took another sip from her glass. She brought her face close to mine and kissed me. She wanted to know that I loved her and her alone, this lovely woman who'd promised to stay a week, maybe two, absolutely no more. Three children later and she was still with me. Her golden-brown hair was cut short as mine. Her waist had thickened. Those hips that had been so heavenly were three-children matronly, yet still as beautiful, still as delicious, and I loved her for how she used to look and how she looked now and how she would keep changing. She had big eyes, a big smile, big lips, big breasts, and a big behind. Men stared at her in the street; that had never changed. The other thing that wouldn't change was that big heart of hers. She was forty-one now. I blessed the day I met her and every day we spent together. She'd never left me, not in the highs and lows of a decade. She'd stayed and she wanted to stay some more. With me.

With *me*.

Sometimes I compared Gabriella Zazò with Irina. It was something I couldn't control. I would think of Gabriella and how she had written that she couldn't trust me. That I hadn't earned it. I'd think of the way she'd disappeared and sometimes I blamed her, I really blamed her. Hate would rise in me, and a rage, and I would wish her dead even while knowing she already was. The mind plays games. Gabriella herself would walk into my dreaming sometimes, sometimes when I'd been thinking of her and thinking of Irina, and she would say in English, with her sweet Sicilian accent clear as it ever was, Don't you dare compare me. Don't you dare compare me, you bastard.

Yet the other truth was that sometimes Gabriella just didn't measure beside my wife, no matter how many caramel-flavored kisses she gave me in my sleep or how far she flew me with her wings, over those starry cities of Heaven.

Now we were kissing on the couch like kids, Irina and I.

The magic happened, shortly, in the way it sometimes does in conjugal life. We'd had enough to drink, and some snacks, and I'd gone into the bathroom to clean my teeth for bed. Somehow Irina was in there with me, her heavy body already completely naked. Somehow she was sitting herself up on the bathroom basin beside the sink with its still-running tap, and her thighs were open, and she pulled me by the waist to stand between them. She smiled, her arms entwining around my neck. Her skin was a fine light chocolate. My slow moves seemed to bring me closer and closer to her heart, but also closer to my own broken-nosed face in the mirror behind her head. It was comical, to be making love like that, with my own crooked and dented nose so close to me. It was comical but wonderful too, as if, in Lorca's words, I were seeing myself in the whiteness of her breasts, though hers weren't white but dusky, with dark strong nipples. In the glass the normally olive-skinned me was red, flushed; mid-thirties features with a ruined nose never properly fixed and silver in the black hair—but I could look at myself these days. I could look myself straight in the eye and not be revolted. I could look at Irina and know love. I could look at Natalie and Annie and Lara and feel my soul swelling.

Irina held me, her teeth grinding, then her beautiful mouth was clamping to mine, her arms trying to crack the top of my spine, and when I heard the words "I can't sleep" I thought Irina sent the thought into my mind by telepathy.

As one, we twisted ourselves to look at the bathroom door.

Which was open now, and with our littlest, four-year-old Lara, standing there in a pink cotton nightie. She was rubbing her eyes and saying again, in her baby voice, "I can't sleep. Mummy had a bad dream. Daddy there a old man. Horrible old man."

I Wish I Knew Her

I STAYED IN THE background during the service and the electric whirring that rolled the loved one in his walnut-stain-shiny coffin into the furnace and the fire.

Many of the people in the chapel knew me and I them, but I exchanged few words with these folk who'd been so much of my life back in the New Farm days. It's fair to say that these people kept away from me. I nodded to Gabriella's mother and father and from a distance they nodded back to me, but it was as if they were affirming, in case I had any doubts, Salvatore, don't think we're about to welcome you.

The passage of time hadn't been kind to them. They looked far older than my parents, far more tired, far more worn down by the weight of the sky. They had the look of people starving, and who wouldn't understand after what they'd had to bear? Gabriella's older brother Michael was there with his wife and children, and his mobile telephone went off while the priest said the words "Lord we beseech you" and then again in the middle of the Ave Maria. Once, in a supermarket aisle, him twenty-one and me already a flop at nineteen, he'd said, "Fucken cunt," and then moved on into the dog-food and pest-control aisle.

Sandy Zazò was the most incongruous of everyone gathered in this little nondenominational chapel. I saw that like Gabriella it was as if at least one of her parents wasn't her parent at all. Sandy was nearly six feet tall. In a bunch of Sicilians that made her an Amazon. She was very striking, with her long, long legs in a straight black dress without adornments. Her lipstick was the opposite of demure, as bright red as the best tomatoes I purchased by the carton for my restaurant, and both her ears were clipped with trails of little studs that made you think you could tear along the dotted line. When she turned a certain way the light caught some kind of precious stone, small and delicate as a hope, pinned in her nose. Her hair was naturally jet-black and whereas once it used to flow in luxuriant childish locks now it was short-spiked and dyed fire-engine red, the same as her lips. She even had some kind of eyeshadow in the same hue. For all the strangeness of her appearance she held both of her parents as if she would never let them go. She was the one who started the congregation crying when the coffin slid away.

I N T H E S U N S H I N E, a green plain descended to the main road, where I'd hail a taxi.

While I waited alone everyone started to emerge into the crematorium grounds. Watching the hugs, the handshakes, the standing shoulder to shoulder of them all, I wished, I really wished, that I could have been up there doing the same. The roadside was an outcast's place. There was the noise of traffic and the pungency of belching fumes but worse than that was the absolute apartness of the position. It was unfair—then, as if she had the ability to hear bad thoughts, Sandy Zazò was walking down that green slope bordered by beds of daisies and jasmine and azaleas. Her black dress was a little too short for mourning and she seemed all flesh, her thighs long and white and her arms ivory and slender.

"I wanted to speak to you," she said, giving me a quick kiss on the cheek that I didn't expect. "Thanks for coming."

"It was good you rang."

"Everyone will be at the house in a little while. Do you—"

"I have to get back to the restaurant."

"Not even for a coffee?"

"Not today."

Sandy said, "If you made the first step."

I said, "I don't believe that."

Instead of being put off, Sandy took my arm. Her manner was poised. She didn't have to search for words. She knew what she wanted to say.

"I'm sorry that we never had the chance to know each other. My grandfather, well, he really loved you. He wasn't allowed to mention your name around the house, but I knew how he felt."

I watched her for a trace of Gabriella, but there wasn't one. If anything, Gabriella's presence was clearer in me than her.

"You're trembling," she said.

"Funerals. They . . ."

"You did love him?"

"I don't know. I knew him a long time."

"He loved you, Sam." Sandy squeezed my arm and was warmly against me. "Have you heard I'll be moving to Sydney soon? Probably not. We're finding it too hard to get recognition here. Our manager's got us a lease on a terrace in Newtown and we're all going to move in. My parents are *dying*."

I didn't have a clue what she was talking about. It was hard to settle myself down. The funeral to me meant the end of everything that had to do with Gabriella Zazò. No, it was even more than that. I wished that like Sandy I'd been able to sit in that chapel and weep openly but I'd thought that everyone would have known what I was really weeping for, the true end of my adolescence—even if I was mid-thirties. Enrico Belpasso's flashes of remembrance about his granddaughter had faded back into *la notte* years ago. The gorgeous lights he'd said he lived in had dimmed. We'd never really mentioned Gabriella again, not after that night of his turn and the story he'd told me about the old bomb shelter under the Zazò house. Whenever I brought up her name after that he'd stiffen and go silent. It was as if, in remembering that place again, it hurt him too much. In fact, he became very pensive and stayed that way till here, the end of his days. He'd taken to being a grumbler and even more of a loner; many times his welcome to me was forced and I had the impression he would rather have stayed alone. His thoughts were clouded and troubled but he was still a storyteller, and the days when things were easier between us he would sit on a bench and watch my three girls playing chasey on some sultry Sunday afternoon, and he'd tell a little tale of Sicily that didn't involve Gabriella. Still, the old man was a rope to my past and now that was broken I felt heavy inside.

I kept an eye on the traffic for a taxi; that was all I wanted, to get away now and return into my safe world. Sandy made me nervous because her grip on my arm was like an anchor to something I knew I should let go of.

She said, "I wish I could talk to you."

"I have to find a taxi."

"I have to talk to you about my sister."

"Why do you have to?"

She pressed closer, her breasts firmly against my arm, using them the way some women do, aggressively, and it still felt good.

"All I know is what my family tells me, but I've got a different feeling about her. I want a sister. I want my sister. I just want to know what she was like. Michael's nice but we can't talk and my nieces and nephews are great but I feel cheated. I wish I could talk to you about her."

I tried to move my arm but Sandy wasn't letting go.

"Please. Wouldn't that be all right, Sam?"

In that place, on that subject, with everyone who despised me so close by and watching, Gabriella was the last thing I wanted to speak about. Gabriella was gone. Sandy knew my discomfort but she didn't let that put her off; she didn't even let herself wilt under the disapproving stares coming from outside the chapel. If it had concerned any other subject, that trait would have made me like her more. But stories of Gabriella Zazò were off limits to me. That was my old, old promise to myself, and it was a promise that had let me find a real life with Irina and my children.

So I said, in that easy way of deflection, and freeing my arm from the firm warmth inside her dress, "You've really grown. I remember someone telling me you wanted to be a model."

I noticed the color of Sandy's eyes. They were green the way Gabriella's had been, but perfectly, even scarily so. They were without flecks or imperfections in them, and being so close I saw that she had contacts in as well. Then I realized it was the contacts that were so green and that I'd known all along her eyes were as brown as mine.

"No, modeling's too superficial for me. What a terrible way to have to live. I like eating. When I was thirteen maybe."

"What then? The thing about going to Sydney?"

"How famous do I have to be before I can get your attention? I'm in a band. Electronic ambient dance. We play everywhere. Pop Party?"

I shook my head.

"Haven't you heard our singles? They're on the independent stations. Our last one was number sixty-six on the Triple Z top one hundred for last year." She was looking at me curiously, trying to see if any of this rang a bell with me, which it didn't. "Well, so much for my ego. You should come and see us."

"I guess you can see I don't really know anything about music."

Sandy looked glum. It was obvious that "electronic ambient dance" and Pop Party were everything to her.

"So—this band, it's an all-girl sort of thing?"

"No, the turntable guy is a guy."

I had no idea what that meant either.

"And his name is Guy. He's my boyfriend."

"Right. But aren't you—?"

"I'm eighteen," Sandy said with a trace of defensiveness. It only lasted two words. "But yeah, I am the youngest in the band. By a long way, really. Guy and I have been going out fourteen months. That's when I joined. We've got a contract with a record company and everything, and we'll be touring nonstop for like a year or even two. Stop looking like that, Sam. It's really great. If it works out we'll be recording in January. I write the lyrics. I'm the singer. The album's completely worked out in my head. Guy's nearly your age and he's got lots of experience with producing. We're going to live together. The others in the band will be living with us too but it's sort of romantic, isn't it? Do you know what it's going to be called, our album I mean?"

"No."

"*I Wish I Knew Her.*"

Yes, despite her ham-fisted little seduction tricks I liked her. It was just that I wasn't sure what she wanted to seduce me into. Sandy was young and what she was living was a mystery to me, and her band and her interstate move were probably breaking the hearts of her parents all over again, but she herself was very easy to like. She had enthusiasm, an eighteen-year-old's optimism, and I wondered if that was something you could really hang on to all your life. Looking at my girls playing, sleeping, eating, running like the wind, I always found myself hoping that I would be able to teach them how to stay so fresh-faced and so open, so believing of the world and the good that was around every corner.

Sandy looked straight into me now and I was unsettled once again. There was something just a little too knowing in those fakely green and unquestionably sensuous eyes of hers.

I had to escape or succumb. That's the power of femininity, even when possessed by an eighteen-year-old. Sandy radiated a vibrancy, in that particular way that only comes from someone so consciously, so conspicuously, sexy. It wasn't so much in the extraordinary way she looked but in the impression she gave that she was prepared to swallow life whole. I thought of Enrico Belpasso, now no more than invisible smoke particles dissipated in a blue sky, and Gabriella a set of memories, and Sandy right here and so different to all of that. She crackled with the electricity of life and because of that I wanted to tell her not to worry about her sister. I wanted to tell her that she should stop this futile wishing that she knew her, because it was nothing but a romantic fantasy about an older-wiser-dead sibling. It was a very gothic idea: Oh God, if only I'd known her, uttered by a beautiful and tragic mouth. What difference would it make? I really wanted to say that she should wave sweet adieu to all things and all people long gone, even if it was her own flesh and blood. For Sandy everything was ahead. There was no Book of Fire already written for her. I wanted to say to her, as one day I would say to each of my girls until I was absolutely certain they understood, Never look behind, my darling, forget what's over with and go on. Just please go on.

When I saw a taxi cruising I shot out my hand and waved until it came to the curb.

"Did you love her, Sam? Did you really love my sister?"

"We were children. We were younger than you are now. Who knows what we felt?"

"Did you used to be alone with her? Did you kiss her? Did you used to really kiss her?"

"Sandy—good luck with everything."

"I wish I could talk to you about Gabriella. Let me ring you. Can I ring you at home?"

"I'm pretty busy." I had the taxi's yellow door open and was climbing into the back seat. I said to the driver, "Spring Hill," then, seated, I looked out the window at Sandy Zazò leaning there, an Amazon of long legs and a piercing gaze made hot by the sunlight and all her own scarlet hues.

She said again, "Can I? Please? Give me the number before you go. Only the stupid restaurant's in the book."

Irina and I kept a silent number at home so that people wanting to know about the restaurant, or wanting me to write more silly food and Sicily articles for free street magazines, couldn't bother us.

"So what is it? I've got an eidetic memory. Do you know what that is? Test me. Just say it now, Sam, I won't forget it."

The taxi pulled away and I didn't look back or wave. Sandy could hear about the sister who'd died before she was born from someone other than me. I would not relive it. My new life had made me greedy—

greedy to keep it. The years of equivocation and wandering were over, and bless every star in the heavens because I had Irina and Natalie and Annie and Lara, all my women—all my women who would never disappear.

Then, despite myself, despite wanting to push all thoughts of helping Sandy deep underground, another thought struck me. It struck me as we approached Ristorante Notte e Giorno in the blinding glare of the afternoon. Heat rose from the street. The view of squat office buildings and people lumbering in the hard light shimmered in that haze. In the un-air-conditioned taxi I sweated into my shirt and collar.

But Sandy didn't need to ask me my home number. Especially with the memory she claimed to have. For hadn't she already rung me there, the day the old man died, and spoken to Irina before she finally found me at the restaurant?

A Gift Out of Nowhere

IRINA'S REHEARSALS STARTED A few days after that and in the way that goes with family life everyone pitched in to take up her absence. My ma, my papà, friends, and hired babysitters, me—at first we all seemed to become ridiculously occupied with the simple procedures of getting the girls to bed, to school, to dance classes, to tennis lessons, to music practice, to the park, to the next kid's party, to the next sleepover, to wherever and whatever came next.

Until we found a rhythm that worked.

I left most of the running of the restaurant to Larry Rowe and let the cleverer staff loose on the morning markets, and in a couple of weeks discovered just how little Notte e Giorno needed me. A funny feeling took over. I started to look forward to not having to leave the house at five in the morning and instead being able to hover around the kitchen making sandwiches and washing pieces of fruit and packing those three lime-green plastic lunchboxes with extra things, such as carrots and celery. It was a lot like when I'd been living as a prince in that beautiful St. Lucia apartment, only this time it was better because I had a purpose. While Irina slept in I'd make the girls their breakfasts and check that their faces were clean and their hair neat and their uniforms fresh and ironed. Just before leaving they'd go in and tease their mother in her bed, then Ma and Papà would arrive in their car to take them to school. Once the house was cleared and the kitchen cleaned I'd bring Irina a cup of tea and slices of toast with honey and jam, and she'd be propped up with her pillows, the script and a pen in her hands.

"Listen," she'd say, and give me some lines. "Does that sound right?"

The *Blood Wedding* rehearsals started later in the day and went into the night, and Irina would arrive home either in a state of exhilaration, preoccupation, or sheer exhaustion. I loved seeing her so connected to the outside world again. She'd always had a brightness about her, especially when she was with the children, but now it was as if she'd recaptured that zest that had made her so exquisite to watch singing on the stage. The mornings became our time, and with the restaurant looked after and the girls gone until three, and me in no hurry to leave, Irina and I took to making love more slowly and sweetly than we ever had since first meeting. On the one hand we would indulge ourselves like randy teenagers, but on the other hand these randy teenagers had absorbed enough of life to know that there was plenty of time to explore all of the physical senses.

Later, Irina would sit in the garden with the sun on her face. I'd watch her from a window, watch her not reading those pages or making little sideline marks with her pen but instead gazing at the treetops, at the colors of the flowers she'd planted, at the vegetable garden beds that come Sundays and her other days off she'd till with a hand shovel in order to root out the weeds. Some days she worked there with my papà, him in ragged trousers and stinking of stale sweat and her in a bright sundress or a halter top and shorts. I never loved her more than in these moments. Later she would disappear to her rehearsals and the house would be quiet and creaking without my women.

Maybe it was those idle hours between when Irina left for the day and my ma and papà brought the girls home in the afternoon that made things turn. Those idle hours when I should really have gone to the restaurant but more often than not spent wandering in the house and gardens and playing old vinyl records and reading old books.

Because it was during one such afternoon that I opened the front door to go check the mail and sitting on the doorstep by the welcome mat was a child's toy, a plastic kaleidoscope. There were always other people's children running through our house, and toys that didn't belong to the girls getting mixed up with their own, but when I bent down and picked that thing up I knew it was meant for me. I held it to my eye and saw all the swirly-whirly crazy colors and that was enough to make my head go dreamy with memories. Everything came back to me and perspiration soaked my shirt and my trousers as if I had a sudden fever. I had to sit down but I couldn't sit down so I left the house and paced a shopping center instead. That night I gave the kaleidoscope to Lara to play with and she promptly broke it and started to cry, and the next day when I was alone again in the house I did what I was crazy to do and picked up the telephone and rang Sandy Zazò.

H ER VOICE ON the telephone sounded very subdued.

I said, "When do you leave?"

"Sunday," she replied, "if I'm going. We're all supposed to be driving down."

"Why wouldn't you be going?"

"I don't know."

There was a pause that said she didn't want to add anything else.

"All right. I've got something to ask you. It might sound a bit strange, but did you come here, Sandy? I mean, did you leave something on my doorstep?"

"No."

"Then who did?"

"How would I know?"

"I think you know."

That was the prompting she needed. I had to remember she was only an eighteen-year-old kid. Sandy started to speak softly, as if she were afraid of being overheard. It was like the old whispering Gabriella and I used to do as a game, where you put your mouth right next to the other's ear and whisper straight in.

"Sam, do you believe there's one special place where you can see the world completely? Not just the world either, but—I don't know how to explain it—the universe? Do you believe it's possible to find a place like that? Do you think you could see everything, like you were God or something?"

"Sandy—"

"And if you had a place like that and then you lost it, Sam, wouldn't you turn yourself inside out to find another one?"

Sandy started to cry. She really wept, and an ice was growing in my belly because if I didn't understand what Sandy was saying then no one else ever would.

"Where is she, Sandy? Have you seen her?"

She didn't answer. I heard her sniffling some more.

"All right. I want you to come and see me. Do you understand me, Sandy?"

"I wanted to see you all along."

"I didn't understand before but now I do. You should have explained. Come and see me."

"When?"

"Today—no, tomorrow. Tomorrow, that's better."

"Where?"

I didn't want Sandy to come to my home. I didn't want to have a conversation like this here. I didn't want to meet her in a coffee shop and I didn't want to meet her on a street corner like some illicit lover. The next day was a restaurant day off.

"Notte e Giorno. Midafternoon. It'll be quiet."

"Three?"

"Three o'clock."

I put down the receiver because there was nothing more to be said by telephone. I stayed where I was and tried to pull myself together but that wasn't going to work, so finally I stood and went into the little room of the house that I used as an office. In an obscure daylight of curtains drawn and papers strewn, I dug under my bookcase for the secret place where Gabriella's diary had remained untouched but not forgotten for the years and years that my life had been so blessed.

Dear Diary

Gabriella's Book of Fire

I READ SEXUS the way Salvatore wanted me to and it was nothing, just a man bragging about the women he took to bed, and somehow Salvatore sees something about life in this. In the detailed descriptions of sex and even rape. I can't lower myself to call any of it lovemaking. Not one episode has a thing to do with love. If that's what love is supposed to be in the adult world, well, *vaffanculu a tutti*.

It all had to do with a man who blustered his thing could swing heavy as a hammer and that an erection is a lump of lead with wings. What have I missed? I ask you that, Salvatore. What can't I see? This man who wrote this book, he doesn't aim for much, that's what I think, and so to Hell with him and others like him; just to describe the rites of the flesh, and the twitches and moans in people's faces, and to make gullible readers call this something of the spirit and the senses, and sell, sell, sell, buy, buy, buy, this surely is evil somehow, isn't it? Or at least a most excellently discharged deception. Am I too stupid to understand,

and should I therefore break my pens and never set anything to a page again?

Then there was the next thing, a completely opposite thing. It's funny how a person like Salvatore can think that he is putting you in the one direction and his very act pushes you somewhere completely different.

Because that book made me sick and so I had to seek out something better.

In the New Farm municipal library last Saturday morning, where I go alone when all the boys and girls of our area have gathered together with their bicycles or whatever and are making their plans for the weekend, I found something by a writer born in Buenos Aires, Argentina. It was a book called *The Aleph and Other Stories*, translated into English from the original Spanish. I don't know what made me pick that particular book up. I don't know what made me interested once I flicked through the pages. Maybe it was the simple writing and the biographical note that said Mr. Borges, the writer, was born in 1899. Maybe I liked the idea of reading something written by a man born so close to the time of my nonno, who'd lived through the same eras. Or maybe I impressed myself by knowing that the Aleph is the first letter of the Hebrew alphabet, for I'm sure I was the only person in that library who knew something as obscure as that.

When I was home I didn't read any of the other stories, only the one, the main one, "The Aleph." It puzzled me and still does. This is a strange little tale and I discovered that the title meant something very different to what I'd arrogantly decided it must have been.

THE STORY STARTS as if it's about many matters—unrequited love, for instance—but the real point of it is that a pompous poet by the name of Carlos Argentino Daneri tells the writer, Borges, about a place he has discovered that is really all places. He calls this the Aleph and it exists in his house. The Aleph can be found under the nineteenth step of the staircase into Daneri's basement, and to see it you have to lie down there in a special position. So Borges does this. To his utter amazement he truly does see a phenomenal thing. It turns out to be a sphere two or three centimeters in diameter and inside it he sees, well, the whole universe. Past, present, and future too, all at once, and as a living thing with every facet of existence perfectly clear and visible all at the same time. Borges sees the earth and the sea and all their creatures, he sees all people and all things, he sees the fine detail of countries and cities and he sees a spider's web inside a pyramid. This made me so excited to read. The possibilities of this really made my head swim. This writer who is writing sees everything, everything, everything. He even sees himself, and the rotting flesh and bones of the woman he loved, and he sees us too, the readers of his story. Borges says that in the Aleph he sees what everyone has dreamed of, "the inconceivable universe."

The story confused me and it frightened me and it thrilled me. I read it three more times and that didn't stop me thinking about it all day and all night. The next morning Salvatore was at the door and he had some plums for me. We felt so reckless because of each other's presence that we couldn't wait to run off to some secluded spot, and so instead we kissed against the invisible-making thick trunks of the great deciduous trees in our street. His lump of lead with wings was ready to take flight all right—but while our tongues crossed and our blood sang my mind started drifting somewhere else again. I dreamed about the possibility of a place that is all places.

Salvatore was bold. He squeezed my breasts hard and he jammed his hand down the front of my shorts, getting his fingers under the band of my briefs and touching my hair and dampening his fingers inside me. I shivered. I felt my spine turn to water and my flesh want to melt with that slight-light-slow touch of his fingertips. That was the first time he touched me there. I let him, I pushed against him, I discovered a mouth that was hungry for his fingers. Why did I let him do that? Why didn't I fight? Why did I want him so—finally? Because it came to me even while we were kissing what that old writer must have meant. His theme was an old-fashioned one. A prosaic one and even a foolishly romantic one—

like with things you find in the Bible, Old Testament and New. What he
was expressing was the sort of idea that you have to have lived many,
many years before you can have the true faith to believe in. It helps—I
think—if you've seen several wars.

He meant of course that we are ourselves and everyone. We are here
and everywhere. Our special individual moments are everyone's
moments. We live inside ourselves and we live through others, and
there's no such thing as death because not everyone dies at once, quite
the opposite, we all stay alive together forever, joined into eternity, and
that's why life is so much a mystery and so utterly beautiful it can ache
in your soul.

This was a step forward for me. I used to think that only good angels
and bad angels fight for supremacy inside of us, but to have the whole
cosmos—what a responsibility that is.

After that I set my mind to a series of tests. I inspected my house
inside and out, to see if there was an Aleph. There wasn't and so I felt
despair. There had to be one. I knew that there had to be one because of
all the thoughts that I'd been thinking and all the writing I'd been doing.
What's another word for writing? Feeling. And what I've been writing
I've been feeling from inside and out and so I deduce that this Aleph
thing has been calling me. It might be out in the street somewhere, or
under a petrol station pump, or by the ice-cream freezer in Mr. Harry's
corner shop, or lost in the outback where not a soul will ever discover it,
but what good would that do me? In those places I can never discover it.
So what chance do I have?

Days later I realized I was being foolish. I woke one morning knowing that the obvious was right in front of my eyes. Hadn't Mr. Borges's
story directed me? Hadn't he told that the Aleph was in that bombastic
poet's basement?

And so I knew where it was and that it was waiting for me. Maybe
it's been waiting for me or someone like me for hundreds of thousands
of years. I ran down there in my flannel pajamas, into my secret room
underneath the house and underneath the sad earth, and I stretched out
on the raggedy mattress to see. Soon I felt myself having to open like a

flower because that's the way it is down there. I let the shadows come falling down on me, and the weight of the sky again, making me raw with its fire, but I kept my eyes fixed up, looking for the sphere as described, searching for that tiny coin-sized span where all of existence was assembled. My mouth stretched but my teeth wanted to grind themselves together. The fire burned me raw, again, again, again.

But imagine if I'm right, that an Aleph is right here!

No need for me to imagine. In this Book of Fire I want to write it down. I saw it. I found it. I'm not two feet away from it right now, but of course it's impossible to see it from here because I'm at the wrong angle, my head's in the wrong position, I haven't set myself out just so.

In a second I'll put my pen down. I'll kneel on the mattress and then lie on my back and stretch myself out. No matter if the shadows come to fall onto me or if they don't come. No matter if the weight of the sky sinks down on me or if it doesn't. I'll look into God's face that is my face and yours Salvatore and the naked starving child who bathes in a stream of heat in Biafra and the faces of strangers who lived somewhere in history and were forgotten until now.

I'll see all of Enrico Belpasso's stories entwined with the stories of everyone we have known and the multitudes we haven't. My grandmother Fortunata will smile at me, and her mother, and her mother's mother, then back the other way I'll see my own babies wailing, and then theirs, and so on. I'll look at cities and countries and plains and fields I never imagined existed, and see the stars in their birth and the planets in their dying, and I'll go into them and discover if I do have a home, and one day I'll return—should you ever get to read this, Salvatore Capistrano—because with all this before me I know one thing, and it is that love and eternity are as real as hate and dying, so if you can just dream of me, and hold me in your heart, some day I'll be sent home from this inconceivable universe that an old writer has conjured for me, and having journeyed on angel's wings into the kaleidoscope that is Heaven, and followed the trail of your thoughts back to my home, whose will I ever be again, if not yours?

On the Art of Conjuring

"DIDN'T YOU SLEEP LAST night? Your eyes look terrible."

"Yeah—I got up and watched the PGA championship or something."

"Is that golf? You hate golf."

"I just couldn't sleep."

"I wish you'd come with me," Irina said while Natalie, Annie, and Lara sat in front of the television with their sandwiches, soft drinks, cereals, and playthings. Our daughters were in a communal sour mood and I wasn't in the mood to indulge them. They wanted to stay home and watch whatever rubbish was on television. Forever, they said. Irina, exasperated by the lot of them, the whingeing, the whining, the retreat into baby moods, was looking forward to getting out of the house. As if I could blame her. She said, "It's the first full run-through today and I'd really love you to see it. Maybe you could give me some pointers."

"You don't want me there. What do I know? I'd make you nervous."

Irina said, "You would. Yes, you would. It's my first run-through today and you're the one who couldn't sleep."

She came and kissed me, her own tiredness and lines now barely even there. That's what joy does to you, it lifts you up, just like that. My hands were sticky with the banana smoothies I was about to whiz and share out between the girls, but I would have loved to have run my palms all down Irina's back and over her buttocks.

Turning away from her wet kisses, I called out to the children, "Hey! You know what time it is? Are you still eating?"

Irina leaned against me, looked over her shoulder. "We won't have time, will we?"

"Thanks to them. Anyway, Ma and Pa Capistrano will be here soon."

The horn of their car blared as they came up the driveway.

My parents came inside. It was some day off for them. They were going to take their grandchildren to the school fête and spend the afternoon there with them. The girls didn't want to go because they thought it was a rip-off to have to spend a non-school day at the same place as always. I kissed my mother and my father and tried to press a fifty-dollar note into my papà's big workman's hand.

"What are you doing?" he said in Sicilian. "What's the matter with you?" He was offended, wouldn't take the money, and then he was nearly tripping over, what with the way the girls ran at him and ringed his legs, tightening their hold on him as if they were strangling vines. They were squealing. Angry at me, they showered all their enthusiasm on their grandfather. He shouted, top of his lungs, in English, "Wildcats! Devils!" and he started chasing them through the sudden pandemonium of the house.

The spell of petulance was broken. Papà was making them scream with delight.

"Until he loses his temper," Ma said, knowing grandfathers and grandchildren. Then, looking at my eyes: "What's the matter with you? What will you do today?"

IS IT ANY wonder that I denied Gabriella all these years? Is it any wonder that those last words she'd written down filled me with ten years' worth of bile? At her, for her, at the so-called inconceivable universe? I'd tried to understand and hadn't. In the end the anger was just too unreasoning and I had to let her go. Letting go of her let me make something new and worthwhile for myself. There was no such thing as an Aleph and I was certain that Gabriella had been speaking in a metaphor, in her own special code, for some purpose I didn't understand. She would have come back to her Book of Fire and explained it all but what had happened at Nocturne had taken away her chance.

No wonder I couldn't sleep.

Twenty years later her sister Sandy was coming to Notte e Giorno to hear what I knew about this, but the question that plagued my mind now was how did she know about it? At first, like the idiot I was, I'd jumped to the conclusion that Gabriella Zazò had waltzed back from the dead and had a nice long conversation with her sister, Sandy. Then, when I got over that, when I realized that after all these years I still hoped for the impossible, the obvious answer was that old man Enrico Belpasso had filled his second granddaughter with stories of Gabriella he had not told me, and so she knew things I didn't—and that scared me, it really scared me. Exactly why I couldn't say, but there were things about Gabriella's diary that had always troubled me, words that went together and said one thing so that I thought I read them right when in my heart I worried I read them wrong.

ſ ANDY WAS DUE at three.

I was at Notte e Giorno by midday and made myself a sandwich and a cup of freshly brewed coffee in the deserted, stainlessly steel–clean expanse of the kitchen. The air-conditioning wouldn't come on and it bothered me that no one had told me about this.

Then I found that the sandwich wouldn't go down my throat. The bread was cardboard and the fillings paper. I set it aside with the cup of coffee, which could go cold. It was like stone or rock or gravel that had been whizzed in a great blender and made into a thick and ugly liquid, and it had all the flavor of dirt. My temples throbbed and there was a sourness in the pit of my stomach that I couldn't explain. If only Irina and I could have had the chance that morning to be alone. The tension would be gone and the day would be lighter. I felt all at sea; dumbstruck, confused, anxious, all because Sandy would soon arrive.

Larry Rowe had dutifully laid out the receipts and the bills, the notations and the cash books, on the table in the office for me. The restaurant's silence was infinitely more oppressive than those myriad numbers, and from my comfortable leather chair I could see through my open doorway to the now uninhabited expanse of the dining room. The tables were stripped of their white cloths and crockery and cutlery; there were no flowers, and no memories of parties and good nights and music. A restaurant when it's closed is like a palace where all the kings, queens, courtesans, princes, princesses, jesters, guards, and priests have been sucked into the ether. I pushed my glasses higher on my nose and investigated the additions, subtractions, projections, and unwritedownable hubris that would tell me how the future looked. There were a few solid hours' work in those permutations but I was yawning after ten minutes, eyes drooping inside a half-hour, half asleep close on the heels of that.

What did I see?

One time, twenty years ago, toward the last time I was alone with Gabriella, my family and her family both happened to be invited to a rainy Saturday's Sicilian wedding. I'd had a fever or something and got to stay home. Gabriella made some excuse, I can't remember what. She came into my bedroom in her yellow raincoat fifteen minutes after our families had driven away to the wine and song. We stood in front of one another and she took off her blouse and pulled my shirt over my head. My hands and my forehead were hot and my eyes all watery but I unsnapped her flimsy brassière; she helped me out of my jeans and unzipped her little skirt; she got on her knees and slid my underpants down and then I fell onto my own knees and kissed the beautiful dark red wedge a hand's width down from her belly button. I held her against my cheek, the heat in my palms pressed into her cool buttocks. The summer storm beat against my windows. Then Gabriella was touching me, rubbing her hand over and around me, in a dreamy sort of spiral, but that was almost all of it. She kept sighing my name, Salvatore, oh Salvatore, but maybe I'd really been too sick that night. We must have thought we had all the time in the world and that this night would be only one out of thousands. I remembered Gabriella's legs, no longer girlish in that short skirt but womanly in their nakedness; I remembered her nipples standing out from her white breasts. To a green teenage boy Gabriella's buds had been soft yet firm, pink at the edges but so dark red in their center they were purple as figs. It's true what Lorca had written in the play Irina was going to perform; I saw my reflection in those young, not yet truly loved breasts. Gabriella had lain in my bed and lifted her knees but her hands on my shoulders were firm, holding me back; she hadn't wanted what I wanted. She'd let me slide down and put my cheek against her belly and then my tongue where she said it wasn't supposed to go, and though her body seemed to tremble and to sing, after that there was nothing, nothing, nothing.

But even in the fever of my sickness and the fever of being held away from her there'd been something I'd known very well. The world was absolutely mine now, and Gabriella would always be in it with me.

THE COMPUTER COLLAPSED before I did. The screen faded and the whirring in the processor stopped. My office had darkened and I looked around at the lights that weren't working. The electric calculator wouldn't calculate, but anyway, in that new dimness, what did it matter? It was a relief to have a reason to get away from my desk. I left my glasses behind. The fuses in the mains were all right and because there was no light anywhere in the building I had to use a torch down below. I tried to ring the electricity board number tacked on the wall but the telephone was mute as a stone.

So I went out into the hot street. The air was dry and the traffic quiet, footpaths deserted. There was a milk bar across the road and Mr. Mikalou told me business was slow but the power and telephone were fine. I returned to the restaurant, where it was still and muggy, shadowy and silent. For a few minutes I amused myself by throwing wide every possible window for air and every curtain and blind for light, and when I looked at my watch it had also stopped and a tremor went through me.

A kitchen is always the best place to kill time. All the electric appliances were quiet and I worried about the food we had stored, but I'd never known power to go out in this area for longer than an hour. The last thing I wanted was technicians wandering around spoiling my talk with Sandy. I had Gabriella's diary with me and I was going to give it to her. Then we'd see what we would see. She deserved the chance to read her sister's thoughts, and it crossed my mind to make sure that after I passed that diary on it never returned to me.

All the kitchen burners used gas and when I turned the knobs there was that reassuring hiss. It wasn't so dark in the kitchen that I couldn't see what I was doing; I opened the vents in the ceiling using the manual push-pull levers and without really thinking about it set to work. What Sandy and I didn't end up eating I'd take home for tonight's family dinner. I opened a bottle of South Australian red and started to set everything out on the counters and wooden cutting boards, rolling up my sleeves.

Time was off on the electric clock of the microwaves and frozen at 1:12 P.M. in the flip-over clock of the giant oven. I looked at my own wristwatch again; none of the hands had moved. So I got my own down to good dirty work.

Dear Diary

Gabriella's Book of Fire

I F   Y O U   H A V E a kilogram of topside mince, and three eggs, and a
tablespoon of finely chopped garlic, and the same of parsley, and
ground pepper and some salt, and one and a half cups of grated
pecorino pepato cheese, and you mix all this very well in a bowl, and
make little entities that look like golf balls, or larger if you prefer, then
you've nearly got proper Sicilian meatballs coming out of your kitchen.

You still have to fry them of course. Do that in the best extra-virgin
olive oil you can buy. With one big chopped-up onion too. Do it slowly;
don't rush; take a drink or listen to some music. Make sure the meatballs
get cooked all the way through and then put them aside with the glistening onion. Don't let the meatballs be anything less than golden. Why
would you, unless you were lazy and didn't care what you were going to
feed your family?

To make the sauce you get three hundred and fifty grams of tomato
paste and boil and peel and take the seeds out of some nice juicy toma-

toes. Maybe eight or ten of them. And then you chop them up. You get one and a half liters of water in a big saucepan and you mix and dissolve the paste and tomatoes in that water, using a wooden spoon. You put the saucepan over a strong gas flame, and then go ahead and have some fun: add the meatballs and the onions; put in a quarter of a cup of sugar; put in two whole cloves of garlic and a half a cup of peas and a half a cup of sliced mushrooms and one chopped carrot. Put in the salt and pepper you like. I never use salt anywhere, but that's just me. Some people are so sweet they never take sugar and I'm so sour I never need salt. You just go ahead, do what you think your body needs. Then stir what you've got in that great saucepan of yours and then let it simmer with the lid on, and I mean simmer, don't get lazy and turn that heat up. Simmer it slowly for two full hours. I'll tell you again, don't turn up that flame, don't get lazy. What's your hurry?

All right, after the two hours I want you to do this: get three medium-sized potatoes, wash them and peel them and quarter them. Get one big bunch of Italian or Greek basil (you know the difference, don't you?) and put all that into the pot and then let it simmer for another twenty minutes.

Nearly there.

Boil a kilo or a kilo and a half of your favorite pasta in plenty of water, that could also be salted. The old Sicilians say it has to be, but again I don't care for it, but am I you? By the way, have you had at least two glasses of something rich and red yet?

Now, my new Sicilian chef, dig in that pot for the meatballs and pota- toes. Gently. Separate them from the sauce and serve them in a nice ceramic dish on their own. Note the beautiful rosy color they've taken. Rinse in a colander the pasta you've boiled—we call it the scolapasta— and then mix it with the sauce. Serve it up to your family on big, big plates and give them parmesan cheese or more grated pecorino pepato to sprinkle over it. Get them to eat plenty of meatballs and potatoes. After all, you've been cooking all afternoon, when do they expect this again? Plus you've made enough for six hungry Sicilians. In Australia that probably means you've got enough to feed ten to twelve ravenous people—tell them loudly and wave your right hand, play your role to the hilt. *Mangia, mangia!* Eat, eat!

This dish is called, properly, *polpetti al sugo*. In our Sicilian dialect it's *puppetti o suco di carne*. Keep serving that red wine through the dinner, that's what my mamma does. And she doesn't show it too much— whereas everyone else does of course, because they're all smiling with this big peasant feast they're eating—but when she cooks this dish she's happy. Inside, I know she's singing. Well, I don't have to keep it inside. When I cook this dish, over its hours and hours, I do sing. Silly radio love songs that make you want to cry even with their moon-June-spoon little rhymes, and full-blooded Maria Callas arias I'll never have the voice for. You go ahead and do whichever one you want, but I assure you, one way or the other, your heart will be lighter.

Puppetti o Suco di Carne

IT WAS HOT IN the kitchen and the red wine didn't help.

My shirt was soaked and perspiration ran down my forehead and face, but I felt good. I did feel lighter. This was what I wanted—to lose myself in an earthbound fulfillment; to live in pulsating senses; to make, create; to be. Though this was Gabriella Zazò's way of cooking, the heat and the floating flavors of the ingredients and the pungent garlic still on my hands made me think instead about Irina and the birth of our children, about the way she'd been soaked in sweat and exhausted with strain, in-out delirious with the pain and agonized pleasure of bringing those lives into our hands.

I wondered how I'd become so lucky with the things time had given me; so lucky, yet still so prone to dragging a weight behind me.

Because I hated myself for the hopes I could never stop hoping. Why did I try to fool myself? I knew why I was in Ristorante Notte e Giorno and it wasn't to see Sandy Zazò and help her, it was to hear Gabriella's voice again. I knew she was dead and I still expected her to walk in the door. That was it. In my mind I saw that it was Gabriella who had come to my doorstep and placed the kaleidoscope there. That was her talisman. In my mind I saw that it was Gabriella who had spoken to Sandy about the Aleph, not Enrico Belpasso. In my mind I heard her speaking to Irina on the telephone the day the old man died. Yes, I imagined that she was back, and more than that, that she was thinking about me. These ideas had never gone away. These hopes had always been with me, behind everything I said and everything I did. It was the same since finding the Book of Fire, it was the same since being a confused teenager standing at Nocturne's wire gate and staring hauntedly around at the heat-shimmery intersection.

No wonder the lights in the restaurant were out. Notte e Giorno was in the shadowy half-world between night and day. No wonder the telephone was dead. Here the only words worth hearing were those you were willing to tell yourself. No wonder my wristwatch had stopped. Because time in its tyranny isn't a line but a circle, always taking you back to where your hopes are born.

How long before she arrived?

It was the red wine and the heat and my tiredness from not having slept, nothing else. I half smiled, half sighed, feeling drunk. Fat beads of sweat ran down my face and my forearms and my fingers, and it was like that old once-upon-a-time when I'd been playing in the family backyard with bones and murdering weapons and dead dogs' teeth. When I'd learned to buy kisses with caramels and licorice and tutti-frutti, even with dark plums and Valencia oranges. When I'd learned to love in silent dark places, in rickety cubby-houses, and while perched in the high boughs of neighborhood mango trees. We'd sit like crows watching down on our weedy, cracked, steaming little streets, always leaning close; that had been Gabriella and me. Then I'd learned to wait and to hate, to weep inside and show nothing outside, to dream of angels and lie down in gutters. I'd learned to be a fool until somebody saved me, until somebody truly saved me, and it was my Irina, and then our children, Natalie, Annie, and Lara.

So how would I find the strength to leave them behind, now that Gabriella Zazò was nearly home?

·   ·   ·

TIME WASN'T PASSING at all, at least not in a way that was recorded by the restaurant's dead clocks. Yet the gas flame flickered and licked and the huge pot performed its everyday voodoo, and I dreamed in the dusky quiet while the aromas and flavors slowly entwined and expanded and transformed.

Looking back, I remember perfectly that there was no sense of an arrival. There was no door opening and closing, no footsteps creeping spooky-scary across the polished floors, not even an unexpected blast of wind that filled the rooms with uncanny promise. No. She'd come and there wasn't a cataclysm, only little words as wide as a universe.

So what's gone wrong so far?

It was said so softly it might have been a voice from a far corner of my mind. My hand, stirring in the bubbling orange-red of the pot, stopped. My body became as immobile as the clocks. I didn't turn; instead my shoulders stayed square in front of the gas stove. It even seemed unreasonable to want to take a breath, for fear this spirit conjured right out of my memory would want to drift back into the depths of her dark, dark night.

It came again, weightless and insubstantial.

So what's gone wrong so far?

A shiver went through me, from top to bottom, for that old secret language of Sicilian light still carried the never-forgotten scents of Brisbane rain and wet herbs in the herb garden and freshly mown, hilly backyards that you rolled and tumbled down with all your friends following. Those few words, really, in all their beautiful shadows, said, Hey, are you all right? Do you miss me? Will you come and meet me later in the park, by the rose gardens?

She repeated it a third time, that introduction of 1975, when our neighborhood first came alive with the fact of her and the summer sun on my face made me start to dream of forever.

So then she knew to wait and give her old friend time, time to accumulate the twenty years and figure out what to do with them.

I put down the wooden spoon and leaned with my hands on the counter, my head hanging and the sweat falling in heavy drops onto the polished tile floor between my feet. I was overwhelmed, terrified to move my head and look at her. I'd expected this and not expected this. For twenty years I'd waited to turn some corner, to open some door, to wake one morning and there she would be.

This time her voice wasn't a thought. She said very clearly, one last time and with a hint of irritation, with a hint that if I didn't answer now she would take herself back into *la notte,* where I wouldn't find her again,

"So what's gone wrong so far?"

She sounded different. Not the way I remembered. Not the way little Gabriella Zazò was. My head hung and my throat was constricted. I couldn't think at all. It was like the eighteen-year-old Enrico Belpasso being confronted with the inexplicable fact of Fortunata and her desire for him: all he could think of was running away to a place where he could—think.

I answered in a tight bad mutter, Nothing yet.

"What, Salvatore?"

"Nothing yet. I said nothing yet. Nothing's gone wrong yet. All right?"

There was a little pause, and I knew without having to see that she was smiling in that old way of hers.

"Wrong," she said, with a funny intonation, and despite the fire in my head I started to smile too.

So time takes you in its circle, to where you're helplessly young.

Sometimes You Fall

IN THE STEAM OF the cooking all my pores were open. The air was heavy with the wholesome sweaty essence of Sicilian food. It took effort to reach for a fork and gently search through the bubbling, simmering sauce for the long stalks of the basil, those things now brown and weedy, their buds having long since softened and melted to do their good work. The fork danced to the quivering of my hand.

"Salvatore," she said. "Aren't you going to turn around?"

There was a heaviness in my face. A smile couldn't last a second, not with the way those muscles and tendons were working. When this new Gabriella who was the old Gabriella came close, and then entwined her meaty arms around me, it was as if a spirit had come to lift me from this world into a place so lovely I had no right to even look at it. The body that pressed to me was the opposite of what I remembered. She was voluptuous and womanly. At the points where she met me there was heat. She kissed the side of my neck and the side of my face, and my head and my hair, and her perfume was her own salty damp skin, and she held her palm against my sweating cheek, and that was too much, just too much.

Until she made me turn.

Then we were kissing.

Somewhere in this breathing-as-one, lips-as-one, ragged-thoughts-as-one, I looked at her, searching her face for her every feature, and of course it was Sandy Zazò, twice the size of her long-gone sister, and she was so entranced by what she thought she knew about her that she was playing this game, and I thought, You bitch, you mind-fucking bitch, then almost at the same time, What does it matter? and I played the game too, because I'd been cheated all those years ago, I'd never got to make love with my Gabriella, only to dream of her, and if Sandy was going to want me to do that to her in Gabriella's name, then why should I stop it? Why shouldn't I take whatever scraps this fart of an inconceivable universe sent me?

She was, after all, as everyone liked to say, the replacement daughter.

Sandy Zazò pushed herself away from me and leaned on the opposite counter, the electric oven behind her head and the digital clock frozen at a time that wasn't the present. She studied me, she took me in. How strange and familiar we were to one another. For me it was the same as the way it used to be. My heart tolled a hurtful, heavy beat. I felt that beat in my groin and armpits, in my throat and temples. She made me all flesh and bone and blood.

"You always had to buy Gabriella's kisses with something, didn't you? So what have you got for me?"

"Her pasta sauce. The way it's written in her diary."

"Have you got it? I've heard about it. I'd like to see it. Will you give it to me?"

"It's here."

"I want you to say the name Gabriella. I want you to call me by her name."

"Why? Why do I have to do that?"

"Because I want you to make love to me the way you would have made love to her if you'd had the chance."

I stared at Sandy, trying to understand her.

"Call me Gabriella."

"How do you know so much about me and her? How could you possibly know?"

"Give me something to buy my kisses first, then I'll tell you." Sandy tilted her head a little and half closed her eyes. "This smells good. Basil, and I think—I think you've put some chilli in too."

"That's my touch. It's not hers."

"You mean mine."

"All right, I mean yours." I hesitated. "Why are you doing this?"

Sandy's lips curled into a smile and she didn't answer.

I asked her another question. The real one. "You've seen her?"

"I want some of your food, Salvatore. What you've made is exactly what I want you to give me."

I turned to the pot and started to lift out the meatballs and potatoes. Every now and then I looked to make sure Sandy didn't run away, which she didn't, today in very faded and slightly torn canvas men's trousers and purple-black Doc Martens and a crumpled, too-tight T-shirt that said "Blam." She'd toned down the redness of her lips and her eye-shadow and her hair, but it was all still there, and so were those amazingly fake green eyes, and her positively twice the size of a slip of a fourteen-year-old girl named Gabriella Zazò.

"I haven't boiled the pasta yet."

"Put it on bread then."

I found a big Italian loaf left over from yesterday. It wasn't stale. I cut thick slices and used a spoon to soak the bread with the very red sauce. Then I put a meatball on top and broke it open with a fork. I put all this on a china plate and handed it to Sandy. There was something about the action, handing that to her, that made me weak. I wanted to fall down on my knees and explain how I felt about a girl who was a ghost. Our hands touched as she took the plate and the charge that passed from fingers to fingers was more electric than kisses. I watched Sandy take a bite and close her eyes, and then all my wild fury was back and my fists knocked the plate out of her hands and it smashed on the floor.

"What do you think you're doing? What kind of a game is this? She was a fucking little bitch who never came back and you want to be her? Why? Tell me that. Why?"

"She's told me all about you. She's told me everything. It was the most exciting thing I ever heard. How you'd buy her kisses, how you'd send each other messages from your bedroom windows—"

"No! It's not possible—"

"She wants to see you." Sandy was breathing hard, just like me.

"What?"

"She wants to see you."

"You're lying. You're a liar just like she was."

Sandy shook her head, her fake green eyes wide and scared and excited too. "Can't you see I know everything about the both of you?"

"No, you don't. You haven't got a clue."

Sandy waited, then she said very evenly, "So what's gone wrong so far?" and I immediately answered, "Nothing yet," and she picked up a bowl to replace the plate broken and bloodied on the floor. She ladled in sauce from the pot and meatballs and potatoes and all. Then she said, "Put out your arm."

She took me by the wrist because I wouldn't do it and she dipped her index finger into the bowl, and very carefully, dipping again and again, she inscribed "Zazz" on the soft inside of my right forearm.

"Now write your name on me."

"No."

Sandy paused before she said, "She wrote 'Gabriella' on your arm but now she's known as Zazz."

I kept staring at that name, in red, right there on me.

"It's not true. It is not true."

Sandy dipped her finger in the bowl again and this time she touched her lips with the sauce. Then she stepped close and kissed me, her mouth open and sweet and me sinking and falling.

Then I was on the floor and crying for twenty years of absence, and Sandy was with me saying, It's all right, call me Gabriella, you can call me Gabriella if it makes you feel better, over and over, and over and over again, and I couldn't imagine such longing and such loss, not like this, not all at once.

Zazz

IT WAS THE NICE rhythm of the rain that made me open my eyes and pull myself out of my dreaming. The rhythm of the rain and the rhythm of Sandy Zazò stretching herself and pulling on her things.

The couch was comfortable and the square pillows under my head still redolent of the way we'd used them to lift her hips. I remembered every kiss, every thrust; every smell of her young body against mine, every sigh that came out of her throat. I remembered the kitchen and the cold red-stained floor in there; I remembered Sandy going to find the bathroom with sperm running down the insides of her long thighs, her breasts full and pink with how hard they'd been handled. I remembered her returning to me in my office and on my couch; in one hand she'd been carrying the bottle of wine that kept me company through the cooking and in the other were two wine glasses. We even ate, dipping Italian bread into big bowls of the sauce, and we'd talked a little bit too.

I watched her tying the laces of her dark little boots, her breasts now held inside a sweetly patterned but very strong brassière.

There was only one subject worth remembering.

"How did you see her?"

"She came to find me after Nonno died."

"Has she gone again?"

"Yes."

"Where? Where does she live?"

"On a beach. On an island."

"No. Where?"

"North Stradbroke Island."

"You're trying to tell me she's that close?"

"She hasn't been there long. Maybe a year. But the thing is—"

"What?"

"It's what I said. She wants to see you."

"So why hasn't she?"

"Aren't you married? Don't you have three children?"

That was like a rock to swallow. A rock for my guts to go with the rock in my head.

Sandy straightened and arched her back. She stood and found her tight Blam T-shirt and said, "I don't know. Do you want this to happen again?"

"It shouldn't have happened this time."

"So why did it?" She smiled. "Don't let it kill you. Anyway, I'm Sydney-bound. For a while I thought I'd stay for Gabriella but that's not the right thing for me to do."

Sandy's scent was on me. She left my office and went into the restaurant where she was out of my view, but her scent remained. It was everywhere. From where I was lying on the couch I imagined that the entire restaurant would reek of food and the unmistakable fragrances of lust. Sandy returned with her bag. She took out a notepad and a pen and scribbled left-handedly. Gabriella was right-handed. The sisters were so dissimilar I knew I was guilty of only one thing, described by that blunt and soul-destroying word, adultery.

"Here," Sandy said, tearing the page out and about to hand it to me, but when I reached for it she flicked it away.

"What is it?"

"I don't know what you're going to do, but if you want her this is where you can find her."

"Then give it to me."

"Don't we have to exchange?"

So her game wasn't finished. I rose up out of the couch and went to my desk. The diary was beside my computer and I picked it up and handed it to her with a strange feeling of—not release, but of emptying myself.

Sandy weighed it. "There's a lot here."

"More than you'd expect."

"No. She's a writer. That's what she does. She uses her new name."

"What is it?"

"It's here." She gave me the note and the name and the address meant nothing to me. I said, "Zazuella? Zazuella O'Connor? Who the fuck would believe that? This is a joke. Zazuella's not a name."

"Isn't it?" Sandy laughed. "Is Zazò? Or Capistrano?"

"Give me the telephone number."

"No telephone."

"I'll be checking." I read the address again. "This is still a game, isn't it?"

"No. I don't know. I've seen her and I've talked to her and I still wish I knew her." Sandy put her bag over her shoulder. "Guy'll be wondering why I'm not at practice."

Sandy left the office and from where I remained I watched her walking to the front door. She looked back and said, "Good luck," and for the rest I didn't stop her. The door fell shut and I didn't know what to think. This was the type of bizarre dream that leaves you completely spent and exactly as I was now, standing naked and stupid in a place I was supposed to know well.

Heavy in the head, I wandered around the rooms of the restaurant. They were dark. The power hadn't returned. The telephone was burring but the clocks were still. Rain pattered against the windows. I used soap and water in the bathroom to wash the name Zazz off my forearm and the smell of Sandy Zazò from my other parts. When I looked in the mirror I saw a face that I didn't understand. Dressed again, I spent a lot of time in the kitchen clearing and cleaning things up, then I sealed the lid on the pot and wrapped it up in a tablecloth, and knotted the cloth twice at the top in the proper way.

Zazuella O'Connor. *Bull*shit.

I went to the telephone. Directory assistance told me there was no listing anywhere in the country. Then I dialed again.

"Larry, something's wrong down here. The power or I don't know what. Can you come and see what's wrong?"

It sounded like the ordinary me but Sandy was gone and so was my fidelity to my wife. I wondered if when I arrived home my little girls would know that the man they were hugging wasn't their father but a stranger. I felt such a weariness and letdown. I'd always dreamed that hearing Gabriella Zazò was alive would release me from a world of disappointment, and now I knew that was just another lie in a life of lies. I didn't leave the restaurant yet; I dragged things out as if a solution might arrive. What could I check: bookshops and libraries. My insides felt worse than ever. I'd given Sandy what she wanted and she'd given me what I wanted. I could make all the checks on earth but all that was left was to go to Gabriella; I really would. And when I did, when I broke the bond with my family, she would finally trust me.

That was what she was waiting for.

I returned to my office, having forgotten that Gabriella's diary wasn't there anymore.

After living with it so many years it felt as if the Book of Fire had gone missing, but maybe it was wrong to think of it that way. The book had gone to a new rightful owner. Still, it struck me I wasn't lightened of a burden but stolen from yet again.

The Two Parents, the One Wife,
and the Three Demanding Daughters
of Salvatore Capistrano

LATER THAT EVENING MY papà was in a bad mood with the littlest, Lara, and she clung to me, all sad-faced and whingey from the moment I walked in the door. The day at the fête had been too long and too hot, and then they'd got stuck in the crowded car park in the rain, and my papà and his youngest granddaughter were overtired, and then grouchy and resentful with one another.

It was always the same between those two. The eldest of our family was always at loggerheads with the youngest. It was also true that there was a very strong bond between them. Still, he'd make a face at her and she'd burst into tears. She'd be too demanding with her games and her songs and he'd lose his temper. Sometimes she ignored him as if he didn't even exist. Other times he'd carry her around on his shoulders from room to room to amuse her, for hours that never ended, for afternoons that flowed into evenings, happy enough to horsey her around or get on the marble floor of the rumpus room and play with her crayons and dolls just so she wouldn't be lonely. That was the Sicilian man's way with children. Tough in one way and a lamb in another. It infuriated me beyond reasoning.

Ma took the wrapped-up pot from me and said, trying to make light of things, that she would make the pasta seeing that her son had done the hard part. I hurried into the bathroom and shower to rid myself of whatever traces of Sandy were still on me.

No sooner did I have myself soaped up all over and the family shampoo in my hair and running into my eyes than Irina came in. She leaned against an opposite wall and stayed there with her arms folded while she talked to me through the blistered glass. That day she and the other actors and crew had been given the news that their production of *Blood Wedding* had shut down before it had the chance to get going because the company, SmashtimeCrashtime Theater, had smashed and crashed financially, like so many of its predecessors. As Irina told me this she didn't try to be stoic; she had to let it all out. So I rinsed all the soap and shampoo off me and emerged from the shower dripping wet and wrapped her up while she cried and cried.

"There'll be something else. Something else will come up."

I knew how much it meant to Irina to have something that was hers outside the realm of wifehood and motherhood, and now she hadn't even had the chance to prove herself. It took a while before she could pull herself together.

She said, "I'm glad everyone's here tonight, even if they're in a bad mood. It's good to have everyone around."

Then Irina's line of vision dropped a little, to near my shoulder.

"Sam," she said, the pupils of her eyes completely dark and dilated, "who did that to you?" and when I looked in the misty mirror that mist couldn't hide the bite mark, the *horse*bite, just below my collarbone.

The only thing I could think to say was this:

"Gabriella Zazò is back," and then Ma was shouting from the kitchen for all of us to come sit down to eat.

W E   S H A R E D   T H E   pasta around and some ate noisily, especially my papà, who liked to suck the slippery red noodles down in the old loud Sicilian way and whose lips were rouged with sauce. Ma was more genteel but she talked and talked and showed the food chewing up in her mouth with complete ignorance of the more delicate sensibilities of those around her. I couldn't eat anyway and Irina couldn't look at me, and the twins, Natalie and Annie, played with their food like it was alive. Their bellies were probably full of licorice and sweets from the fête. Then Annie was showing Natalie how she could lift the scab off a sore on her elbow and reveal the pink fresh wound below.

"Annie!"

She jumped in her seat and stared at me with big terrified eyes. She was this close to crying and probably would have if she hadn't been so shocked. Then the moment passed and she went back to petulantly pushing a meatball from one corner of her plate to the other. From then on Annie was as miserable as her mother. Ma put her hand on my hand to tell me to not be so tough. The rain was coming down outside but the night managed to stay muggy all the same. My papà drank rough Stanthorpe red wine and Lara was whingey in my lap so that it was hard for me to eat anything because of the way she kept rubbing her face into my shirt and kicking her feet against my shins and whining, whining, whining. Her little body was hot and uncomfortable and she wouldn't stay still. She wouldn't get off me either. Halfway through his loud pasta sucking and the smacking of his red wet lips after every sip of Stanthorpe red, my papà leered at Lara in his usual dumb teasing way and Lara burst straight into tears and started to sob and to kick as if her best Barbie doll had broken into a million pieces.

My hand slammed the table and all the cutlery and plates jumped.

"What are you doing?" I shouted at my father from across the table. "What are you doing? Leave her alone! Can't you leave a little kid alone?"

At the shouting, Natalie and Annie joined Lara in the veil of tears. The wailing was deafening. My ma got the children away from the table and out of the room. I could hear her off somewhere placating them in her grandmotherly way, in exactly the same manner as she used to do with me.

My papà, meanwhile, kept eating, and then he laid his fork down and he wiped his mouth with the back of one hand and the back of the other. He looked first at Irina. His old eyes were browner even than his sun-dark Sicilian skin, and after he'd studied her he turned to me. He didn't say anything for a long time and I stared back at him, full of fierceness and defiance. Anger at everything and nothing must have made the veins stick out in my temples. My papà considered me for as long as he wanted to. He was in no hurry. Eventually he said, having taken every bit of me in, and speaking in a more gentle manner than a raging bull like him had probably ever spoken in his life, *"Figlio, cosa c'è?* Son, what is it?"

There was not a time in my life that I'd heard the old peasant dialect of ours sound so loving. That dialect of the fields and the mountains, untouched by Sicilian literature or culture, was a language for berating donkeys, for screaming hate or shouting passion, but this—this was something new. How many times had I trembled when my father had gone into one of his rages, shouting at me and the injustices of the world? Yet this now was somehow more frightening than any of that could ever have been.

Because it made me ashamed.

I looked down at my hands and what I saw was the way they'd squeezed Sandy's breasts and held her vulva and lifted her buttocks to better get me inside her.

Irina reached over and she tore my shirt so hard three buttons popped across the dining table, one landing in the serving bowl of pasta.

My ma had returned by then. The kids had quietened. She and my papà, their eyesight no longer so good, had to look hard. My ma put on her glasses and then she passed them to her husband so that he could see what she saw. They looked at my horsebite and they looked at Irina.

She said, "Your son tells me that Gabriella Zazò is back."

"Gabriella Zazò?"

"That's what he says."

Ma, showing every line on her face, said to her husband, taking him by the forearm, "We have to go."

"No," Irina said. "Stay. Why should you go?"

My papà's mind hadn't slowed in his later years. He still understood enough to know how men are. He remembered little Gabriella Zazò as well as anyone did, and he and Ma of course blamed her for the slide their promising son's promising life had taken way back then.

He said, "She's not back. She's dead. Some other witch did that."

Irina said, "Who did it, Sam?"

I said, because in a way it was true, but only in a way, "Gabriella Zazò."

My papà said, "That girl's nothing. You were always thinking she should come back. Look what she did to you. You could have ended up in jail because of what she made you do. She should have stayed dead. All right, she was your friend, but that was twenty years ago. She nearly ruined your life. Have you ever let yourself see that she wanted to ruin your life? Why did she leave you there with the old man? Why didn't she ever come back? So no one took her. She never got kidnapped. She ran away, is this the story? There are people like her in the world. Witches, gypsies, they cast spells. If it wasn't for her you'd be a lawyer or a doctor. But look what you've got here anyway. In spite of her. In spite of Gabriella Zazò. Look what you've got in this house. If she comes back again spit in her face. I know I will. So will you do that, will you spit in that little witch's face?"

I said, "No."

Irina said, "Are you going to see her again?"

Ma said, "He's not!"

I said, "Yes."

Ma said, "He is under a spell. Virgin Mary, the poor boy is."

Irina said, "How many times did you fuck her?"

My ma said, "What fuck? Who's talking about that? He never did that."

"How many times today and how many times yesterday and how many times last week?"

Even my ma didn't want to answer that question for me.

"All right," Irina said. "Just tell me this. How long has it been going on?"

I said, "Today, that's all."

Irina said, "Today—is that all?" and struck me across the face. I kept looking down. Neither my ma or my papà tried to stop her. She said, "Where is she now?"

Ma said, "How does he know? How can he know where she is? He doesn't care. Tell your wife you don't care. Tell your wife you won't see her again. He won't see her again, Irina, don't you worry. That whole family's bad. What does he care about any of them?"

I said, "Gabriella lives on a beach on North Stradbroke Island. I don't know what she does there. Maybe she's a writer or something. Her family thinks she's dead just the way I did. Her whole family except for her sister. What's-her-name, Sandy."

"Sandy's in on this too?"

I half nodded, too afraid to say anything unless I blurted out the truth.

"You saw them today? Both or just one? You said you were going to do the accounts."

"I gave Sandy that diary I found, all those years ago."

"You kept that?"

"Yes."

"Where?"

"It was in my room here."

"Hidden."

"Yes—hidden."

Irina stopped staring at me. She lowered her eyes and said, "You've been living with this ghost all the time you've been living with me. And now you know where she lives. Some beach—"

My father shouted, "And who cares?"

Irina said, "You're going to her. You are actually going to her."

Lara returned and when I looked I could see Natalie and Annie hiding badly behind the corner, listening to every word, terrified and wanting to come in and be held.

Lara said, "Daddy, are you going to the beach?"

I took her back onto my knee, full of shame. But not enough shame to stop me from saying, "Yes. Daddy's going to go to the beach."

"I want to come. I like the beach."

Irina reached over and took Lara off my lap and held her on her own. Lara's arms went around her neck and she looked at me with a dismal face.

"You can't come, baby. Daddy's going alone."

"It's not fair." Lara rubbed her eyes. She said in the same insistent tone she used for telling us she was very hungry or had to wee, "I want to go."

Natalie and Annie sort of drifted into the room. Natalie, who sometimes was the most serious and mature of the entire family, said, "Why do you get to go and we don't?"

Annie said, "We want to go. We always want to go. You never take us. You never ever ever take us."

My papà was still looking at me, shaking his head. Ma was holding my wife's hand and tears ran down her face. Irina was comforting Lara, stroking her pink cheek, and meanwhile in her own eye a fat tear balanced like a rock on a cliff. I wanted to run out of the house and down all the streets of our neat little suburb. Meanwhile, the rain lightly caressing the windows was like a hundred thoughts at once, asking to be let in.

My papà looked at me some more and then he pushed his plate away. "If your son's any sort of decent man," he said to my ma, "he'll take his family to the fucking beach."

Natalie and Annie were startled by that word he used. It was as if they expected some sort of catastrophe to immediately come falling down on the house. When nothing happened they hid their mouths behind their hands. I knew that by tomorrow they'd be saying "fucking" every chance they got.

Lara kicked her feet at him in an annoyed manner. She said, scrunching up her nose, "Horrible old man. Horrible, horrible old man," and Irina pushed her chair back.

She said to the girls, extending her hands, "Come on," and all of them crowded around her as they left.

So I sat with my ma and my papà, who kept looking at me in their sad and strangely innocent way, trying to understand exactly who and what their son was.

I TOOK MYSELF out of bed and started to dress.

Irina said, "Say good-bye to your children before you go."

"They'll be asleep. I don't want to disturb them."

"That's what a coward would say."

I put some things into a bag. Irina switched on the bedside light and came to help me.

"Here are a few clean shirts. Will you want underwear? You forgot that. Swimmers? You'll do a bit of swimming, won't you? There's your sandals. You can't wear shoes on a beach. Don't forget your shaving things."

She went back into the bed and switched out the lamp.

I walked out of the bedroom and down the corridor, carrying the fattened bag, going by the rooms where the girls slept. Their doors were ajar but I didn't look in. I went on down into the kitchen and turned on the light, the starkness of it making me flinch. When I poured a glass of water and drank it down my hands shook so much I needed both to hold the glass up to my lips. Through the window I could see that summer rain falling and falling and falling. Once, high up in a mango tree in New Farm, Gabriella and I had huddled on a branch during a sudden heavy shower, getting sprayed and shivering because of it, but cuddling and kissing and laughing because it was fun too.

On the kitchen table were three crayon drawings on big sheets of white butcher's paper.

The first, a colorful clown with a big banana for a smile. That was Lara's.

The second, a fat yellow sun shining over an ocean where a whale was swimming. That was Annie's.

The third, a family at the beach. Natalie was the best drawer. For some reason she always drew me wearing my glasses, though I didn't wear them very often, not unless I was working. I could always tell myself in her drawings. In this scene, the man with the glasses was standing on the beach while black and gold heads floated in the water in front of him. Hands were in the air, fingers spread like sticks and drawn in every color. Everyone had upturned mouths except for him. There was a ball in the air, and it was striped. It was floating above the black and gold heads, who were Irina, Annie, Lara, and of course Natalie herself.

I went to the front door and opened it and something about that rain on my face was like Gabriella Zazò's kisses. Fragrant, sweet, never-ending, soft lips meeting mine and going on into eternity. When I turned around Irina was standing in the long cotton T-shirt that she used as a nightie.

She said, "Sam—"

I said, "What if you stop loving me while I'm gone? What if the girls have some kind of problem? What if one of them disappears? What if you won't let me in this door again?"

We kept looking at each other.

"Please, Irina," I said, "let me come back."

"Oh you idiot," Irina sighed. "You haven't gone yet."

An Overdue Visit with
Tony Solero

BECAUSE OF THE TYPE of low-security prison farm it was, way out in the country, I was able to sit with Tony Solero on a bench in the sun. Across the prison yard groups of men played basketball or touch football and others wandered in ones or pairs, talking softly or laughing at some joke or smoking alone. Others were hoeing rows in a little field of vegetables, where stalks of corn and green vines looked healthy and abundant.

"I thought you'd come more often. Don't you like it here?"

"Well," I said, "it's all right."

"Thanks for writing anyway. Not many people bother to. Anyhow, by next year I'll be on work release and if everything goes all right, year after that I'll be out for good." Tony stretched his legs. "It keeps you going, thinking about that."

"The restaurant will be waiting for you."

"Still okay?"

"Better than that."

He nodded his large head, squinting at the light.

"So you keep saying in your letters. But I've been thinking about that too. It's not everything to me. In fact, it's not anything. I got what there was to get out of La Notte. There's plenty of money in my family's trusts. The courts didn't get their hands on all of it, not even half. Good, huh? You've got your family to think about. Notte e Giorno is legally yours, let's keep it that way."

"That wasn't what we agreed."

"It is now."

Two fat men started to argue on the basketball court. The others pulled them apart, and then there was a general shaking of hands. It struck me that there wasn't a single guard anywhere and the fences seemed to be a long way off. It also struck me that Tony didn't want another word about the restaurant.

So I said, "You look good, *cumpari*."

"Yeah, I've lost some weight the last few months. I like the gym. Learned how to box again too. You never really lose it and sometimes it comes in handy here. You know Bob Dylan boxes? Can you imagine that old fart duking it out? Most of these white-collar guys here are pussycats but you get the odd group of bastards. Nighttime's the worst. They wait for you. One time, one mutant tried to stick his salami into my rear in the showers but I got him in the second round of a match we organized. Boy, did I feel good when I put him down." Tony grinned, remembering. He'd lost two teeth somehow, the ones next to his front teeth, on the right. He saw me looking, "Don't worry, I haven't been chugging. They haven't got me doing that."

I said, "I wasn't thinking you did."

"And what's the attraction of a man's hairy bunghole anyway?" he asked. "That's what I'd like to know. Doctor had to check my prostate a few weeks ago and if there's anything fun about that I don't get it. All I keep dreaming about is tits. Tits tits tits tits tits, day and night."

"Fresh breasts," I said.

"Fresh breasts?"

"It was something someone used to say."

"Tits and fresh pasta more likely. The food they try and cook here is disgusting and the bastards haven't let me have a conjugal rights visit with Santina yet. They've got these caravans set aside for it. I grow the best fucking beans and tomatoes in this place and they still say I haven't earned ten minutes alone with my wife. But I keep asking."

In the heyday of La Notte the good life had worked its usual way on Tony and he'd become a lot heavier, his neck thick like a bull's, and though he was still on the big side his arms and shoulders had gained the density of muscle. As we'd walked to the bench I'd noticed a certain lightness to his gait. I believed him when he said he liked learning how to box again, and maybe thinking constantly about breasts gave him that extra bit of energy to keep lifting weights in the gym—or was it because of the mutants who lay in wait in the dark, who could tell?

I said, "You remember Gabriella Zazò?"

"Huh. I haven't thought about her for a while."

"I think she's turned up again."

"What are you, mad?"

"I don't think she's dead."

"Bullshit."

"No."

"What do you mean, you don't think?"

"I got it secondhand."

Tony said, "Never trust strange information that comes secondhand. Believe what you see. What's it, twenty years?"

"Twenty years. Her grandfather died. You remember Enrico Belpasso?"

"Soft in the head, but he got better, didn't he? So now he's dead and she comes back." Tony's brow creased as he remembered it all. "No, it's not true. Fucking hell. Are you saying she didn't get snatched or what?"

"I think she ran away."

"Why?"

"Something about the universe."

"What?"

"I don't know."

"What do her family say?"

"They don't know yet, except for her sister, Sandy. She's the one who told me, it was only yesterday."

"Sandy. I never met her. She was born later, wasn't she? But you know, she has to tell her family. You have to tell them. If there's even the slightest chance—what are you waiting for?"

"There's something I had to check with you first."

"Me? What's it got to do with me?"

"Nothing, but there's this thing I've been wondering about. It's niggling me. It's got to do with what you said to me once, first time I visited you here."

"What?"

"About Pietro Pierucci."

Tony turned and stared at me.

I said, "You told me you were thinking when you got out you might retire to a secluded beach somewhere. You said you might do that just like Pietro Pierucci. Do you remember that?"

Tony sucked his teeth and made a face.

"You weren't just talking. You weren't just imagining that's what he'd do."

"Sam, don't listen to whatever bullshit I crap on about."

"No, you knew what he wanted. So even though all these years he's dropped out, somehow the both of you . . ."

"He wrote to me."

"He wrote to you?"

"Yes."

"Where from?"

Tony cleared his throat and looked at the blue of the sky, making up his mind. "What does it matter now? Back then I think it was Adelaide, or some little town near there. He said he didn't stay long."

"After that did he find himself a beach?"

"But what do you want to know for? You know it's more complicated than that. After everything he did, for him to write to me . . ." Tony shook his head. He rubbed his eyes and then his cheeks. "First you're talking about little Gabriella and then you're talking about fucking Pierucci. What does it matter if he found himself a beach or not? It was just something he wrote once."

"Once. Or are you still in contact with him?"

Tony shifted. He wasn't supposed to tell. He said, "But don't go spreading it around, all right? It's hard enough for him to keep a low profile."

"What do you care whether he does or not?"

"I do. I suppose now I do."

"Where is he?"

"*Cumpareddu,* his days of worrying about little Gabriella Zazò are over." Tony shook his great head, now smiling, still a little disbelieving. "Ex–Senior Detective Pietro Pierucci. Funny how that name keeps coming up. People in here talk about him, you know. They'd scream their heads off if they knew I was hearing from him. But what let you know we've been keeping up the contact?"

That was a good question, and all I had to fall back on for a decent answer were those old ties that bind and that don't really get broken.

"Because you were friends. Because he probably hasn't got another friend anywhere."

Tony nodded, half laughed, but it wasn't a laugh at all. "A corrupt bagman cop who turns and dobs everyone else in so he can have legal immunity is going to have a hard time making new friends, that's for sure. Most people, whether they're cops or not, would probably rather pull out their dicks and piss in his mouth. That's what I wanted to do."

"So I'm right."

"He started the letters. I wouldn't have known where he was."

Tony shifted and reached into the back pocket of his jeans. He pulled out a dirty envelope that had been folded into quarters.

"He wrote for a long time before I bothered answering him. Two years, more or less. But I kept thinking about what he had to say. It wasn't that interesting really, but what got me in the end was that he wanted to say it at all. 'Sorry, Tony.' So now we write. He doesn't say anything about what he does now other than to say that he's scored himself a baby. Imagine at his age. He just goes on and on about every-thing that happened to him. He doesn't mention you and he certainly doesn't mention Gabriella Zazò."

"But why do you think he keeps writing to you?"

"Sam, if he hadn't sold everyone out, if he hadn't given his evidence and made a deal, he would have gone into a mid-to-max security jail and a man like him wouldn't have lasted long. There aren't many pussycats in those prisons and police turncoats are on a par with child molesters. There's nothing lower. I've heard stories even I don't want to believe. Pierucci would have had a screwdriver in the heart or a bit of barbed wire wrapped around his throat soon enough. Or if he was too tough for that, at the very least his dance card would always be full, if you know what I mean. So he made his deal. I would have done the same. But do you think an old tough guy like him would have swallowed being such a coward so easily? You know what he wrote once? He wrote that he always thought he'd end up falling in the line of fire in New Farm to save some stupid one of us kids or something, and in the end all that happened was that he proved what a coward he was. He wrote that from that moment he wished he was dead. He actually put it on a piece of paper and mailed it to me. Can you imagine? Him?" Tony sighed. "What am I supposed to do, sit in here all these years hating Pietro Pierucci?"

I reached for the envelope.

"His name isn't on the back but the address is. They don't check mail here." Tony pointed. "See, that's it. He's out of circulation and intends to stay that way for life."

I stared at where Tony pointed. I didn't have my glasses so it was an effort to read the writing, but it wasn't the effort that made my head grow light. It was the surprise of seeing just how right I could be.

"That's a beach over on North Stradbroke Island. Deadman's. It's a pretty good place, really quiet and peaceful from what I remember. Except for holiday times. I'm going to bring the family to stay with him one day. Or maybe just Santina, and I'll leave the kids at home. I think about tits all the time and when I'm not thinking about tits I think how my wife didn't leave me when the shit hit the fan, or through all the court cases. They nearly killed her, you know."

"I know."

"When we got married, *she* had a great chest. Remember?"

"Who'd forget?"

"I was a fucked husband. I feel like I've got a second chance. Funny. You ever feel that way?"

I squinted at the burning sun. It must be burning over that long and quiet beach of Pietro Pierucci's and Gabriella Zazò's right now. It must be making them want to get naked and swim in the cool clear crystal waters close at hand.

"Sometimes."

Tony joked, "So what's the connection, according to you?"

I took out the dog-eared little slip of notepaper that Sandy Zazò had written an identical address on and handed it to Tony. He read it and thought a minute and said, "Shit."

"She wants to see me."

"Does *he* want to see you too?" Tony thought some more. "Maybe you should just write to her."

"No, I'm looking forward to a weekend at the beach."

Tony shook his head and showed the space where some nighttime prison horror he wouldn't discuss might have knocked out those two teeth. Maybe it had been in the ring after all but I couldn't help wondering if it had been different from that, and if his new boxing skills gave him much protection, and whether it was any recompense to go down fighting.

"She's not there. That kid's long dead. You have to be prepared to find that out all over again." Tony licked his lips. He was thinking it through. "Maybe it's a good idea, Sam. Go over there and get it out of your system finally. Convince yourself little Gabriella Zazò's dead and gone once and for all. And when you see him, when you see Peter, just try and shake his hand and forgive him. Really forgive him. The chaplain here's always saying that's what we have to do. Father Max says it himself when he gets you with his right hook. He knocks you down in the ring and helps you up and says, 'I forgive you, son.'" Tony paused. "But what will you do if she really is there?"

We exchanged a glance, and Tony looked off at the court where the basketball game was winding up. Fat men playing that sort of a game only made it look clunky and graceless. Yet Tony wouldn't laugh at their efforts. He had a certain grace himself. Maybe he was planning to go join them after I left. It was funny. For the first time in twenty years I liked Tony Solero; I really liked my old friend again.

And From Here You Can See
Whatever You Want to See

ON THE RED RUSTY lumbering old car ferry that took us the fifty-five-minute journey over to the island, Irina and I had tea in styrofoam cups and watched Natalie, Annie, and Lara play with two children they'd made friends with in the first five minutes of the trip. The ferry was stacked full with cars and utilities, panel vans and people movers, and trucks, big ones, even an eighteen-wheeler going back to the island to work on one of the sand-dredging operations. Added to these vehicles there seemed to be fishing equipment everywhere; the island's surrounding sea and its secluded lakes and waterways were well known for how generous they could be.

But that of course wasn't what occupied either my mind or Irina's.

She reached down and took the slim paperback from out of the bag sitting between us. The book was our local library's edition of *Big News from a Bad Planet* by Zazuella O'Connor. Irina turned to an inside page.

"'Zazuella O'Connor is a ceramicist who writes for children.' So?"

"She's got four books published and they're all out of print. This was the only one they had and it came out more than three years ago. They told me she's not very well known."

"Do you think this writer is her?"

"I don't know."

"Have you finished it?"

"Last few pages. Natalie and Annie might like it."

"I'm reading it next."

Irina handed the paperback to me and I returned it to the bag. Despite what she said it was wrong to have that book with us, wrong and yet ridiculously essential. The funny thing was, Irina had been the one to pack it, whereas I'd been ready to leave it at home, in my office, anywhere it couldn't intrude. But the fact of it did and that was that. So Irina wouldn't let it hide. What I'd read was a story that was simple and direct, and it was about a girl named Emma who was born six and a half feet tall and who dreamed bad things were going to happen only to find that whatever the worst was she imagined, the exact opposite of it would occur. So it was a book about believing in hope, if you wanted to look that far. I did, and I looked for every sign of Gabriella Zazò too. Was the girl meant to be her? I couldn't say. What I could say was that the children I identified with the fictional Emma were in fact my own, Natalie and Annie and Lara.

Irina was watching them run around the busy deck.

"Why did you take me back?" I asked. "Why did you forgive me for Gabriella?"

"You mean for Sandy," she corrected. "Sandy and Gabriella."

"Yes," I said.

She took off her five-dollar sunglasses, purchased at some service station, so that I could see her eyes. She didn't smile or try to lighten the question. She stared into the blue-green horizon while holiday-makers in baggy shorts and colorful shirts and big sun hats milled by, most of them carrying magazines or the Saturday newspapers.

"Because of everything we've gone through together."

"Is that all?"

"Isn't that enough?"

I nodded, but Irina thought about it some more. There were times she was so serious it was impossible to picture her laughing, or singing, or dancing sexy on a stage, or playing I Spy or hidey-go-seek with her daughters.

"Because of the way you looked after me when I left Julián all those years ago. I was a bitch to live with but you let me live with you. You never said, But you promised to stay a week, maybe two, no more. One day, you know what I found? I found your makeshift Filofax. Remember that stupid thing? You used to always carry around a sheet of A4 paper that you folded in half and in half again, and that was where you kept your reminders and your grocery lists and the new addresses you needed and all the new telephone numbers you came across. You'd torn it up, and the one before and the one before that. They were in the garbage when I was looking for something I'd lost somewhere. I was curious. I put all those pieces of yours together and what I read were lists of girls' names. Your Friday and Saturday night La Notte girls. God knows who they were. Sharon, Shauna, Joan, Jean, Jane, I'm just making them up, I can't remember the names. It was so soon in knowing each other that we weren't even kicked out of your big apartment yet and there you were throwing all those names and telephone numbers into the garbage. Do you remember? Do you remember when you decided to throw them all out?"

I didn't have a memory of it. Absolutely none. I couldn't picture that moment I'd chosen Irina over a wonderfully free-wheeling, drunken young life of absolute emptiness. It had just been the way. She was thinking well of me for something that was so easy to do I didn't even remember it.

"I forgave you because I'll never forget the day you came home to that little flat we had, what was it, three years later, and by then we were fighting a lot and even discussing whether we should break up, and I told you I was pregnant. You smiled and then you laughed, and then you made love to me on the floor and gave me the worst carpet burns, and almost as soon as you came you said, 'This is no place for a kid, we need to get a house with a yard in a street with lots of trees,' and that's what we did. You made me laugh, you really made me laugh. And when I found out it was twins I couldn't believe you were happier. And when I found out it was girls coming you had tears in your eyes. I saw them just kind of growing. Do you think I'd forget that, Sam?"

Seagulls were chasing the ferry. Some walked cockily around the deck like the children and holiday-makers. All of them scavenged for food. I saw Lara run to try and catch one, and that seagull scampered and then took to the wind currents, graceful wings barely beating.

"I forgave you because you've got a past just the same as I've got a past, and I don't own you anyway and I don't own the things that you think or the things that you dream about. It makes me love you more that you do think, and that you do dream, because nothing is easy in life except for stopping caring and living like you're dead, and that's something you haven't done, no matter how hard it is to run a restaurant and bring up three children and see your wife so unhappy because she doesn't know what else she can do other than be a wife and a mother. You know how many of my girlfriends have got husbands that are dead as doornails? Can you imagine what these women tell me about their men?" Irina shook her head. "And then there's another thing. Another thing I want to tell you."

"What?"

"I forgave you because of Gabriella. Because you wanted Sandy to be Gabriella. All right. I don't like what happened or the way you tried to hide it but I'm trying to understand. I'm trying to understand it the way you understand it. I forgave you because you remember Gabriella and you still love Gabriella, because you cherish her memory and you wish good things for her. Don't you ever look around, Sam, and wonder about everyone else? Look at me. I was married to Julián for eleven years, and I was young and impressionable, it's true, but not as young as you were when Gabriella disappeared, and when the time came to get him out of my life that's what I did, just like that. I cut him out. I wiped him out. And it was easy to do because it's what other people do, they just use people up and then wipe them out, just like that, don't try and tell me it isn't so. After eleven years together he was out of my mind and out of my heart. When people are done with other people they break away, they turn their backs, and they repeat words and platitudes they hear on American talk-show programs about letting go and setting one another free, but what they're doing is covering over the fact that they don't really care. Oh, of course they care for a bit, they care that they hurt someone, to see something as intense as a relationship fail is always painful, but when the point comes where they want to go, they go. What else can they do? And the person left behind is just left behind. They've got no comeback for having their guts kicked out. Every promise that was ever made to them by their loved one means nothing. Everything they ever saw of themselves in their loved one's face seems like the worst kind of lie, now and forever. Whenever they hear the words 'I love you' from then on they hear instead 'I'm going to use you up.' Human nature is greedy, and cruel, and when people go it's because they've taken what they want and there's nothing left to interest them, or they see something better ahead and want that instead, or they go just because it's too hard to love another human being for a long time. I forgave you because you kept your love for Gabriella and because I dismissed Julián with a wave of my hand. You've wept for that girl over years and years and I've congratulated myself for being smart enough to get rid of a used-up husband. I know you loved Gabriella. I know I never loved Julián. All right. That's why I forgave you. I forgave you because to you Sandy was Gabriella and Gabriella was Sandy and you couldn't control the emotions you've been carrying. When Julián's in town and I see him for a coffee all I think about is how wrinkled he looks, and how someone should tell him to cut his nose hairs, and how hard it would be for a woman to be made love to by such a slow old Spanish bull."

I grinned at Irina but then I stopped, because her joke wasn't a joke, what she said was real.

"The thing is I envy you. I do in a way. Nothing's guaranteed, Sam. I forgave you because if you can love Gabriella forever, maybe you can love me forever. And if you can't love me for that long, then I believe, I really believe, you'll at least love Natalie and Annie and Lara forever. What more would a wife and mother want from her man? What more is there for me to look for? What more do you think I could ever want?"

The first gray-green-brown outlines of the island were becoming visible in the distance, beyond the spreading strait of choppy sea.

"Well, there's one thing, Sam. There's one big thing I want. Never lie to me again. If you do find Gabriella Zazò here and you love her enough to want her, really want her, you have to say. That's it. All right?"

"All right."

"You know what else? To hell with acting. When did I suddenly decide I was an actor? I think I could sing again. I'm a singer and that's what I should have let myself keep believing in. My throat is fine these days, even if I'll never have the greatest voice in the world. I'll have to have lessons to make sure I don't hurt it, but it's not impossible. If I get up on a stage and sing it doesn't mean I'm still tied to Julián Luna and His Orchestra. I think that's why I've stopped myself so long. I think that's why I denied myself the pleasure of doing it. But to tell the truth, Sam, it is what I really want to do. There have been nights where I've just dreamed about it, just to sing. I dream about it in exactly the same way I used to dream about giving birth to the babies when I was pregnant. My dreams are full of music. I feel like I could really be that music again. Does that sound stupid?"

"No, Irina, no."

"I think it means I'm happy. I think it means I'm really, really happy. The fact of Gabriella or the maybe of Gabriella can't make me unhappy. She's a part of you, Sam, dead or alive, and that's the way it is." She bit her bottom lip and took my hand. "So will you help me be a singer again? ¿Puedes ayudarme? Will you help me?"

Irina must have liked what she saw in my face. She was smiling now. Really smiling. Despite everything, she had a gaiety about her. White teeth in her brown face, nice dark almond-shaped eyes crinkling at the corners, and the type of smile that you can't fake, or put on like lipstick, or act. There was something else too. Her palm, holding mine, was very damp. It wasn't because of the hot morning. Irina was really perspiring and it was because all of this she said came from deep inside her. It meant so much to her, and it had all been thought out so hard, and her heart was such a full thing.

From this hard deck vibrating to the great heaving engines and propellers you could see anything you wanted to see, the blue and the green of the waves, the hazy outline of the coming island, the sun burning down out of an azure sky. You could even see forever, to tell the truth, if you were so inclined; it was in that spreading, never-ending sky all right, but mostly it was closer, in the faces of all the children scurrying and laughing and squealing across the iron decks below.

"What do you want to sing? Latin, salsa, jazz, blues?"

Irina leaned her head on my shoulder. "Oh, who knows? Dreamy things," she answered. "Beautiful, dreamy things."

The Dead Man's Dream

IN THE HEAT OF a southeast Queensland island's midafternoon I found the street and the number and walked through a scrubby front yard to a weather-beaten beach house, the number of which matched Sandy's, matched Tony's.

All the windows were wide and the front door was open for any rising breezes, this entrance guarded only by a screen door with broken hinges and a diagonal rent in the netting. I saw all the way through the place to the back, where a whole half-wall of louvres starting at about the height of a knee were open, giving onto very high sandy slopes that led down to the undulating world of Deadman's Beach. It was as if the house were made of glass and so couldn't conceal the green sea beyond. A baby was wailing and I had to knock on an outside wall and rattle the screen door several times, my heart pounding.

First, a very ugly small dog came to investigate, giving me two dry *arf-arfs* and sitting himself down behind the screen and doing nothing else. Second, a man's voice testily called, "Wait a minute."

After more than a minute Pietro Pierucci came to the door carrying a baby in a brilliant white nappy. The baby was pressed to the left side of his chest and shoulder, and with his right hand Pierucci was gently tapping the baby's back. For the time being the wailing had stopped but I had the feeling that it might start all over again at any minute. At the sight of me Pierucci's hand fell still. He became quite still, staring at me, standing behind the broken screen door in bathing trunks and nothing else, his eyes round and wounded like a beast that's taken a heavy blow. It appeared as though, if not for the baby, Pierucci would have let his legs collapse under him.

He didn't say anything and neither did I.

With as little as a look I understood everything Tony Solero had told me about the letters and their contents. This man was not the same as our old local hero or even the unpredictable bagman-turned-informant of the eighties. He was brown and hard-lean but gone very, very old, his hair white and buzz-cut, the tight skin in his tanned face etched with deep long vertical lines, and apprehension already in his eyes. Maybe these days it was always there. The last time I'd seen him was as a force of defiance and anger and insolence striding in a beige suit past pressing journalists and television news crews, 1989 or 1990 or both, and this tiny fistful of years later he couldn't have seemed more different.

After more silent moments which didn't wipe the complete astonishment off his face, he looked as if he might speak—but nothing came out.

So I said, "Is she here?"

H IS HANDS WERE full but he kicked the bulldog out of the way so that I could open the screen door and let myself through. He led the way down the short corridor to the back room. The walk seemed to take forever and I searched for signs of Gabriella in every thing and in every space we passed. The kitchen was stifling with the way something in a pot simmered and steamed on the stove, but we didn't stay in there. I expected of course to be tricked at the last turn. I suspected I was already tricked and there was no Gabriella. The stubby bulldog wandered off to some other place. The back room where the air circulated nicely was much cooler and very bright because of all those glass louvres, and busy too, with a little playpen and a multitude of yellow building blocks loose or put together into various architectural designs, and an old mahogany rocking chair, and a well-lived-in sofa with flattened pillows turned strangely sideways into a rectangular picture window, and a cradle shrouded by a much mended mosquito net.

Pierucci said, nursing his baby, "Joshua's not very happy, he's had a bit of colic."

"Is she here?"

"Not now."

"Is he hers?"

"Ours."

"Can I hold him?"

"No."

He carefully put little Joshua down and this energetic boy who had now forgotten his tears and wailing crawled to the building blocks, bulldozed over them, went onto the rocking-chair and took it by a leg, and started to shake it furiously. Actually, quite proudly, and this was for my benefit, I thought. The rocking chair crashed backward and stayed that way and Joshua didn't cry but looked spectacularly surprised. He wriggled out of his clean new nappy and sat naked in the center of the room and picked at the foreskin of what seemed an inordinately long baby penis. Every now and then he babbled whatever words he could say.

His father said, "Good, stay there," then turned to the louvres and shaded his eyes at the sea. "Of all the people I've been expecting to turn up at my door, I wasn't expecting you."

"I had a message that was supposed to have come from Gabriella Zazò."

"You did?"

"Yes."

"Where?"

"At my restaurant."

"A message at Notte e Giorno?" Pierucci shook his head as if he couldn't imagine what this fantastic thing might mean, but his wounded eyes said he understood immediately and all too well at that.

Silence—and he watched the green soaring sea.

"By the way," I said, because of the stultifying aroma from the kitchen, "you've got your heat turned too high. What is it—chicken and rosemary or something?"

"Yes, exactly."

"I thought so. You're trying to simmer it too fast. It'll be too tough if you don't go a little easier."

Pierucci ignored me and my advice. Maybe he liked his chicken meat hard and stringy. I didn't speak again but instead chose to endure his mute staring at the world past Deadman's Beach until he himself felt the urge to say something.

It was this: "Got a wife and twins, Sam?"

"There are three daughters now."

"Three, I heard, and they're all girls. I keep up with what's happening. Three girls'll end up giving you a heart attack one day."

"Probably."

"And so you reckon Gabriella Zazò called you at your restaurant and she asked you to come over?"

"No, her sister Sandy gave me the message."

"The rock-star Amazon. She's been here."

Pietro Pierucci laughed so humorlessly it came out as the type of dry bark his little bulldog would have been proud of. The lines in his face deepened with either rage or hurt or both.

"*Accussi sunu i cosi, chi ci putemu fari?*" he said, knowing I would understand. It was the common, thousand-year-old fatalistic rejoinder of Sicilian men sitting in wicker chairs smoking and gossiping with their friends about a world they couldn't hope to control: "That's the way things are, what can you do about it?"

His hand played with one of the louvres, tilted it, put it back, tilted it again so that it caught the sunlight. We could have stayed like that all afternoon. It was time to push him.

"Gabriella wants to see me, Peter. You can't stop it."

The old Pietro Pierucci would have made a person pay with a little blood for saying something as bald as that but this new one, this gray one, said, "Well, as you can see for yourself, the lady's not here."

H OW WAS I supposed to think of Gabriella as a lady? In my mind she was fourteen, or perhaps even fifteen, but no more, forever.

Yet it didn't matter one way or the other, for of course she wasn't there. She wasn't anywhere. For some reason these monsters were pulling a trick on me, these monsters being Pietro Pierucci and the rock-star Amazon Sandy. That badly cooking chicken with rosemary wasn't for Gabriella Zazò. She of all people would have had the sense to teach a man better than that. Maybe Sandy and Pierucci were sadists working together, or researchers researching how many games the human mind can deal with before it collapses in on itself. And the baby wasn't Gabriella's. There was nothing of her features in little Joshua's eyes or hair or skin. Maybe it was Sandy's. Maybe big fleshy Sandy was hiding in one of the rooms holding her sides to keep the laughter in. Maybe that eighteen-year-old and this lean gray man were lovers; maybe Sandy Zazò was in fact Zazuella O'Connor, a writer so unimportant her books weren't even in print anymore. I thought of every crazy permutation to try and explain things but none of them seemed right at all.

A ND NOTHING WAS helped by this silence that kept falling between Pierucci and me; every word felt as if it had to be dug out of a grave. Except for the creaking of that louvre's hinge and the crashing of the incoming waves down against that curving strip of sandy beach there was little else to listen to. Pierucci seemed to think that if he pretended I wasn't there soon enough I'd get bored and go away.

"Peter," I said, "why don't you tell me what your story is."

"You think you deserve to know?"

"If it involves Gabriella. Is that how it is, are you really trying to say it involves Gabriella?"

"I haven't said a thing."

"But don't you want to? Don't you want to get it off your chest? If you don't tell it to me who else will ever listen?"

Pierucci turned to me with equal parts hate and hurt. "Plenty of people would like to know."

"But who else would understand? Who?"

Little Joshua sneezed wetly and lost his balance, falling sideways and then laughing about it. Pierucci leaned down and set him straight and wiped the baby's leaking nostrils with his fingers.

He wasn't the same anymore. He had to write letters to Tony Solero and God could only say who else in order to try and find some sort of absolution for himself. It was a good thing to do but the fact that he wrote so incessantly said that he would never let himself find it. The hardest man I've ever known was weak from the twists and turns of his life, and with the very fact of me in front of him he was diminishing by even greater degrees—or maybe it was his love for Gabriella and her ghost that finally made him tell his story.

"You know how stupid life is," Pietro Pierucci started.

And so I gave myself over to listening, and in a way I imagined I felt the same as Gabriella must have felt listening to her nonno Enrico Belpasso's stories so long ago, and that was the way I put Pietro Pierucci's words together—the way my Firehead would have written them.

B UT DO YOU really know how stupid life is, Sam? When I was on that stand in the middle of the police commissioner's trial and I was giving my evidence that's exactly when it came to me. After all those years here we were in the Supreme Court talking about family trusts and how people hide their assets and how bank accounts can be opened and maintained in false names and that was when it clicked, that was when the possibility of a line of investigation I'd barely investigated hit me again. False names. I didn't follow it because I didn't know a reason for it but now I saw that just because I didn't understand the reason didn't mean it couldn't be so. The fact is it's hard to find someone who doesn't want to be found and I was so blind I'd always assumed that if Gabriella wasn't dead then of course she'd want to be found.

But what if she didn't?

In the early days of Fitzgerald and then Drummond I still had colleagues who would do favors for me even though I was already out of the force and a private citizen and giving evidence. These friends did broad-query searches through all the databases at their disposal, on a new name. Not Gabriella Zazò anymore but G. O'Connor, a female. A female who would have taken the family name of her biological father. There were plenty of first names that started with a G to go with the last name O'Connor and there were one hundred and twenty-four Gabriel O'Connors in the country that they found. Not a single Gabriella but maybe that was just a fine point. I had my colleagues initiate police contact with every single one, even though all but five or six of them were supposed to be male, just in case, to cover everything and everyone.

None of them turned out to be her and I was in another dead-end street.

I daydreamed through the court trials. I was there on the days I had to give evidence but in a way I wasn't there because I had something bigger and better to occupy my mind. I was always writing the names Zazò and O'Connor and one day toward the end it seemed like they were married, Zazò+O'Connor. By the time that jump happened my name was ruined in the force and the community and there was no friendship or loyalty left between police officers or detectives or support staff and me, but I had a last contact in transport and he had one database he could investigate and that was driver's-license issuing and he came up with a lovely match.

O'Connor, Z., born 1961. First name Zazuella.

The Witness Protection officers hated my guts but they gave me one break and that was they asked me where in all of the country I might like to be relocated to and I said Adelaide, because that was where

Zazuella O'Connor was registered with a South Australian license to drive, but I didn't tell them that and such a move was all right by them because most of all I just had to be out of Queensland.

After years of dead-end streets now I was in a dead-end city. Nothing I did in that new place turned her up. A year passed and then close to two and I was sitting in a beer garden one Saturday afternoon and Gabriella walked in and my heart wanted to explode. After so long I didn't truly believe it was possible she was alive. Not until the split-second I saw her.

Her hair was like a man's and jet-black and she was taller and not scrawny but she was still who she was. She was with a woman. She didn't see me. Neither of them saw me for the week that I followed them everywhere. It was the most interesting thing I did for years and I would have kept doing it for longer just because it gave me so much pleasure. I didn't know when I'd let her see me but the right time came very quickly and that was the night I watched her in bed with this woman.

I smashed that little flat to pieces and even though I hadn't planned it that way I beat Gabriella just about senseless and I beat that woman raw whoever she was. I beat Gabriella for everything she'd put everyone through and for having short black hair and a new name and for being alive when everyone cried that she was dead. I beat that woman for having her. I did whatever I wanted to do and two things inspired me the one being how I was ruined in the force and the newspapers and the second being that I knew I would be safe here doing whatever I wanted to do because how can a person who's made herself so anonymous and so new for so long run for help to any authorities? I put the fear of God into that other woman I don't even remember her name the silly bitch and Gabriella begged her not to say anything to anyone anyway. She begged and begged her even more than she begged me.

Why did she beg her so much and not me so much? Because in her sly smart sharp little way she knew she'd find a way to get the better of me. That's little Gabriella Zazò for you.

So I visited her every day and watched her making ceramics in her little rented half a house and watched her writing little books and one day she changed her hair color to blond like a Swede's and she tried to light out of Adelaide and the fear of exactly that was why I was making sure to keep her under my constant surveillance. I ended up dragging her by that short blond hair into my car and I decided to drop every pretense about any of this so I took her into my brick house in Glenelg, which as you might know is a beach suburb at the edge of the city of Adelaide. Eventually she had to give in and I made love to her for the first time and that was pretty much against her will I admit that but then she asked me to turn my bed toward the sea and every next time her face would drop to the side and she would do that she would watch the sea and not mind what I did.

Of course with someone like her it wasn't easy but in the end I thought I'd won. Really it was just a deal that we didn't speak about. I would keep her secret if she would stay with me and if she ran away I would shoot my mouth off and this was exactly what she most feared so that was the pact. I'm not saying I didn't wonder what was right and what was wrong. I had to think to myself do I still want to bring her home to her family even to Sam Capistrano do I really want to make everyone happy but what I decided was that I deserved to be happy and what would make me happy would be to have her even if she did have to watch the sea like that and even if there was this unspoken pact and so that's what I did I made sure I would have her.

She got pregnant very fast but from the first time I was doing it to her I was thinking even then get her pregnant get her pregnant just get her.

What I didn't think was that the fact of me and the fact of a baby would make her want to come home finally after so many years. It was either give in to this new idea or I knew she'd say damn the consequences and so run away again because now that was her pattern in life. The other thing I didn't think was that she herself would not be able to make it into the old hometown. First I made her laugh about our Catholic background and I called her Eve and I was Adam and we were kicked out of the Garden. We mixed it up with the Moses story about the promised land and how Moses couldn't cross the threshold even after all his trials and tribulations. This—this island here is as close as she could get to the place she started calling home with a sort of wistful sound in her voice. So we're just across the water. We're settled.

The truth is it suits me best of all to be here. I like it.

And then the final twist came and with Gabriella you know it's always like the world's craziest and most dangerous roller-coaster ride. This twist was that Gabriella or as she is called now Zazz saw the death notice for her grandfather in the newspaper. That was the last thing she had to get over because of the whole story with the old man and so now I can see she really believes she is ready to go home. Understand?

You don't believe me. You don't believe a word of this, Salvatore Capistrano.

I T WAS DIFFICULT and eerie to listen to an insanity that was quite so insane.

Pierucci turned and chewed his lips and again took up his stance at those louvres, watching the sea. Then I saw I was wrong, it wasn't the sea he'd been studying all this time, and not the incoming tide, or the swimmers. It was the long strip of sand and who might be walking along it. Pietro Pierucci was looking and longing for Gabriella or more likely her ghost.

I said, disappointment battling victory, "I was nearly believing you. Maybe you did find some person in Adelaide who was a lot like Gabriella. Maybe you did end up making some sick sort of perverted relationship with her. I don't know and I don't really care. I don't believe you because you've got it the wrong way around. Because if she was alive there'd be one thing most of all that she'd come back for. The old man. She loved him. They had this special thing. Enrico Belpasso not being there anymore would be one good reason *less* for going back."

Pierucci shook his head at the louvres. It was almost like sympathy and it only lived for seconds.

"Enrico Belpasso," he muttered.

Then Pietro Pierucci turned and gave me a stare that was as cold and empty as his insides, and to my complete surprise that was the thing—the absolute—that finally filled in every space in Gabriella's Book of Fire.

His face seemed to melt in front of me. The burning in my ears started. Or was it a roaring? And the strength went out of my arms and out of my legs so that I had to sit in a chair. Perspiration gathered in fat beads on my forehead and then started to run. My hands were wet.

Pierucci refused to look at me a moment longer.

S HE'D TOLD HIM about it, but it was in her diary anyway, the words that told the story, if you only knew how to read them right.

I never did, never imagined, never saw what was in front of my eyes. The shadows coming down on her and the fire burning her insides. The mental escape into a dream she called the universe and the universe she called the Aleph. Why didn't I ask myself what sent her into such extraordinary flight? Why did I need Pietro Pierucci's dead-eyed stare to awaken me? Then there were the stories about old loves in romantic Sicilian fields and an old man telling a little girl, You say, Gabriella, Fortunata can't come again. Isn't she here already, Gabriella? Isn't she standing in front of me?

And what had Gabriella herself said to Mrs. Veronica?

Maybe you could ask one of them to call herself Fortunata.

What she meant: Because I can't be Fortunata again. I'll pay someone to take my place. Happy birthday, Enrico Belpasso, but this gift is for me.

Ten years later Enrico Belpasso never spoke about Gabriella again. That was after he told me about the hiding place; everything must have come back to him and so he never mentioned her name or told stories of her one more time. What absolution, if any, had that old man sought? How would I ever know? Pietro Pierucci ate himself up inside but the heart of a man I'd been closest too would stay locked in this mystery.

Pasta: 1995

What I did know was that he was dead and so I was supposed to believe Gabriella Zazò was back.

JOSHUA WAS STARING at me from his position on the floor. His wet loose baby lips were open and his big eyes perfectly round, and a little line of drool was flowing down onto the creamy white of his chest. He gurgled and started to eat his own chubby fingers because that's what innocence does when it knows no better.

Pierucci moved from the view and wiped Joshua's chin and straightened his cotton singlet and let him stand up and hang on to his leg.

"She's gone for her afternoon walk down the beach. When you've got a kid you need your quiet time or else you go mad. You know that three times over. My quiet time's around seven, so why don't you come back then, if you have to come back at all. I go up to the beer garden for a few drinks. You can visit while I'm away and plan whatever you want to plan with her. All right? Why don't you get out of my sight and do what you have to do behind my back?"

So that was his equal parts of hate and hurt; that was why he'd never taken the time to tell me Gabriella Zazò was supposed to be alive; he knew that if I came here it would only be to take her away.

Even through the howling black that filled my head I could see how he longed for me to let his dream dream on, and his dream was that he and his woman and his baby would stay like this, the emotionally mutilated Gabriella Zazò turning her face to the side and gazing at the sea every time he moved his shadow down on top of her.

My God, but what was I to believe?

Pierucci tried his first and final appeal to me because there was nothing else he could do. He said, "She's got a life, Sam, she's got a baby. She's got work, she's got me. Why does that have to change? Leave her be, okay, leave us be."

That well-lived-in sofa with the flattened pillows that was turned so strangely and obliquely against the rectangular picture window, against the universe of sky and sea, kept drawing my gaze. If any of Pierucci's story was true it was a monstrous thing.

I said through my teeth, "So she's happy?"

"She's content."

W HEN I PUSHED the chair and it tumbled over Pierucci took a step back and the baby fell on his bottom and started to wail. Pierucci took that step backward but then straightened himself and stayed where he was, the crying going on and on.

It didn't matter to me that the man still had some dignity.

For this little dream he'd forged for himself was almost unraveled. Gabriella was making her moves to come home, and once home what threat did he have to keep her with him anymore? It was bizarre—now I almost believed him. His insanity was spreading to me. Gabriella Zazò was alive and here was her wailing child and her name these days and for twenty years was the ridiculous Zazuella O'Connor. Wasn't a *zarzuela* some kind of old Spanish music that had to do with love and courtship, the type that Julián Luna would still be playing somewhere with one of his many orchestras? I picked up a white porcelain vase, then a water jug made of blue glass and with a huge twisted handle. When I turned both these things upside down their imprints read "Zazz."

"Where does she make these?"

He'd fallen too far to stop. Pierucci nodded to a wooden shed that was all rickety and bent on a scrubby sandy hillock fifteen meters from where we were standing. White nappies flapped in the breeze, strung on a clothesline that went from the shed to the house.

"Her sanctuary."

It occurred to me that this at last was something I could understand better than he, Gabriella and her need for a place of solitude and retreat.

I said, "Do you know what an Aleph is?"

Pierucci stooped and picked up his baby, who had stopped crying murder and now sobbed and coughed. He nursed Joshua, rocking him

in his arms with care until the baby changed attitude and started to gig-
gle and gurgle, white plump feet kicking and little claw hands reaching
up to touch the gray face.

Pietro Pierucci said, "A what?"

The shed's tin roof reflected in the sunlight.

The Dreamer in Her Dream

GOING OUTSIDE, THE SUNSHINE seemed too bright and my shirt far too wet for this to be a dream, but that was what it had to be, a dream of the type that brings you terrors and truths in equal proportions.

I stopped and had to get myself together. Look at the sea look at the sky look at the scrubby grass and sand between your feet. As I did so the ugly little bulldog with the droopy, flabby, smashed-in face came to investigate me again. He waited and I felt vaguely foolish, then he followed my steps across the backyard. When he was certain I was going into the shed he scampered ahead as if to welcome me into Gabriella Zazò's workplace. There was a pottery wheel and broken ceramics, a small wood-fired kiln with a hand bellows, and a million mounds of raw clay that might one day fit the shapes in Gabriella's head. Charcoal hand drawings were tacked to several walls, illustrating ideas for what she or her ghost might make next.

And Zazuella O'Connor's short oeuvre of books were in multiples on a shelf. I looked at the one I already knew and the three that I didn't and they were all roughly the same and without biographical details or a photograph.

The wall that faced the sea was made mostly of glass louvres, in exactly the same fashion as the beach house. Against it there wasn't a sofa or a bed but a newly varnished oak desk. It was very busy but very neat too, clean though speckled with sand, with six deep bronze-handled drawers, and papers and notebooks stacked in asymmetric piles on the top. If there was a Gabriella she used one of her own home-turned coffee cups to house her many pens. They stood there, waiting to be picked up, so that she could come and sit and write two words or two hundred or two hundred thousand. I reached out to touch the papers for the simple reason that after twenty years' living without her I still half imagined Gabriella Zazò had never seen the inside of this so-called sanctuary.

The bulldog panted and looked up at me, then scratched furiously at one ear.

It took me a moment to realize that the Book of Fire was on top of some stacked notebooks. Seeing it there was like seeing it for the first time down in the musty shelter under Gabriella's old family home. It was strange that the diary had left my hands only days before, yet here it already was. How must Gabriella have reacted reading her child-woman's thoughts? GabriellaGabriellaGabriella—her very name was a question that sent my mind into confused spirals. Out of the spiraling came another question: was Sandy and her changeling game just a little sexy charade this "ghost" had planned in order to get her diary back?

Beside the Book of Fire and the stacked notebooks a pile of loose papers was weighed down by a kaleidoscope. This one was by no means a child's toy but something heavy and clearly expensive, made of bronze and polished wood and glass lenses instead of plastic and cardboard. It was Italian-made, I thought, for the name inscribed on the side: Poli & Co. I held it to my eye and the sea cracked into a nebula of shooting stars and planets exploding and comets leaving fiery trails through the heavens.

I put it down with care. These things in this sanctuary made a sort of sense.

Rummaging around like a bad spy, I found those loose-leaf papers and heavy notebooks were filled with handwriting, in blues and blacks and greens, and every careful notation and correction was done with a thin red ballpoint pen. Gabriella's Book of Fire had never come to an end. What I'd had in my possession had only been a beginning, yet even with all those myriad scrawled dates cascading before my eyes—to the end of the seventies through the eighties, the nineties, a continuous unfurling of narrative and thought—I was clouded with doubts. Whatever force was directing me, it wanted me to believe that in the twenty years since the events at Nocturne Gabriella had always kept writing her story, her grandfather's stories, and the stories of her own little island so far away in the Mediterranean. Either Gabriella had done so or—come on—Sandy Zazò, not a rock-star Amazon but the young writer of four children's books, who for reasons known only to herself, and of course Pietro Pierucci, had taken up the interesting creative task of *continuing* a lost sister's story.

This was the possibility that joined every thread.

If the handwriting was different, from beginning to end, there would be the answer. As was always my tendency I'd forgotten my glasses, which I only really needed for reading. I gave the pages and pages and pages of handwriting as close an inspection as I could, yet those sentences flowing so unrelentingly into one another seemed ridiculously hard to judge. The writing at the start was more or less the same as the writing at the finish, wasn't it? The loops, the whirls, the punctuation. In my inexpert way I thought there were only the changes you'd expect from an adolescent growing into maturity.

So I had to clasp my hands together just to keep them still.

There was a final thing to take note of. Gabriella's Book of Fire wasn't called that anymore. The title had been crossed out and in its place was written another word, *Kaleidoscope*.

The bulldog sneezed.

I lifted my eyes from the utter disarray those writings spun for me and gazed instead at the view through that expanse of glass. Salt had dried on the louvres but the panorama was so clear and sharp—the infi-

nite tract of sea and above it the wide sweep of sky—that it hurt, it physically hurt to look at it so.

Then I saw her.

JUST AS PIETRO Pierucci had said, Gabriella Zazò was walking
along the beach, now returning from however far she'd gone, her
feet splashing in the swirling wavelets of the shallows. Her hair wasn't
cut short and dyed black or blond or anything. It was her natural color
and her natural style.

Others were scattered far and wide across the white sands, families,
children, dogs, beach umbrellas, what have you, but she seemed to walk
inside a space of her own, untouchable and untouching in this world,
her wild red hair marking her as the Firehead forever.

She stepped further up toward the loose dry sand where the water-
line didn't reach at this time of day, and she seemed to step right out of
her clothes into a pink nakedness. She made a pile of her things and
turned and dashed into the waves, making a shallow dive as a curler
poised breaking over her. I saw the flash of her buttocks disappearing
into the churning-foaming green and blue and then she emerged further
out, her hair wet and now clinging straight, her head and pale shoulders
bobbing among the white crests of the waves.

I threw my clothes beside hers and the bulldog sat down on his
haunches, tongue hanging, ready to wait. He must have waited like this
for Gabriella or for Pierucci or for both every day. No one noticed me
run like a demon into the sea after Gabriella—no one on the beach, that
is, but I had a sense that Pietro Pierucci might still be at those glass windows back of the beach house, holding his baby and making sure to
never miss a thing that Gabriella Zazò did.

Desperate inside, flooded with happiness and relief and deliverance,
the nice bitter taste of saltwater already in the back of my throat,
already stinging my eyes, I swam out strongly. I wanted to laugh and to
shout, for what else is *allegria*? Gabriella was a good swimmer; she

seemed to cut through the waves and into them, sometimes diving and then reappearing past a set of new rumbling roiling crests. It felt good to be inside that current and to fight the strong beating-into-shore waves. It felt right to be naked, miraculous to be swimming toward my ceaseless dream. How long was it since I'd swum in the sea? The water was cool and there was no industrial or natural scum. People said there were often dolphins close to the shoreline and whales passing in the spawning season, but not today. The sun on my head and shoulders was warm without being burning. I was renewed; the leaden feeling that had come over me while with Pierucci was gone. The spiraling years of confusion and frustration were ended. There was an inner rumbling roiling of my own, and even the weight of what I now knew to be true about Gabriella and Enrico Belpasso and Pietro Pierucci couldn't drag me beneath the surface of those beautiful waves.

When I was closer I had to call out Gabriella's name three times. She was treading water, then lying back, floating. I was almost touching her when she turned.

We stared at one another through the space of two decades.

Then she pushed herself into my arms and cried out into my shoulder. As the waves breathed back our feet could touch sandy bottom but when they swelled we floated upward.

"My God," Gabriella said, "you look like a ghost coming out of the water."

To me of all people it was the strangest thing she could have said, but my *allegria* only made me all the hungrier for her. There was the smallest inflection of that old Sicilian accent, just a touch that turned the end of her words around and marked her as forever from somewhere else.

"Are you real? Gabriella, are you real?"

"I'm real—by God how I'm real."

She wanted to kiss me, really cover me with her kisses, but we were out too far for holding one another without drowning.

I said, when I had the chance, when I'd turned her around and around and kissed her and touched her and told her how mad I was for her, "Baby—I've seen your baby."

"Isn't he beautiful? Can you believe he's mine?" She held and pressed her breasts as if to show me, laughing. "Can you believe I nursed him with these little things?"

Gabriella was so desirable in the sea. Twenty years hadn't passed, not even twenty days. The way her hair was slicked back and down, the way her white arms and legs flashed inside the water, the way her breasts with their coral-pink nipples were caressed by the cooling waves. She was a woman in her thirties and the child of fourteen was still somewhere in her eyes. I couldn't stop staring at her, caressing her, feeling her. The lines in her face accentuated her old prettiness in a way I couldn't have hoped to imagine, making her beautiful with maturity. But "beautiful" wasn't the word to use. She was breathtaking. Not in the way of film actors or catwalk models or photogenic specimens whose perfect features adorn the covers of magazines, but breathtaking in the way that she carried years of living. Living, real living. That's what made my heart soar so high—Gabriella's living.

I saw too, in an overpowering rush, that her body had filled out. She wasn't skinny and scrawny and all knees. Her breasts had weight and were lined from her feeding, and when we came together they pressed to me, just an imprint on my cold skin, the waves taking her away again. Her belly was soft and her thighs too. Her skin had deepened in color and was no longer perfectly pink or white but in places very softly tan; her face wasn't smooth as a girl's anymore either. She showed every single one of her years and they were full of heartbreak and hope, and I wanted to know what made up each of those things.

The breakers roared behind us.

"Can you tell me, Gabriella? Can you tell me what happened?"

"Already?" she said. "Does it matter?"

She came toward me again and I took her in my arms, and she cried, "Oh!" and I didn't care that she didn't want to say or even that we sank under the surface, both of us trailing bubbles, both of us spinning in the salty water. Her legs wanted to wrap around my hips; we kissed and kissed, tongues licking saltwater, not the old caramel and licorice and citrus tastes of old. Yet those beating waves wanted to spoil things, and Gabriella groaned playfully and laughed again, and I was light-headed and hard with desire and salvation—and with our eyes widening and our mouths opening a breaker like a building reared up and crashed down, smashed down, and broke us into a million pieces of forgetfulness.

W E DIDN'T GET out of the water and go dress ourselves. We were still coughing with the way we'd been tumbled and thrown about, and we dropped in the shallows in a nice seclusion from all the others who occupied the late-afternoon beach. Gabriella told me I was bleeding and I watched red drops fall into the clear water beside me. I liked the way that she and I and blood all went together. The wound on my cheek stung and she came close and pursed her lips and kissed it, holding my face in her hands. Her breath was as sweet as the ocean breeze. I wanted to cover her right there, to lay my body over hers and bear down and forget all the things that made up my blessed life.

Gabriella said, "You see what this place is? It's Heaven. It's like a corner of Heaven for me."

"But do you really want to come home? Is that what you really want?"

"Will you help me?"

Hadn't Irina asked me just that question this morning, on the rusty car ferry on the way over?

And I had to remember too the last time Gabriella asked me that, asked me to help then left me to carry the weight of the world. Her hand was still touching that bleeding graze. I had to move my face away.

Gabriella's hand stayed poised in the air and then, thoughtfully, she touched her lips with her fingertips. She said, "I'm ready to see my mother and my father. They should meet their grandson. I'd like to go for a walk through our old suburb. Maybe even live there."

"It's pretty different these days."

"Sandy too, I want to feel close to my sister, even if she is leaving."

"But how could you have left? And how could you have stayed away?"

"Come on, I'm sure you know enough now," Gabriella said, not responding to the accusation in my voice. Her face said she wasn't going to go any further.

So the sun glistened and reflected in the waves and their frothing crests were exactly like the thoughts that could keep me awake at night—busy and churning and never completely destined for rest. It was a shimmery sort of world we sat so close together in, Deadman's Beach not still and quiet like a place of graves but languidly moving toward an evening of sweet-scented air currents carrying the crash of ocean waves. And talking to this ghost who wasn't a ghost but little Gabriella Zazò as a woman in her mid-thirties, that had an imaginary quality too, as if I were dreaming an everyday dream, me, the sea, and the lost girl come home.

But Gabriella had to relent. It was me after all. She hadn't gone so hard that she could deny me completely.

"What I mean is—with Sandy visiting you and Pietro up in the house, you do understand enough?"

"About the old man? If I'd known back then, or even later, I would have . . ."

"You would have what?"

Something twisted inside me and the last bit of *allegria* was gone, but I didn't want to put words to such feelings, not yet, not to spoil all this.

"This is what I want to say. After you went, Gabriella, I was his friend. That's the lie you left me to live."

Gabriella's fingertips touched the graze on my cheek again. She wanted to soothe the loathing away as if it would be something very easily done.

"You don't have to touch me like that. Just tell me why it had to be."

It wasn't easy for her. She lived with betrayal and disappointment but all hope wasn't dead either. If it was she would never have reappeared, not out of her own sense of *la notte,* and that was why I had to press her.

She said, "Stories can be seductive just like wine and food. Maybe that's all you need to know. It means that even the ugliest storyteller becomes the most beautiful, if the story touches you deeply enough."

I shook my head. It was too hard to keep the good, the imaginary, the dreaming quality going. Inside I was cursing the memory of an old man; inside I was this far away from cursing her for her absence—but I had to stop myself, really stop myself. What brutality would help me here? And rage and romanticism and retribution, Gabriella, wouldn't they have pushed you further away?

Instead I said, "All those stories, I read them in your diary."

"There's so many more and that's what makes my writing so hard. *Kaleidoscope* could be the book I want it to be but for too, too long now"—this time she really smiled—"it's been the same old diary-doodling. Everything's in it but there's so much that in the end it turns into nothing. At least I've discovered what my real theme is. Now I'm getting somewhere. Do you want to know what that theme is?"

"What is it?"

"Belonging."

"I'm nearly finished your last children's one, Zazuella."

"Really?" She still smiled, even more so at the sound of her wrong name. "The books get published and they get gobbled up by young readers and then they disappear. I don't think that's so bad but the people who should know say it could be better if I did some promotion." She shook her head. "*Kaleidoscope* will stay without me, that's what I really want."

"So you can stay invisible. In your diary you wrote that one day people would cheer your name."

Gabriella gave herself the time to slowly study my face. I liked her doing that; I liked her looking at me. It made me feel like I was a center for her.

"Am I the only who's changed? Look at you," she said. She laughed. "Look at your nose."

Then between the competing elements of the sea and my changed face, the sea had to win. She was already watching it in a dreamy sort of way when she said, "You want to understand."

"I deserve the chance."

Despite herself Gabriella seemed to shrink. Her shoulder stopped touching my shoulder, a barely perceptible move that put the distance of a sea between us.

"I lived all around the country, if that's what you want to know. I let myself be myself, getting lost and turning around and finding new roads—but it was really just confusing movement for progress. The main thing I've been doing for twenty years is writing different stories down. I'm getting close to finding a structure that works." She looked at me with a little defiance. *"Va bene?"* she said, which means, All right?

It was only the first visit of our old secret language and that made it clear how far apart we were.

"I want to hear about what happened before that," I insisted. "You left because of Enrico Belpasso."

Nothing could have stopped me from bringing it up again but as soon as I did I was sorry. With the mention of his name a blush traveled down Gabriella's throat, and spread further, making the skin around the horizontal thrust of her collarbone look as if it had been exposed to the sun too long. It was a blush but you could call it a burn, like the memory of a young girl's flesh frying at a terrible touch. That at least was how I wanted to see it. She held her hands between her breasts and pressed hard. I thought she'd swoon, just like in old movies, but when I reached for her she didn't want my comfort. Gabriella's eyes were very green when she looked at me. Green like the ocean. Ocean eyes deep with vulnerability, hard with defiance. She shook her head, then her red wet hair, letting it straggle and fall.

She didn't want to speak.

So I said, "You were just a kid, Gabriella, it was so wrong to you."

Gabriella shook her head. "Sometimes. Sometimes it was right. Sometimes I was who he wanted me to be and that part of it made me happy."

Ossi dei morti. Skeleton bones. Why did they come back to me then? I was thinking of skeleton bones, those hard old Sicilian biscuits that Gabriella used to break in her hands to save her nonno's three rotten teeth. But it wasn't the biscuits I was thinking of but him, and the way his own skeleton bones were now cremated and turned into dust. On the annual Day of the Dead—the second of November of every year from here on in—they would be free to return. And what gifts would Enrico Belpasso have to bring his Gabriella but the same old decayed sack of disillusions as always? I had to sit where I was and clench my teeth for fear of howling the damnation of a dead man's skeleton bones.

Gabriella seemed to need to uncloud her thoughts. Or maybe, finally, she was deciding to trust me.

"There's something else. It was about the way we used to live."

"What?"

"About what I called it before, belonging. That's what I never found." Gabriella pressed her chest. It hurt her to even mention it and I understood it straight away. It was the hurt of what happened in her secret hiding place coupled with the hurt of what happened in that outside world we used to know; her breath barely seemed able to drive what she had to say next: "All those people who hated us, they taught us a lot of shame, didn't they? Shame—that's such a word."

"You should have told me."

"In Sicily I wasn't home because of this." Gabriella flicked her hair. "And my face. My freckles. My Irish looks that everyone knew the reason for. Back there they taunted me to enrage me and that's what I did, I used to let myself catch fire. Then when we made our escape this was supposed to be my place of hope. I needed all these new people surrounding me, I really needed them, and instead what were we? Wogs dagos eyeties. They were stupid and ignorant and I couldn't stop wanting to join them. They made me feel dirty and ugly and I kissed dirty and ugly boys to fit in. Do you think I'm proud of that?"

"But everyone wasn't the way you say."

That seemed to stop the conversation. That seemed to make Gabriella think I could never understand her.

She said, "I asked you before. Will you help me?"

And then she stopped very hard on that question too. It was easy to see why. She knew I didn't want to answer and she knew she was the firehead. Somewhere along the line of her life she'd learned that there were times she had to quell her anger—or explode into the same flames as always. She seemed to hate me now for not saying that I would help her; maybe that showed how complete her self-absorption was. Yet I didn't want to believe it was completely like that.

Gabriella swallowed once, twice, as if there were something dry in her throat. Her eyes seemed to grow larger.

"Now I wonder about other things. Things like how many people suffer the same way today. I like to call them my brothers and sisters. The nice Australian middle road is very, very wide, but if you're outside of that—"

"No, you're wrong, you're too bitter. Things are different."

"Do you read the newspapers?" Gabriella spoke more quietly. "Tell me something. You and Tony Solero and all the others. How did you make a home with strangers? How did you make them believe you're like them? How did you tell them that you need them?"

The truth was I didn't have an answer. I didn't have an answer because these were the questions from twenty years ago. We'd let go of all that. There'd been the good and the bad and in the end the enmity had just sort of run out. We didn't have to try to be like anyone anymore. I couldn't have expressed it any other way. Or maybe I was too simple and there truly was more than self-absorption to what Gabriella was saying. Yes, I did read newspapers but in the way a man preoccupied with his life and family and business does, looking for the little snippets that interest and amuse and can then be forgotten. Maybe these days I was too much in the nice fat center of Australian life myself and I didn't see what happened around me—to the different ones who were supposed to be Gabriella's brothers and sisters, to the ones she wanted to tell me were my brothers and sisters too. I looked at Gabriella with something new, a certain sense of true understanding.

"What's this book *Kaleidoscope* supposed to be about?"

She changed when I asked that, changed into the Gabriella I used to know. A light of old seemed to come on inside her, her face growing luminous, and these slow things told me that just as in the old days we could share one another's secret thoughts, if we gave it enough chance to happen.

"I keep telling you. Black white brown yellow, richmanpoorman-beggarmanthief. Washer-woman child-woman businesswoman crying-woman, and mothers too of course."

This was the part of her that was all too easy to like. The part that could seduce and amaze and make you want to love her forever.

"You think it's too romantic?" she said.

"It's everything you are."

"No," she said very definitely. "Everything that I should under-stand." Then she paused as if she were afraid to ask it again: "Will you help me?"

But we still weren't far enough.

"All right. Don't speak," she said. "Don't speak."

Gabriella breathed a deep sigh. Her smile softened and then went away and her eyes seemed to keep searching out the ocean. Whenever she watched it her body would relax. Her gaze would glaze and the lines of her face would smooth themselves so that she looked—like a child-woman.

WHATEVER IT WAS that she wanted or expected from me, my ardor toward her had finally settled. The old desires were old desires after all. We were naked in the cooling water and caressed by sunshine too, but I wasn't fifteen anymore. I wasn't blinded by those aching, all-permeating longings for physical release. Had those things only distanced me from her all those years ago? I had to wonder. I had a million more questions for her too, but I knew they couldn't be answered now. She was Gabriella and she wasn't Gabriella. I was scared that her life of escapes left her poised for escape just that one more time; I thought about what I'd learned from Pierucci, of her head falling sideways so that she could watch the sea whenever his shadow came down over her. Maybe every shadow sent her into that inconceivable universe. Maybe that's why her writing came so hard: she couldn't look her great theme straight in the face.

Or maybe things were as she'd said; now she could.

And she was my Gabriella and she wasn't my Gabriella; she was my first love; she'd reshaped herself and I didn't know enough to say whether it had been right or it had been wrong. All I cared about, when I came down to thinking about it clearly, was that I was with her again. I moved a little closer to her, then touched her breast with the backs of my fingers so that she looked at me curiously, wonderingly, then I put my arm around her, and she was warm and she sighed again, and then she laid her head on my shoulder.

"You ran away from the things that hurt you, and I was one of them."

"Please don't talk. Don't talk at all."

T HE POOL WE sat in was becoming a part of the sea. The shallows would not be shallows much longer. The water was nearly to our chests and the incoming waves could now rock and sway our bodies so that it was difficult to stay together.

Gabriella was the first to rise to her feet. She took a deep breath. Behind us the little bulldog barked, excited for whatever reason dogs get excited by the actions of their owners. I looked up at Gabriella, at her woman's body, at her dark red little lawn a palm's width below her belly button. Once upon a time I'd gone onto my knees and kissed her there. I looked at her nice breasts and hard nipples and imagined how she'd used them to make a baby strong.

"I want to swim alone now," Gabriella said.

"You're going to disappear again."

Gabriella almost laughed. "What, out there?"

"The last time—just tell me this. How was it that you disappeared? No one can disappear so completely. No one. You were waiting inside

Nocturne with me, the old man had that turn of his, and you were gone. You had no money, no clothes hidden away, you must have ended up a street kid or something? Invisible. How did you cope? How did you live?"

Gabriella looked down at me. She ran her tongue over her lips.

"Don't you remember the eldest boy I used to let kiss me?"

I shook my head. "What—?" I tried to think of it, tried to see it.

"He knew what was going on at Nocturne. I told him about it. He was very angry that I chose you to help me and not him. He came there, really, to save me."

"Mrs. Veronica and her daughter always said there was a car outside, someone staring at the front of the place. But it was a man."

"A teenage boy behind the wheel of a car can look like a man, can't he? When everything went wrong I panicked. The pressure was too much. I remember I ran out the back way and then somehow I was disoriented and confused and I was in the main street. I thought I'd killed my nonno. I must have run as hard and fast as I could but all I really remember is that my head was on fire and there he was waiting."

"And then?"

"And then he took me to his house. His parents were away. If they hadn't been away, who knows? That's how things work."

"His house. You mean his house in New Farm?"

"Maybe that's how things always happen, one thing leads to the next and you don't plan it to be that way but before you know it that's the road of your life."

I had to think about Irina when she said that, I had to think about our first meeting in the nightclub, the kisses in my kitchen, the one week, at most the two that she would stay, until ten years later there we were with three children and one life.

"I never meant to run away from you. I never meant to be saved by him. I never meant to go to his home. I never meant for something to break inside me, but it did, I felt it, I felt it break. It was as clear as that. And it didn't get better when he told me that my nonno was perfectly all right and alive. By then I didn't want to go home anymore. By then I was thinking, Nobody knows where I am so finally I'm free. It was as if the hardest part was already done. I didn't want anything except to cease to be. To start again and make myself into someone else. He tried to talk sense to me but I couldn't hear, couldn't listen, but then when I realized he was in love, infatuated, however it was for him, I knew I could make him do what I wanted."

There was that name to dig out of the grave of the past.

"Scholar-mouse-key."

"Bobby Skolimowski."

"You stayed with him? You were right there in New Farm?"

"I gave him what I knew would make sure he'd stay quiet. I knew how to do that. He repaid me by hiding me and feeding me and getting me clothes. You could say I was hidden in plain sight, but that's not true, I didn't go out. It was only a few days. We planned what we'd do and then we just left in his car."

"Mrs. Veronica used to say it was Japanese and yellow and her daughter said it was a Chrysler and silver."

Gabriella held her face until she remembered a piece that would help fill this bitter little join-the-dots game.

"A white EH Holden rusted nearly all the way through."

I shook my head. But for the bad memories of a brothel-keeper with bad colors and her horse-faced daughter, Gabriella Zazò would have been back to all of us inside of a week.

"He wrote a note for his parents and put it on the kitchen table. He used to ring them and they'd beg him to come home but they didn't know about me. They didn't know to go and tell Pietro Pierucci that their son had gone away. A nineteen-year-old boy leaves home to make his way in the world—it happens ten times a day. When we were over I don't know what he did."

"Where did you drive?"

"Straight to Melbourne. That was our goal. That was a nice big city to get lost in. We became new people and I stayed with him until I was eighteen. I planned my way and made myself the new me and when I was secure with who I was I left him behind. All the rest is the rest, until Adelaide."

I still shook my hanging head; I was again the demolished adolescent I used to be. Was it the flatness of Gabriella's intonation? The join-the-dots game of it? Was it the callous this and this and this that had gone on so smoothly while we'd all been tearing out our hearts? Or was it that not even once had she said she used to think of me day and night?

"You could have come back."

"Salvatore," she said, finally with some gentleness, adding, to be nice, the old Sicilian version, *"Turiddu."* That was more intimate than the way she now reached out to stroke my hair. "Not everyone's like you. Not everyone finds a home." She smiled. "Pietro's old contacts gave him your number and your address. I found them in his papers. I've spoken to Irina. I've seen your children."

When I looked up at her she was already watching ahead.

"At least I love the sea. I love to walk into it and lose myself in it. It makes me feel like I'm a part of something. Of course I'm not, but it's a very seductive lie. Belonging—that's what I've always looked for. But what I've found is aloneness. In a way I seek that too. I think I've come to love it—and too much. I can't be that way when I've got a little boy to care for. I have to change. But still. When I'm in the sea I just feel so beautiful. I feel like I can see the whole universe, and everything that's ever been dreamed, and everyone who ever dreamed it." She paused. "It's not enough."

Gabriella put out her hands and she strongly pulled me to my feet.

"Will you help me?"

It was such a question, and getting worse.

"If this time . . ." I said.

"What?"

"If this time you come to me."

Gabriella looked down at her small feet a moment and wriggled her toes into the wet sloppy sand. In some cubby somewhere, a million years ago, I'd bent down and caressed those feet and then taken her white toes into my mouth, making her shout with the sweet pain of it. Yet it had all been sweet pain. Gabriella Zazò had been too young and too lost to really love me.

"So go to your family," Gabriella said. "Now that you know what I'm like. You're not that impressed with me anymore. But do me a favor, please Salvatore. Sometimes—remember me the way you used to. I used to feel it everywhere I went. And when I felt it, I just loved myself that way."

It was like a little knife in my side, her finally saying that, and here she was about to run into the waves again.

"Wait," I said.

"Why should I wait?"

There were still things to ask, to say, to state, to claim, but until she came to me, or not, what I had was this: "Is there such a thing as an Aleph?"

That made her smile, smile as if her heart would never stop aching.

The breeze had well and truly risen, making the waves crash in more powerfully, making Gabriella's hair whip around her face. She looked at me then kissed me quickly, just a peck on the lips and her small hands briefly pressing against my chest. The kiss was different from any that I remembered from her. In a way I still wanted to sink deep into Gabriella and lose myself in her even if she preferred to swim in the sea and be its eternal child. But the price of having her was too high; what she still carried I'd left behind—all that bitterness and loneliness in the big dreamy streets of our big dreamy past. Now she planned to use those things to make herself strong. What I was left with was exactly what I had in the beginning. I would never lose her, not when she was in me this way. I wished I could have told her but it was beyond me. It was truly beyond me.

Gabriella thought about my question long enough.

"I used to have my own but then I lost it and I stopped believing it was real." She said, "But when I'm standing here I do see it again. When

I'm writing at my desk I do. It's the sense of being alone yet not being alone. Look." She stretched her body as if offering herself to the sun and wind. "And . . ."

"And?"

"And. Why is there always an and?" She liked, at least, to be light. "*And* that's why I think I'm a writer, because I think such thoughts."

Gabriella Zazò gave me our old secret smile, but that was all, then she walked naked back into the sea, her dream.

Kaleidoscope

WHEN I RETURNED TO our rented little flat by the waterside of
Cylinder Beach, which is of course not very far from Deadman's, the
rooms were full of cases and clothes and toys and children's books, all of
these things scattered everywhere. In the bedrooms the bedclothes were
heaved apart as if a great wrestling match had proceeded like a hurri-
cane from room to room. The remains of a late lunch were still in the
kitchen. Nothing had been put away and ants crawled over the bread,
the pickles, the slices of tomato and beetroot, the chicken and cheese,
the lettuce, and one fat ant had even drowned in the open jar of mayon-
naise. There was a bottle of sparkling mineral water open and going
flat. Greasy plates sat unattended in front of the television, which
silently showed an animated cartoon about an amorous skunk trying to
make passionate love to a sleek and sexy black female cat. I started to
clean and wipe down the counters, and wrap things in plastic for the
refrigerator, and I wanted to lean with my hands against the wall and
ask some spirit out of Heaven to come save me from the loneliness eating me alive.

That was when a little note fell down from where it had been pasted on a shelf, supposedly at eye level. I picked it up off the floor.

In many colorful crayons it read: THE BEACH!!!

I left things where they were and stepped out onto the balcony. The air was cool and somehow raspy, as if it were a tactile force full of salt and sand. Our weekend rooms were at ground level and I climbed that balcony's railing, heading across the well-tended apartment-block lawn and then over some dunes, and then down a slope where the warm silken sand massaged my feet. The breeze was stronger here and scented with only one thing—like Gabriella's breath—the freshness of the sea. Few people were still out in this late afternoon before evening's impending fall, though couples were walking hand in hand toward the grottoes where the rocks started, and a fisherman was casting a line deep into the surf.

Near at hand, a naked child was just in front of the shallows, making a sandcastle with a pail and squealing every time the rushing, lapping waves happened to heave too far into shore and bring her construction down as slush. She was wearing a big white and blue Foreign Legion–style sun hat and nothing else. It took a moment to realize that this little girl was mine. The absolute futility of her work seemed perfectly balanced by the delight she took in it.

Past Lara, bobbing like corks in the water, were a small group of swimmers.

My heart lifted and I felt it as Gabriella's, broken and aching yet curiously light with love too. I didn't think it was too romantic to believe that she forgave Belpasso, Pierucci, and our old dreamy streets too, because not to do so would have kept her from finding that thing she said she'd always longed for. She wanted belonging, or at least a road that might lead her to that particular corner of Heaven. It didn't make me feel guilty that I'd found a way to beat her there.

I ran further down the windy beach to where the last sunlight of the day was still bright in the silver waves, cracking the beautiful black and gold heads of my wife and children into what they are, a multitude.

Acknowledgments

THIS BOOK WAS WRITTEN with the assistance of a writing development grant from Arts Queensland, to whom I am grateful.

My deepest thanks to Consigliera Bettina Keil for her enthusiasm, insight, and friendship; to Fiona Inglis and Linda Funnell for their support; and to Susan Ballyn of the University of Barcelona and Maria Vidal Grau of the University of Lleida, the two wonderful points of the Catalan railways system between which this book was born. For excellent editorial input I'm indebted to Meredith Rose, Rosemary Forster, and Susanne Rikl of List-Verlag in Munich. To those who helped in Sicily I express my warm appreciation: to Ylenia Fazzio, her father, Nello, her mother, Camilla, and brother, Orazio; to Leonardo Giacobbe and Margherita Milceri, and to Signor Catino Viscuso and Signora Francesca Armanno-Viscuso. I was assisted in the writing of this book by Alberto Manguel's excellent article "Eternities of the Heart," which appeared in *The Australian's Review of Books*, volume 3, issue 2, March 1998.

All characters are fictitious, though some events are based on fact.

Federico García Lorca's play *Blood Wedding* is quoted on page 236 from *Lorca: Three Plays*, translated by Gwynne Edwards and Peter Luke (Methuen, London, 1989).

VENERO ARMANNO was born in Brisbane, and has studied at the University of Queensland; the Australian Film, Television and Radio School (AFTRS); Queensland University of Technology; and the Tisch School of the Arts, New York University, New York City.

The son of Sicilian immigrants, he has traveled and worked widely throughout the world. In 1995, 1997, and 1999 he lived and worked in Cité Internationale des Arts, Paris, and he is frequently invited to speak about his work in Spain and Germany.

His first book of short stories, *Jumping at the Moon*, was equal runner-up in the prestigious 1993 Steele Rudd Award, and his novels *The Lonely Hunter* (1993), *Romeo of the Underworld* (1994), *My Beautiful Friend* (1995), and *Strange Rain* (1996) have all been critically acclaimed. Several of these books, including *Gabriella's Book of Fire* (2001), have been published in the USA, South Korea, Israel, Germany, Switzerland, Austria, and France—with selected titles in film pre-production.

His new novel, *The Volcano*, will be released in 2002.